## HEIGHTENED SENSES

*Where are you tonight?*

As if in answer, notes from an alto sax trickled down from a window somewhere up the street. Pure and sweet: a soulful, lonely sound.

All the buildings in that direction were dark. The music stopped almost as soon as it had started.

The rain came down harder, a curtain of clear beads in a doorway. Laura stood under the arch, feeling the chill draft as rain blew inward. With the rain came the stench of death.

Suddenly, she could feel him: his essence leaking out of the wet cement, the air around her. Controlled rage. A predator. For a moment she knew what it was like to be a rabbit in the shadow of the hawk.

Was he watching her now?

# Darkness on the Edge of Town

## J. CARSON BLACK

A SIGNET BOOK

SIGNET
Published by New American Library, a division of
Penguin Group (USA) Inc., 375 Hudson Street,
New York, New York 10014, USA
Penguin Group (Canada), 10 Alcorn Avenue, Toronto,
Ontario M4V 3B2, Canada (a division of Pearson Penguin Canada Inc.)
Penguin Books Ltd., 80 Strand, London WC2R 0RL, England
Penguin Ireland, 25 St. Stephen's Green, Dublin 2,
Ireland (a division of Penguin Books Ltd.)
Penguin Group (Australia), 250 Camberwell Road, Camberwell, Victoria 3124,
Australia (a division of Pearson Australia Group Pty. Ltd.)
Penguin Books India Pvt. Ltd., 11 Community Centre, Panchsheel Park,
New Delhi - 110 017, India
Penguin Group (NZ), cnr Airborne and Rosedale Roads, Albany,
Auckland 1310, New Zealand (a division of Pearson New Zealand Ltd.)
Penguin Books (South Africa) (Pty.) Ltd., 24 Sturdee Avenue,
Rosebank, Johannesburg 2196, South Africa

Penguin Books Ltd., Registered Offices:
80 Strand, London WC2R 0RL, England

First published by Signet, an imprint of New American Library,
a division of Penguin Group (USA) Inc.

First Printing, January 2005
10 9 8 7 6 5 4 3 2 1

To the memory of my father

In the sun on my face
The scent of a desert rain
The shifting leaf shadows on a wall,
You are always with me

# ACKNOWLEDGMENTS

No one can write a book alone. Many people have given generously of their time and expertise to help make this book possible, including:

*Florida Location:*
The good folks at the Florida Department of Law Enforcement in Tallahassee, Florida: Jennie Khoen, former FDLE Public Information Officer; Kristen Perezluha, FDLE Public Information Officer; Mike Phillips, FDLE Special Agent Supervisor; and Apalachicola historian, Laura Roberts Moody.

*Arizona Location:*
Leslie Boyer, M.D., Medical Director of the Arizona Poison and Drug Information Center; Michael Crawford of Chandler, Tullar, Udall & Redhair; Lieutenant David Denlinger, Arizona Department of Public Safety; DPS crime lab criminalists Ron Bridgemon (retired), Sue Harvey, John Maciulla, Curtis Reinbold, Seth Ruskin, and Keith Schubert; Ron Thompson, Tucson Police Department; and the folks at the La Posta Quemada Ranch (on which the Bosque Escondido is based), Karen Bachman and Pam Marlow. Also thanks to Alice Volpe, Tracy Bernstein, Claire Zion, Leslie Gelbman, and Kara Welsh. To my friends, family, and the people who just plain helped me out, not exclusive to but including: Sinclair Browning, J. R. Dailey, Pete Hautman, J. A. Jance, Mary Logue, Carol Davis Luce, Cliff McCreedy, Barbara Schiller, and Allegra Taff; writers' group members Sheila Cottrell, Elizabeth Gunn, J. M. Hayes, and E. J. McGill. And to my aunt, Evelyn Ridgway, my mother, Mary

Falk, and my husband, Glenn McCreedy, the only person to read my first draft—at his peril. Special thanks to my three go-to guys: Arizona Department of Public Safety detective Terry Johnson, Tucson Police Department detective Phil Uhall, and Cops 'n Writers consultant John Cheek (TPD retired). Without you, there would be no book.

Any and all mistakes are mine.
No animals were harmed during the writing of this book.
I'm available for birthday parties.

All of the above is true, except for the birthday party part.

# 1

*Vail, Arizona*

Francis X. Entwistle showed up in Laura Cardinal's bedroom at three in the morning, looking world-weary.

"Don't get up, Lorie. Just wanted to give you a heads-up. A bad one's coming."

Frank's complexion was pale and there were shadows under his eyes. In life, his face had been dull red from the high blood pressure that had killed him. A bottle of Tanqueray gin sat on the window table and the tumbler in Frank's hand was about a quarter full. Laura didn't own any tumblers and she didn't drink gin.

Laura wasn't entirely surprised that her old mentor was sitting in the straight-backed Mexican chair in her bedroom four months after his wife had buried him. Maybe because she knew she was dreaming. Or maybe because he was her last link to her parents, and she didn't want him to be gone for good.

Frank Entwistle leaned forward, the night-light from the bathroom illuminating the scroll of white hair above his side part. "You're gonna have to pay attention, and keep *on* paying attention."

He stopped to scratch the tip of his nose. Laura Cardinal

realized the absurdity of the situation: sitting in her bed at three in the morning, watching a dead homicide cop scratching his nose.

"I'm talking about the kind of thing, you aren't careful, could come back around and bite you in the ass. The key word here is *vigilance*."

She wanted him to clarify what he meant by that, but he was starting to fade.

He held his glass up in a salute. "Watch your back, kiddo."

When she caught the case the next day, there was no doubt in Laura's mind that it was the one Frank Entwistle had alluded to.

It was the weekend and she was at her little house on the guest ranch where she lived rent-free. The owner, a friend from high school, liked the idea of having a criminal investigator from the Arizona Department of Public Safety living on his property.

The dream about Frank Entwistle remained with her, vivid and unsettling. It didn't feel like a dream. When she got up this morning she had sleepwalked into the bathroom. In the dim glow of the night-light she saw a ring on the table left by a sweating glass. Instantly she was wide-awake, her heart rate going through the roof, until she realized the real culprit was Tom Lightfoot. Tom never remembered to use a coaster.

It was Tom who had been on her mind all morning, Tom who had preoccupied her since he left two days ago on a packing trip to New Mexico.

This was because of the note stuck to the refrigerator:

Maybe we should live together—T

Not "Love, T," she noticed. The word "love" scared her, anyway, so she wouldn't hold that against him. What she did hold against him was the fact that he had blindsided her, leaving that note on her refrigerator and then creeping out of town. She couldn't reach him in the backcountry. She couldn't tell him they'd only been together two and a half months, that his house was just over the hill, that just because he spent every night with her anyway he shouldn't think he could move in. Living together was a whole different proposition from sleeping together. The last man she had lived with had been her husband, and that had not turned out well.

What bothered Laura most, though, was the part of her that leaped at the thought.

Restless, she went outside to water, the day already hot enough she had to run the hose a while to avoid scalding the plants. Her mobile rang and she retreated into the shade with the phone.

It was Jerry Grimes, her sergeant. "You busy?"

"What's up?" Knowing that whatever plans she had for a quiet weekend were about to be blown out of the water.

"Bisbee PD's asked for an assist on a homicide."

As she listened, Laura forgot about Tom's note. Frank Entwistle had warned her it would be bad, and it was. A fourteen-year-old girl had been found dead in a small town south of here.

"Mike's talked to the chief down there and we all agree," Jerry said. "You're the lead investigator on this. So don't take any shit."

He always said that, although Laura had never taken any shit yet. She knew the pep talk was just his way of showing support for her, a woman doing a man's job. But being called in to assist on investigations in other jurisdictions—mostly small towns—Laura knew that petty politics were far more obstructive to an investigation than any effect her gender might have.

"Victor will meet you there as soon as he can. You know where the ADOT yard is this side of the tunnel?" Jerry said. "They'll have someone from Bisbee PD there to escort you in."

Fifteen minutes later, Laura turned her 4Runner onto Interstate 10 going east, dread pressing into her throat.

Fourteen years old.

# 2

Once on the road, Laura punched in the number for Jerry Grimes to get some background. Now she'd have time to absorb what he had to say.

"A girl named Jessica Parris was abducted yesterday from the street near her house. They *think* that's where it happened—there weren't any witnesses."

"What time yesterday?"

"After school. She didn't come home for dinner. Place is kind of out in the sticks. According to Bisbee PD, she lives—lived—at the end of West Boulevard." Jerry paused. He reminded her of an old-time union boss: tough and gruff. This case, though, would get to him: He had three daughters of his own.

Jerry said, "A girl fitting the Parris girl's description was found this morning in City Park. You know where that is?"

"On Brewery Gulch."

"That's right. Tourists went to see the band shell and got a big surprise."

She thought of how the tourists must have felt, that sudden drop in the pit of the stomach. "She was in the band shell?"

"Propped up against the back wall. Kind of like a doll on a bed, the woman said. The witness's name is Slaughter." He paused to let the irony sink in. "Doris Ann Slaughter. Said the girl was dressed up in some way, I don't know, like a doll dress." He paused again: This was hard for him. "Victor's coming from Marana. Should be a half hour behind you."

Laura signed off and pushed the 4Runner up to eighty, mesmerized by her own thoughts as the freeway unraveled before her. She hoped the storm would hold off until she got a look at the crime scene. The day was sunny but the sky to the south and east was an ominous leaden blue.

The monsoon season had started July 4. They'd had a thunderstorm every day this week: uprooted trees, downed powerlines, roofs torn off, the north-south streets of Tucson turned into flooded canals. A whole city held hostage by rain-swollen streets, many of them uncrossable. Ask a man who has been plucked by a helicopter from the roof of his pickup in a Tucson intersection just how quickly nature can trump progress.

This morning, the heat hadn't yet built up sufficiently to produce the cumulonimbus clouds necessary for a thunderstorm, but Laura could feel the electricity in the air. She stopped at a fast-food place in Benson for a breakfast sandwich—fuel—then drove south into the gathering gloom that seemed to press down on the mountains like a weight.

She felt both dread and anticipation. Needing to get there, see it for herself, but knowing that when she did the image would haunt her for the rest of her life. The sight of the dead girl would be imprinted on her eyeballs as if it were caught in the flash from a camera.

It would have plenty of company.

Laura reached the ADOT yard, where the Arizona Department of Transportation kept road machinery, at a little after ten a.m. A Bisbee PD Crown Vic was parked just outside the Mule Pass Tunnel. The officer—female, twentysomething—leaned against the Crown Vic's door. When the officer saw Laura's unmarked 4Runner pull in behind her, she walked up to the window. "I have to advise you that you are not allowed to park here." Her face was peeling from a severe sunburn.

Laura showed her badge and told the officer—her name-plate said DUFFY—that she would follow her. They drove through the tunnel and down into town and parked in a lot populated by law enforcement vehicles from four different agencies. Everybody and his brother was here.

Officer Duffy was out of her car in an instant. She strode across the lot without looking back, headed toward the staging area set up outside the mining museum across the street. Laura was used to this kind of rudeness. A state agency, the Arizona Department of Public Safety could only assist small town police departments if the chief requested it. The chief usually asked for help either because his force was too small, or they weren't equipped to do the job. Laura encountered resentment every time she set foot in one of these small towns.

Sometimes she thought her job description should read "professional pariah."

She opened up the back of her vehicle and took out her camera bag, wishing she hadn't worn dark clothes that absorbed the heat. The sky above was an unrelenting blue: no sign of the storm clouds she'd seen on the way down. The mountains above the town were so high they probably hid them from view. Laura entered the park and introduced herself to the cluster of men in the roped-off area.

Rusty Ducotte, who served twenty-five years with the DPS before his current stint as Bisbee police chief, spoke in the subtle Arizona drawl that Laura had grown up with. He was long-faced, with receding hair and red-rimmed eyes that reminded her of a rabbit's.

Ducotte made it clear that she was the lead, that it was now her scene. "I'd like Detective Holland to walk the scene with you, though, if that's okay."

Although the chief put it in the form of a request, Laura could sense steel behind it. He wanted his detective to work the case with her. Laura didn't see why not, as long as he didn't get in the way. She couldn't depend on Victor: His wife had just had a baby and he'd already told everyone who would listen that he wanted to stay close to home.

As she listened to the first officer at the scene describe how he had secured the area, Laura assessed Buddy Holland. He had the cop look: hair clipped short, razored whitewalls, mustache. He also had a grim jaw and watchful eyes. Wary.

He didn't say much. Just kind of sat back and waited. Figuring out with those small narrow eyes which way to jump?

Officer Billings, the responding officer, paused in his dissertation. Looking at her for approval.

"You've made my job a lot easier," she told him. He deserved praise. By her standards, a lot of street cops weren't careful enough at crime scenes, mostly because they weren't trained well. Officer Billings had probably trained himself.

"I plan to be a homicide detective someday. That's my goal."

Buddy Holland smirked.

Twenty minutes later Victor breezed in, trailing expensive cologne behind him. "I guess you're wondering why I called you all here today," he said, crisp white shirtsleeves already rolled up. He walked up to Detective Holland and held out his hand. "Victor Celaya."

The Bisbee PD detective straightened up from the tree trunk on which he had been leaning, his face instantly animated. "Buddy Holland."

They shook hands like long-lost brothers. Victor had an unerring sense for which person in a crowd needed to be won over. Now he paused and shot a glance at Laura, just to be sure she was still charmed by him. Impossible not to be.

It was decided that Laura, Detective Holland, and Officer Billings would walk the crime scene and Victor would interview the two female witnesses, detained in a conference room at the Copper Queen Hotel. Victor usually did the interviews. He was the best interviewer/interrogator in the unit.

Laura glanced up the street lined by two-story brick buildings: Brewery Gulch. From their vantage point on OK Street, news photographers aimed their telephotos down the hill at the park. OK Street marked the eastern boundary of Bisbee; after that, there was no place to go but straight up. This odd topography had the effect of making the corner of Brewery Gulch and Main Street both the city center and the edge of town.

They walked up the Gulch, Officer Duffy leading the way. The narrow canyon seemed to telescope until Laura's gaze was trained solely on the blue uniform of Duffy ahead of her, twenty pounds of duty belt and service weapon and flashlight and handcuffs shifting from side to side on her compact girl-body. Duffy seemed sure of herself, as if she knew exactly where she was going. Laura got the impression it wasn't just Bisbee the officer was sure of, but her future as well. Laura envied the girl's certainty. Her own future seemed to disappear somewhere up ahead in the mist; she'd suffered too many body blows to take anything for granted in her personal life. Or maybe her personal life and her professional life were one and the same. The only thing she seemed to be good at was this job.

Ahead, yellow crime scene tape blocked the road, leaving space for people to turn their cars around. Their little group passed the open door to a bar. The beer smell billowed out, enveloping Laura in a dank, underworldly current.

The closer she got, the greater the dread she felt. The game of push and pull went on full force inside her: the urgency to see the scene, the equally strong desire to turn away. Whatever Jessica Parris had been thinking, feeling, or doing—stuff as simple as hanging out with a friend or planning what to do for the weekend—all of it had been cut short like a snipped thread.

At least nothing could hurt the girl anymore. Her family was another matter. In the aftermath of the tornado that took their daughter's life, their entire world would be blown apart, shattered into tiny pieces. Laura knew from experience that you could pick up the pieces but you could never put them back together. She was here to get Jessica's family the only thing left that had any meaning: justice.

A knot of people had gathered at the edge of the tape. A uniform held them back, unassailable as a block of granite. She saw he had been assigned to keep the crime log.

Laura took photographs of the people crowded near the tape, making sure to get every face. You never knew who would be there, thinking they were invisible.

A hot wind spiraled up the canyon, bringing with it the smell of impending rain.

She let the camera hang down from the ribbon around her neck.

Her stomach tightened.

Time to begin.

# 3

When she was in grade school, Laura's parents took her to the Tucson Metro Ice Rink for ice-skating lessons. She remembered walking gingerly on her blades across the black rubber apron to the edge of the rink. The delineation between rubber and ice was inviolate, a law of nature. First you were clumping, and then you were gliding.

Like an ice rink, a crime scene was something apart. City Park had been transformed forever from what it had once been. The evil that had visited here would linger in the hearts and the minds of the people who frequented it, long after the body was carted away and the crime scene tape taken down. Legends would grow up around it. The crime scene was hallowed ground.

Laura was about to step across the threshold into a new world with new rules, and she saw what she did there as a sacred duty. Mistakes could never be recalled, so she had to take her time and do it right. She ducked under the tape, followed by Holland and Billings. Officer Duffy followed suit.

"Officer Duffy," Laura said firmly, "it will be just the three of us."

Duffy blushed furiously and stepped back. Laura didn't bother to explain something the officer should already know: the fewer people inside a crime scene, the better.

Cops were the worst offenders when it came to trampling evidence, drinking from water fountains or flushing toilets at a crime scene.

Now they were standing at the entrance to City Park, which was actually one story above them and accessed by a flight of dingy brown steps climbing up to the street above. Bisbee was built on hills, and concrete stairs like these were everywhere, connecting to the winding roads above and below like a game of Chutes and Ladders.

According to Officer Billings, there was an entrance into the park halfway up. The witness had led Billings up this way. The place made Laura think of the inner city, Chicago or New York: a park made of concrete, suspended above the street on the backs of three locked-tight shops, their windows blank.

She looked up and saw the finials of a wrought iron fence and some treetops. Wondered how trees could grow there. She glanced at Officer Billings. "That street, where does it go?" She pointed to a street that curved up the hill around the edge of the park.

"Opera Drive? It makes a half circle around City Park, doubles back up there." He motioned to the road above, high on the mountain. Houses were strewn down the hill like items in a jumble sale.

"Let's start here and walk the perimeter," Laura said. Behind her, Buddy Holland snapped on latex gloves and young Billings followed suit. Buddy looked over at Laura, then pointedly back at his hands. Laura crossed her arms, tucking her hands under her armpits. She didn't wear gloves until it was time to collect the evidence; wearing them tended to make her complacent.

They walked north on Brewery Gulch and followed the curving street up the hill, Billings filling them in on the witnesses' discovery of the body and his subsequent trip back with them to the band shell—any and all observations, large and small. Halfway up the curve they came to an entrance into the park. From here Laura could see a long concrete oval with a basketball court, a playground, cement bleachers cutting into the hill on the right, and the band shell.

Billings's voice trailed off into silence.

Inside the band shell, propped up against the back wall, was a tiny forlorn figure. At first glance, it looked like a doll. From where she was, Laura couldn't see features, details, but she could see the figure's static nature, its lack of life. She felt the shocked presence of the men with her. The whole canyon seemed quiet, insulated from the world like a soundproof room.

She wiped sweat out of her eyes. Suddenly she wished the storm would come, bringing with it cool rain.

After a moment that seemed like a prayer, they continued up the hill. Sunlight glared off silver-painted roofs down below on the Gulch. Laura realized how thirsty she was. When they got back down she'd ask for someone to send up some bottled water. They followed the wrought iron fence, looking at everything, paying particular attention to the ground. She could hear her own ragged breathing; they were up at five thousand feet. They could see into the band shell, the horror closer now. It was unsettling how much the girl looked like a doll. Still too far away to be sure if she was real.

At the top of the road, they reached the flight of stairs that descended the hill along the south side of the park. If they walked down these stairs they would have gone full circle. In the corner, next to the steps, the tar-paper roof of the band shell gleamed in the sun, a shallow puddle from a recent thunderstorm in the center. Beneath, unseen, was the girl. The stench of death condensed in the humid air, cloying and undeniable.

The three of them stood at the top of the concrete steps, looking down at Brewery Gulch below.

A breeze touched Laura's face and she smelled wild fennel. Behind her Buddy said, "I don't think he came from up here. He'd block the road. It would be hard to get in and out. He'd have more of a chance of being seen."

Laura thought he was probably right.

A cicada buzzed, hard and violent.

She was aware of the two of them looking at her. "Let's go down the stairs."

As they entered the park, Officer Billings headed for the band shell steps.

"Officer," Laura said. "Stay with us."

He blushed at his lapse of judgment. "Sorry," he said, quickly rejoining them at the entrance.

Laura stood still, facing out into the park. The body of the little girl would wait. Wordlessly, the two men stayed with her. She could see Detective Holland out of the corner of her eye. She hated dividing her attention between two people she didn't know and the crime scene. If she had it her way, she'd be here alone.

Looking at the park with her back to the band shell, she measured with her eye the distance to the other end—approximately two hundred feet, maybe a little more. Inside the long oval of the park, the basketball court formed a smaller, concentric one. Near the wrought iron fences there were cookie-cutter scraps of dirt, where the trees grew. She realized that she was in a natural amphitheater, houses all around, many of them looking down from the tall hills—a ready-made audience.

Laura closed her eyes, trying to summon the thoughts of a killer. Sometimes, if she narrowed her field of vision enough, she could see things from his perspective.

Laura knew he craved an audience, knew it from the evidence he'd left behind. Even as she tried to draw him in, *think* like him, her analytical mind ticked away underneath, logically picking up and discarding theories: the easiest way for him to enter the park, if the girl was dead or alive when he brought her here, and what he did last, just before he left.

The reason he had to dress her up like a doll.

A scrape of shoe on cement—Holland or Billings. Whoever it was, her concentration broke. The killer had something to say to her, but she couldn't hear him. Maybe it was

Detective Holland, his disapproval of her jamming the frequencies.

She would come back later, alone.

She turned and faced the band shell.

The 1916-era band shell was small and shabby—stuccoed-over cement. The stage apron stood a little over waist high. Under the arch, the shallow interior had been painted pale blue—to represent the sky?—but was now overpowered by graffiti.

The body of the girl had been placed in the center, propped against the wall, legs out. Flies zoomed around her.

Finally, Laura looked directly into the girl's face. Shocked, she thought, *I know her.*

# 4

The barriers of time and place dissolved, and she saw the grainy newspaper photo of the two-tone sedan and the headline above it:

### CAR USED IN ABDUCTION OF LOCAL GIRL FOUND

It wasn't Julie, though. Of course not; it couldn't be. And now that she really looked, she saw that the girl was not an exact match.

Laura owed it to this girl not to get sidetracked. Her resemblance to Julie Marr was just a coincidence. Looking for a distraction, she glanced at Buddy Holland.

His face had turned deep crimson. He stared at the child, eyes fixed, a vein pulsing in his jaw. For a moment she wondered if he was having a heart attack. She opened her mouth to ask him if he was all right.

He turned his head to look at her. For a moment the bleakness in his eyes reminded her of Frank Entwistle staring across the hospital bed at his own death—what one guy in her squad referred to as the thousand-yard stare. Then his eyes turned stony, unreadable.

Laura looked at the girl. She was barefoot and dressed in an old-fashioned white dress. A little girl's dress: babyish.

Something a seven-year-old would wear to First Communion. If this girl really was Jessica Parris, she was fourteen
years old—far too old to wear a dress like this.

"I wonder where he got the dress," Laura said. "Who
would sell dresses like that for a girl that age?"

"It looks small on her," Buddy Holland said. His voice
was thick with emotion. She liked him better.

Laura took inventory. The girl's hands had been placed
neatly in her lap. Her fingers were clasped together. Her hair
had been brushed. Her legs had been slightly but not overtly
spread. This last could indicate sexual motivation. Dressing
her up was also most likely sexually motivated.

She had been arranged in a tableau.

Buddy's voice echoed her own thoughts. "He staged
this—put her on display. I'll bet you dollars to doughnuts
he's done this before."

"Probably." Either the bad guy had killed before or he
had worked his way up to this, probably with rape.

God, she wished she had some water. She led the way to
the band shell steps on the other side farthest from the street,
the ones she believed the killer did not take.

She was pretty sure the guy had come up from below.
That would have been easiest. He would have come up the
steps from the Gulch, entered the park and headed right up
the steps to the band shell.

Up on the concrete stage, Laura scanned the inside walls.
There was a door opposite, probably a storage area, pad-
locked closed. On the padlock someone had written
"FTW"—Fuck the World. Bad guys, but likely not the ones
she was looking for.

The floor was so clean it might have been swept. Clearly,
he was an organized offender. He made very few mistakes.
The guy she was looking for had probably read the same
books she had, books on criminal investigation and forensic
science. Laura stared across at the entrance to the park, just
down the steps from the band shell, already picturing him

coming up from the street. It would take him ten minutes, tops, and that included clasping the hands.

In, out.

Arms still folded, she hunkered down next to the girl in a catcher's stance.

The girl looked nothing like Julie from this angle. Her eyes were too close together. Her hair was a lighter blond. It looked dyed. There were holes in her earlobes, but no earrings. Did he take them? There was a tiny butterfly tattoo on the fleshy part of the right hand, just below the thumb. At odds with the dress. The dress itself was white but appeared shop-soiled, as if it had been packed away for a while. She could see the creases. She leaned to look at where the girl's back departed from the wall. The dress had been zipped up only halfway. No tag.

Laura took a deep breath and looked into the girl's eyes.

She had seen many people who had died violently. It seemed to her that the eyes of a large percentage of these victims had been stamped with fathomless terror, as if they had seen their deaths coming for them.

But in this girl's eyes Laura saw no emotion, just broken blood vessels in the whites—petechia—which hinted at death by strangulation. Brown and brittle as acorn hulls, the girl's eyes showed nothing at all.

Laura hoped it meant she hadn't suffered, but the petechia told her otherwise. Either way, she would never know the truth for sure.

She stood up and walked around to the other side, looking at the girl from that angle.

Laura always felt that the victim could tell her something. There was usually some evidence that the dead kept to themselves, a secret that they had taken with them, a secret the killer forgot. In every homicide case she'd investigated, there had been something that the dead had held back. She just had to find it. To recognize it when it looked her in the face.

"I figure the lividity points to the fact that she was

moved," Officer Billings said behind her. "Down by her ears, the bottom of her neck, see?"

She tried to block him out, concentrate on the girl.

"Looks to me like she was prostate when she was killed."

"Prostrate," Laura said.

"Prostrate, sorry." He laughed nervously. "That's funny, prostate. Anyway, I knew it the minute I saw her."

"Would you shut the fuck up?" Buddy Holland snapped.

Hurt, Billings said, "Hey, I was just—"

"I don't fucking want to hear it."

Laura was aware of Buddy's legs, spread in a fighter's stance. She thought he was very close to the edge. When the chief introduced them, he'd mentioned that Buddy Holland had been with the Tucson PD a long time before coming to Bisbee. Why did this death affect him so much? He must have seen his share of corpses—even young girls.

He squatted down beside her. She could feel his breath as she studied the girl's hair near her ear.

That was when she saw it.

*You slick son of a bitch,* she thought.

*You missed something.*

# 5

After Musicman logged on at the Earthling Café, the first thing he did was check his mail.

There were two messages from CRZYGRL12@synerG. net.

Fingers tapping rapidly on the table, he tried to think it through. Hard, because his mind was rushing a mile a minute. Although his rage had not abated one bit, he felt the overwhelming need to know what happened.

Out front, another police car went by, this one from the sheriff's department.

He tapped his fingers some more and then brought her picture up on the screen. Maybe he could find a clue in her eyes.

The waitress, a scarf-haired girl wearing heavy white linen tied around her waist, set his iced tea down. She glanced at the picture. "That your daughter?"

He lowered the laptop lid so she couldn't see. "Uh-huh."

"Pretty girl."

He nodded, acknowledging but not friendly. She took the hint and threaded her way back through the cramped café to the stand-up counter. Only then did he push the laptop's lid back up.

She smiled out at him—his girl.

Like a tidal wave, the desire—the *need*—came rumbling up from deep inside him. He could feel it in the trembling of his hands, the prickling saliva in the corners of his mouth. The adrenaline rush, the beating of his heart, the answering chime in his groin.

If she *was* his girl.

He had to know. No way could he leave it like this—not when he was this close.

He opened the first message.

Where wer u? I waited 1 hr. I thought for sure this was the day and I walked 3 Miles. Did I get the wrong day? Let me know. Luv, Your Muse. PS I looked it up, it's really cool to be your muse.

He closed the first e-mail without replying and opened the second one.

Y haven't I heard from u? Write me!

The same. She was the same. Or at least she *seemed* the same.

Another cop car went by, lights on but silent. That was seven, total, since he'd been here. He poured two packets of sugar into his glass and stirred, having to use a regular tea-spoon because they didn't have the long ones.

Suddenly, he wanted to throw the goddamn spoon across the room.

*His* girl. Who was he fooling?

He wasn't stupid—far from it. He knew he couldn't dismiss what he'd seen. There came a time when you had to trust your instincts. He had always been fully aware of the dangers, and that was why he was so careful. He'd always had a sixth sense for trouble.

Until now.

# 6

Dusk had fallen by the time one of the lab techs, Danny Urquides, motioned to Laura from the band shell stage. "The ME's gonna take her now."

For the last half hour, Laura had been waiting for the crime scene techs to finish their work. Now she realized how dry her lips were—a chronic problem. She fumbled in the pocket of her slacks, momentarily afraid she'd left her lip balm in the car, relieved and grateful when her hand closed around the small tin. When she worked a crime scene her field of vision narrowed so much she forgot about things like thirst, hunger, and dry lips.

It had been a very long day. There had been so much to do, and she trusted no one else to do it—even the stuff some might label scut work—because this was her case and she had to build it painstakingly. In her mind she thought of it as a Popsicle-stick house, placing one piece of evidence atop another until she had a case so tight no defense attorney could knock it down.

One thing Frank Entwistle had drummed into her: Think about the endgame. In police work, the endgame was a conviction. Whatever she uncovered would have to stand up in court.

Since this morning, she had walked the crime scene

twice. She had marked and collected evidence, measured and drawn the crime scene to scale, and shot seventeen rolls of film from the ground and an additional two from the DPS helicopter. Laura hated flying in general, and flying in helicopters—where the world tilted crazily—in particular. But it was part of her job and she white-knuckled it.

Laura dropped the lip balm into her slacks pocket and went up to supervise the removal of the body.

A tech from the medical examiner's office was in the process of gently moving the girl away from the wall. Laura photographed the part of her that had been concealed until now, from head to heels. Other than residue from the dirty wall, there was nothing new. The one thing the killer had missed—a mesquite leaf Laura had found on the girl's neck—had already been photographed, bagged and removed.

By this time they had made a positive identification: The girl was indeed Jessica Parris. Victor Celaya had made the notification earlier in the afternoon.

A familiar twinge started in the small of her back. At five feet nine, she was on the tall side and had a long waist. A car accident during her time at the Highway Patrol had weakened her back despite the doctors' assurances to the contrary, and she felt it every time the job required long hours and standing around. She couldn't even lean against a wall until they were done with the crime scene.

It had rained scantily off and on for about an hour—not much of a storm. The air smelled of wet earth and wet cement, nothing like the seductive perfume of the creosote desert where she lived. But it had cooled her down, blown some fresh air into her.

As they lifted the girl, Laura looked at her face. Despite the deterioration already beginning to erode the hopeful image of youth, the face that once belonged to Jessica Parris seemed unconcerned with the indignities of death—as if she were already an angel.

Laura thought of the parents, glad that they could not see

her now. How did you deal with the death of your own child?

Anguish stormed up into her chest, the wanton destruction getting to her. Why? Why take this girl's life? She knew the conventional wisdom, the explanations given by psychologists and FBI profilers, the charts and statistics and probabilities, but at this moment they rang hollow.

The firestorm of emotion took her unawares, blowing up through her soul like a crown fire. Just as quickly it burned out, leaving only cold, bitter anger.

*You think you can get away with it,* she said to him. *But you won't.*

*I will find you. I swear to God I will.*

*I will make you pay.*

Going back down Brewery Gulch, she passed the bar she'd gone by this morning, what seemed like a hundred years ago. Heavy metal music spilled out along with the beer smell. Several Harleys were parked out in front of the bar. Bikers, tourists, and stray dogs populated the shadowy street, flickering in and out of lights from open doorways. They were joined by hippie types who seemed at the same time flamboyant and insubstantial, slipping through the night like ghosts of a long-gone era.

Laura was tired, dirty, drained, and hungry. Earlier today she'd seen the sign in the Copper Queen Hotel lobby for prime rib. She hoped the restaurant would still be open after the briefing at the Bisbee police department. Maybe grab a bite with Victor. She hadn't seen him since this morning. He'd spent most of his time canvassing the streets around the park or up at the Copper Queen Hotel conference room, doing what he did best: talk. Interviewing witnesses, being interviewed himself by the news crews from the Tucson and Phoenix network affiliates. He could have them.

Laura was almost past a redbrick building when she saw something in the store window, partly shielded by an old-fashioned canvas awning, its candy stripes faded to pink: a doll, propped up against a metal trunk, legs splayed, hands together on her lap. She wore a Victorian-style little girl's dress. The dress looked like it had once been white but had been faded by the sun.

The sign above the door said COOGER & DARK'S PANDE-MONIUM SHADOW SHOW AND EMPORIUM. The antique shop sold twentieth-century kitsch: Melmac, Buck Rogers space ships. A dim light came from the back of the store.

Taped to the door's window was a faded poster depicting whirling leaves on a dark sidewalk. Laura remembered it from her childhood, the cover of Ray Bradbury's book *Something Wicked This Way Comes*.

Evil had visited Bisbee in the middle of the night, like the locomotive in Bradbury's book, bringing the dark carnival to the edge of town.

She knocked on the door and it rattled in the frame. No one answered.

The shop next door was open, though, a tattoo parlor. Laura asked the proprietor about Cooger & Dark's Pande-monium Shadow Show and Emporium.

The heavyset woman looked up from tattooing the Virgin of Guadalupe on her customer's forearm. "Oh, that place. Guy doesn't show up much, kind of like a lot of shop owners around here. No set hours, just every once in a while the door's open. Name's Ted." She shrugged. "That's all I know."

Laura could find out who owned the shop tomorrow. All it would take was a look at the city records. She was about to walk out when another thought occurred to her. "Did you do the tattoo for Jessica Parris?"

"Hold her steady, Ramon." The woman put down a tool that looked like a dentist's drill and bustled over to a filing cabinet behind the counter, handed Laura the file. "She wanted the butterfly—very popular with young girls. Turned out real nice."

"Don't you have to get parental permission to tattoo a minor?"

She gave Laura a look. "In this case, her mama brought her in. Her mama and her boyfriend."

"Jessica had a boyfriend? You know his name?"

"Cary Statler. He lives with them. They took him in when his own mom left town."

"So what do we know about this guy?" Chief Ducotte said.

Laura, Victor Celaya, and the eight members of the Bisbee PD were crammed around a table in the police department conference room, an airless cubicle smelling of microwaved pizza.

"The creep likes to play dress-up," muttered Sergeant Nesmith.

Nervous laughter.

"I bet he's done it before," said someone behind Laura. Sandwiched as she was between a young police officer named Noone and Detective Holland, she'd have to turn herself inside out to see who had spoken. Holland had thrown his weight around, literally, making the most of his space and practically pushing Laura into Noone's lap. The molded plastic chair didn't help her back much, either.

She didn't mind the chair so much as the feeling that this briefing was an exercise in futility. Chief Ducotte had asked that the briefing include all of the Bisbee Police Department. Laura remembered his exact words: He wanted "to foster an inclusive atmosphere" and make sure that everybody "was on the same page."

Bottom line: He didn't want his people to feel left out. Even though they would be.

Laura was well aware of the pressures the chief faced. The safety of a city dependent on tourism had suddenly been breached, and logical or not, the chief would be blamed. His job was to keep the town running smoothly, bring in revenue in the form of traffic tickets and fines, and maintain a comforting presence in the community. These were his priorities, and he needed to get the town back up on the rails as quickly as possible. That meant he had to get his cops back out on the street.

But he also had to think about morale.

In Laura's opinion, this briefing was unwise; it would raise expectations in the rank and file that they would be integral to the case, and other than helping in minor ways, that just wasn't true.

Officer Billings, one of the few here who had seen Jessica Parris's body, was enjoying his three minutes of fame. "You know what she looked like?" He paused dramatically. "Judy Garland in *The Wizard of Oz*. The girl was too old for a baby-doll dress like that . . . damn, it was spooky."

Sergeant Nesmith leaned back and folded his arms over his considerable bulk. "Haven't heard of nobody dressing 'em up like that. Sounds like something you'd see on *Most Wanted*."

What no one said but everyone thought: This guy might be a serial killer. Either there had been other murders before this, or Jessica Parris was the first. Everyone here had some knowledge of FBI profile techniques. They knew as well as she did that when a person employed ritual in his killing, he would do it again.

Victor said, "The dress was too small. He must have had the dress first. Why'd he have the dress *first*?"

"Maybe that's all he could find," said a scrawny cop with a rust-colored handlebar mustache like Wyatt Earp's. His nameplate said DANEHILL.

Laura said, "We need to check the resale and antique shops in the area."

"He could have gotten the dress anywhere," said Victor. "Also, there was no tag on the collar."

"Maybe he tore it off."

"Or it could be homemade."

"What, you mean like sewed? From a pattern or something?"

"My wife sews," Sergeant Nesmith said. "If I could get a look at the dress I could probably tell. I could get on the

Internet, check out dresses like that, see if there are any patterns."

Laura shifted in her seat to relieve the pain in her back, caught Officer Heather Duffy's eye. Duffy was glaring at her.

Victor crossed his leg at the knee, played with the tassel on his Italian loafers. "We'll get photos of the dress and pass them around to everyone. I wonder what he did with her clothes?"

"Took 'em for a souvenir?" suggested Officer Billings. "A trophy?"

"Or threw them away."

Chief Ducotte said, "You have someone on that? Checking all the garbage cans around here?"

"We're on it," said Nesmith.

They discussed the mesquite leaf found on Jessica Parris's neck, stuck like a piece of confetti behind her ear—something the killer had missed. This pointed to the possibility that the girl had been killed outside of Bisbee, since mesquite trees were rarely found above five thousand feet. Unfortunately, the surrounding valleys—some of them only a mile or two away—were thick with them.

Then they came to the doll at Cooger & Dark's. "I'm going by there tomorrow and talk to the owner," Laura told them. "Maybe he saw somebody, someone too interested in the display."

Chief Ducotte nodded, blinking his rabbity eyes.

Victor said, "Another thing, we're all agreed he took her up there after she was dead. That means we have three crime scenes. The one where she was abducted, the one where he killed her, and the band shell. Any ideas on that?"

"His house?"

"A motel, if he isn't from around here."

Laura glanced in Duffy's direction and noticed she was looking at Noone with an odd expression. She tried to pigeonhole it—Longing? Anger? Something in between?

Duffy's short, compact body looked like it was about to explode.

Something between Duffy and Noone.

Buddy Holland, who'd seemed preoccupied throughout the proceedings, followed Laura's gaze. One corner of his mouth came up. Whatever was going on with Duffy and Noone, he knew about it.

Victor was saying, "Motels, bed-and-breakfasts, apartments, what else?"

"If it's his crib it'd be pretty much impossible to find," said Danehill.

"I got some photographs of the crowd by the crime scene tape this morning," Laura said. "Our guy might not have been able to stay away. As soon as we have them, I want to canvass the neighborhood again. Maybe somebody noticed something unusual, maybe someone they knew did something outside their routine. That is, if he's local. But I have my doubts about that."

Detective Holland picked at some invisible lint on his sleeve, stretched his long blue jean–clad legs out and stared at his feet. "I think he *is* local."

"You do?" asked Noone. "From here in Bisbee?"

Holland shrugged. His watchful eyes scanned the room, landed on Laura. "Why would he come here? We're a little off the beaten path. It just doesn't compute."

Officer Duffy spoke up. "I think Buddy's right."

Chief Ducotte looked at Holland. "Go on," he said.

Buddy Holland paused, waiting until he had their undivided attention: *When E.F. Holland talks, people listen.*

"This is a local guy, been working up to this a long time, peeping in windows, maybe caught masturbating outside some little girl's house. I see it as opportunistic—nobody was around, he saw her, he grabbed her. Maybe it got out of hand. He's fantasized about this for a long time." He pushed his chair back, almost pinning Laura's arm between them. "I think what Ms. Cardinal here said was telling. The doll shop. He could have got the idea from the doll. A local would know the park really well, know how easy it'd be to get up and down with a db without being seen."

"How many people from out of town know where West Boulevard is?" demanded Heather Duffy. "Nobody."

"He could've grown up here and come back," said Dane-hill.

"It's one theory," the chief said. "But I've been thinking there might be an Internet connection. It could be what drew the guy here, like maybe he met her on the Internet. Buddy's been raising concerns about this—his daughter—" He looked at Holland. "You're the logical choice, why don't you look into it?"

"Okay," Holland said. "We have to cover all the angles."

Laura knew she should say something before the chief took the briefing over and started making assignments. "Looks like we've got a plan." She looked at the chief. "I know you're shorthanded, but if you could spare an officer to help canvass the houses facing the park once I get the photos from the scene, that would be helpful."

Chief Ducotte stood up. "No problem. My people are your people. You want Detective Holland to coordinate that?"

Code for: He wanted Detective Holland to work closely with her.

"No," she said. "He'll have more important things to do."

If she'd expected Holland to be grateful, she would have been disappointed.

As the briefing broke up, all of them crowding around to squeeze through the door of the conference room, Heather handed Laura a tampon still in its package. "You drop this?" she asked.

Her voice had the exaggerated sweetness of a bully.

Laura became aware of men shuffling, coughing, some of them amused, no one looking at her. Mention a tampon and you're back in second grade, never mind most of these guys were married and had umpty-ump kids.

Laura took the tampon, thought briefly about stabbing Duffy in the eye with it. "Thanks, Duffy. I never turn down anything that's free."

It took the drive back to the Copper Queen Hotel to get her heart rate back down. Hard to not show how humiliated she was. It took her right back to grade school.

It had been her experience that there were certain women who knew just where the soft underbelly was—an instinct they were born with. A toxic form of cunning. She supposed there were men like that, too, but she hadn't met any.

Victor didn't help, reliving the scene more than a few times. "Jesus, I bet you haven't been razzed like that since you were a rock at the Academy."

"Fuck you, Victor."

They ate in the dining room at the Copper Queen just before the kitchen closed, then headed for the bar. She wanted to talk about this guy, bounce some things off Victor. This was a bad bad guy. He was on a roll, and she knew he wouldn't stop with Jessica Parris.

A man was playing the upright piano in the bar—"Rhapsody in Blue." On the table next to him was a jar for tips. Laura loved "Rhapsody in Blue," so she put some cash in the jar. He nodded to her as she and Victor went out onto the terrace.

The moment they sat down, Victor produced the photographs. Laura had been expecting them. Victor's daughter Angela had been born a week ago, his fifth child.

Laura oohed and ahhed over the baby, who looked like a red thumb wrapped in a bandage. The baby did look cute in her little green blanket with the yellow ducks.

The rest of the roll was from the get-acquainted barbecue at Lieutenant Galaz's a couple of months ago. There was Let's Go People! himself, holding a meat fork and wearing an apron emblazoned with the words GOT CARCINOGENS? Detectives and their wives playing volleyball, chowing down on burgers and dogs, holding plastic cups of beer and smiling hazily at the camera. A couple of group photos, Laura conspicuous by her absence, Richie Lockhart's fingers forming bunny ears behind Let's Go People!'s head.

"A great time had by all," Laura commented.

"You should have been there," Victor said. "It was fun."

"I was busy, remember?"

She had been working the most disturbing case of her career. A Safford man had shot his wife, his mother, and four children. At first they thought he had taken the youngest—a little girl—with him. But it turned out she had crawled under the house and died of her wounds. The little girl had been alive for at least a day.

"How did the notification go?" she asked Victor, not wanting to think about that case.

"You know it's never good. On a scale from one to ten, maybe a seven. No hysterics." He took a drink of his Chivas Regal. "The mother was pretty weird. Too busy kowtowing to her husband, making sure his dinner was still hot—can you believe it? When I did get her attention she seemed embarrassed. Like the kid made her look bad. Could be just shock. She kept saying stuff like, 'I told her something like this would happen,' and 'That's what happens when you don't listen,' as if the kid skipped school or something. Almost like she expected her daughter to turn up dead."

"They've been living with it since yesterday afternoon," Laura said. "If they've been watching cable at all, they know the drill." Hungry for filler, the cable news channels had blown stranger abductions up into epidemic proportions, the experts drilling it into the American psyche that children abducted by strangers were killed within three to five hours after being taken.

One cable TV network had labeled this "The Summer of Fear." The spotlight had moved on in recent months to three separate grizzly bear attacks, and a reasonable person might assume that the child abductions had ceased altogether.

"Did you meet the boyfriend?" she asked.

"Boyfriend?"

"According to the tattoo artist next door to the doll place,

Jessica's boyfriend lived with her family. His name is Cary Statler."

"Nobody mentioned him, and I didn't see anyone matching a boy her age." He took out his notebook and wrote the name down. "He lives with them?"

"Uh-huh."

"Cozy—just another modern American family." Victor sipped his Chivas. "There's someone else we should look at, just in case Sherlock Holmes in there is right and it was a local. A neighbor—a friend of the family. Chuck Lehman. Guy was over there in the role of concerned friend, but there was something . . . I dunno, avid, about the way he was tuning in. So I checked him out. Two DUIs in the past three and a half years—one in Colorado and one here. Also, he broke into his ex-wife's house, tore up some of her dainties. Felony trespass and criminal damage, both DVs. They pled the felony down."

"How old is he?"

"Early forties. I know, I know. He skews old for this." He lit a cigarette, even though he knew Laura didn't like it.

Victor turned his head and blew out the smoke, and also held his hand away—his try at meeting her halfway. "It's a lead. Don't worry, we'll get a match on this creep somewhere, you'll see. Jesus. Dressing her up like it's her First fucking Communion."

The pianist had finished "Rhapsody in Blue." Even though they were outside, Laura applauded with the rest of the bar patrons, Victor following suit. The door was open and it was possible the pianist might hear.

"With Lehman, there are some serious stressors," Victor said. "Guy's divorce was finalized a month or so ago, just around the time he got laid off from work." He saw the question in her eyes. "He worked at the mine—well, what's left of the mining operation out here."

"Where'd you hear this?"

"I asked around. Danehill was the one popped him for the

DUI and the DV. I've got the number for his probation officer if you want it."

"Sure. We have to look at everything." The story de-
pressed Laura. "How's Elena doing?"

"Fine now. At least she's not cursing my name anymore.
There was about eight hours there where she seemed a little
pissed off at me."

"No kidding."

"Come on, it's not all my fault." Victor showed her his
most irresistible grin, no doubt the one that had snagged
Elena into motherhood five times. "She was the one who
wanted another one." He took a sip of Chivas. "Some
women actually want kids. It's the maternal instinct, something you'd appreciate if you ever grew up, found a nice
man, got married—"

"Hey, I put in my time."

He laughed. "Seven months? That's a slap on the wrist."

"I got time off for good behavior." Laura realized that
she'd never told Victor the whole story about her marriage.
Maybe because, logic to the contrary, she still felt embarrassed.

"One of these days you'll find the right guy and you'll
know what I'm talking about. I got the impression you
didn't agree with Buddy back there, about the guy being a
local."

Laura sighed. It didn't feel local to her, but her gut could
be wrong. "Who knows? Maybe there's an Internet connection, like the chief said. In that case, it could be someone
from anywhere. Buddy Holland says the guy wouldn't know
Bisbee, but it's not that big. It wouldn't take much to figure
this place out."

"But why here?"

Laura shook her head.

Why anywhere?

Victor left for Tucson soon afterward, wanting to get home
to his new baby. Laura would stay here and go directly to the

autopsy in Sierra Vista tomorrow afternoon. The Copper Queen Hotel was full up, but after calling around, she found a place on the main drag through town.

The storm that had been threatening all day finally unleashed its fury during the short drive to the motel. Rain hit the windshield like a fire hose, but she managed to spot the neon letters spelling out THE JONQUIL MOTEL. She got out and ran through the downpour to the office.

The Jonquil Motel was a white-stuccoed motor court, circa 1930, situated on what was once the main highway through town. For Laura, it was love at first sight. In her job as a criminal investigator, she'd spent many nights on the road, and the motels often stuck out in her memory. After a long day she'd close the door to her room and give herself time to unwind. Many times she'd find the answers that had eluded her when she was on the job—something would just click. She remembered asking a maid for towels at a Holiday Inn in Flagstaff and abruptly remembering a piece of evidence essential to the case.

The motels also reflected the peripatetic quality to her job: always starting over, working with someone new. She was invariably seen as an outsider, but Laura didn't mind that. She liked working her way into the warp and woof of a town, picking up its easy rhythm, slowing down for the odd yellow dog crossing the street.

Every small town had its own personality.

She got into bed without bothering to change out of her clothes and lay there thinking about Jessica's killer. When she wasn't thinking about the killer she thought about Tom and the idea of living together, her mind going around like a carousel.

## Traffic Stop on 92

Rain tapped on the roof of Officer Duffy's patrol car as she sat in the Safeway parking lot, keeping her eye on the blue BMW Z4 through the streaming windshield. She'd already run the plate; it came back to a Darrell Lee James, 2452 E. Silver Strand Drive, Gulfport, Mississippi. No wants, no warrants—

*Great* car.

Duffy glanced down at the laser-printed photograph on the seat beside her. In the orange light from the sodium arcs, raindrop reflections from the windshield crawled across the picture like ants. The photo showed a good-looking man leaning against a blue BMW Z4. Hard to believe he could be a child-raper, a great-looking guy like that. Still, when she'd spotted the Z4 on her way out to Tacho's Tacos for a late dinner, she'd had no choice but to check it out. If it *was* him, and she was the one who caught him—oh, man. That would show them all up.

Her thoughts turned to that stuck-up detective the chief had saddled them with. Imagine being kept out of the crime scene, like she was a first-year rookie. She smiled at the picture on the seat and said, "You stupid bitch. You don't know everything."

If this was the guy, she'd be a hero. She pictured how impressed Randall would be if she and Buddy ended up on *The Today Show*.

This daydream kept her occupied until she spotted a man carrying a grocery bag in each hand splashing through the parking lot toward the Z4. She couldn't see much of him: He wore a hooded raincoat. When he drove out of the parking lot, she pulled out right behind him.

He made it easy for her by speeding. Couldn't blame someone with a car like that for putting on the afterburners. She stopped him on 92 just south of Tintown.

The rain was coming down hard now. Mud sucked at Duffy's shoes as she walked up to the driver's side, careful to approach him from an angle. Safety first. Darrell Lee James buzzed his window down.

She flashed her light on his face. It wasn't him. This guy was fifty if he was a day.

Duffy kept her face impassive, but her disappointment was deep. She knew she should feel more than disappointed. There was a monster on the loose. The problem was she didn't feel things deeply the way other people did, with one exception. Love was the most important emotion on earth, and that she felt in spades. Everything else paled in comparison to what was going on between her and Randall—even catching a killer. Love could be sweet torture, or a burning agony, and she couldn't live without it.

"Sir, put both hands on the wheel where I can see them."

"Officer, I know I was speeding—"

"Reach down with one hand and remove your wallet. No quick moves."

Carefully, Darrell Lee James reached into his coat and produced his wallet, holding it high and away from his body. The move was automatic; he'd been caught speeding before.

"Slide the license out of your wallet, sir."

He did so, and handed it to her, then put both his hands back on the wheel.

"Do not remove your hands from the wheel, sir. I'll be watching."

She took her time walking back to her unit. Since she had already run his license, she sat there for a couple of minutes, looking at the photo on the seat.

Now *that* was a good-looking man. A total fucking creep, but good-looking.

When she felt she'd waited long enough, she got out and trudged through the mud, handed him back his license, and opened her ticket book. "I'm going to give you a warning this time. But keep to the speed limit from now on, okay?"

"Thank you, ma'am." Eyes like a Pekingese, shiny and moist in his fat pink face.

Duffy watched him pull back onto the road, driving like a little old lady.

A shame to see a Z4 being driven like that.

# 7

At two a.m. the clock radio came on. Laura got out of bed, pulled together what she needed, and walked through the rain-slick streets to City Park.

Ducking under the crime scene tape, she stopped on the sidewalk below the park and looked around.

The light from a sodium arc lamp tinted the street and buildings apricot. This had a flattening effect, making it harder to see. Most of Bisbee was sleeping, but she saw a few rectangles of light in the old buildings up and down the hills.

She looked up the tall flight of steps to the street above.

Laura had always thought it was most likely the bad guy had parked down here on the street and carried the girl up the stairs. She pictured him driving up around the park once to make sure no one was around. On the second pass, he parked right in front of the steps, the passenger door only a few inches from the curb and five feet from the bottom of the steps.

Were his lights on? Would he leave the engine running?

Yes to the lights, no to leaving the engine running. The best way to hide what you were doing was to act normally. Drive down the street with your lights on, park, turn off the lights along with the engine. If anyone happened to be awake and looking out the window, they would see nothing suspicious in someone parking a car. People worked night shifts.

It was doubtful that he had been seen at all. At the briefing, it came out that there were very few houses from which you could actually see the band shell. This had surprised her. There were a couple of houses right on the road facing the park, maybe one or two across the way up high on OK Street, although the trees blocked the band shell from view.

Laura stood in the street where the driver's door would be, pantomimed walking around to the passenger side, leaning down and picking up the girl. He could be up the steps in less than five seconds.

*One step into the park. Three more steps to the band shell stairs. Four steps up. Set her against the wall, clasp her hands together, stand back to look at what you've done. Admire your still life.*

Water from rain earlier tonight dripped from the band shell arch.

Just the act of carrying Jessica up here and placing her against the wall would cause him to shed fibers, hair, skin, and some of that would stick. How would he deal with that?

Would he sweep up?

Or could he have used one of those sticky rollers, the ones people used to pick up pet hair? Lab techs now preferred the sticky rollers to vacuum cleaners when they looked for trace evidence.

Water dripping from the band shell roof: tap tap tap.

*Where are you tonight? Holed up in a motel, or have you moved on already?*

The wind rose, whipping the treetops. Their restive shadows danced on the band shell wall beside her. Rain started up, speckling the concrete.

*Where are you tonight?*

As if in answer, notes from an alto sax trickled down from a window somewhere up the street. Pure and sweet: a soulful, lonely sound.

All the buildings in that direction were dark. The music stopped almost as soon as it had started.

The rain came down harder, a curtain of clear beads in a doorway. Laura stood under the arch, feeling the chill draft as rain blew inward. With the rain came the stench of death.

Suddenly, she could feel him: his essence leaking out of the wet cement, the air around her. Controlled rage. A predator. For a moment she knew what it was like to be a rabbit in the shadow of the hawk.

Was he watching her now? She looked around but saw nothing. Imagined she heard footsteps, but it was only the rain.

The wind blew harder. The tree shadows lashed back and forth on the wall of the band shell in tortured shapes, as if they were being strangled.

She stared out at the park.

Something caught her eye in the gleam of the streetlight, wet and shiny at the edge of the stage. A matchbook.

Laura had been over every inch of this stage earlier today, and she knew the matchbook had not been there when they removed the body. The crime scene had been clean. The matchbook could belong to anyone: kids, tourists, curiosity seekers. The morbid.

Donning latex gloves, she hunkered down beside the matchbook. The words THE COPPER QUEEN HOTEL were stamped on the front. Holding the edges with her fingertips to avoid smearing any prints, she pried it open.

On the inside cover, someone had written a message in block letters with a rollerball pen. The cardboard was so soggy it threatened to come apart in her hands, the letters starting to blur where the raindrops hit them.

Laura scooted back under the overhang. Holding the matchbook open against the concrete, she aimed her flashlight at the block letters.

CRZYGRL12.

The rain hissed, chortled, murmured.

CRZYGRL. Short for crazy girl? The twelfth in a line of crazy girls?

She caught a movement in the corner of her eye. Suddenly, a bright light shone in her face and a voice demanded, "What are you doing?"

# 8

Laura squinted into the glare of a Maglite.

"What are you doing?" Detective Holland repeated. The Maglite steady on her face.

She wondered if he was keeping it on her purposely. Letting her know she was the trespasser here rather than the lead on this case? It made her angry, but it also goosed her heart up a notch. What did he think—she was planting evidence?

"What's that?" he said, motioning at her hand with the light.

She stood up and brushed off her slacks. "What are you doing here?"

"Checking on the crime scene, same as you."

"Earlier today, did you see anything like this?" She held the copper-colored matchbook up to the light.

"Nope."

"Take a look."

"I don't have gloves."

"I'll hold it for you." She opened the matchbook as carefully as she could. "Crazygirl 12. What do you think that means?"

He stared at the letters on the matchbook, his gaze stony.

But she could tell that something was going on behind his eyes, the cogs turning.

Laura said, "I need a paper bag for this."

He just watched her.

"I have plastic evidence bags but no paper. This thing's falling apart and it's wet. If we're going to put this into evidence, I've got to have a paper bag. I've got some in the 4Runner. Would you mind running down and getting me one?"

She tossed him the keys and he caught them. But he made no move to go.

"I'm parked outside the Jonquil."

"Is that an order?"

"It's a request." She added, "Don't you want to catch this guy?"

He stood there for a moment. Drawing it out—that she needed a favor from him. Then he shambled down the steps, in no hurry.

Way down the block she heard the big engine of his Chevy Caprice start up.

Laura wondered how long Buddy Holland had been up here. She would have heard him if he'd just driven up. If *she* could have planted the matchbook, so could he.

The rain kept coming down. After a while, her back started to hurt and she needed to sit down. She sat against the band shell wall, as far away as she could get from where Jessica Parris had been. She tried not to look at the spot. Breathed through her mouth and let her mind wander.

She remembered someone telling her that before the citizens of Bisbee built City Park, this place had been a cemetery. Where did she hear that? On a trip down here a few years ago? Probably. She used to come down overnight with her boyfriend, a member of the Pima County Sheriff's SWAT team. Mostly they came down to cool off from the Tucson summers and make love. It didn't work out because he had an ex-wife who kept tabs on him even though they'd split up years ago.

Counting Tom Lightfoot, that made six serious or semi-serious relationships since college, if she included her ex-husband Billy, who was before, during, and after.

Suddenly she flashed on the night two months ago at the Vail Steak House, going off to the bathroom with Karen, who did the books for the Bosque Escondido. They'd run into each other in the bar on Laura's first foray out into the world with Tom. Tipsy, blundering into the vinyl-walled cubicle, verging on conspiratorial giggles, Laura asking: *What do you think?* Like asking someone off the street to tell her if she ought to buy a certain car. On cue Karen said what Laura wanted to hear: *He's so good-looking, and he can't keep his eyes off you. You guys make a really cute couple.*

*It doesn't bother you that he doesn't have a real job?* Laura asking this as if Karen's opinion was more important than her own.

*Who cares? You earn enough for both of you.*

A car cruised up the street and the engine died. Buddy appeared at the steps to the band shell a minute later. He pulled a folded evidence envelope from his pocket and handed it to her.

"Sorry it took so long." He didn't tell her why.

She placed the matchbook in the envelope and marked it with a pen. "To preserve the chain of custody, I'll keep it with me tonight and take it to the crime lab when I get back to Tucson." Looking for a reaction. He didn't give her one. "Do you have any ideas who Crazygirl 12 is? Is she a local?"

"Not that I know of."

"Anything come to mind at all?"

At first she thought he wasn't going to answer. Then he said, "It could be something to do with the Internet."

"What, like an e-mail address?"

He rubbed his nose. "Or a nick."

Looking at her for some sort of reaction. All she could offer was confusion. "Nick?"

"Nickname. In a chat room." He stared out at the park. "Are we about through?"

"Why did you come up here tonight?"

"Same as you. I wanted to see the place how *he* saw it."

She didn't get back to the Jonquil Motel until a quarter of four. The rain stopped on the walk back.

A fluorescent bulb sizzled above the yellow-and-green door to her room. The glare of the light was so harsh she had to blink. When she stuck her key in the lock, it didn't turn.

She jiggled the key in the lock, cursing under her breath. Stared down at the stubborn lock. Funny—her hand didn't look like her hand. It looked strange, but she couldn't figure out why.

Brain fart. She'd gone without sleep for long periods before—the job required it. Forty, sometimes sixty hours straight. She was young, she was healthy, but tonight she felt every one of her thirty-one years bearing down on her like a weight.

Abruptly, the lock turned. She got the door open, stripped off her clothes, and crawled under the covers. But even when she closed her eyes the light from above the door seemed to sizzle behind her eyelids, little fireworks popping in the dark.

# 9

## The Birthday Celebration

Musicman bought a cupcake and a box of birthday candles, even though the box of candles was a waste of money because he used only one. He chose a blue candle because blue was her favorite color. He set it down next to the present even though the present was not for her. He'd wrapped it with care, beautiful eye-catching paper with a bright golden bow.

While waiting at the checkout counter he'd picked up a paper. Jessica Parris's death made the front page. Lots of strokes and attaboys. He was disappointed, though, that cable hadn't picked it up.

Back inside with the shades drawn, he lit the candle and sang "Happy Birthday," surprised when it made him cry. She would have been thirty years old today. He remembered the last time he saw her, in 1998, two years before her boyfriend beat her to death during a drunken binge. Musicman liked to think she had provoked the cretin into killing her because she could not live with herself.

It still troubled him, her ending up like that. He hated thinking about what had happened in Alert Bay, but sometimes it just reached up and grabbed him, pulling him down into that bad time.

He had been surprised how warm the village on the west Canadian coast was in midsummer. While browsing through the drugstore on the main drag, he'd even had to take off his jacket and wrap it around his waist.

Alert Bay was about as far away as you could get from where he lived—so far away it was even in another country. It was almost as if she had drawn a line on a map. He didn't blame her, after what she'd been through.

There were plenty of knickknacks on the half-empty shelves. Most of them had a Native or marine theme, which was fine except Misty had lived here awhile and none of it would be new to her.

*Who are you trying to impress?* It didn't matter what he bought. He knew that. She would know what was in his mind, and that was what counted.

He glanced at his watch. If he was going to surprise her, he'd better get a move on. She got off work at two. Hurriedly, he picked out a ceramic orca and a card, one of those soft-filtered ones showing two cute little kids together. He also grabbed a roll of breath mints.

He walked fast, worried he might miss her. As he rounded the bend he saw the yellow clapboard building housing the Midnight Sun Hotel and Restaurant. He'd just started up the steps when a woman pushed the door out, struggling with a kid in a stroller. The woman looked used up, your basic white trash: stringy hair, tattoos on her bare arms.

He waited for her to get through the door. She made a big show of wrangling with the stroller, but he refused to help. She gave him a dirty look and he returned her gaze serenely, not letting her know what he was thinking: *She looks like a hype.*

"Thanks for your *help*," she said.

He ignored her and went inside. The place was empty except for a woman he presumed worked there, sitting at a table by the window. He asked her pleasantly if Misty Patin was there.

"She just left."

"Could I get an address?"

The woman parted the curtain and then looked at him. "She's still there. Didn't you see her when you came in?"

He felt his heart drop, the funny feeling you get when an elevator goes way up. "I didn't see anybody."

The woman looked at him as if he were crazy. She shoved back the curtain again and pointed. "She's right out there."

He leaned down and peered out. He saw the hype and her kid across the street. A brand-new navy pickup pulled up. The driver looked like an Eskimo, although that wasn't what they were called around here. He wore a tank top, shorts, and flip-flops. A little girl, maybe ten years old, hopped out right behind him. She was blond and didn't look anything like the man or the kid in the stroller. The girl ran down to the rocky beach and threw rocks into the water.

Looking at her, he knew it was true.

She looked just like Misty.

He felt a wall in his gut give way, the dam he had carefully built up over the years. He could feel something dark and toxic seep out, the resentment and anger that had always been there but had managed to control up until now.

The woman said, "You better hurry if you want to catch her."

"Shut up."

"No one talks to me like that. You'd better go, mister—"

"Shut the fuck up or I'll make you shut up, you dried-up old hag!"

For a second, there was quiet. Then the woman catapulted to her feet, her chair screeching across the floor and ricocheting against the wall as she made a beeline for the kitchen. "I'm calling the police. Nobody talks to me like that."

He ignored her, pulling the curtain back and staring out the window. He watched the little girl, the delight she took in picking out stones and hurling them into the bay. She was fruit of the poisoned tree but still innocent, like an angel. The way Misty used to be.

He let the curtain drop. Looking down, he realized he had crumpled the paper bag holding his recent purchases. Also, he'd forgotten to take a breath mint.

It didn't matter now.

# 10

When Laura arrived at the Bisbee Police Department the next morning, she looked for Buddy Holland, but he wasn't at his desk. She'd planned to divide up the phone work, but that didn't look like it would happen now.

Chief Ducotte had scrounged up a phone and phone jack for her computer and given her the table by the window where they kept the coffee urn. Fortunately, the coffee urn had been moved so she'd have some privacy. She sat down in the folding metal chair, thinking that if she sat here very long, her back would be in agony. She scanned the list of contacts at other law enforcement agencies in the state. Might as well get started.

In the next hour she reached close to a dozen of her counterparts in other jurisdictions, but none of them had encountered a similar crime.

She knew this wasn't this guy's first kill. Dressing the victim up was the killer's signature—something he'd do every time. It would have taken him time and practice to perfect a ritual like this one. Unfortunately, looking for one piece of information in the staggering wave of data from VICAP was a daunting task. VICAP—the Violent Criminal Apprehension Program—was only as good as the agencies entering the data. The FBI database cross-referenced violent crimes nationwide, but participation was voluntary and many smaller jurisdictions didn't use the system.

Somebody standing at her elbow—Officer Noone. "Ma'am?"

She straightened up, felt a twinge in her back. Smiled at him.

"I heard you were looking for a saxophone player? My sister dated a guy who played the sax. I heard he lived on the Gulch, so I asked around and I found him. Name's Jeeter."

"Jeeter who?"

"Just Jeeter."

Through the window Laura saw Buddy Holland and Officer Duffy approaching from the parking lot. Duffy looked pissed. Laura got the impression that was a permanent condition.

As Buddy approached the window he ducked his head to look in at her. No, not at her. He was looking at himself.

"Jeeter doesn't have a last name?" Laura asked Noone.

"Apparently not, ma'am." He looked chastened, as if Jeeter's not having a last name was a reflection on him.

"What's Jeeter's story?" she asked.

"Guess you could say he's a night owl. Itinerant musician, takes up the slack with odd jobs."

Laura glanced at Buddy Holland's desk, at a faded but eye-catching photo of Buddy, a woman, and a little girl posing in front of Old Faithful at Yellowstone. "Did Jeeter happen to look out his window?" Laura asked Noone.

"As a matter of fact he did. He likes to sit next to an open window when he plays. Feel the night air."

"Great for his neighbors. Did he see anything?"

His broad handsome face lit up—what he had been building up to. "He saw a motor home." He consulted his memo pad. "He noticed it for a couple of reasons. Almost nobody drives down the Gulch in the wee hours of the morning. And, this motor home went up and back on the Gulch twice."

"What time was that?"

"Between two and three."

"Did he notice anything else?"

"Just that it went slow. He wasn't thinking make, size, anything—just noticed it driving down the street a couple of times. Here's his number." He handed her a "While You Were Out" slip, the name "Jeeter," his phone number, and his address neatly printed on it.

He lingered.

"Yes?" Wishing he would go so she could think.

"If there's anything else I can do—"

She glanced at her watch, thinking she should get out to see the Parris family soon or she'd have to wait until early afternoon—and that would be cutting it close. She was meeting the owner of the Cooger & Dark shop at eleven and the autopsy in Sierra Vista was at four. She looked at Noone. "As a matter of fact there is something you can do. I want you to look up motor homes—you can do it on the Internet. Go back at least fifteen years and get a representative sample. Go show them to Jeeter and see if anything jogs his memory."

"Yes, ma'am. I'll do that right now."

"When does your shift end?"

"Three o'clock, but—"

"You'd better ask your sergeant if he can spare you, otherwise it will have to wait."

After he was gone, she thought about the motor home. Saw it in her mind's eye, cruising down the Gulch in the early hours of the morning.

It made sense. A motor home was an ideal vehicle for a sexual predator: portable, self-contained, window shades so no one could see in.

She glanced at Buddy Holland's desk. He must have come in and gone again while she was talking to Noone. She powered down her computer and went looking for him, catching Officer Danehill at the coffee urn, which had been set up outside the bathroom. "Have you seen Buddy?"

"Buddy? He just left."

Laura decided that could be a good thing. She doubted Buddy would be a help and might be a hindrance. She headed up-canyon to see Jessica's parents.

David and Linda Parris lived on West Boulevard, the last house before vacant land. Three hundred yards up, West Boulevard bottomed out in a hairpin turn before slanting up the mountain. According to Laura's map, this road, old Route 80, switchbacked up to the top and then down again to connect up with the main highway on the other side of Mule Pass.

On the left side of the road just before the hairpin turn were a couple of houses. It might be worth talking to the owners of those houses, to find out if they saw anything. She'd do that after her interview with the family.

It was going on nine in the morning. She'd debated calling first, but decided it was better to just show up. In her job, Laura always looked for the upper hand with everyone— victim or perpetrator—so she could get a better read on the personalities involved.

The Parris house, a Craftsman bungalow, had a three-foot-high base of dark volcanic rock, with red brick above that. The porch, windows, and doors were painted white. A picket fence flickered in and out of the shadow of a massive sycamore tree, and an American flag hung dispiritedly from the porch roof. Blinds in the front windows were shut tight.

The day was steamy after the rain and the sun blindingly bright. Laura was grateful for the shade of the porch. She used the deer-head knocker, preparing herself.

No answer. A breeze shuttled a few oak leaves across the floorboards. She knocked again, scanning the street while she waited, then tried the doorbell.

"They're out."

Laura looked up and saw a bare-chested man watering his plants next door. Was this the neighbor Victor had told her about?

"You with the police department?" he asked.

"Laura Cardinal, Department of Public Safety." She held her wallet badge up for him to see and approached the fence.

She studied him as he looked at her badge: five feet nine, average build, tattoos on his arms, head like a bullet. Intense eyes.

He shook her hand over the fence. A grip like a mountain climber. "Chuck Lehman."

"Do you know where they went?"

"Dave mentioned making funeral arrangements yesterday, so I'm guessing they're at the funeral home. You just missed them."

Laura tried not to show her disappointment. "Do you mind if I ask you a few questions?"

He picked up the hose and started watering again. "Sure, go ahead."

"Did you notice Jessica coming home from school day before yesterday?"

"Nope. I was in the back room, on the computer. Stock trading."

"You didn't hear anything, see anything? Maybe earlier? A car you didn't recognize, maybe going slow? Someone hanging around?"

She was plowing old ground; Victor had already asked him questions like this, but she wanted to hear his answers for herself.

Chuck Lehman was willing. He gave her a thumbnail sketch of the family (father, authoritarian; mother, a pretty doormat; boyfriend, probably will end up being gay; Jessica, a cute kid; younger brother, a little shit). He pondered at length how her agency could use its resources to better advantage; they needed to get the media involved "on a national level," put up roadblocks. "You don't even have the Amber Alert."

"You sound like you're in law enforcement."

"Me? No. I'm a carpenter." He touched his forehead. "But I have good powers of observation."

She noticed the tautness in his face, the slight trembling

in his body; he seemed to be on an adrenaline high. Was he excited about being included, or covering up something?

"Did you talk to Jessica much?"

"Me? No." He waved at the air vaguely. "Hardly ever saw her." Mister Amiable, suddenly closing up.

"You know of any of her friends I could talk to?"

"How would I know that? If you haven't noticed, I'm a *big* kid." Confident smile.

"All the days she's walked home from school, nobody, nothing stuck out in your mind?"

"I don't notice who comes and goes. They're just kids."

He seemed increasingly uncomfortable. It occurred to her that he could be hiding an interest in young girls.

Something not right about him. She remembered what Buddy Holland had said, that CRZYGRL12 could be an e-mail address or a chat room name. She lowered her voice, her inflection friendly: *You and me in this together.* "You said you have a computer. Do you know anyone with the e-mail address Crazygirl 12?"

He blinked. "What?"

"Crazygirl 12? Maybe Jessica's e-mail? You wouldn't know if she had a computer, would you?"

"Why would I know that?"

Angry. Offense was the best defense.

Without conscious thought, Laura shifted her weight to her back leg. Aware of the gun under her jacket. She made her voice even quieter, nonthreatening. "Sir, could you tell me about your conviction?"

His eyes turned hard. "You can call my probation officer."

She waited.

"Criminal damage," he said, his voice as hard as his eyes. "I broke into my ex-wife's house and tore up her clothes."

"Her underpants," Laura said, sounding as if it was something that happened every day.

"Right. Her underpants. Satisfied?" Anger radiated from him, making him seem bigger.

She stepped back, hand near her hip. "Sir—"

Suddenly he crossed the space between them, so quick she had to back up another couple of steps. His chin thrust out like a drill sergeant. "I *said,* are you satisfied?"

"Yes," she said. Keeping the calm in her voice, though she was anything but.

He glared at her, his eyes like twin blue flames.

"Good." With a jerk of the head for emphasis, he walked into his house and slammed the door.

Laura stood there for almost a minute, shame and anger riding a river of adrenaline. She had reacted in an acceptable way—stepping back to allow space between them so that she had room to draw her weapon—but couldn't help feeling she'd looked weak. Would Victor have retreated like that?

Lehman got a big charge out of intimidating her: In his mind, he had won. She looked back at the Lehman house. One of the blinds moved in the front window. He was watching her. She straightened her back, trying to ignore him. She'd planned to do something. What was it?

The houses at the hairpin. That was it. Someone there might have seen something.

She started up the road, careful to stay to the asphalt, scanning the ground on either side. She doubted she'd find anything; the general consensus was that Jessica had been picked up coming home from school, which would mean she didn't get this far. But Laura looked at the ground anyway, trying to concentrate. Trying not to think of Lehman staring at her back. A hundred yards up, she noted a clearing on the left side of the road, and another turnout on the corresponding side. Several cars had turned around there.

A dog barked at her from behind the redwood fence of the first house. She knocked and got no answer, stuck her card in the door with a request that the homeowner contact her when they got home.

The second house was set back from the road, a faded

green cinder-block. The drapes were closed. A swamp box cooler rattled like a cement mixer. She thought she heard a TV set going, but no one answered her knock. Many people these days didn't answer their doors—a safety issue. She left another card.

On the way back to the car, Laura stopped at the turnout and examined the tire tracks. Many of them overlapped. One set of tread marks in particular caught her attention. A heavy vehicle, judging from the way the tracks sank into the ground. She could see corresponding tread marks on the other side of the road; he'd had to back and fill.

The mud had dried, hardening into bas-relief. They'd make excellent plaster casts.

She squatted down and stared at them. Double wheels. From looking at both turnouts, she thought the vehicle had a big wheelbase.

Like a motor home.

The sun bore down on her neck like an iron and flies buzzed around, lighting on her face and arms, tickling her. No telling if the tracks here belonged to a motor home at all, let alone the one Jeeter had seen on the Gulch. She knew what Frank Entwistle would say: When in doubt, be thorough.

She walked back to the 4Runner and got a spool of yellow crime scene tape and blocked off the area around both turnouts. She called the station and asked to be patched through to Officer Noone.

"What are you doing?" she asked him when he answered.

"Looking up motor homes." He added hastily, "The chief said I could."

Laura glanced at her watch. She had to be at Cooger & Dark's in ten minutes. "I've taped off some tire tracks up at the end of West Boulevard," she said. "I want you to come up here and keep an eye on them until I get back. Can you do that?"

"Yes, ma'am. I'm on my way."

*        *        *

Ted Olsen, the owner of Cooger & Dark's Pandemonium Shadow Show and Emporium, looked nothing like his Viking name. He was a short balding man with a ZZ Top beard that had been buttoned into the neck of his short-sleeved shirt, as if he wanted to keep it out of the way.

Cooger & Dark's shelves were cluttered with fringed lamp shades, art deco radios, and old lunch boxes. A gas pump from the early part of the century stood in the corner. But Laura's attention was on the dolls suspended from the ceiling. They made her think of trapeze artists caught in midswoop.

They reminded her of the Cabbage Patch craze years ago, only bigger—much bigger, their long flour white limbs like sausages. They were dressed in gingham pinafores, dotted swiss baby-doll dresses, gunnysack dresses. White, pink, yellow.

"You've got a lot of dolls," she said as Olsen went through the shop turning on lights.

"You like them?"

"Very nice." Actually, they creeped her out.

She wondered: Could this be the guy? She didn't get anything from him except matter-of-factness, but she wasn't psychic.

"Where did you get them?" she asked.

"My girls? I make them."

"You do?" Her next question would naturally be, "Why?" Instead she asked him if anyone had shown interest in the doll in the window.

"She's not one of mine. She's plastic. I use only natural materials."

"But has anyone asked about it? Or any of your dolls?"

"Tourists."

"Any men?"

"Men?" He stroked his beard. "Usually the men are interested in stuff like that gas pump. I can't recall anyone . . ." He coughed up something into a handkerchief that he kept in his gray pants, pants that reminded Laura of the custodian at her high school years ago. "There *was* a guy interested in a dress. Wanted to buy it."

"Why?"

"People never cease to amaze me. Been in this business for twenty years, and you never can figure out what they're gonna ask for. He wanted to take that dress up there right off Daisy, but I told him no."

Laura's gaze followed his long crooked finger.

The doll wore a pale pink tulle dress with baby-doll sleeves.

"If I sold him the dress, Daisy would have been left in her birthday suit," Olsen explained. "I couldn't do that. When I explained it to him, he got mad."

"Mad?"

"He didn't make a scene but you could tell he was steaming. Like he was counting to ten."

"Can I see the doll?"

"Sure." He grabbed a long pole with a hook on the end of it and pulled at a rope hanging down behind him. Laura realized that it was a pulley system, kind of like at a dry cleaner's, from which the dolls were suspended. He pulled the doll around, then expertly hooked her off by the neck and set her down on the counter. She noticed he had a U.S. Marines tattoo on one arm.

Laura eyeballed Daisy, thinking she was approximately the same size as Jessica Parris: one big damn doll. "What size dress is that?"

"Size three, junior."

"What age would that fit?"

"Thirteen, fourteen years old."

"Tell me about the guy."

According to Ted Olsen, the man was white, average-looking except for a black mustache, and he had blue eyes. Olsen remembered the eyes because the guy was so mad. Asked to describe his clothing, Olsen thought he might have been wearing a ball cap, and "probably jeans."

"Nothing seemed unusual about him?"

"When he first came in, he didn't seem like somebody who would get so mad."

"So how did he strike you? When he first came in?"

"Well, see, I didn't really notice him until he found me. He was the kind who blends in—just a regular guy."

"When did he come in?"

"Day before yesterday. I was open that night, which I do sometimes when I'm working on a doll in back. Stayed open until nine o'clock."

Nine o'clock: three to four hours after Jessica Parris was last seen.

Laura told him she'd be back with a photograph of the dress Jessica Parris had worn, in case he recognized the style. "In the meantime, if you remember anything else about this guy, please call me." She handed him her card.

As she crossed the street to her car, she finally got hold of Buddy Holland.

"Where are you? I've been looking for you."

"Running down some things on my own."

And avoiding her, she thought. "We need to compare notes. I'm headed up to take some plaster casts on West Boulevard right now, but—"

"I'll meet you there. I'm going up there anyway."

"You are?"

"I just talked to Dave Parris. Thought it would be a good idea if we took a look at the girl's room. Unless you're too busy."

# 11

The window to Jessica Parris's room was open, sunlight pouring in along with the warm summer air. It was clear from the posters on the wall that Jessica favored Josh Hartnett, Shakira, and Nelly. Laura had done stupid things in her teenage years, but worshipping a guy who wore a Band-Aid on his cheek wasn't one of them.

Someone had written all over Jessica's sheets with permanent markers. "Stay cool!" "You're my best friend ever." "You and Cary are the coolest people I know."

"Her friends wrote those things," Mrs. Parris said from the doorway. "We had a slumber party and they helped her decorate her room." She hugged herself as if by doing so she might hold herself together, her nervous gaze straying to Buddy Holland, who was poking around the room as if it were a garbage dump. "Do you need anything else?"

Laura said, "I notice she doesn't have a computer. Do you or your husband?"

"No. We're not computer literate around here. Excuse me. I have to check the cookies."

A dresser drawer screeched as Buddy opened it with latexed hands.

Laura looked up sharply. Holland returned her look, eyes devoid of all expression. She'd seen that look before, had used it herself. Cops who detested each other still had to work together, so they did it with as few words possible, just enough to get the job done. No one did cold as well as a cop.

Laura said, "No computer in the house, but she probably has access to one at school. You really think Crazygirl 12 has something to do with the Internet?"

"Could be." Then he did something she didn't expect: volunteered. "Let me check it out. I know my way around the Net pretty well. If she's there, I can probably track her down."

It was the longest speech she'd ever heard from him. "What would you do?"

"Check out Internet Relay Chats, see if I can find her there."

Laura seized on the one word of the three she understood. "You mean chat rooms?"

"Uh-huh." He didn't elaborate. "You want me to or not?"

She nodded. "I think you should."

A photograph on the dresser top caught her eye: Jessica and a young man she assumed was Cary Statler. Jessica was pretty in a short denim skirt and halter top. Statler was a skinny, sleepy-looking kid in a black T-shirt and dirty-looking jeans. His hair looked like a pineapple top.

Buddy had gone back to searching, rummaging through a makeup caddy, then moving on to a velvet-lined box holding her earrings, bracelets, and anklets. A tinny sound as an anklet hit the floor. Doing it to annoy her.

"Buddy."

"What?"

"Why don't you interview Mr. Parris?"

Shrug. "Fine with me."

He snapped off his gloves and left the room.

The stillness contrasted with all his banging. Now maybe she could get a feel for the girl.

Jessica had a thing for girly stuff: flavored lip gloss, smiley-faced colognes with names like Cool Diva and Cha

Cha Chica, and at least a dozen tubes of Sungirl—sun care products with glitter.

Laura looked at the photo again, wondering what about it nagged her.

It would come.

She looked through the dresser drawers and closet: blue jeans, peasant blouses, halters, clogs. Jessica's underwear was neatly folded in her dresser drawers. Bikini underwear in pastel colors, a couple of bras—Victoria's Secret type stuff. They looked sophisticated for a fourteen-year-old girl, at least the fourteen-year-old girl Laura had been. A different era. She found a few homework assignments jammed into a bookshelf, most of the answer spaces blank. Round handwriting with hearts to dot the i's. No diary, unless Jessica kept it in a secret place. No books other than schoolbooks and the Harry Potter series, which was lined up in the bookcase like those leather-bound classics people displayed for show. Laura couldn't say for sure, but she doubted that Jessica had cracked one of them.

Lots of *stuff*. Laura had read somewhere that tweens—eight- to fourteen-year-olds—had so much discretionary income and such expensive tastes that they drove the whole economy. Not just the U.S. economy, but the world's.

She noticed a newspaper clipping from a modeling agency tucked into the frame of the dresser mirror. Mrs. Parris had told her Jessica had wanted to be a model or a rock star.

Now she would be neither.

Laura walked into the kitchen, where the smell of baking cookies was overwhelming. Mrs. Parris fluttered back and forth through the sunny kitchen like a bird trapped indoors, her movements increasingly frantic.

"How are you doing?" Laura asked.

Mrs. Parris checked the heat on the oven. "We're okay. I mean . . . it's horrible, but . . ." She wiped a strand of red hair from her eyes.

"I'm sorry, but I have some more questions." Laura set her mini–cassette recorder on the kitchen counter.

"I know. You have to ask your questions. We want to find the guy who did this." She said this last brightly.

"Mrs. Parris, do you know if she used a computer at school?"

Her brow wrinkled. "I think so."

"She never talked about it? You know, e-mailing her friends?"

"I wouldn't know e-mail from a hole in the wall. I'm not the least bit technical." She stared at the oven. "Jessica loved to bake cookies. That's why I'm doing it today. Kind of in her memory."

"Where's Cary?"

"Cary?" Linda Parris looked stunned.

"Her boyfriend. Doesn't he live here?"

"Oh." She floundered for a moment, as if she'd dropped a thought and had to consciously pick it up again. "We're kind of like his foster parents, even though there's nothing official. You must think that odd, but it really isn't. He needs us. We love him as if he's our own son."

"He and Jessica were boyfriend and girlfriend, though?"

"I know what you're thinking. We had very strict rules, her father did. Cary lives in our travel trailer out back. Not in the house. But he's a nice boy."

"Were they sexually active?"

Defiance. "Yes. I found out about that a couple of months ago. And you know what I did? I marched her down to Planned Parenthood and got her birth control pills. You might think I'm a bad mother, but I did what I had to do, and I didn't want our child *having* a child."

"I'm not judging you, Mrs. Parris."

"Please don't say anything to her father. He'd have a fit if he knew."

Laura thought that he probably did know. "I see no reason to tell him. So you don't know where Cary is?"

Mrs. Parris frowned. "Come to think of it, I haven't seen him for a while."

"Since Jessica was missing?"

"I'm not . . ." She didn't finish her thought.

"You don't know when he was here last?"

"He comes and goes. He has an uncle in Tucson—sometimes he stays there weeks at a time, especially after—" She stopped. Her eyes widened slightly.

"After what?"

"After a fight." Linda Parris looked past Laura, out the window.

Laura took note of the present tense and decided to stick with it. "With Jessica? Do they fight a lot?"

"No, no, nothing like what you're thinking. Just arguments. Jessica can be—she could get dramatic. Cary just stayed out of her way, let her cool down. That's all it was."

"When was their last fight?"

"I know they weren't talking earlier in the week."

"And you haven't seen him since?"

"It's not like that. David and I would never bring someone into our home that we thought would be dangerous to our daughter."

"Mrs. Parris, I have to know. When was the last time you saw him?"

"I think it was . . . two, three days ago. But it's not what you think. He keeps to himself a lot, likes to go for long walks. Sometimes he stays with friends. That's what Jessica loves most about him, even though it drove her crazy sometimes. She said he was a free spirit. I know what you're hinting at and you're wrong. We would never put our own daughter in danger."

"I understand that, but it's important I talk to him. It's very likely he doesn't know Jessica is gone. Don't you agree he should know?"

She nodded reluctantly. Laura asked for the uncle's address and phone number, and Linda Parris found it in her address book and copied it on paper from the memo pad stuck to the refrigerator, a flag at the top above the phrase "United We Stand."

Linda moved back to the sink and carefully washed the mixing bowl and set it in the dishwasher. She stared out the window again. "We had so many good times. Last Saturday we spent the morning weeding. Jessie and her dad went to the Arctic Circle for hamburgers. She got mine with mustard but not ketchup—she knew I didn't like ketchup. That was a great day."

She continued to stare out the window.

Something brushed Laura's ankles. She looked down. A Siamese cat rubbed against her trouser legs.

Laura was attracted to animals the way some people were attracted to babies. She hunkered down and stroked the cat.

"That's Princess, Jessie's cat." Linda Parris's voice broke. "Jessie found her in a Dumpster at the school. Half starved, sick. Her father told her Princess was her responsibility—she couldn't keep her unless she did everything. Feed her, clean the cat box, use her allowance to get her spayed . . ." She was rambling.

The cat climbed up into Laura's arms and onto her shoulder. It felt natural to Laura: the small vibrating body, the warmth. Comforting.

Holding the cat, she thought of Jessica. Jessica, who liked Josh Hartnett and Nelly. Jessica, who took such good care of her cat. Something crumbled in her chest, and tears pricked the corners of her eyes.

She turned away so the mother couldn't see, and set the cat down.

As Laura left through the front door, she glanced up the street at the roped-off area where the turnouts were. Officer Noone stood in the road, hands on his waist above his heavy duty belt, the yellow crime scene tape quivering behind him. When he saw her he waved. If he was bored by his new duty—waiting for the tire cast to dry—he didn't show it.

Buddy appeared from around the corner of the house,

where David Parris, Jessica's father, was hammering away at something.

Buddy nodded toward Noone. "You about done up there?"

"Might be another half hour. How's Mr. Parris?"

"Wouldn't talk to me. We put up three sections of rain gutter, though."

"Wouldn't talk at all?"

"The only thing he said was, if Cary Statler ever showed his face around here again, he'd kill him."

As Laura reached the turnout, Noone said, "They're almost dry."

Beside the metal-framed cast lay a couple of sticks, all that was left of a sampling of twigs, grass, and debris Laura had instructed Noone to collect from around the site. These Laura had used to reinforce the plaster. Not only would it make the cast stronger, but it would also supply a soil and debris sample for the crime lab. Laura picked up a stout twig and wrote her initials onto the cast, along with the case number.

"I never saw anyone take a tire cast before. It's pretty interesting," Noone offered. "Too bad there weren't any footprints."

It was clear Officer Noone had made the leap from the motor home sighting on Brewery Gulch to the abduction of Jessica Parris on West Boulevard, concluding that the killer had used a motor home.

"These tracks could belong to anyone. I wouldn't get my hopes up if I were you."

"But it could be his."

"Could be." Emphasis on the *could.*

# 12

To business.

Musicman wrote:

D—Your shipment has come in.

Immediately, a reply popped up.

DARK MOONDANCER:   Hello, friend.

Musicman's fingers flew over the keys.

MUSICMAN:   I have that special order you requested.
DARK MOONDANCER:   Same price?
MUSICMAN:   Two thousand more.
DARK MOONDANCER:   Verification?
MUSICMAN:   Turn on the local news.
DARK MOONDANCER:   That one? You're in my jurisdiction! Let's meet.
MUSICMAN:   I never meet my clientele. It's not good to mix business with pleasure.
DARK MOONDANCER:   You do it all the time, mix business with pleasure LOL. But seriously, we are an exclusive club, you and I. Please come visit. Bring a friend.

MUSICMAN:   My plans are fluid at the moment.

DARK MOONDANCER:   Fluid? There's a pun. So you ARE still here. I would have thought you'd be a thousand miles away by now.

MUSICMAN:   Parting is such sweet sorrow.

DARK MOONDANCER:   Don't be cryptic. I'd love to know what's going on in your mind.

MUSICMAN:   Shall I make the shipment or not?

DARK MOONDANCER:   By all means. As before, payment is forthcoming. But if you're planning an extended stay, do give serious thought to my invitation. You might not come this way again.

Musicman thought, *We have less in common than you think.*

Dark Moondancer's desires were base, his enthusiasm clumsy. He didn't get the subtle distinctions; he was just another cretin saturated with bloodlust, looking for a vicarious thrill. The guy reminded him of a comic book character—way over the top.

Still, he paid the bills.

Musicman pulled up the photograph he intended to use: baby ducks following their mother across a lawn. Beautiful, the play of sunlight and shadow on their soft yellow down. So innocent. And yet beneath the surface resided a dark secret.

A secret that, truth to tell, shamed him.

He wouldn't do it if he didn't need the money. So far he'd ignored Dark Moondancer's hints about escalating the violence—it just wasn't his way. Even with this one—who'd made him so fucking angry!—he'd stopped short of fulfilling Dark Moondancer's requests. Partly because he didn't like the sight of blood (although he'd proven that he *could* deal with it if he had to), and partly because he didn't like Dark Moondancer or anybody else calling the shots.

This was *his* show.

Musicman knew, though, that Dark Moondancer was getting impatient. The gravy train wouldn't last forever.

Utilizing a user-friendly software program he had downloaded from the Internet, Musicman embedded the first photo into the picture of the baby ducks. He pulled up another scenic from his photo library: boats in a marina.

He would send four pics in all. Each pic would be encrypted and require a password to open. Dark Moondancer would have the baby ducks, but he would not have the real picture underneath until Musicman got his payment. Only then would he send back the encrypted password.

He pictured Dark Moondancer looking at the little duckies, wishing he could see what was underneath.

" 'Water, water everywhere, nor any drop to drink,' " Musicman intoned. He hit the SEND button, consigning the ducklings and their invisible cargo to the ether.

# 13

"Her hyoid was broken," Cochise County ME Carmen Sotomayor said as she snapped off her gloves and dropped them into a biohazard container.

The smell of sawed bone clung to Laura's nostrils, almost as bad as the odor of death. The last thing Carmen Sotomayor had done before sewing Jessica Parris back up was to use an electric saw to open up her cranium to examine her brain.

Laura thought the killer had been crafty, but now she knew to what extremes he had gone to avoid detection. He'd bathed the girl's body and washed her hair, clipped her fingernails, even given her a douche.

The douche was necessary. He had sexually assaulted his victim after death, not before. Postmortem sex was another indication that the killer didn't want to risk abrasions to Jessica and to himself. Whoever he was, he knew something about the collection of evidence.

She looked at Jessica Parris, small and forlorn on the stainless steel autopsy table. Gutters running around the edge of the table gleamed in the light, still holding the residue of blood from the autopsy. The girl who had reminded her yesterday of a Victorian doll now looked more like Raggedy

Ann, big ugly stitches forming a Y down the length of her body.

"When you measured her—you said she was small for her age?" Laura asked.

"And underdeveloped."

"You mean more like a little girl than a teenager, anatomically?"

"There's a phenomenon we're just beginning to see in the physical development in girls. They're maturing at a faster rate than, say, when you and I were their age. But this girl is on the immature side, although it appears she had enough pubic hair for him to shave."

"He shaved her so he could think of her as younger," Laura said.

"And to destroy evidence—her pubic hair and his." Carmen Sotomayor stared at the girl, her eyes sad. Laura noticed she had bitten her lip: a little gash, dark lipstick edging her teeth.

Carmen added, "If he did it to make her seem younger, it wasn't too much of a leap—she's pretty flat up top. She wasn't wearing a bra. You'd think a fourteen-year-old girl would wear a bra, whether she needed to or not."

Laura thought of the bras in the top drawer of Jessica's dresser. "He took it."

"But he left the bikini underwear."

Laura said, "I wonder if he had a replacement pair and they didn't fit."

"What would he replace them with?"

"Maybe something more modest."

Two vertical lines appeared between Carmen's dark brows. "You think so?"

"Who knows? It was just something that occurred to me." Laura divested herself of the paper booties, the gown, the gloves.

She knew not to jump to any conclusions. Her method had always been to disprove a theory, rather than prove it. That way, she avoided making leaps in logic just to bolster a theory that might not pan out. She liked to look at evidence as if it were a disassembled car spread out on a tarp, making damn sure that whatever parts connected weren't forced into place.

Something didn't fit here. Maybe it was the girl herself. She seemed out of place, although Laura couldn't figure out why. Maybe it was her age; maybe it was more than that.

"That dress is homemade," Carmen Sotomayor said. "No tag anywhere, and those darts looked like they were from a pretty simple pattern. So that ought to narrow it down."

By the time Laura left the ME's office in the Sierra Vista Community Hospital, it was going on six o'clock and looked like it would storm. She rolled down the window, inhaling the scent of the impending rain on the dense air. The area had greened up a lot since she'd been down here a couple of weeks ago. Johnsongrass lined both sides of the road, lush and green, soaking up the runoff. Ocotillo on the hills looked like dark green pipe cleaners.

The evidence for the DPS Crime Lab resided in the back of the 4Runner, each piece packaged separately and bearing her initials: head and pubic hair samples from Jessica, fingernail clippings, scrapings from under her fingernails, swabs from her body, and her clothing. And, of course, the tire tread moulage and the matchbook in its paper evidence envelope.

He had been pretty sure of himself to go back and leave the matchbook—another taunt. He was playing with them. In a way, that was good. Laura knew that when you got cocky you made mistakes, and she intended to be there when he did.

The dress intrigued her, the idea of it having been run up on a sewing machine from a pattern. Did that mean he could sew, like Ted Olsen? Did he have someone in his life who sewed for him—a girlfriend, wife, or mother? He'd tried to buy a dress that would fit a fourteen-year-old girl because his own dress didn't fit.

It would be time-consuming to locate the company that produced the pattern, and track back from there to the outlets. Laura was even less optimistic about tracing the material, the zipper, the thread, the lace, and the ribbon.

If he didn't purchase those in the area, you could forget about that.

The storm hit just as she reached Tucson. She took the Valencia Road exit and drove west to the Department of Public Safety on Tucson Boulevard down the street from the Tucson International Airport.

Lightning sizzled across the sky as she turned into the parking lot. Built in the sixties, the DPS building reminded her of a grain elevator. In the blowing rain, the concrete building darkened to the same slate color as the sky. U.S. and Arizona flags whipped in a wind-driven frenzy, their chains rattling. Laura waited for the automatic gate to roll back and drove in, taking note of the cars in the inside lot. Victor's truck wasn't there. She doubted she'd see anyone at this hour.

She booked the tire moulage, the matchbook, Jessica's clothes, and other items from the autopsy into evidence, filled out the paperwork, and requested the types of tests she wanted from the crime lab. On her way to the squad bay she passed Mike Galaz's office and noticed something new: two rows of photos on the wall by his door. Mostly of the Tucson social scene, Let's Go People! and his wife standing in groups of three or four at various fund-raising events. Expensive coifs, more expensive smiles.

Laura had never been part of that social circle, and knew by now she never would be. Fortunately, she didn't need an expensive evening gown to send her check to the Hermitage No-Kill Cat Shelter.

Everybody had gone home except for Todd Rees, the youngest and newest member of the squad. His desk was catty-corner to hers, facing the other direction. She liked that, because it kept their interaction to a minimum. He looked up and then back at his computer.

Her plant was looking a little dry. She prodded it, filled a coffee cup with water from the bathroom sink, and gave it a drink before checking her messages and her voice mail.

One message had been placed on the center of her desk in Rich Lockhart's handwriting: "Call Myra Maynes at the Medical Examiner's office."

"When pigs fly," she muttered, tossing the note into the wastebasket.

A California detective named Barry Endicott of the Riverside County Sheriff's Department had left a message on her voice mail, "regarding your child homicide in Bisbee."

She didn't recognize the name. One of her contacts at another agency must have made some calls. As she picked up the phone, Todd Rees slipped on his suit jacket, picked up his briefcase, and ambled past her. He always dressed in a suit and tie.

Tall and thin, he reminded her of a praying mantis. Now he craned his neck over her shoulder, looking at her notes.

She put her hand over the mouthpiece. "Watcha need?"

"Nothing." He slouched past her, but she could feel him lurking in the doorway. Todd had a reputation for keeping his mind on other people's business, always looking for a way to ingratiate himself with the brass. "You have a good time in Bisbee?"

The phone started ringing on the other end and she broke the connection. "'Good' is not the way I'd describe it."

"The lieut kind of wondered why you didn't come back with the techs."

So that was it. What, he thought she turned it into a vacation?

One of the new rules Galaz had instituted was financial: He wanted to see a justification of every expense over a hundred dollars. This affected overnight stays. If at all possible, he wanted his detectives to drive back rather than stay the night.

"I used my own money," Laura said, mad at herself for letting Todd put her on the defensive.

"Did you use your own time?"

It was a parting shot; he was already out the door and halfway down the stairs. Todd had a habit of sniping at people and then running for cover. Still, she knew she'd have to smooth it over with Jerry Grimes, and he in turn would smooth it over with Galaz.

She wasn't going to worry about it. Jerry knew she got results. Maybe her methods were a little unorthodox, but that had always been the way she worked.

Lieutenant Mike Galaz had been here for five months. Other than his watchful eye over the budget, he was an unknown factor, generally considered to be a good (if political) administrator who left the sergeants to run their own squads.

His first official act was to institute weekly briefings where everyone in the criminal investigation division got together and discussed their cases. Galaz himself didn't take part, but stood at the front of the room listening intently. At the end of each meeting, he'd give a short speech about the importance of their mission, ending with a phrase he must have picked up from a TV show: "Let's go, people!"

Laura punched in Detective Endicott's number but got his voice mail—gone for the day. She looked at the clock: seven thirty. Next she called Cary Statler's uncle. No answer, no machine.

Where was Cary Statler?

It nagged at her, even though Laura's instincts told her he wasn't Jessica Parris's killer. Strangling a person face-to-face showed rage, which would fit a domestic abusive relationship. But Laura worked under the assumption that the killer was older. Dressing her like that didn't fit with a boyfriend-girlfriend relationship. And the way he'd cleaned her up, so careful not to leave evidence—it was possible Cary could have done all that, but unlikely.

Still, she wished she knew where he was.

When she looked at the clock again it was eleven thirty.

By this time there were stacks of papers all over her desk, some on chairs, some on the floor: transcripts of interviews, autopsy results, her own notes torn from a yellow legal pad. A sea of information, including a printout of City Park drawn to scale. She had looked it over three times now, worrying that she was missing something. Now she was staring at it without really seeing it.

Time to go home, and sleep—if she could.

# 14

The 4Runner's tires rumbled over the cattle guard marking the entrance to the Bosque Escondido Guest Ranch. The storm had gone, leaving a few luminous clouds and a full moon that turned the dirt road white, a chalk line through the desert.

The moment she drove onto the Bosque Escondido, Laura felt something give in her chest. She loved her job, but it wasn't natural to have to look at so much ugliness day after day. The evils people visited on one another—the unspeakable cruelties she saw almost daily—had the cumulative effect of a house of cards, one insult building up on top of another until over time the whole thing threatened to come crashing down. She was almost to that point now. She could feel it, tiny cracks running through the wall she'd put up.

Structural damage.

Tonight she had nothing to go home to except the flat-roofed Mexican adobe in the middle of the desert.

Normally she liked being way out at the edge of Tucson, in a shallow indentation in the desert where she could not even see the city lights, but tonight she didn't want to walk into an empty house. Putting it off, she drove past the main ranch house, the guest bungalows, the cantina, then turned onto the short loop road that took her by Tom's place: a tin-roofed adobe with a screened-in porch. The place was dark—no welcoming light. She wondered if he was thinking about her.

Right now—at this moment—she wanted him to move in and never leave. It was almost physical, this need she had. She wondered how she had managed to go so long without someone. When you had someone everything was better. You had a mate in a world where most people had mates. You went more places, and there was an aura to being in love, like you had God's blessing. People saw you differently.

She thought of all the places she wanted to go with him. Just overnight stays because she worked so much. But good times. Good times piling up one on top of the other, photos in an album.

She wished he was here right now. She wanted him to hold her, she wanted him to make love to her, see if that could wipe out the image of Jessica Parris, dehumanized and left like a piece of meat on display in a shabby band shell in a concrete park. Obliterate it from her mind. Tape over it with something good.

She didn't want to be logical and look at the long run. She wanted them to live together. Hell, if he asked, she'd go to Las Vegas with him right now. Why not just abdicate responsibility, do something for the pure thrill of it? Like getting married to a man you've only known for a few months.

The two of them against the world.

"Good thing you're in New Mexico," she said to the dark house.

She followed the road back into the desert, the road dipping down into the Agua Verde wash and out again—a quarter mile to her place. Just where the dirt lane right-angled, there it was: *Mi Nidito*. It looked like a hacienda in Mexico, whitewashed by the moonlight, almost hidden by mature mesquite trees.

*Mi Nidito*. My little nest. Laura didn't know who'd named it, spelling it out in Mexican tile by the door. Someone else who had lived here for a while? She saw it as her house but she knew it wasn't, that someday she'd have to move on.

Stepping out of the car, she was careful to avoid the cow pies; the ranch cows went where they pleased. She did step on plenty of mesquite bean pods, though, soft, yielding crescents on this hot humid night. The old metal gate creaked as she went through.

Laura was serenaded by cowlike crying: spadefoot toads. She smiled, remembering how her mother had told her that the noise, which always came after a summer storm, came from rabbits who'd lost their homes. Now she knew better, but she loved the sentimentality—the Irishness—of her mother's story better.

She walked up onto the deep porch and stopped to listen, hoping the bobcat kittens who lived on her roof were back. They hadn't been around for at least a week.

The place was quiet.

She had it all to herself.

Looking at the cemetery and sky was like peering through a sheet of bright yellow cellophane. Laura knew where she was: the Mexican cemetery on Fort Lowell Road down the street from her parents' house. The cemetery belonged to *los fuerteños,* the community of Mexicans and Mexican Americans that grew up around the abandoned fort on the rich bottomland of the Rillito River. Laura used to walk by here every day on the way to school.

The graveyard was both stark and beautiful, an anthill riddled with plaster and iron crosses, statues, and heaps of flowers both plastic and real. Graves alternated with cactus and creosote bushes.

Julie Marr was standing outside the wire fence by the curve in the road, looking at Laura. From where she was, Laura could see the old car coming. The picture in the paper was black and white, but in this bright yellow world she knew the car was orange over ivory. She knew the make, too, thanks to her experience with the Highway Patrol: a 1955

Chevrolet Bel Air sedan. Primer on the rocker panels, a crucifix hanging from the rearview.

Laura sat up in bed, her pulse hammering in her ears. Her dreams had always been vivid and easily recalled. In recent years, she'd had one recurring dream: going home to show off her DPS Crown Vic to her parents, just a few weeks out of the Academy. It always relieved her to see that they'd come through the months of intensive care, physical therapy, and countless operations with flying colors. Dad didn't walk so well, and Mom was forgetful. But they'd made it through.

Except it wasn't true.

Laura's mind veered back to the dream. She remembered how her parents had freaked out when they heard about Julie Marr on the news. "But for the grace of God, it could have been her," she'd overheard her father say. Julie's kidnapping had affected her mother strangely, leading to an obsession with true crime—the grislier the better. It sent her to a journal-writing group, which she attended faithfully, and a year or so later she started receiving letters with New York postmarks. Laura's mom never told her what was in them, but she guessed they were rejection letters. Maybe writing about crime was Alice Cardinal's way of facing her fears.

The car—the 1955 Bel Air—had been stolen specifically for the purpose of abducting Julie Marr on that terrible spring day in 1987. Julie had never been found, but there had been blood evidence in the car.

Lots of it. That didn't show up in black and white, either.

She got on the road early the next morning. The faded moon hung in a clear indigo sky as she drove off the ranch and through the little town of Vail, over the railroad tracks and onto the freeway going east toward Bisbee. Ahead, there was a blush over the far mountains. Julie Marr's death faded from her mind like an old photograph in a scrapbook.

# 15

## Officer Noone Investigates

Randall Noone—he hated the name "Randy"; people might as well just go ahead and call him "Horny"—parked a little way down and walked up to the turnout on West Boulevard. He'd just started his shift and wanted to check on the tire tracks and see if the same vehicle had come back. He was sure those tire tracks had something to do with Jessica Parris's death. Otherwise, why would Laura Cardinal bother to take casts of them?

At seven in the morning, this part of the canyon was still deep in shadow. There was a hushed feeling to the air, which was actually cool for once, thanks to the overnight rain.

His favorite time of day.

Even though he'd enjoyed the thrill of working nights, he never could adjust completely to the night. Working the day shift in Bisbee wasn't big on excitement, but he enjoyed talking to folks—the place was like Mayberry. He was good at giving speeding tickets, too; he made people feel so good about getting a ticket that they were practically thanking him before he was done. Randall thought that if he'd really wanted excitement, he could have joined up with the sheriff's department, which had become a war zone in the last few years. With the Feds clamping down on the border crossings in California and Texas, Arizona was a hotbed for illegal aliens. One of his friends in the sheriff's department had personally discovered three decomposing bodies in the desert just this year, and had nearly been run down during a routine traffic stop when a vanload of illegals jumped out after putting the van into reverse, right at him.

Nope, he liked Mayberry just fine. Especially with the baby on the way. He and Marcie had picked out the name already: Justin. A good strong name.

The only bad thing about days—Heather Duffy was on days, too.

The Duffy trouble began when his wife had a cold and couldn't make it to the year-end party. After downing five Tabasco shooters, he'd ended up making out with Duffy, and she'd never let him forget it. She sank her teeth into him like a Gila monster. When one of them clamped onto your fingers you might as well get used to having a new clothing accessory.

He reached the yellow tape and looked at the area. He'd made a mental note of exactly how it had looked the night before and was happy to see that the area had not been disturbed.

Glancing back at the Parris house, he said a brief prayer. Man, that was tough—imagine losing your kid like that. The chief had mentioned a possible Internet connection. That was bad stuff, the way some freak with a computer could reach right into your house and lure your kid right out the front door. When Justin grew up he'd have to watch him like a hawk. He'd get AOL. They had safeguards for stuff just like that.

He walked across the road to look at the other turnout. A raven flew over, making a nut-cracking noise deep in its throat.

As he reached the road's shoulder, the smell hit him.

He realized that off and on yesterday afternoon he had

smelled it, too, had thought it was coming from the Dumpster. But it wasn't really a garbage smell.

It was a death smell.

He looked up and down the road but saw nothing. Probably some poor animal had been hit by a car and crawled into the underbrush.

A thick screen of trees ran along the east side of the road. His uncle Nate called them cancer trees because they spread like a fast-moving tumor. He stepped to the side of the road and peered between the trunks. No animal that he could see, but there was something—a solid patch of gray through the trees. Couldn't be more than ten feet from where he stood.

An abandoned shed? No, it had a pitched roof. It looked like a little cabin. Suddenly he remembered something else Uncle Nate told him, that there were some old tourist cabins around here from the twenties, back when this road was the highway through town.

As he recalled, it had an Indian name. Cochise? No. Geronimo. The Geronimo Tourist Camp.

Randall Noone squinted at the shack, holding the tree limbs away from his face. The trees made him feel claustrophobic. They gave off a cloying odor, like peanut butter, that mixed with the death smell and made his stomach queasy. Breathing through his mouth, he made his way through the underbrush, the limbs springing back like boomerangs when he let go of them, until he was standing outside the shack.

The doors and windows to the cabin were gone, leaving it open to the elements—just a shell with a rusted stovepipe lying in the corner across floorboards pretty much rotted through. Place couldn't be much bigger than a roomy bathroom.

He noticed another ghostly square to his left, maybe fifteen feet away, and went to investigate.

This cabin looked like a kids' hangout: There was a candle, an old rug, throw pillows, rolling papers, and a boom box. A faint odor of pot.

This was *interesting*.

He spotted another cabin, this one farthest away from the road and backed up against the hill. He picked his way along a faint trail littered with junk: a roll of hogwire, broken glass, a sink with a hole in it.

Darker here, shadowed by the ridge and oak trees. Damp. The raven flew to an oak and chortled at him as he approached the open doorway.

The stench hit him with almost physical force.

He stepped back, his mind reeling. Something dead here. Steeling himself, he breathed through his mouth before peering in.

At first he thought it was just a pile of black rags. No, it was jeans and a T-shirt. Naturally, his gaze wandered up the T-shirt toward the face.

His disbelieving eyes registered the green fright mask for just an instant before he reeled backward out the door, gulping for air.

Officer Randall Noone found himself on all fours, the scrambled eggs Marcie cooked for his breakfast ending up in a steaming pile on the grass.

# 16

"What do you think?" Laura asked Victor. Early afternoon now, and the crime lab techs had finished collecting evidence and the ME's people were on their way to remove the body of Cary Statler.

Victor sighed. "Whoever killed Jessica probably killed him."

Laura knew what he was thinking: more trouble. Just seven hours ago he'd been making arrangements for a studio portrait of his family, including his new daughter, and now he'd been dragged back here in this heat to look at the corpse of Cary Statler, which in his view only complicated the case.

Laura agreed with Victor that there was a high probability that Jessica and Cary had been attacked at the same time. With a body this far gone, it would be impossible to fix a definitive time of death, but Laura didn't believe in coincidences. The fact that Cary Statler and Jessica Parris had both been victims of homicide was just too big a coincidence to ignore.

Detective Holland said, "He wanted the girl and this poor sad bastard was in the way. So he bashed him in the head and took the girl where he could have his fun without being rushed."

Laura kept her gaze on Statler, although it was hard to do. He was riddled with maggots. One eye had been pecked out, and several fingers had been torn from one hand, probably dragged off by animals. It was fortunate he had ID on him, because skin slippage and a hardening and darkening of his complexion made his features unrecognizable—his face was marbled lime green and black.

But Laura knew who it was the moment she saw the Megadeth tee and the yellow pineapple hair.

She straightened up, feeling the twinge in her back. The shade, which had stayed with them most of the day, had given way to full sunlight coming in through the southern window. The air was stifling, the stench almost unbearable. Victor and Buddy had shared dabs of Victor's jar of mentholatum to block out the smell, but Laura had made it a policy not to use the stuff, since she knew from experience that the stink would linger in the mentholatum long after she had left the scene. She breathed through her mouth, but could still feel death lying on the membranes on her tongue, in her nostrils, on her skin.

Victor cocked his head. "Man, that was some hit he took." The force of the blow had broken Cary Statler's neck, even though the wound itself had been higher up to the side of the head. One blow. It had come close to separating his head from his body.

"Had to be someone who knew about this place," Buddy was saying. "You can't even see these cabins from the road."

"Could be." Laura kept her voice neutral.

Buddy had the ball and he ran with it. "I think he knew them. He wanted Jessica, she fit his fantasy. My guess is he followed them, or knew about their little hangout—"

"If it was their hangout." Laura could feel sweat trickling under her hair. She wanted out of this cabin *now*. She desperately wanted to go back to the car and get to her purse, scrub her face and hands with hand sanitizer and salve her dry lips.

"If it was Cary's hangout, this guy would know they hung out there. He'd be able to keep tabs on them, look for his opportunity. I think he planned it," Buddy said.

"What I still can't figure out though—why the dress?" Victor asked. "Why did he do all that? He leaves the kid here, like so much garbage dumped out by the side of the road, but he's careful about the evidence with her."

Buddy said, "He didn't think anyone would find the kid. That's why he brought him to this cabin, farthest from the road. Nobody comes out here. That's also why I think he's local. He knows this place. He had to act fast and move this kid, and he knew exactly where to put him."

"And then what?" asked Laura.

Buddy looked at her and his eyes narrowed. "He takes her to his place."

"So he's parked up on the road?"

"I guess he would be."

"Wouldn't he be afraid that someone would see his car? Or see him come up to the road with the girl?"

"He's pretty bold—you said so yourself, dressing her up like that and putting her in City Park. If you don't like him taking him somewhere, he could have killed and raped her up here, came back later that night, cleaned her up and planted her in City Park."

"Why?"

"To taunt the police. To show us up."

Buddy's theory was logical. Still, something about it bothered her. She had spent a large part of yesterday talking to various law enforcement agencies in Arizona. No one she'd talked to could even remember a case like this one, but there was the phone call from that detective—Endicott—in Indio, California. She'd tried him twice today, would have to keep trying.

If he was a local, she guessed that he had not lived here long. A year or two at the most. She knew he had done this before. He had built up to this.

The mesquite leaf, too, bothered her. She didn't recall

seeing a mesquite tree anywhere up here; it was too high up.

And there was the matchbook she'd found at the band shell, CRZYGIRL12 written in block letters on the inside cover. "Why would he leave that behind?"

Buddy stared at her. "We don't know for sure it was his." Gauging her reaction.

"No, we don't know he was the one who put it there. We have to consider it, though. We have to consider everything. This might have something to do with the Internet."

"That's how he could have met her."

"But you think he knew her from here."

"He knew her from here and he knew her on the Internet. They were probably e-mail buddies."

She could tell he was getting steamed. She saw Victor grin—the first time today. Victor understood Buddy's frustration, maybe even sympathized. He'd often said she was *too* evenhanded.

"Besides," Buddy said, "I talked to her teachers. She was carefully supervised and never left alone on the computers. No way someone could have reached her—they'd know. I think Crazygirl 12 doesn't have anything to do with it."

Laura didn't bother to reply. Instead, she stepped outside the cabin. She couldn't stand the stench in there and she couldn't stand Buddy Holland's attitude. His barely veiled belligerence. His hints that she'd planted the matchbook.

Concentrate.

She walked out beyond the crime scene tape. From here, she could see the Dumpster near the road. The lab techs had removed the Dumpster's contents and already taken it to the crime lab in Tucson, even though they had found nothing overtly related to Cary's murder.

What Laura hoped for was a bloodstained towel or T-shirt. There had been evidence that Cary's head had been wrapped in something to keep his blood from getting all over. This dovetailed with her theory that Cary was moved to the cabin from the spot where he'd been killed.

The killer had probably taken the shirt or towel with him. Maybe he knew that it was possible to get latents from cloth. Or maybe it was his natural neatness.

He was still being careful.

She did agree with Buddy on one thing: Cary had been in the way, and the killer had not foreseen this. He had taken some pains to hide Cary's body, but had been too much in a hurry to clean up.

He had made a big mistake.

She caught a movement down below: Chuck Lehman walking in the direction of the crime scene tape stretching across the road. An unleashed Rottweiler accompanied him.

Officer Noone walked down to meet him. Reporters zeroed in on him like ducks after bread. Voices drifted up but she couldn't hear them. She didn't need to; Officer Noone was telling Lehman he couldn't go past the tape.

Lehman whistled to his dog and turned on his heel. He walked back in the direction of his house but didn't go far. Arms folded over his chest, he watched the ME's van pull up behind the other vehicles. Laura couldn't see his expression, but she could sense his excitement even from here. It was evident in the tense way he held his body, pitched slightly forward, as if he were absorbing everything about the scene with all his senses.

She thought about the word Victor had used to describe him.

Avid.

After the body was removed, Laura, Victor, and Buddy headed down to the road. As they reached the crime scene tape, a female reporter thrust a microphone in Laura's face.

"Is it true the body you found belongs to Cary Statler, Jessica Parris's boyfriend?"

"We don't have a positive ID yet," Laura said.

"But you're pretty sure it's Cary Statler?"

"We won't know that until we get a positive ID."

"If it was Cary Statler, can you comment on what they were doing in here?"

Someone else shouted, "Did he die trying to save Jessica's life?"

"We don't know what happened. We're just beginning this investigation."

"But Jessica Parris was here?"

"It's too early to tell that."

She finally got past them and walked to her car.

It was going on three o'clock when the news vans pulled out, following the ME's van down the road. Laura scrubbed her hands and face with hand sanitizer and applied lip balm to her lips. Then she reached into the backseat and tore open the plastic covering on the case of water bottles she carried there, grabbed a new bottle, and drank. Water never tasted so sweet. Ducking into the back of the 4Runner, she stripped off her shirt and replaced it with the blouse she kept on a hanger for emergencies. She ran a brush through her hair, hoping she looked respectable enough to meet people.

Victor took the houses on the east side of the street, and Buddy took the houses on the west. Laura headed up to the two houses at the bend in the road.

Again, she got no answer at the first house. But a man answered the door to the green house. Frail and thin, he was bent over a walker. It was clear he was not going to invite her in. The house smelled of boiled cabbage and unclean cat boxes. A TV set blared in the background. She asked him if he had seen or heard anything unusual the last few nights.

He looked at her blankly. "I've been in bed all week with a septic throat."

He hadn't heard anything and didn't know Cary Statler or the Parris family. Laura asked him her whole list of questions, but it was clear he didn't know anything and didn't *want* to know anything.

"Does anyone else live here?"

"Nope. Have a girl comes in three times a week."

Laura finally nailed it down: The "girl" worked on the day Jessica had been kidnapped. When Laura asked for her name and phone number, the man sighed and clacked his way into the darkness, returning with a slip of paper that had been torn off the edge of a *TV Guide*, one inch by one-half inch.

"Is that it?" he demanded. "I'm not supposed to be out of bed."

"Have you noticed any unusual vehicles drive this road in the last few days?"

"I keep my drapes drawn. Don't want to fade the furniture." The door closed in her face.

From her vantage point in the 4Runner, Laura watched Victor get in his vehicle and drive off, and then Buddy. Neither one approached her, even though she was in plain sight. She assumed Victor was going back to the Copper Queen Hotel for a swim and to call his wife. They would meet later at the hotel restaurant and compare notes.

Buddy—who knew what he was going to do?

Laura took out her camera and stepped onto the road. She wanted to be in this canyon at the time of day that Cary died and Jessica was taken.

She guessed that Cary had been killed somewhere between five and seven o'clock in the evening on the day Jessica disappeared. This would fit the timeline for Jessica's abduction.

The shadows stretched down from Mule Pass, coming from the opposite direction. The trees on the left side of the road were all in shadow now.

Laura stepped into the woods and worked her way over to the cabin that had contained the drug paraphernalia.

She pictured herself sneaking up on them. Tried to move quietly, but it was impossible given the leaf litter underfoot and the whiplashing limbs.

They would hear an intruder, but would they care? They might not be afraid of strangers. Mellow on pot, Cary and Jessica might not see the danger until it was too late. Would he lure them up to the other cabin, farther away from the road?

Or did he arrange to meet them here?

She leaned in through the cabin door and inhaled the smell of pot, which to her smelled like a cross between a burned-out campfire and old grass and gym socks in a school locker.

The lab techs had removed the pillow, the boom box, the rolling papers, the rug, soil and debris samples—everything—as possible evidence. They'd also vacuumed the cabin for fibers and hairs, to see if they could place Cary or Jessica or both of them here.

If he did encounter them here, how did he overpower them? Two young, strong kids—that would be hard to do.

She retraced her steps back to the road, looking for any sign where the killer might have come in, and nearly walked right over a couple of divots in the sand north of where she thought he would have gone in.

She squatted on her heels and examined the shallow impressions. They could be drag marks—the divots could be a sign of heels digging in. She followed the trajectory of the marks down into the trees, feeling more excited the more she saw. The leaves on the ground were scuffed, a broken line running in roughly an east-west direction. Not, she noticed, in the direction of the hangout. Plenty of broken limbs and branches—the kid had been dragged by a whirlwind—and swipes and spatters and smears of blood.

Eventually the scuff marks led to where she thought they would: the cabin on the hill.

She was now sure he did not meet Cary and Jessica at the first cabin.

Laura absorbed the warm stillness of the canyon, thinking. Cary had been dragged down from the road. That meant he had met the killer up there, or at least gone to his car. But where was Jessica during all this?

A raven flew over and settled in a tree farther up the hill, chortling at her.

She returned to the 4Runner for latex gloves and evidence envelopes and retraced the killer's steps up the hill. She was nearly to the cabin on the hill when she spotted something red on the ground: a rectangular plastic tab. She recognized it as one of those savings cards people used at grocery stores—a Safeway Club Card. It fit on a key ring; the hole punch looked as if it had given out from use.

These cards had a bar code and a number, one reason Laura had never signed up for one despite the savings. She didn't like the idea that her purchases could be tracked by someone she didn't know.

She bagged the card. At the edge of the road where Cary had been dragged into the woods, she took several soil samples and marked them as evidence.

Some of the soil looked dark, almost black. It could have been oil spots from a car.

Or it could have been blood.

Back at the Bisbee Police Department, Laura photocopied both sides of the Safeway Club Card, then looked up Safeway in the phone book. There was one in Bisbee. She took the photocopy and drove out to the strip mall where the Safeway was located.

She asked to speak to the manager. A sallow young man with a few thin hairs on his upper lip came to meet her and they walked back to a dingy, fluorescent-lit office at the back of the store. She guessed he was *a* manager, not *the* manager.

"Is it possible to get a name and address from this card?" she asked, handing him the photocopy.

The young man, whose nametag said GERALD, looked dubious. "I don't know . . . that information is confidential."

Sure it was. Laura knew these cards were used to track shoppers' purchases, and that the company shared this information with other companies.

Laura had to be careful, here. She wanted Gerald to give her the cardholder's name without tipping him off that it involved a homicide. She didn't want it getting out what kind of evidence had been left at the scene—information like that would make a defense attorney's day. She cleared her throat.

"I could really use your help. The person who dropped this is an important witness to a serious crime—"

The boy leaned forward. "What kind of crime?"

"A missing persons case." Technically, that was true.

"Do you think it's connected with those murders?"

"This concerns someone we just need to talk to. You'd really be helping me out."

She could see the wheels going around in his head. "I think it's against regulations, you know, unless you had a search warrant or something like that." He drummed a pencil on the desk blotter and looked tortured. "Are you sure it doesn't have anything to do with that girl getting killed?"

"We haven't ruled that out—tangentially."

"I thought so." Pleased with himself. "So you really need to talk to whoever owns this card because he might have witnessed the killing?"

"Gerald, I can't really say."

"Damn, that's scary. Two people getting killed like that. I saw it on the news." His eyes turned regretful. "I wish I could help . . ."

Laura glanced at her watch. "Damn."

"Ma'am?"

"I'm just thinking, I've never run into this kind of situation before. I can get a warrant, no problem—I just hope nobody gets hurt because we took the extra time to hammer this out." She shook her head. "I just can't believe this is happening." She stood up. "I hope I can find a judge at this time of day. If this turns bad, I sure don't want this on my conscience."

Gerald squirmed in his chair. "Maybe I should look it up, just in case. I can't remember if there's a hard-and-fast rule."

"That would be a *big* help."

Five minutes later she emerged from the Safeway into the parking lot with the name and address. She didn't need the address, though. She already knew where Charles Edward Lehman lived.

# 17

Victor Celaya showed up at the Jonquil hours after their dinner at the Copper Queen Hotel. He leaned against the door-jamb, gamma-rayed by the fluorescent light above the door to her room, waggling a six-pack of Bohemia.

Well, almost a six-pack. One was missing.

"Can I come in?"

"Sure. Just let me wake up."

"You were in bed already? I'm sorry." He walked past her and put the six-pack on the table. "Want one?"

She glanced dubiously at the six-pack.

"They're cold. Just got it from Circle K. I'm sorry I woke you up but I had to tell you my idea."

Laura sat on the bed, trying to focus. She'd just made it into deep sleep when he pulled her out of it. "What idea is that?"

"Kind of stuffy in here. You want to go outside?"

"Sure." Why not? She wasn't going to go back to sleep now.

Laura went into the bathroom and changed out of the long shirt she wore to bed. Back into today's clothes, wrinkled as they were. She could hear Victor whistling a familiar-sounding *corrido,* pure and sweet. Wondered what his idea was and why it couldn't wait until tomorrow.

Whatever he'd come up with, he was excited about it.

They crossed a bridge over the narrow channel that ran through Tombstone Canyon and sat down at one of the outdoor tables. Laura was almost glad he'd awakened her; it was a beautiful night. Cool compared to Tucson. The sky full of stars. Runoff from the rains tumbled through the canal, catching the glow of the streetlights.

He quickly spoiled the mood. "I thought of a way to get in Lehman's house. We go through his probation officer."

"We could do that," she said slowly. As a probationer, Chuck Lehman did not have the rights regular citizens had. Probation was a substitute for prison, and there were a number of restrictions on him: what he could do and not do, who he could associate with. If his probation officer suspected he was violating his probation, his house could be searched. Usually it required concurrence by the chief of probation, but essentially, Lehman's house could be searched without a warrant.

Laura didn't like this for a couple of reasons. One, Chuck Lehman's link to the crime scene was tenuous. He lived right near the vacant land. He had a dog and probably walked around in there often. The key tab could have come off anytime. She'd bagged it because she was thorough, because if their investigation pointed to Lehman, she'd have other evidence to back it up.

And two, going through the probation officer could cause problems down the line. She could just hear the defense attorney: overeager cops. Abusing the privilege—using a probation officer to gain access to a house when they couldn't get a search warrant through regular channels.

That could cause problems if this ever went to trial.

Frank Entwistle had always taught her to think of police work as a pool game, always setting up the next shot and the shot after that. Thinking about the endgame—the trial. The ultimate shot should land the bad guy in prison.

This strategy made her a lousy pool player but a good investigator.

Victor was talking, excited about the case for the first time. She knew he had a pool game of his own in mind: getting home to his wife and family.

This was not the first time Victor had cut corners. He saw everything in terms of exit strategy: close the case, boost the solve rate.

Laura said, "We can't do that, Victor. We don't have enough evidence."

"That's the *beauty* of it. We'll *get* the evidence, once we're inside."

"You really think he's the one?"

"Don't you?" Suddenly his mouth flatlined. "Shit! You don't. You don't think it's him, do you? You're still fooling around with that motor home idea. Nothing can be easy for you, can it?" He stood up and walked around in a circle. "I *knew* you were gonna do this."

"Victor—"

"What, afraid you'll lose your membership in the ACLU?"

She tried not to lose her cool. "It just won't work."

"Of course it'll work. You just don't want it to."

Suddenly, it dawned on her. "Did Buddy Holland have anything to do with this?"

"Oh, that's great. You never give me any credit, do you? What, I can't think for myself?" He set the bottle down on the table so hard that beer sloshed up—a sharp yeasty smell.

"Victor, I don't want to say this, but—"

"Then don't."

"It's my case. Like it or not, I'm the lead. I say we're not going to do this."

He smiled at her sadly. "Too late."

"What do you mean?"

"It's a done deal. We're meeting Sylvia Clegg over at Lehman's tomorrow."

It shocked her so much, for a minute she couldn't speak.

He stood up. "Sorry you're not happy about this. I came here as a courtesy. We're meeting the probation officer over at Lehman's at eight a.m. See you then—if you want to be there."

# 18

Driving up West Boulevard the next morning, Laura resolved to do the best she could to hold her case together.

She knew when she was beat. The probation office had agreed to this search, and if she objected now, it would only send a signal that the right hand didn't know what the left hand was doing. That in turn would be communicated to other jurisdictions on many levels, and would affect her ability to get things done.

Perception *was* reality.

Victor and Buddy had made an end run around her. She had to salvage what was left of her case and go on.

When she reached Lehman's house, the first thing she saw was a new black Suburban parked two houses down. The vanity plate said RICOPRZ. She knew it: The Suburban had been seized from a Mexican American drug lord under the RICO laws. It was driven by Lieutenant Mike Galaz.

What was he doing here?

Laura remembered a difference of opinion she'd had with Victor about the new lieutenant. Victor insisted that Galaz was a control freak. But as far as she could tell, Galaz seemed detached from the job, letting the sergeants run the day-to-day—which suited her fine.

She suspected that Victor resented Galaz for other reasons, more amorphous stuff, like his expensive home in the foothills; his constant talk about his golf game; his breedy-looking second wife, a high-powered Anglo lawyer.

Laura glanced at Galaz. The fact that he was here really didn't surprise her. An important case like this, it wasn't unprecedented that the lieutenant would want a piece of the pie—especially since this lieutenant was already unofficially running for mayor of Tucson.

The Suburban, a Bisbee PD patrol car, and Buddy Holland's Caprice were all parked on the street half a block from Lehman's house. A small group had collected near Victor Celaya's shiny black truck. Laura recognized everyone except a skinny bleached blonde in Guess? jeans that molded tightly to her ass, and an older Hispanic male: Sylvia Clegg and the chief of probation, Ernie Lopez.

Victor leaned against the front fender of his new GMC, the window open so he could get his last few minutes of Rush Limbaugh. A Mexican dittohead—who'd've thunk.

Galaz nodded to her, his brown eyes assessing. She wondered why he was so interested, put it down to the fact that he hardly knew her. He explained that later today he was speaking at a law enforcement seminar in Sierra Vista, and he decided to come by and see how "his people" were doing.

Those inscrutable eyes, weighing her. Laura turned to Ernie Lopez.

"Is he home?"

"His car's there."

They headed up the street, the Bisbee PD officer, Chambers, leading the way. Galaz hung back—not sure of his role? He'd come up through the administration side of DPS, with a long stint in Internal Affairs. Not a cop's cop.

Laura glanced back, uncomfortable that her lieutenant was walking behind her. When he saw her looking back he transferred his gaze from Clegg to her and flashed a smile. Galaz was one of those people dirt didn't stick to: manicured nails, expensive suit, immaculate white cuffs crisped to a razor edge, micromanaged haircut. With his patrician good looks and Spanish elegance, even at eight a.m. he looked ready for a thousand-dollar-a-plate fund-raiser, a world Laura knew existed but would never in her life see firsthand.

She could smell the products that went into him: shampoo, cologne, mouthwash, body wash, hairspray. His expensive shoes clicked on the sidewalk behind her like a metronome.

Officer Chambers rapped on the door.

Laura was aware that Lieutenant Galaz remained near the curb. Was he worried there might be shooting? Laura's own hand hovered near her weapon—automatic.

Lehman came to the screen. Shirtless again.

He took one look at them and said, "Oh, *shit*."

Sylvia Clegg said, "Chuck, I'm informing you that I am here to do a search."

Lehman glared past her at Laura. "This is *your* doing. You trying to get back at me?"

Unperturbed, Sylvia said, "Chuck, you know that under the terms of your probation, you have to allow me in to search."

For a moment it looked like there would be a standoff. Chambers shifted his weight slightly, his hand near his gun.

Lehman stood in the doorway, arms folded, looking like an angry Mr. Clean.

"What did I do?" he demanded. It took Laura back to the other day when he'd yelled at her like a drill sergeant. "What did I *do*?"

A powerful engine started up on the street. Laura looked back to see Mike Galaz pull out and drive away. Why had he bothered to come at all?

Clegg said quietly, "Chuck. May I proceed with the search?"

"And if I don't, you'll arrest me."

"Come on, Chuck, this isn't such a big deal," Clegg said. "Take a deep breath and—"

"You're gonna arrest me, am I right?"

"No one's going to arrest you. If you just let me take a

look around, we'll be in and out in no time. You know I wouldn't—"

He shoved the screen door open so hard it slammed against the wall of the house. "Go ahead. I have nothing to hide."

"First you need to secure your dog," Clegg said.

"Oh, for Christ's sake!" He whistled for the dog and took him outside, returning a few moments later. "I put him in his run, that good enough?"

Clegg smiled like she'd won the lottery. "That's great, Chuck."

They traipsed in: Laura, Victor, Buddy Holland, and Sylvia Clegg. The rest remained out on the street.

Buddy Holland cruised the room, eagle eyes taking in everything. Laura was worried that he was going to piss Sylvia Clegg off, but it appeared they were friends. Buddy must not have seen anything incriminating, because he joined them and stood there with a bored look on his face.

Chuck Lehman lived well. Blond hardwood floors, Oriental carpet, Danish furniture. Doggie bed in the corner, near a river stone fireplace. Colorful kites hanging from the walls.

Sylvia Clegg, gloved in latex, started a low-key but thorough search. Her movements were deliberate and efficient. Laura noticed she had a calming effect about her, which was well appreciated.

Victor said to Lehman, "Mr. Lehman, we'd like to ask you a few questions." He glanced in the direction of the sunny kitchen. "Why don't we go in and sit down, while your probation officer looks around."

"Am I under arrest?"

"No, sir."

"Then I'm not answering any questions."

Victor smiled. "We'd appreciate it if you would. We just want to clear up a couple things."

"I can't *believe* this! I'm calling my lawyer."

"You're not under arrest. We're only asking for a little cooperation."

"You can fuck that." Lehman picked up his cell phone from the kitchen table and turned away from them.

It was a short conversation. When he was through, he closed the phone with a snap and slapped it on the table. "Lawyer's on his way."

"Can we at least sit down?" Victor asked him.

"I can't stop you, can I?"

They sat in the breakfast nook. Lehman leaned against the refrigerator, arms folded.

Victor set his mini-recorder on the table. He spoke into it, giving the time and date and Lehman's name.

Lehman ignored him, staring straight ahead, his eyes like two holes in his face. She could feel his rage under the surface—he hummed like a power line.

"Did you know Cary Statler?" Victor asked Lehman.

Lehman didn't answer. He was in his own zone, his breathing short and rapid. Staring so hard at a spot on the wall she thought he'd go cross-eyed.

The way he'd tried to bully her . . .

"When was the last time you saw Statler?" Victor asked.

Lehman transferred his gaze to the ceiling.

"Do you remember where you were the evening Jessica was kidnapped?"

It went on like that for a minute or so before Victor gave up.

Usually he could charm people with his easygoing nature, his sympathetic ear. But Lehman was immune.

Laura looked around the kitchen. Everything was spotless, gleaming. The stove, refrigerator, and cooking island were all stainless steel and modern. There was not the usual clutter you'd see on shelves or near the sink; in her house the dishwashing liquid sat next to the sink, but here, the kitchen counter was cleared of everything except a bowl of fruit.

Not much in plain sight.

Buddy leaned in the doorway, looking at her. A self-satisfied smirk on his face. Laura ignored him and concentrated on the kitchen.

Place reminded her of a model home. She thought of the way the bad guy had washed the girl, washed her hair, clipped her nails. This guy was that neat. Would there be trace evidence in the shower? She knew that the probation officer's search wouldn't extend there, but if she found something else incriminating, they could get a search warrant.

What would that be? Dress patterns for little girls?

Sylvia poked her head in the doorway. "Can I get in here?"

Lehman shot her a virulent look and launched himself away from the refrigerator like a missile. He went out the kitchen door into his yard, letting the screen door slam behind him. Laura, Victor, and Buddy Holland followed.

Out into the steaming summer heat. Brick patio. Immaculate propane grill. Lehman turned on the hose and began watering the potted plants. The smell of the water mingled with the scent of wet earth.

Laura knew that Clegg could not do a comprehensive search. She'd noticed how Victor had worked certain words into his conversation with Clegg as they'd walked over here. He asked her if she knew how to sew. Mentioned his own mother's sewing machine. Asked her about actors, too, what she knew about makeup, wigs, dress-up. How as a kid one Halloween he'd gone as Snidely Whiplash, twiddling his big black mustache.

Broad hints. Clegg had gotten it.

Now Clegg spoke through the screen door. "All I have left is the bedroom."

Laura glanced at her watch. Victor would have to leave soon; he had Cary Statler's autopsy in Sierra Vista. She wanted to get out of here, too. She needed to go to Tucson to notify Cary's uncle about the death in person. The man might know already, although the police had not yet given Cary's name to the press.

She glanced at Lehman.

His intensity scared her. All this time and his anger had not abated. A hard smell to him—could you smell testosterone?—mingling with the smell of water and earth.

This was Victor's show. Victor's and Buddy's.

"I've got to go," she said to no one in particular.

Neither Buddy nor Victor said anything.

Laura let herself out the gate just as a Lexus pulled up to the curb. An ugly little man in an expensive suit emerged, holding a calfskin briefcase.

Lehman's lawyer.

# 19

Tucson-Saguaro Auto & Body, near the corner of Palo Verde and Twenty-ninth Street, was a cinder-block building with three roll-up work bays, a parking lot surrounded by a ten-foot-high chain-link fence, and a corrugated iron shed that served as the office. The traffic here was a six-lane river of cars and SUVs flowing past a median on which a person dressed like a chicken waved a sign for a fast-food place called El Pollo Grande. Every car window was up, the air-conditioning going, people with cell phones attached to their ears. All of them isolated from one another in their speeding steel-and-glass capsules.

The chicken looked jaunty, even though he must be smothering from the heat—a real trouper. Laura wondered how much he was paid.

As she stepped onto the curb, she felt the familiar tightening in her stomach that came whenever she notified people that their loved ones were dead.

She knew what it felt like. The memory was always close at hand, a penance of sorts. A counselor at the university had explained to her the concept of survivor's guilt. It ran through her head like film: drifting off to sleep, her thoughts on Billy and the fun they'd had in Nogales, turtle soup at La Rocca's, coming home late and not feeling like going to her parents' house for dinner. Making love, Billy having to leave because he had to be at work early tomorrow. The stutter of the sprinklers outside the open dorm window. The bed-clothes smelling of sex. That last happy day.

Someone knocking on her door. She opens it to two men in suits, who look as if they've been lurking in the hallway trying to get their stories straight.

Knowing right then something is wrong.

The older one with the florid complexion clearing his throat . . .

She walked along the weedy curb to the shed. The heat was like a convection oven. The door to the shed was open and a table fan blew sporadically in her direction. It took her a moment to adjust her eyes to the darkness of the shed after the blinding desert sun.

"Help you?"

The man sat at a metal desk facing the door. Graying ponytail, a red T-shirt washed so many times it had faded to pink. Behind him, a Tecate poster of a sweaty girl with a bare midriff and cutoffs was tacked to the faded wall.

The minute he saw her his smile faded. She realized that he had been expecting this visit.

"Are you Beau Taylor?"

There was still a hopeful quality to his expression, as if there was a chance that there had been some kind of mistake. Laura remembered going through the same thinking process when detectives Jeff Smith and Frank Entwistle came to her door. It went like this: As long as nothing was said, you were all right. But the moment the words spilled into the air, there was no way to call them back. So the thing was to try and stop those words.

"If it's about the Coupe DeVille—"

"No, sir." Best to tell him flat out, no ambiguity. "There's no easy way to tell you this, sir, but your nephew Cary Statler was found in Bisbee yesterday morning, dead."

His face crumpled. "I thought it was him. The news said they found a body, but they didn't identify him."

"Why did you think it was him, sir?"

"Jessica was killed and he disappeared. If he was missing, he was either hitchhiking his way here or someone got him, too. He didn't show up, then they find a body right near her house. You might as well tell me what happened."

She did.

"Do you think he suffered?"

She went for the white lie; for all she knew it was true. "I don't think so. It was a massive head injury."

"Poor, sweet kid. He wanted to be a vet. His grades were piss-poor, he dropped out of school, but he was always talking about getting his GED and then trying to get into vet school." He snorted. "Like he could get through a science degree in college. Didn't talk about it so much lately, though. I grew up in a time when drugs were cool, but I tell you, I've seen more kids lose their ambition, smoking pot . . ." He trailed off, looked down at his clublike fingers. "Probably never would have gotten anywhere."

"Did you ever hear him talk about a neighbor, a man named Chuck Lehman?"

"Sure. He and Cary made kites. Kind of strange, a forty-year-old man and an eighteen-year-old kid."

And a fourteen-year-old girl, Laura thought.

"Cary was a funny mixture of a kid. Never could stick with anything, had that attention-span problem, what do you call it? ADD? Plus, he got put off easy."

The shack rattled—the thundering whistle of two A-10s from Davis-Monthan on final approach. Laura glanced out the doorway and saw one of them over the strip mall across the way, a giant mosquito looking for a place to alight.

She wondered how Cary's uncle could stand it, here in the flight path of the A-10s and C-130s—and worse, the F-16s—just an iron shed between himself and the stifling heat that killed one or two illegal aliens a day a few miles south of here. He noticed her discomfort and aimed the fan in her direction. Must have been a floor model; it still had the streamers.

"You said he was put off easily?" she asked him.

"Say if somebody hurt his feelings, he'd withdraw. I think it was because he was shy. Somebody said one wrong thing to him, he'd just clam up. Just up and leave. That's why he was always bouncing around between Bisbee and here. He didn't like being criticized, took it to heart."

"He ever get in fights?"

"Nope. When something bothered him, he'd pack up his stuff and take off." Beau Taylor stared at the shimmering white heat beyond the open doorway.

"You're sure he was friends with Chuck Lehman."

"Oh, yeah. It was always Chuck this and Chuck that. Guy knew everything. Nobody else knew shit. But that all changed a couple of weeks ago."

"They had a falling-out?"

"Kid wouldn't talk about it, but you should've seen the look on his face when I asked about him."

"This was a couple of weeks ago?"

"Last time he came down here."

"Could you pinpoint the date?"

"I think it was a Sunday. We're closed Sundays, plus we go to church." He rolled his chair over to the counter under the window and consulted a greasy-looking desk calendar. "Sunday. End of June."

"Did he fight with his girlfriend much?"

"They had their set-tos. But he was in love with her and in love with her family—couldn't say what he loved more. His mother wasn't worth much, and he always wanted a family."

"Cary was eighteen. An adult. How come he wasn't out on his own?"

"He attached himself to people. He was needy and a loner at the same time."

"Was Jessica a friend of Lehman's, too?"

"I'm pretty sure she was. Cary mentioned a couple of times they did things together."

"Didn't it seem strange to you? A man that much older hanging out with kids?"

"I didn't have a say in it. As you said, he was an adult."

Laura opened her mouth to say that Jessica wasn't an adult—and that was when her cell phone chirped.

Sylvia Clegg, standing on a chair in the closet, felt hard plastic behind the piles of folded blankets stored for the summer.

She pulled down a videotape just as she heard the toilet flush.

The tape was called *Pubic Enemy No. 1*. The heartwarming story of a gangster who finds love in a hot-sheet motel with two vertically challenged girls.

"What's that?" said Detective Buddy Holland from the doorway.

"Buddy, you didn't use the bathroom, did you?"

He held up his hands, gloved in latex. "You gotta go, you gotta go. What's that? Porno?"

"You're in here now, you might as well come and look at this."

She held the tape out to him. He didn't touch—just looked. "What do you think?"

"Girls could be twenty, or they could be sixteen. Hard to tell these days."

"Definitely not little girls, though." She stepped back up and reached into the closet, pulled out more tapes.

Buddy remained in the room, hands on his hips, watching her.

"Where's Chuck?" she asked him.

"He's still out back, stewing." He added, "The DPS guy left, has to witness the autopsy."

"You really aren't supposed to be in here."

"I know." He made a slow circuit of the room, peering at things without touching. "Anything besides the porno?"

"Not that I can see."

"Too bad." Buddy shone his Maglite at the back of Chuck Lehman's dresser.

"Buddy, what are you doing?"

"There's a gap between the dresser and the wall."

"So?"

He looked at her. "Did you look to see if anything fell back there?"

Sylvia felt a twinge of embarrassment. "I'm not done yet."

Buddy continued to stand over the dresser. He was looking at something.

Sylvia got down off the chair and set the videotapes down on the floor. "What is it?"

Buddy pointed his flashlight behind the dresser. She came to stand next to him and peered down. Something there. A cylinder.

She went and got a videotape, which was just narrow enough to fit behind the dresser. She caught the thing with the corner, scooting it toward her.

"Bingo," Buddy said as a lipstick tube rolled across the floor.

# 20

They served the search warrant for Chuck Lehman's house at six o'clock the next morning, pulling Lehman out of bed. He slept in something that looked like a karate *gi,* and for a minute Laura wondered if he was going to launch an assault at them. He looked mad enough to bust a brick with his hand.

Anger boiled out of him, his eyes burning pure hatred, like twin gas flames.

Nudging the red line.

A lot had happened since Buddy Holland found the lipstick. Most notably, a partial print on the lipstick matched Jessica Parris's index finger from the print cards taken by the Sierra Vista medical examiner—an eight-point match. Laura, Buddy, and Victor had spent most of the night hashing out what they wanted on the search warrant, which Laura and Buddy would get from a judge in Bisbee. It was important they didn't leave anything out—any area not spelled out by a warrant would be inaccessible to them. And so it became a name game: books, diaries, computer disks, the computer itself. Anything in the sewing line. Makeup, hairpieces, spirit gum, and false mustaches. Kites. Indoor and outdoor trash. All cleaning products. Personal grooming products and grooming products for the dog: shampoos, soap, nail scissors, pet-grooming equipment. Financial records, receipts, checkbooks, credit card information. Tools. His car, his yard, his garden shed.

Victor remained in Tucson, catching up on the paperwork they'd accumulated so far.

Buddy took the bedroom. Laura started in the living room and moved on to the kitchen.

The stainless steel appliances would show fingerprints, smudges, if they had not been wiped clean with glass cleaner. She didn't know if he had cleaned everything recently to cover up Jessica's presence in his house, or if this was just the way he was. The place had been neat when they'd come here yesterday. Maybe he was just a neat kind of guy.

She got on her hands and knees, looking for hairs or other evidence. Found several graying hairs and some dog hairs but nothing long or blond. She took them as evidence.

Now for the refrigerator.

Lehman favored health foods, green leafy vegetables, white wine. A healthy guy. A neat guy and a healthy guy.

Expecting to move on pretty quickly, she slid out the crisper.

A chill crept up her back. The only occupant of the crisper was a screenplay: *Candy Ride*.

She hunkered down on her heels and aimed the Maglite at the script. After fixing its position in the crisper, she reached a gloved hand in and lifted it out.

She felt breathing on her neck. Buddy.

"Why would he keep a screenplay in the crisper?" Laura muttered.

Buddy shrugged. "To hide it, I guess. I wonder what's so bad about it he has to hide it."

Carefully, Laura pushed back the cardboard cover and read the first page.

Buddy, leaning over her, whistled, low.

The scene started with the abduction of a teenaged girl.

Buddy said, "Sick fuck."

"You could look at it another way."

"How?"

"I don't know."

"He hid it in the crisper."

Laura stared at the first page, thinking that it could go either way. People wrote what came from their imaginations; it didn't mean that they did what they wrote about. "Maybe he's serious. Maybe he's trying to sell a screenplay."

Buddy just stared at her.

"Are you done with the bedroom?" she asked.

"I wanted to tell you. Couldn't find anything in the bedclothes. He changed the sheets."

"You sure?"

"They were black yesterday and they're blue plaid now."

She absorbed this. "He was afraid we'd come back."

Buddy looked grim, which prompted her to ask, "What else?"

"What do you mean, what else?"

"There's something else. What is it?"

"I think he vacuumed the bedroom. Place is so clean it's sterile."

Laura thought about the appliance surfaces. "He could just be a neat kind of guy."

"Yes, except I checked his vacuum cleaner. And his hand vac. New bags."

"So what he did, the minute we left, he vacuumed." She thought of something. "Why'd he leave the screenplay in the crisper?"

"He didn't think we'd look there."

"If it was me, I'd get rid of any evidence of it. He'd have to know we'd look in the refrigerator. He'd have to know we'd be thorough this time around."

"How else do you explain it, then?"

"I don't know. Did you find any floppy disks?"

"I found a box of them. Didn't look at them, though. Some of these guys have a program where they can destroy everything on the hard disk if someone unauthorized logs on. No way I'd turn that puppy on."

Laura concealed her disappointment. "He could hide e-mails on those disks, right?"

"Oh, sure he could." He straightened up and she heard his knees crack.

Forensics on a computer would take weeks, sometimes months, depending how careful he was in getting rid of any incriminating evidence. Just deleting files wouldn't protect him for very long. Most of what was on his hard drive would be retrievable through various means, but it would take a long time.

She wondered if they'd finally find CRZYGRL12.

Ted Olsen stroked the beard lying on his chest as if it were a pet ferret. "I don't know," he said at last. "The mustache made a big difference."

The owner of Cooger & Dark's Pandemonium Shadow Show and Emporium squinted again at the row of six photographs on the table in the conference room at the Bisbee Police Department. He wore a polyester short-sleeved shirt, so thin Laura could see the individual hairs on his back. She noticed his odor, a peculiar combination of chicken soup and pencil shavings.

Buddy Holland alternated between leaning over him and pacing the small cubicle. "You sure?" he asked now. "Do you know any of these men?"

"That's Chuck Lehman."

"Think about what he'd look like if he had a mustache."

Trying to influence the witness.

But Ted Olsen wouldn't be influenced. His shifted onto one buttock and removed a snot-caked handkerchief from his back pocket, blew his nose. Leaned back and looked. Leaned forward so his eye was close to the photo. Leaned back again and scratched an armpit.

Milking it for all it was worth.

Finally he shook his head. "It could be Chuck. But I can't tell without the mustache. He has blue eyes," he added helpfully.

"What about his voice. Did his voice sound like Chuck's?" Buddy asked.

Laura shot him a warning look but he ignored her.

Olsen considered this, but finally shook his head. "I'm not sure and I can't put a man in jeopardy if I'm not sure."

"I think we're done here," Laura said wearily.

She was surprised at the virulence in the gaze Buddy shot her. He reached down and swept up the photos.

"Thank you for your help, sir," Laura said.

He looked up at her. "Sorry I couldn't help."

"You did the right thing. If you could give me your opinion on these." She showed him photographs of the dress Jessica Parris had worn in death. "What about this dress? Do you recognize the pattern?"

He stroked his beard, then clasped his hands over his stomach. "Looks familiar . . . I never made that one."

"Why not?" asked Buddy.

"Because I don't like the sleeves. Too puffy."

"But you've seen something like this before?"

"It could be in the catalog. Online."

"And that would be?"

He marked them off on his fingers. "Inspirational Woman, Satin and Lace, Lynette's Originals, Darcy's Dress Shoppe . . ."

Laura wrote them down. "Must be a popular style."

"It's kind of alternative clothing, you know? The stuff girls wear today—kids in thongs, those midriff blouses."

"You don't like that kind of thing?" asked Laura.

"Nope. I should have been born in a different era. When women didn't show everything they had."

As Laura headed back to Tucson later in the day, she replayed her interview with Ted Olsen. After agreeing with him on the sad state of teenagers today and their lack of modesty, she'd eased into specific questions about his actions on the evening Jessica Parris disappeared. If he recognized that the thrust of the interview had changed, Laura didn't see any evidence of it. He answered her questions innocently and with painstaking thoroughness, supplying the name of at least one person, a local woman, who had been to his shop that night. Her follow-up call to the customer corroborated his story.

Even though he made dresses and his shop was close to City Park, Laura found it hard to imagine this man killing Cary Statler and overpowering Jessica Parris. His shop was cluttered and dusty, his personal hygiene abominable. She couldn't picture him scrupulously cleaning up Jessica with an almost scary attention to detail.

This driving back and forth between Bisbee and Tucson was getting old. Laura got some cheese crackers from the vending machine and headed to the squad bay. On the way, she ducked into the bathroom and gave herself a strip wash, using liquid soap from the dispenser and a half dozen small sheets of brown paper towels. It didn't do much good. Her blouse was wrinkled and she still felt stale. She salved her lips, combed the sweat more evenly through her hair, and decided that was as good as it would get today.

Victor wasn't at his desk but he'd left her a copy of his autopsy notes.

It occurred to her that Victor wasn't around much at all these days.

He seemed to be disconnecting from the case. She knew he was preoccupied with his wife and new daughter, not to mention his four other kids and the mistress everyone knew about but didn't acknowledge. But it was more than that. He was acting as if the case were already solved and he had moved on.

Victor had always been a lazy investigator, but his charm made up for it. He was a brilliant interviewer and interrogator—had gotten some astounding confessions over the years. On the cases they'd worked together, his laxness in certain aspects of an investigation had never bothered her. She'd picked up the slack without complaint, not because she was a saint—she sure as hell wasn't—but because she liked to keep her finger on the pulse of every case. She wanted to possess a case, know it up and down and inside out, the car parts on the tarp, so she could pounce down on any piece at any time. For this reason she liked being teamed with Victor. He never got in her way.

But that had all changed when he went behind her back and set up the search with Sylvia Clegg.

She'd just started reading Victor's autopsy notes when the phone rang: Doris Bonney returning her call. It took a moment for Laura to place her, the "girl" who worked for the old man on West Boulevard. Doris Bonney sounded much older, sixty at least.

Accustomed to doing two things at once, Laura skimmed the report as she asked Doris Bonney about the previous Friday. "Do you remember what time you left there?"

"Had to be six fifteen, six twenty at the latest."

"Are you sure?"

"Mr. Toomey eats at five thirty every evening. I have to be across town for a class I'm taking by six thirty."

"Did you notice anything unusual when you left?"

"I can't think of anything."

Laura's eyes ran down the report. Cause of death: a blow to the head. Well duh.

"Think hard," she said to Mrs. Bonney. "People walking their dogs, kids, someone driving by?"

Silence. Laura pictured her thinking. Most good citizens tried hard to please. Talking to cops brought out the bright student in them.

"Sorry." Bonney sounded sincerely disappointed. "It was just like any other night."

Once more with feeling. "You're sure? It could be anything out of the ordinary, no matter how insignificant it seems to you."

Laura said this as she turned to the next page of the report, noting that the object used to kill Cary Statler was described as heavy and flat. There was a portion of Cary's scalp where the edge of the weapon had made its mark: a curved indentation. In addition, there was trace evidence of fish, oil, salt, and flakes of metal in Cary's wound. The report concluded that the weapon could have been a frying pan or skillet.

"Well, there *was* a motor home."

Laura straightened in her chair, all her attention now on Bonney. "Motor home?"

"I thought I was going to be late for class. This big motor home was taking its time trying to turn around. I'm sure it isn't important, but honestly, that's the only thing . . ."

"Are you sure it was that Friday?"

"That's the night of my pottery class."

"Can you remember what it looked like?"

"Big. Had to be a mile long. It took him some maneuvering to turn that thing around, let me tell you. There were three other cars waiting. You'd think he'd be more considerate."

"Do you remember which way he was going?"

"When he finally got turned around? Up to the pass."

"Out of town?"

"That's right."

"Can you remember the color?"

"It was light brown—tan, I'd guess is the better word. I had to sit there staring at it for the longest time. Definitely tan."

"Did you get a look at the driver?"

"Nope. It was hard to see in—it's dark up there by six thirty."

After she hung up, Laura pulled out a pad and wrote:

Motor home sightings:
West Boulevard, approx. 6:15 PM July 8
Brewery Gulch, approx. 2 AM July 8

After this she wrote:

Frying pan?

She tried to picture Chuck Lehman walking up the road looking for Jessica and Cary, holding a frying pan.

The phone interrupted her thoughts.

"Laura, could you come by my office for a minute?" Lieutenant Galaz asked when she answered. "Anytime in the next ten minutes."

Laura realized this was the first time she'd seen the inside of Lieutenant Galaz's office since he'd been here.

A big man sat in the leather chair closest to Galaz's desk. He gave the impression of toughness: blond butch cut, muscles encased in fat under a Big & Tall navy sport coat. The ubiquitous cop mustache, ginger gray. Square, gold-rimmed glasses tinted rose that went with his square face. One black-loafered ankle rested on his knee. He did not get up when she entered the room.

Galaz, seated at his massive cherrywood desk, did rise, his smile inclusive, as if he shared a joke with her.

"Laura, glad you could make it. This is Mickey Harmon, with Dynever Security. He's a twenty-year veteran with TPD. We go way back—grew up together."

Laura nodded to Harmon.

"Sit down, sit down." Galaz motioned Laura to the other burgundy leather chair. Watching her with interest. As she did so, she thought how different this office looked from that of the previous owner, Larry Tuttle, who had occupied it for eleven years. The bank of fluorescent lights had morphed into softer, more flattering light. The secondhand furniture, a lot of it cheap office stuff, had been replaced by a thick oriental carpet, cherrywood, and leather. A bookshelf full of books on DPS rules and procedures, one whole shelf devoted to criminal profiling and forensic procedures—not so different from her own library. But the biggest change was on the walls: three nature photos, blown up big. One of them was a close-up of a hummingbird in midflight. The other two were spiders blown up into monsters: a black widow in a glistening web, its eyes magnified to the size of peas; a giant, hairy wolf spider against a shimmering backdrop of green.

Galaz followed her gaze. "Ah, you noticed my photos. It's a hobby of mine. Well, more of a passion." He pushed an *Arizona Highways* magazine across his desk. "Finally made the big time. Page fifteen."

Laura dutifully turned to the photo spread: more spiders and a scorpion or two.

"Very impressive, sir."

His smile was quick, as if he were expecting the compliment.

"I called you in here to see how the case was going. Is it true we're close to an arrest?"

"We're in the process of collecting evidence now. We're hoping the forensics on the computer will pan out."

"But the lipstick with the prints on it? That's pretty solid?"

"The lipstick had her prints on it. It was found in his bedroom."

Galaz frowned. "I'm glad you're taking your time and not rushing to judgment. You remember Walter Bush."

Walter Bush was a local businessman who had been arrested for a series of burglaries based on one witness's identification. He was eventually cleared, but not before he attempted suicide in his jail cell. A lawsuit was pending.

Galaz leaned back, hands clasped behind his head. "Laura here is one of the best investigators we've got. You remember the Judd murders—guy murdered his whole family? Laura was the one who cracked it. She's like a pit bull. Grabs on and won't let go."

Laura mentally squirmed.

"We've been having a little disagreement on what kind of killer this is," Galaz said. "Mickey's convinced he's white, but I'd like him to think outside the box a little bit." He smiled and spread his hands. "You know—embrace diversity."

Laura said, "The majority of these offenders are white—"

"What did I tell you?" Mickey said, winking at her.

Laura added, "But it's a mistake to rule out any one race. Even though there are very few black or Hispanic offenders, I think there will be more as—"

Galaz turned to Mickey, his grin triumphant. "You see, Mickey? She agrees with me. Even though minorities are underrepresented, culturally we're catching up. More of us are joining the ranks of the middle class, are better educated, we're succumbing to the same pressures that the average white guy has. We're developing a taste for it."

Laura said nothing. It was tantamount to saying how great it was that women were catching up and passing men in lung cancer statistics.

"All I'm saying, Mickey, is it could be anybody," Galaz said. "We don't want to limit our options."

"I agree," Laura said. "But likely he is Caucasian." Hoping the lieutenant wouldn't be insulted in some weird way.

"Oh, I'm sure he is. We were talking theoretically." Galaz rolled a Montblanc pen in his long, tapered fingers. "I understand there's an Internet connection to this? You think the perp got to this girl on the Internet?"

She wondered if he got the term "perp" from television. Nobody in her squad or any squad she knew had ever used the word. "We think there could be an Internet connection, but so far we haven't been able to find it."

"Why is that?"

"It's like looking for a needle in a haystack. I've got someone on it, but with the Cary Statler homicide—we don't have the resources."

His eyes were sympathetic. "I was talking about this with Mickey. This Crazygirl thing. You really think that's important to the case?"

"It could be."

"I told you that Mickey here works for Dynever Security. It's one of the top Internet security companies in the United States. Heck, probably the world." He glanced at Harmon.

"You work with the government on all levels, don't you, Mickey? State, federal, you name it. Really impressive."

"We've consulted on a number of high-profile cases for them," Harmon said.

"I forget what all you do," Galaz said, fiddling with his pen.

"Mostly we're Internet security. Countersurveillance. One division creates Web sites and develops networks, another is strictly data management. We also offer Internet security services to small businesses."

It sounded like a sales pitch.

"The point is," said Galaz, "you know as well as I do we're not equipped to handle something like this. If this guy really did lure her on the Internet. You know what our budget's like." He turned to Harmon. "Desert Lakes, this little podunk town in the middle of the state? They have three times the budget per capita we do. They get the shiny new cars, the cyber cops, all the perks. Here we are, the state agency, we're supposed to be *elite,* and we're lagging behind everybody else."

Laura smiled. There was a joke around the investigative division that "DPS" stood for "Don't Pay Shit."

"So we have to improvise." Galaz leveled his gaze on her. "How sure are you that this is the guy?"

"Lehman?" She paused. Not knowing what to say.

"Go on. We're nonjudgmental here."

Laura didn't like the way this was going. She didn't like the "we"—this friend of Galaz's sitting there as if he were DPS. But she had to be honest. "Even though we're moving ahead with Lehman, we're looking at other leads."

"Would it help if we could find this Crazygirl connection?"

"I suppose so, sir."

"What if we outsourced this job to Dynever Security?"

So that was what this was about. She opened her mouth to reply, then stopped. Harmon was sitting right here. She realized belatedly she'd walked into an ambush. She couldn't tell him her real thoughts with Harmon here.

"My guess is, this is going to take some getting used to." Galaz swiveled in his chair, back and forth, smiling at her. "Tell you what. I'm having a little get-together tonight, just a few people. I'd like you to come by, meet the folks you didn't get a chance to last time."

"That would be great, sir."

"So I can count on you?"

"Yes, sir."

"I particularly want you to meet the head of Dynever Security. Great guy. He's like a brother to me."

She nodded, not knowing what else to say.

He glanced at his watch. "I can tell we're going to get out of here late. Nine o'clock for drinks? You can find my house okay, can't you? I don't think you've ever been there."

Laying it on a little thick. Victor was right; she should have gone to the barbecue. She nodded. "I'll be there."

"See you then."

Something in his smile told her that the audience was over.

When the door shut behind her, she felt as if she had been processed through the county jail—her wallet, shoelaces, and belt gone. Folded, stapled, *and* mutilated.

She found herself staring at the wall of photos again. Noticed that most of them included Nick Fialla, the University of Arizona football coach who had led the Wildcats to a Rose Bowl win two years ago. It amazed her how the prominent people of Tucson, the movers and shakers, flocked to get their picture taken with Nick Fialla.

He should rent himself out, she thought sourly. Like the burros in Nogales the tourists posed with to prove they'd been to Mexico.

# 21

The sun had just gone down behind the Tucson Mountains when Laura reached the Vail exit. The lights of oncoming cars were already snapping on, strung out across the pink-purple hills east of Tucson like a necklace of diamonds.

As she drove across the overpass, she spotted a scrawny woman sitting in the open hatchback of a Chevy Vega parked near the off-ramp, holding up a cardboard sign that said BLOWJOBS $2.00.

Everyone had their price.

Laura's was giving in to Let's Go People! Galaz. No way she could get out of going to this party; she'd already missed the barbecue—apparently the only person in the whole department who did.

As she pulled up in front of her house, she spotted something pale in the darkness of her porch. It materialized into a white long-sleeved shirt as she approached.

"Tom?" Her heart quickening.

"Hi, Bird."

"When did you get back?"

"This morning." He stood up from the steel glider near the door. It creaked loudly—sixty-year-old springs.

He was close enough that she caught the scent of his shirt, a combination of starch and the fresh smell of line-drying. Tom didn't own a dryer. He didn't own much of anything.

"I heard about the girl who got killed—thought you might need me."

"Who'd you hear that from?"

"Mina."

"Mina called you?"

"I called her. I was checking on Ali."

Referring to a famous bareback bronc named Old Yeller. Ten years ago, before Old Yeller took the inevitable downward spiral to the dog food factory, Tom bought him, changed his name to Ali ("because he was The Greatest") and towed him around from job to job. Ali was twenty-three years old, swaybacked, and deeply suspicious of Laura.

She inhaled the night air, soggy and laden with the odors of creosote and manure. She was glad Tom was here—*really* glad. "How long have you been waiting?"

"I wasn't waiting. I was sitting."

Zen and the Mystic Itinerant Wrangler. He reached out and touched her lightly on her cheek, which sent her thoughts whirling like sparks from a kicked-up fire, her mind buzzing on and off like an old neon sign. He was aware of his effect on her but had the good sense not to say anything. "I thought we could go by the cantina and get a drink. Mina's beginning to wonder if you're avoiding her."

Mina, the proprietor of the Spanish Moon Cantina on the Bosque Escondido, liked to micromanage the lives of the people who lived and worked here. Laura wondered if she'd weighed in on the living-together issue yet.

"I'd better not drink anything. I have to be somewhere later."

"Oh?"

"A party at my lieutenant's house—it's mandatory."

"Mandatory?"

"For me, anyway. I didn't go to the last one, so I've got to go this time."

"What'll he do if you don't?"

She shrugged. "Probably nothing. It's politics."

"Sounds to me like he set you up."

Great insight from a man whose only possessions were a truck, a saddle, a horse trailer, and one decrepit horse.

Here she'd found a man who was perfect for her in every way except one. In the currency she valued most, the currency that defined her life—career—he didn't even have pocket change. He had no ambition. Thirty-five years old and he wrangled horses on a guest ranch.

He said, "Did you get my note?"

"Of course I got your note. I have to eat, don't I? Lucky for you, you didn't leave it on the cleaning closet."

He had both hands on her shoulders now. "Have you thought about it?"

"I haven't had time."

If she thought he'd be heartbroken, she was wrong.

"Okay, I can wait. If you can't drink, can we at least eat?"

"I was going to have mac and cheese."

He smiled. "Not much food in those little boxes."

"I've got two of them."

Laura drifted in and out of sleep, her body one long smile. Naked in the cool swirl of sheets, the boat-oar ripple of the ceiling fan playing over her body, legs entangled with Tom's long lean ones, the feel of his skin against hers . . . times like these she felt young again. Young in that innocent romantic way before life started cutting away at her. Before Billy Linton blew her romantic ideals out of the water. Before she learned that no matter how strong a bond you had with your family, it could be ripped away from you at any time.

Lying here, she felt like the college kid she once was, infatuated with life, absolutely certain about her future. All she had to do was succumb to her feelings, and she could hold it again, that hope. Allow herself to be swept away by this incredible lover whose touch shot through her like electricity.

Still drowsy, she found herself looking at the length of

his body in the light from the bathroom. It was impossible to keep herself from touching him. She reached out and laid a finger on his skin. Felt a shiver, although it was warm. Traced a line down his muscled forearm, down along his rib cage, the bump where one rib had broken during a bull ride, then down into the hollow between his hip bones.

Another shiver.

*Why shouldn't we live together?*

Because it could go wrong. That was the lesson she had learned from her marriage.

Marriage? the hard-ass in her said. Whatever it was she and Billy had, you couldn't really call it a marriage.

The fact was, love could go wrong. All those good times, feeling you were joined at the hip, that you knew that other person so well, as well as you knew yourself, and then something bad happens and all of a sudden you become enemies. You don't even know how it happens, but one day you meet in the hallway and you skirt around each other, looking away, trying not to touch. Because all of a sudden touching is impossible, you can't stand to feel him on your skin. How does that happen? Just bad luck? Did it happen to everyone who went through a tragedy? She didn't know.

Tom stirred and his arm fell across her.

She couldn't deny how good it felt to be with him. Logically, she knew she couldn't judge Tom by the Lintons. Besides, Tom didn't have a rich family.

She pressed her lips to his and he stirred again.

The sudden thrill of absolute *wanting* always caught her by surprise. Undeniably needy . . . and he always responded.

Now he rose up on one arm above her, settled his lips onto hers.

She cupped the back of his head, and they kissed long and slow.

Exquisite.

But something not so good insinuating itself into her mind—

*"Shit!"* She sat up, grabbed the bedside clock, and turned it so she could see.

Tom, his dark eyes cloudy with sleep and desire and questions. "What's wrong?"

11:10.

*"Dam*mit!"

"What's wrong?" Concern etched into two grooves between his eyes. Realization. "You missed the party."

She hopped out of bed, stumbling in the sheet and having to grab the bedpost to stay afloat. In the bathroom, turning the shower on full spray. Fumbling for her toothbrush. Before or after her shower? What would she wear? What kind of shoes?

Feeling impotent. Unable to make decisions. Duck into the shower, make it fast.

As she scrubbed, she tried to remember. How did she let this happen? The two of them sitting on the porch eating macaroni and cheese. Watching TV, starting on the couch and transferring to the bedroom, hurried and wanting.

Immersed in their lovemaking. Mindless pleasure. Spending themselves, energy dwindling down to a tiny speck, like the dot on her grandmother's old television set just before it went dark. She remembered thinking as she drifted off, *I've got time. Just a few minutes and then I'll get up . . .*

As the hard needles of spray drilled into her skin, Laura thought of something Frank Entwistle used to say.

There are no accidents.

She took Old Spanish Trail, flooring it along the edge of the Rincon Mountains, knowing it was too late. Doglegged over to the Catalina Highway, turning right onto a single lane of blacktop that climbed along the base of the mountains to where Galaz's house overlooked the city. No cars parked outside the closed decorative iron gate, the house dark.

Driving back, Laura was surprised how bad she felt. She sensed that this time, she'd done the unforgivable. Victor always warned her that she needed to pay attention to what was going on with the brass. He'd told her on more than one occasion that she was impolitic. She'd always brushed it off, because in her opinion sucking up wasn't important to the job she did every day.

The moon peeked over the shoulder of the Rincons, a laughing clown.

When she got home, Tom was gone. She was surprised, although she couldn't expect him to stay. If they lived together it would be different. He'd be there all the time.

Too tired to think now, anyway.

She got into bed, was asleep within minutes. Awakened not long after by a loud thump. Hallelujah—the bobcat kittens were back.

Laura sat up in bed, listening to them play on the roof, watching the moonlight and mesquite shadows tremble across the floor. Most ranch houses in the Southwest had concrete floors. This one had been deep red for the majority of its eighty years, scuffed and chipped by generations of cowboy boots, spurs, dragged saddles and bridles. Laura had painted it hazelnut brown, a glossy finish. In the moonlight, though, it was hard to tell what color it was.

She wished Tom had waited. The lack of his presence prickled her, like the ghost pain from a severed limb.

She had not had this feeling since Billy—that heart-thumping, nerve-shattering, high-voltage infatuation. Like two electrical wires touching, igniting feelings both visceral and surprising.

Laura had spent some time thinking about it. She'd known sexier men, better-looking men, more powerful men. Maybe it was the forbidden nature of their relationship. The desire for the forbidden had probably been pummeled into her during catechism—kids being prone to absorb the opposite message as they were. By the time she was a teenager, forbidden pleasure as a concept was in full force. It fueled her poor choices in middle school, high school and college: beautiful boys who knew they were beautiful and had nothing else to occupy their minds except contempt for those who worshipped them.

Her mother wasn't here to disapprove now. But Laura knew she'd adopted her prejudices. An itinerant former bull rider was not the right man for her. The end result was a relationship that tasted and felt illicit—and therefore delicious.

A train horn blared. The railroad tracks ran along the freeway, some five or six miles away as the crow flew. On sleepless nights, which lately had been all too many, she heard every big truck out on the highway and the mournful horn of every train. Those sounds had been woven into the tapestry of her life, the lonely sounds of people going elsewhere, passing in the night.

*If you lived together you'd—*

*Stop it.*

The bobcats, snarling, scuffling, galloping back and forth across the roof. God bless them.

No more sleep tonight. She turned on the light. The chartreuse green walls of her bedroom looked like they had peeled and faded in the sun; she'd taken a course on distressing walls to look old. That and the mesquite mission bed—*hecho en Mexico*—made her room beautiful, to her eyes, anyway.

Her gaze strayed to the photos on the wall opposite the bed, the focal point of the room. Most of them were of good times with her parents and her friends: eight-by-tens of her on her mare Calliope, showing off her ribbons from the Alamo Farm annual horse show; two Ross Santee pen-and-ink drawings that she had found at a yard sale; a wedding picture of Frank Entwistle and his second wife, Pat.

No wedding pictures of her own, though. There hadn't been any.

She liked looking at the wall of photos from a distance, the cumulative effect of them arrayed tastefully, the mellow finish of the gold frames catching the light, but the truth was she rarely got up close and looked right at them. She didn't like how they made her feel.

That was then; this is now.

Those days were as old and faded as the photographs, a half-remembered dream. Someone else's life. She was not the pretty, shy girl perched on the fifty-thousand-dollar Thoroughbred hunter, the teenager giggling with friends at places as diverse as Dairy Queens and rock concerts.

The girl looking out of those photographs seemed confident of her future happiness.

Laura, looking at it from the perspective of distance, thought that was sad.

# 22

She was getting ready for work the next morning when she heard the gate creak out front. She looked out the window and saw Mike Galaz standing just inside the hogwire fence, almost concealed by the large mesquites. He seemed to be looking at her roof.

She came out on the porch. His gaze still fixed on the clay barrel tiles, he said, "Is that a prickly pear growing out of your roof, or are you just happy to see me?"

He didn't sound mad. In fact, he sounded friendlier than she'd ever heard him. "Like it?" she said. "It's the latest in home design." And immediately wondered—was she being too flip? "About last night—"

"Don't worry about it."

A compulsion to explain. "I guess I was more tired then I thought. I fell asleep."

"*No problema.* You missed a good time, but it's no big deal." He removed his coat jacket and folded it neatly over his arm. "You have air-conditioning in that shack? I feel like I'm going to melt."

"Maybe you should trade that black SUV for a white one."

"Why is that?" He stepped up onto the worn brick paving of the portal and wiped his brow with the back of his hand.

"Black attracts heat."

He shrugged. "I've got good air-conditioning. It's just walking from the car to the house that kills me."

He didn't seem to know the basics about living in the desert. Like driving a white car or getting most of your outdoor work done before eight in the morning. She'd seen Galaz go out for a jog during his lunch hour in the middle of the summer.

The Galaz family had been around Tucson since the eighteen hundreds, but the lieutenant didn't act like an native Tucsonan, except in one way. Tucson had a proud tradition of Hispanic politicos and wheeler-dealers.

She offered him coffee and he accepted while she went through the house closing windows and turning on the cooler.

He held his hand up toward the air vent, grimacing at the fishy smell. "You sure it works?"

"Swamp box," she said. "It'll take a while." She had no doubt that Mike Galaz had real air-conditioning in his expensive home in the foothills.

A hundred years ago he would probably have lived in a ranch house just like this one. He looked like he belonged here, with his elegant Spanish features and aristocratic bearing. A man who would look good by candlelight.

He cradled the coffee mug in both hands. "I hope you don't mind me dropping by like this."

"No, of course not." But she started to feel nervous again.

Galaz sipped his coffee. "A shame you couldn't meet Jay."

"Jay?"

"Head of Dynever Security. The main reason I had the party, for you and him to meet."

He was mad after all. What she was about to say would make him a lot madder. "About that." She took a deep breath. "I don't know if it's a good idea to get them involved."

"Because of the chain of custody? Is that what's bothering you?"

"You know what a defense attorney might do with that."

He stared at her, his dark eyes inscrutable. "You're a good detective, Laura. You always think ahead. I like that." He took out a handkerchief and wiped his forehead. "But you've got to give me some credit. There's no way I'd jeopardize this investigation. If you're worried about the forensics on the computer, of course our crime lab does that. No way I'd farm that out. I'm just talking about the cyber stuff. As far as I'm concerned, that's just air."

Air that can kill, Laura thought.

Galaz leaned back and the Mexican chair creaked. "I thought you had your doubts about it being Lehman."

"I have questions."

"I saw the autopsy report. That part about the frying pan. I find it hard to believe Lehman would walk up the road looking for those two kids."

"I can't speak for Victor, but I bet he'd say that Lehman killed Cary in his house and dragged him up to the cabin at night."

At the mention of Victor, Galaz's eyes turned stony. Something between them. She remembered what Victor had called him: a control freak.

He crossed one knee over the other and said, "What do you think?"

"I didn't see any blood evidence of that, and there would have been a lot of blood. Even when you clean a place really well, there's always some residual blood. Nothing came up when we used luminol."

"Crazygirl 12. That bothers me, too. You said yourself Detective Holland hasn't done much."

"To be fair, we've been kept pretty busy."

"But bottom line, you've got your doubts."

She nodded.

He set his coffee mug down. "I think we should try this. Before he gets another girl. Victor and Buddy can work the

Lehman angle." He saw her expression and added, "I promise you, there won't be any repercussions."

"You can't promise that."

"Yes, I can. I'll take the blame if it goes wrong, but it won't go wrong. This guy is good. You'll like him."

She noticed his word tenses. Past the negotiation phase. As far as he was concerned, it was a done deal. It would have been a done deal last night, but she'd messed that up by not showing.

She realized that if she had gone last night, this conversation wouldn't be taking place. He would have asked her in front of this man Jay, and she would have had to agree. In the DPS—as in any law enforcement agency—you never made your boss look weak. Never.

Maybe Victor was right about the lieutenant's need for control. He certainly had it now. Might as well get it over with. She could make a token effort, talk to the guy, then tell Galaz it didn't work out. "Okay, I'll talk to him."

"Good." Galaz reached into his wallet and removed a card, set it on the table.

The card said, DYNEVER SECURITY. MICHAEL J. RAMSEY II, CEO.

She stared down at the pale gray vellum, the embossed letters. Heat suffused her face and her heart started to pound.

"Jay Ramsey?" she said. Her tongue felt stiff.

"You know him," Galaz said. Not a question.

"No, not really. I only met him once."

"Met" wasn't strictly accurate. She'd noticed him plenty. *Watching him whack tennis balls at the Ramseys' tennis court down the road from the stables. Watching him go from the house to his Range Rover, hanging with his friends, driving by in a cloud of dust.*

"He asked about you," Galaz said. "He thinks of you often."

*Occasionally, he'd look her way and nod.*

"But of course that goes without saying," Galaz added.

# 23

Galaz left soon after. Feeling as if she'd been whacked by a two-by-four, Laura walked out onto the porch, wondering what this all meant.

She had no particular objection to seeing Jay Ramsey. She didn't know the man. But it had been eleven years since she had been in that part of town. There were so many memories . . .

Mrs. Ramsey, handing her the papers: *We wanted you to have her. As a thank you.*

A fifty-thousand-dollar thank you.

The phone rang and she jumped.

It was Barry Endicott, the sheriff's detective from Indio. "Sorry I haven't gotten back to you," he said. "I've been working a case that's taken all my time."

"That's okay." Aware of her own breathing.

"I heard you had a girl," he said. "Dressed up and posed, am I right?"

"Yes."

"So did we, five months ago. Girl named Alison Burns."

"What was she wearing?"

"She was dressed up like a flower girl and posed on a bed at a motel slated for demolition. It was pure luck we found her at all. It was kind of opportunistic—guy that found her was taking pictures of abandoned buildings. He said he had his eye on the place and as soon as they cleared out, he went in before it could be boarded up. He was our main suspect for a while, but turns out he was in Monterey around the time the girl was killed—at a photographer's workshop."

"How old was she?"

"Twelve. How old was yours?"

"Fourteen."

He didn't say anything for a moment, probably pondering the disparity in their ages. Laura pressed him for details.

"She was left there after they officially closed the place, but before they removed the beds. The fact the guy found her that early gave us a better fix on time of death."

According to Endicott, Alison Burns had been smothered. She had traces of Rohypnol, the date rape drug, in her system.

"We figured the guy gave her the Rohypnol, then softsmothered her, but that's only a theory. We think from the stomach contents that he held a little party for her."

Laura said, "What?"

"We think he took her to McDonald's. Happy Meal, soft drink, Baskin-Robbins after that. There were balloons in the room and a new teddy bear."

Stranger and stranger. "Like a birthday celebration?"

"Like one. Her birthday wasn't anywhere around that time. We think he made her last day a good one."

Laura was aware how tightly she gripped the phone.

"That's conjecture on our part, though."

"He soft-smothered her?"

"We think he wanted to quote unquote 'ease her into sleep.'"

"Was she molested?"

"Oh, yeah. For days."

"Days? He didn't kill her right away?"

"We think he had her four days, maybe five."

Jessica's killer had kept her only a few hours tops, and

raped her postmortem. Maybe this wasn't the same guy. "Could I see the evidence list?"

"We'll need a written request."

"I'll fax you one, but is there any way we can expedite this?"

"I'll see what I can do. Go ahead and send your request. Make sure you ask for a detailed list. You'll want to ask for photos of the dress, the digital camera—"

"What camera?"

"The one he sent her."

"He sent her a camera?"

"Among other things." He paused. "We think he got to her over the Internet."

Twenty minutes later, Laura got the first fax: a photograph of Alison Burns's dress.

According to the accompanying report, the dress pattern came from an Internet company called Inspirational Woman, which sold clothing designed for the "modest woman and girl." Laura recognized it from Ted Olsen's list. She looked it up on the Net. The dress, called "Winsome," was a lot like the one that had been used for Jessica Parris, but there were a few differences. Alison's dress was plainer, but it had an apron that looked as if it were part of the dress itself.

She scrolled down through the patterns and found Jessica's dress at the bottom: It was called "Charity."

This was good. This was really good.

It got better. The faxes came through at a maddeningly slow pace: a photograph of the camera Alison had received in the mail, two photos of jewelry that seemed sophisticated for a twelve-year-old. But the last picture was the best find of all.

Scribbled on top was a notation by Endicott, saying that the original photo had been printed up on an ink-jet and taped to Alison's mirror. This was a black-and-white photocopy, a poor one—but enough to give her a thrill.

The man was in his early twenties. Dark, handsome,

wearing casual but expensive clothing. He stood before a clapboard house on stilts. Scribbled across the bottom, barely legible in the photocopy, was a note: "Forever True, James."

This was the guy the Riverside County Sheriff's Department believed had corresponded with Alison Burns via the Internet. Unfortunately, they had no more information, since Alison Burns didn't have a computer. Endicott believed she had been contacted by this man during her time on the computer at the public library.

Laura stared at the man, putting herself in Alison Burns's shoes. He did not look like a child molester. He looked like a gorgeous, rich young guy who could fit the bill in the Prince Charming department.

The kind of guy who could lure a precocious twelve-year-old.

Laura looked at the house. The fact that it was on stilts indicated oceanfront property—a beach house? The house was clapboard, a light color, and a saw palmetto grew near the steps. The Gulf Coast? And the man's tanned beauty, the professional quality of the photograph—this could be a photo from a model's portfolio.

She grabbed her notebook and jotted these new developments down:

Alison Burns—similars
Dress patterns—Inspirational Woman
Motor home seen at Brewery Gulch
Motor home seen near primary crime scene
Digital camera, jewelry sent to Alison/Internet connection (?)
CRZYGRL12
The man in the photo—beach house?
Serial killer, organized type
Differences between Jessica and Alison—period of time
    kept, age, manner of death
Postmortem vs. antemortem

There were serious differences: the age difference, the method used to kill the victims, the fact that Alison was kept and raped for days and Jessica was alive only a few hours and raped postmortem.

Jessica Parris's pubic area had been shaved. The dress the killer brought was too small—the ME saying that Jessica was an immature fourteen-year-old. Laura wondered: Could he have realized his mistake after he picked her up? And would the fact that she was older than he expected ruin it for him?

If it did, he might take it out on her. He might strangle her instead of "ease her into sleep," as Endicott had described it.

Laura was even more impressed by the similarities. She had always felt that the answer to this problem was on the Internet.

If the guy who killed Jessica also killed Alison, it would be easy enough to eliminate Chuck Lehman. All they had to do was verify where he was at the time of Alison's death.

*If* it was the same killer.

Despite her doubts about Lehman, Laura added him to her list:

Lehman's friendship with Cary and Jessica
Lipstick found in bedroom
Vaccuumed, changed sheets?
Safeway card found nearby
Screenplay about kidnap and murder of young girl
Porn
Lehman lied about relationship with Cary

It was like looking at two different pictures. A strong case could be made either way.

Frustrated, she closed the notebook and stared out at the desert beyond her window. The answer, she knew, was in the cyber world.

She picked up Jay Ramsey's card and made the call.

# 24

Wrought iron gates set into a seven-foot-high stone wall marked the entrance to the Alamo Farm on Fort Lowell Road. The last time she'd been here the stone wall was waist high and there were no gates. The trees beyond the wall were the same, though: mature mesquite and Arizona walnut. As lush and healthy as she remembered.

As she approached the speaker set into the pole underneath the security camera, Laura buzzed her window down, looking at the wall. She couldn't tell where the old section left off and the new one began. She did notice the embedded glass across the top.

The speaker crackled. "May I see some ID?" a voice asked.

Laura held up her badge toward the camera. She heard a whir inside the camera—didn't know what that was about. She waited for what seemed like eons before the gates rolled back and she could drive through.

The moment the wheels of her 4Runner touched onto the property, Laura's stomach clenched. She should have known all those memories would come back. *Sitting cross-legged on the ground, waiting, the cold seeping up through the seat of her jeans, her eyelids getting heavy.*

*Starting to fall asleep and not wanting to, because she'd*

*been here three nights in a row and just knew the mare
would foal tonight.*

The lane headed south toward the river between the over-
arching trees. Laura realized the wall and the gate were window dressing—the property had deteriorated. It looked
downright shabby.

*The sound of a car engine jarring her from sleep. It
scared her. She was safe on the Ramsey property, at least she*
thought *she was, but her parents didn't know she was here
and Julie Marr had been kidnapped not far from here.*

Laura noticed that some of the trees on Alamo Farm suffered the same fate as others along the Rillito River: a lowering water table as the city grew, putting them in deep
distress. Bare limbs stuck up through the green summer
growth, and the mesquites were snarled with mistletoe. The
irrigation ditch alongside the road, once brimming with
water, was dry. She'd heard on the news that Betsy Ramsey
was killed in a car accident a couple of years ago. Clearly,
no one had used the hunt course since then. It had dried up
and blown away—the jump rails lying on the ground, their
colors faded to the brown of the earth. A dusty halo of grass
and high weeds poked up through the threadbare dirt.

*The droning of the engine, coming closer.*

Laura drove into an S-turn bottoming out in a dark copse
of mesquites and walnut trees. Now the lane ran parallel to
Fort Lowell Road, going west. On one side was a windbreak of Aleppo pines, and on the other, a dry field. The
white board fences remained, but the pastures where Thor-
oughbreds had once grazed were overgrown with more
weeds.

Looking toward the end of the lane, she got a shock.

The stables were gone.

The big cottonwood tree—which gave the farm its
name—remained, but the stables with their spacious box
stalls and paddocks had been ripped out. Knocked down,
bulldozed, scrap lumber stacked in a haphazard pile. Weeds

growing up around a mountain of torn green asphalt shingles, splintered white wood, pipe fencing.

Gone.

### 1987

Headlights appeared at the far end of the lane and barreled up the road, cones of light illuminating the farm trees.

Wide awake now. And scared. Something about the violence of the way the visitors came, flooring the car up the dirt road. Heart thumping, Laura stood up and melted into the shadow of the cottonwood tree beside the mare's stall, uncertain what to do.

The headlights turned in at the house. Car doors slammed.

Laura listened to the rustling of the night creatures, a cricket chirping. Voices drifted out of the house—angry and male. She couldn't hear what they were saying.

Two loud cracks came close together—like an ax splitting firewood. Her disbelieving ears told her it was something else. The door banged open and she heard running footsteps. Car doors slammed. An engine roared to life.

The car slewed around in a fountain of dust, headlights pinning the mare in her stall before it rocketed back down the tunnel of trees.

Laura waited a few minutes but they didn't come back.

She crept up to the hedge dividing the barns from the side yard of the house, followed the path to the open gate and went through, heading for the back door. Partly open, the door was almost obscured by a cloud of bougainvillea until she was right on top of it. Remembering what she'd seen on TV, she pushed the door wider with her forearm, not her hands, so she wouldn't leave fingerprints.

She thought about what the foreman, Rafael, had told her. Both Ramseys were out of town for the summer and their son was house-sitting during their absence.

The kitchen light was on. She tiptoed through the house. "Mr. Ramsey? Are you all right? It's Laura Cardinal. Are you there?"

The carpet in the hallway was surprisingly old, plush and white, and still had vacuum marks. Footprints made deep impressions. She walked around them. The footprints led toward the last door at the end of the hall. Light spilled out from the open door.

Inside the room was a king-sized bed, the rich teal green and white bedclothes piled up. Two mean-looking black iron dogs glowered at the foot of the bed.

It smelled funny in here. A burning smell.

It felt funny, too. Like the air had been sucked from the room. What she had thought were bedclothes now materialized into a pale torso and arm, hanging down off the bed, mostly covered by a pillow. On the carpet beneath was an irregular blotch, as if someone had stomped a raspberry Popsicle into the carpet.

Blood.

# 25

Not as much blood as you would think.

Laura remembered fumbling for the phone (even now she lamented the fingerprints she had probably covered up) and punching 911.

She didn't touch him. Not because she had knowledge that moving him could make him worse, but because she didn't *want* to touch him. As if death and dying would rub off on her.

All these crime scenes later, the best thing she had ever done in her life was *not* do something.

Now Laura let the car idle and stared at the remains of Mrs. Ramsey's stables.

She remembered the way it was: everything in its place. The raked breezeway, the whitewashed tack room, the stable colors. Everything was in green or in a combination of yellow and green: the horse blankets, coolers, saddle blankets, buckets, leg wraps, even the rub rags. Everything. Yellow and green.

Now it looked as if the stables had been torn limb from limb like an animal. Ripped apart by a hungry beast and left to rot in the baking sun.

Sadness seeped down into a place she had thought was sealed up tight.

She was sorry she'd come.

She drove on, turning in at the house. The one-story California Mission–style home built in the twenties looked the same, except there were bars on the doors, and ramps and railings for a wheelchair. The grounds were neatly trimmed, the lawn as green and groomed as a billiard table. Bougainvillea, hibiscus, bird of paradise, royal palm, and agave grew in profusion. Mission cactus formed a tall border around the lawn.

Beautiful.

The cars out front were different. Instead of Mercedes, BMWs, and Jay's Range Rover, there was a large half-van/half-SUV that Laura assumed Jay drove, and an ancient Honda Civic.

This time she went to the front door.

She wondered what Ramsey looked like now. Seventeen years was a long time, and she knew just from what she'd read on the Net last night that quadriplegics suffered from many side effects, many of them life-threatening. She had thought that being paralyzed meant you couldn't walk, couldn't move certain parts of the body—thought of it as dead wood, but reading the articles made her realize that the body was still living tissue, and because it could not do what it was meant to do, there were grave repercussions.

What was he like now? She remembered him whacking a tennis ball, the sun shining on his blond hair, his lean, muscular body darkly tanned against his white shorts. The few times he looked at her, she thought she saw a spark of interest. Flattering herself that a college boy might be attracted to her.

Laura assumed that after all this time the quadriplegia would have taken its toll. Jay Ramsey was in his late thirties now. Galaz had told her he was a C6-7 quadriplegic, having suffered a break between the C6 vertebra and the C7. According to Galaz, Ramsey had pretty good control over most of his upper body, including use of his hands. His life expectancy wasn't much shorter than the life expectancy for anyone.

She knew, though, that there were many dangers: dysreflexia, which could lead to stroke; respiratory problems; kidney and bladder problems; muscle spasms; skin breakdown; pneumonia. According to Galaz, Jay Ramsey's disabilities had not stopped him from starting and building one of the top Internet security businesses in the country.

"He started out as a hacker," Galaz told her. "Got himself into trouble with the wrong people. After the shooting, he straightened himself out and never looked back. Even if his family didn't own J J Brown, he would have made it big-time. Unbelievable intellect."

J J Brown was a discount department store with high-end products, much like the outlets today, started in the 1920s. The Ramseys had been the beneficiaries of that wealth ever since.

She rang the bell, thinking how much she didn't want to be here. *I'll make an idiot of myself. I won't know how to talk to him, I'll stare . . .*

She heard a stirring inside. The door opened and Laura was hit by a blast of refrigerated air. The man in the doorway wore a white knit shirt, chinos, and bedroom slippers. He reminded her of a plump, soft dove.

"Detective Cardinal?" he asked. He looked vaguely disappointed. What was a lifesaver supposed to look like? Superwoman? He pushed open the door and held it as she walked in. "I'm Freddy. Jay has been waiting—he's quite excited. He's in his study."

Laura followed him into the hallway that led off the kitchen.

She prepared herself. With all the dangers, all the bad things that could happen—muscle spasms, cord pain, bedsores, bladder problems—she expected he would already be a ruin of a man.

Freddy opened the door to the room.

The sun spilled in shuttered stripes across the Berber

carpet. Laura could barely see through the dust motes. A massive cherrywood desk, a large computer monitor, a horse statue from the Tang dynasty. And the shape in the wheelchair.

*Hitting the ball backhand, flaxen hair catching the sun—*

Her eyes adjusted to the light.

He looked exactly the same.

In a strange moment of déjà vu, she was a kid again with a crush on the privileged, older son of a wealthy family. Suddenly she was that tongue-tied girl, mouth dry and heart beating fast.

*Jesus. You're a grown woman. You have a boyfriend and everything. Grow up.*

His hair was the same vibrant pale gold. His face would be angelic if it weren't for the amusement in his eyes.

*The same look he gave me when I was fourteen.*

He had the same lean, handsome face, elegant nose, and penetrating blue-green eyes. He wore very expensive but casual clothing, and it fit his lithe body well. Pushing forty, but he didn't look it. It was as if he'd been frozen in amber.

Laura was aware she was staring.

"Laura," he said warmly. "It's good to see you again." Not the voice of a sick man.

She wondered if she could unstick her throat enough to talk. Tried it. "Hello." What a scintillating wit.

A click and a buzz, as the motorized wheelchair came toward her.

"Freddy, you finally get to meet my guardian angel. The girl—the woman, who saved my life." He came closer. "I told you she was pretty, didn't I? But pretty doesn't do you justice now."

Up close, Laura saw that his youth was an illusion. There was a little dip of flesh beneath the chin. His complexion was uneven, the elasticity lost, and there was something brittle around the eyelids. His eyes were bright, but hard, too—the dryest part of him.

"You know, Laura, I don't think I ever thanked you."

*Your mother did.*

He was studying her—amused? Interested? Could he really be interested? Did quadriplegics have a sex drive? She had no idea.

"You're staring."

She stepped back. "I'm sorry."

"That's okay. I'm used to that. There's always that awkward few minutes. Don't be embarrassed."

But his eyes pinned her like a butterfly to a board. "Mike said you need help tracking down a predator."

Laura was relieved to talk about the case. "We think we have an Internet predator." She started to fill him in on the Jessica Parris case, but he held up a hand.

"I watch the news. You're very telegenic, by the way." He smiled. Angelic. "Mike told me all about it. I don't know what I can do to help. You have anything on this guy?"

From her briefcase, Laura removed the photocopies of the young man, the digital camera and jewelry, the matchbook cover the killer had left at the band shell. She started to hand them to Jay, hesitated, and was relieved when he took them from her.

"Freddy?" Jay Ramsey said without looking in the attendant's direction.

The soft-looking man bustled over, took the photocopy and looked at it.

Jay asked, "This is the man?"

"He could be. It's possible he killed a girl in California."

Freddy said, "Definitely the Southeast. Probably the Gulf Coast."

"Freddy was born in Pensacola," Ramsey explained. "What else?"

Freddy handed Laura the photocopy back. "Guy is almost too good-looking. That looks like a publicity photo."

Laura said, "I'm thinking that if we could find the

general area, we could link him through a talent or model agency."

Jay Ramsey looked up at her. "Could happen."

She found herself feeling unusually pleased.

Jay shifted in his chair, winced. "He sent her the camera and the jewelry."

"The detective in Indio thinks he wanted her to take pictures of herself for him."

He turned his attention to the photocopy of the matchbook. "Crazygirl 12. That's interesting." His chair buzzed around to the computer on the cherrywood desk.

"What's interesting?" Laura asked.

"How old was that girl—Jessica?"

"Fourteen."

Jay stared at the computer screen. To Laura's limited knowledge, it appeared to be state-of-the-art. Ramsey spoke but did not look at her. "The number twelve after her screen name—that usually means her age. And since it's human nature for teenagers to want to appear older, I sincerely doubt this girl would lower her age by two years."

"What are you saying?"

He looked straight ahead at the computer. "Jessica Parris isn't Crazygirl 12."

"You think he contacted another girl?"

"That's the most likely scenario."

"He came to Bisbee looking for another girl." Her mind was moving now, all self-consciousness forgotten. "But what happened to her?"

Ramsey's body flinched, and he rolled his head on the backrest of his chair. "A few possibilities, I imagine. He kidnapped her and killed her. He took her and kept her with him. Or he never got to her."

"There are no missing children that I'm aware of."

"Then he probably never met up with her."

Why? she wondered. What stopped him?

Jay Ramsey said, "I have a question for *you*."

"Okay."

"What was it like when you found me?"

She stared at him. "I'm sorry?"

"What happened before and after you found me?"

Laura didn't like the question. It took her right back to that time, and she didn't like to think about the past. She shrugged. "It happened so fast."

"What did I look like?"

"You were unconscious."

"But what did I look like?"

She wanted to tell him this was a pointless conversation, but already felt she owed him. He had given her real insights into the Internet connection. She had to find Jessica's killer, and he might be the one to help her do it. *Keep your eye on the ball.*

"You were . . ." She wondered if he really wanted to hear this. "You were lying in the bedclothes, part of your upper body off the bed. I didn't see blood on you but I saw it on the carpet. I think you were naked."

"Naked."

"I think so. You were partially under the covers."

"You didn't touch me. What made you not touch me?"

"I wanted to—" She stopped. Not touching him had saved his life. The doctors said that moving him might have increased the swelling in the area where the spine had been nicked. She started again. "I was afraid to," she said.

He smiled. "An honest answer. I appreciate that, Laura."

"I don't know why you asked."

"It was the seminal moment in my life. I wanted to see what it looked like from the outside. I was out of it. I don't even remember them coming to shoot me."

Laura knew that kind of amnesia was common.

"You know what happened, don't you?" Jay said. "I wasn't a bad kid, but I was heavily into cocaine. Kind of guys I was dealing with, you don't want to fool around. I thought I knew what I was doing." He sighed. "When I screwed up, they decided to make an example of me—if it could happen to a rich kid, it could happen to anyone."

He paused. Waiting for her to comment?

"You want to talk about your case, though." He returned his focus to the computer screen and said briskly, "This is all we have to start with? Crazygirl 12?"

"Yes. Is it impossible?"

He smiled. "Nothing is impossible. It will take a little time, though. Tell you what. I'm meeting with some people this afternoon and I want to have a rest. Why don't you come back this evening? In the meantime, I'll see what I can do with Crazygirl 12."

Laura felt a strange letdown. "All right." She was aware of Freddy standing at her elbow. He escorted her out— wham bam thank you ma'am.

At the door he said, "He's very excited to be working with you on this. But he had a long night. Give me your phone number and I'll call you and let you know if it will work out tonight."

Then she found herself outside, feeling, illogically, that Jay Ramsey had taken something from her. Which was ridiculous. She understood why he'd want to know what happened. It was probably the thing that made him agree to see her at all.

If it would help catch Jessica Parris's killer, she'd be happy to tell him anything he wanted to hear.

Laura stopped the car on the lane near the ruined stables, letting the engine idle.

She'd campaigned Calliope for three years, winning several working hunter classes in Tucson and Phoenix, placing first in a couple of the big shows. All that time, she thought she owned Calliope. Betsy had "given" her the horse, even providing her with the mare's Jockey Club papers.

One day Betsy Ramsey told her she wanted Calliope back.

Laura's parents explained to her that they could hire a lawyer, but ultimately they would lose. The Ramsey family was wealthy, the Cardinal family—a school principal and a school librarian—was not. And Betsy Ramsey had donated money to build a new wing on the elementary school where Alice Cardinal taught.

It was Laura's first lesson in pragmatism.

Laura remembered how it felt, taking the Jockey Club papers back to Mrs. Ramsey. She'd loved that mare. Calliope had been her best friend. She'd spent hours with her, riding her, grooming her, grazing her along irrigation ditches that were now as dry and dusty as her memories.

Mrs. Ramsey rode Calliope to Reserve Champion in working hunter in the Desert Classic in California that year.

From the day Laura left Alamo Farm, she never went back, not until today. She couldn't even bring herself to say good-bye to her mare. Somewhere along the line she had gotten the notion that clean breaks were best. Laura didn't remember getting this idea from her parents or peers. But she knew instinctively that prolonging the association, that holding out hope, would only hurt her more in the end.

Maybe there had been a ticking clock inside that warned her she'd need that coping mechanism later on. Something primitive, hinting she'd have to face finality early in life. So when her parents died, she'd know how to accept it.

The moment the gate rolled back, Laura felt a deep sense of relief.

She put on her left turn signal and waited for the traffic on Fort Lowell to clear.

"You should have looked at the fine print."

The voice came from inside the car. Frank Entwistle's bulk filled the passenger seat, dressed in a cheap polyester suit jacket and slacks, a brown shirt, and an unfashionably wide tie. He held a breakfast sandwich in one hand. The smell of grease permeated the car.

"You're not real."

"So *you* say." He leaned over and hit the turn signal lever, switching it from left to right.

"What'd you do that for?" she asked, although she knew.

"Aren't you going to go by your old house?"

"No."

"Why not? You're right here in the neighborhood." He glanced over at her, shrugged. "Suit yourself."

"Thanks." Laura switched on her left turn signal and pulled out, going east on Fort Lowell Road, watching her old mentor out of the corner of her eye. He'd never learned to chew with his mouth closed, and apparently being dead didn't change anything. "I didn't know ghosts could eat."

"I'm not a ghost."

"What are you? A figment of my imagination?"

"That's as good an explanation as any." He reached over and aimed the air-conditioning vent toward his face. "Hot in here. Slow down, will you?"

Laura had to slow down anyway. They were approaching the tight curve that bordered the Mexican cemetery.

Frank draped his arm across the seat back. "You ever go in there?"

"No. Why would I?"

"You were a kid back then. You know how kids are, always pushing the envelope, trying to figure it out—about death, you know? When your schoolmate got taken, it would be natural to go there. I know I won't ever forget the first kid in my class to die."

"Who's to say Julie died in the cemetery?"

"Not died. *Taken.* Why don't you pull over?"

Although her first impulse was to resist, Laura turned onto the verge at the last minute, tires bumping on the hard dirt, white dust billowing up behind them. "There was nothing in the paper about exactly where she was taken."

Frank Entwistle crumpled up the grease-spotted paper from the sandwich and shot it at the dashboard. "Then how come you dream about it?"

Laura looked past him at the graveyard. The greasewood and mesquite trees, greener and fuller after the summer rains, mingled with plaster angels, crosses, and graves of heaped dirt and piled rocks. A profusion of flowers—both real and fake—rested on the graves, garish in the unrelenting sun. Laura was parked under a mesquite tree, facing the wrong way to traffic—in the spot where, in her dreams, the orange-and-white car cruised to a stop, the mesquite tree's sketchy shade scrolling over the blocky white hood. The girl, hands clasped around the straps of her backpack, leaning down to talk to the man inside.

In her dreams, Laura always heard the car's rough idling, smelled burning oil and felt the heat from the Chevy's engine—details her imagination had conjured from the nightly news and one newspaper photo long ago.

Entwistle said, "No matter how old you get, you always remember."

"Remember what?"

"The first kid in your class to die."

Julie Marr was a transfer student from North Carolina. She had a strange accent, stranger hair, and even stranger clothes.

Laura had known what it was like to be bullied, picked on. But she'd made it to the other side; she had friends. She'd felt for Julie, but face it: She wasn't about to put her own reputation in jeopardy.

Julie Marr lived in the same subdivision as Laura. Laura hated to admit this, but if she saw Julie walking up ahead of her, she would cross to the other side of the street so they wouldn't end up walking together. It was her damn stride. Her natural stride was long; she covered the ground quickly. So she'd walk on the other side, her eyes straight ahead.

Like Jessica Parris, Julie Marr had disappeared between school and her house. Laura had Press Club two days a week after school. Otherwise, the orange-and-white car might have stopped for her.

The stiff old latches sprang back like little mousetraps. Laura sat cross-legged on the floor of the guest bedroom, the late afternoon sun filtering in through venetian blinds that came with the house, contemplating the old-fashioned suitcase and trying not to sneeze from the dust.

Inside were stacks of files held together by shoelaces. Most of them were marked in ballpoint ink discolored with age, usually beginning with the word "Laura": Laura—school; Laura—artwork; Laura—swimming lessons, and so on.

But some manila folders her mother had saved for herself.

There it was, toward the bottom. The word "Crime" in her mother's spidery writing.

Laura knew exactly where to look, even though she had not seen this file in eleven years. She remembered seeing articles on Tucson murders that her mother had clipped, some of them as early as the forties, including the grisly saga of Charles Schmid, who killed three young girls in the 1960s and landed Tucson in *Life* magazine as the town with the "ugliest street in America"—a killer who wore face makeup and put crumpled-up beer cans into his boots to make him look taller.

Laura had forgotten how serious her mother had been about writing. There were three spiral notebooks full of notes, scrawled slips of paper, photos, phone numbers of detectives and police officers, lawyers and prosecutors, and six chapters of a book titled *Death in the Desert: A Comprehensive Account of Tucson's Most Infamous Murders,* by Alice Cardinal.

She didn't remember *this.* She had been a teenager when her mom started writing classes, involved with her own life. She hadn't taken her mother's interests seriously. "Author" didn't fit with her image of her mom. Her mom was a school librarian who spent most of her time and energy trying to shape Laura's life, not her own.

Laura looked at the first page.

### Chapter One

Tucson, Arizona, had seen its share of murders, but none was as mysterious as the disappearance of San Pedro Middle School student Julie Marr.

On a warm day in late September, Julie Marr was walking home from school as usual, when she vanished without a trace. Two days later a man named Jerry Lee, out hiking in the Redington Pass area east of town, noticed an old car that seemed to have rolled down the embankment off the road and had come to a stop in some brush and cactus. A curious sort, he bushwacked down to the car, and was shocked by what he found. The backseat of the old car was soaked with blood.

Six chapters on Julie Marr's disappearance, then nothing. Laura didn't know if her mom had quit at Chapter Seven or if she'd died in the midst of writing the book, a homicide victim herself.

Laura decided she didn't want to look at her mother's book right now. She put the unfinished book to the side and looked through the clippings of the Julie Marr abduction. Two articles. The first declared

CITYWIDE SEARCH FOR MISSING SAN PEDRO MIDDLE SCHOOL STUDENT

and was accompanied by a school picture of Julie Marr. Two days later, the front page headline said,

CAR USED IN ABDUCTION OF LOCAL GIRL FOUND.

A black-and-white photo of the 1955 Chevy Bel Air, all four doors open, a detective squatting near the driver's side.

She skimmed the articles, jotting down the facts of the case on the inside cover of the manila folder.

The car had been stolen from A & B Auto Wrecking on South Park Avenue. The Bel Air had been in an accident but was still drivable.

Blood-typing indicated that the blood in the backseat belonged to Julie Marr. From the amount, the detectives were sure she was either gravely injured or dead. The lead detective on the case was Barry Fruchtendler of TPD.

Corroborating her mother's account, the article detailed the discovery of the car off Redington Pass Road in the Tanque Verde Mountains east of town. It had been pushed off the road at a curve. The way the road was banked made it impossible for it to be seen from a vehicle driving up or down the mountain.

The search had been concentrated there, but no body, no grave, had been found.

Because Julie Marr's body could be anywhere in rugged, almost inaccessible country, the search was called off the next day.

Julie Marr's parents, George and Natalie Marr, were quoted as saying that if the police had taken her disappearance more seriously, Julie might be alive today.

Laura put the suitcase away but took the file, including her mother's chapters, with her. She dropped it on the kitchen table. An interesting trip down memory lane, but she didn't see any relevance to Jessica's case.

It was possible the killer could have lived here in Tucson all those years ago, and killed both Julie Marr and Jessica Parris. But that seemed unlikely, given the number of years that had gone by and the fact that Jessica was strangled, while Julie Marr had been killed even more violently. It pointed to a different kind of killer: one organized, the other out of control.

Laura called the Tucson Police Department and asked to speak with Detective Barry Fruchtendler. No one there by that name.

Probably retired.

She looked for his name in the phone book and was stymied again. That didn't mean much; cops usually had unlisted numbers. She'd call one of her friends at TPD tomorrow and see if he was still around.

But not now.

She put on a fresh blouse, locked up, and took the path over the hill to Tom's house.

# 26

Jay Ramsey had almost managed to pull his plate onto his lap when it slipped out of his hands and crashed to the flagstones.

"You see?" Freddy said primly as he picked up the pieces of bone china. "You've been out here too long."

"Don't worry about me."

"This was your mother's favorite pattern. You know when you start dropping things—"

"Freddy, enough."

"Fine, if that's what you want." Freddy whisked around them, clearing plates and brushing away crumbs from the tablecloth.

Jay had invited Laura to breakfast. She was happy to get out here early, anxious as she was to get Jay on the Internet and see him work the magic Galaz had promised her, but here they sat. She kept thinking about Alison Burns lying on the bed in the abandoned motel room. And Jessica Parris, posed like a doll in the City Park band shell.

She had to admit it was pleasant here—lush plants and deep shade. Misters on the porch roof cooled the terrace. Across the lane stood the high hedge lining the tennis court, where Jay Ramsey used to play. Laura, a kid, a horse groom, walking by, hoping she'd catch his eye.

Now she had his full attention. Strange how wants and hopes changed over the years.

Freddy was back from the kitchen. He nodded at the thermometer tacked to the pepper tree near the pool. "It's eighty-seven degrees. You've been out here *well* over an hour."

"I'm fine."

"You won't be so cocky if your bladder lets go in front of company."

Jay saw Laura's discomfort and grinned. "Freddy's afraid I'll get overheated. That can lead to dysreflexia, which—"

"Could send his blood pressure sky-high," Freddy said.

Jay leaned toward Laura, his voice conspiratorial. "You know what you have to do if you start to get overheated? Piss your pants." He laughed. "When quads get overheated, sometimes their bladders can back up. You don't want that to happen, so you have a little accident. Relieves the pressure. You have to train yourself to do it—it's amazing how stubborn the mind can be, all that potty training you have to overcome."

Freddy took his stack of still-intact dishes and retreated into the house with a martyr's sigh.

Jay said, "The minute I saw you on the news, I knew I had to meet you. Maybe because we never did." Saw her confusion and added, "Never met."

The Ramseys had been clear from the beginning: They didn't want any visitors. "I understood that. Your parents were looking out for—"

"She was never going to let that happen," Jay said. "Even though you saved my life, she didn't want a *relationship*." He sipped his mimosa. "That's why she paid you off."

Told to her this way, it made her angry all over again.

"You should see your face. I don't blame you for being mad. I would be livid. Especially when she took the horse back. A couple of years down the line, when she saw just how much my condition changed my life—*her* life—she wasn't so thankful anymore."

He shifted in his chair, yawned. Laura wondered if the yawning helped him in some way. "If you want to put it in a charitable light, she was impulsive. Giving you the horse on an impulse and taking it back the same way. Your good deed had outlived its usefulness." No self-pity, just a statement of fact. "But *I've* never forgotten, and now I'm in a position to help you. I know how important this is to you. It would be important to anyone, but considering what you've been through in your own life . . ." He let it hover, the vague reference to the home invasion.

Laura didn't like this. He knew too much about her life.

"I want to apologize for my mother. It's too bad Calliope is gone—I'd give her back to you if I could. Mother sold her foals. For all I know one of them might be in town."

"It doesn't matter now."

He changed the subject. "Did Mikey tell you about my background?"

"Mikey?"

"Lieutenant Galaz."

"He told me Dynever is an Internet security company."

"We've worked with the FBI on cases just like this. One in New York, a pedophile ring. One of my people pretended he was a fourteen-year-old girl."

He wiped his forehead. His complexion looked blotchy and he was sweating. Laura looked around, but Freddy was still inside the house.

"These people are unrelenting. You won't believe what they're like. Pedophiles have fifteen times the sex drive of regular men, did you know that? Fifteen times a normal man's sex drive. They're on the Net every waking hour, just trying to connect with the next girl. It *consumes* them. This stupid cushion." He shoved back up against the wheelchair and twisted. "Five hundred dollars for this stupid lump of foam, and I still get sores. Don't ever break your spine, Laura.

"These guys—they build their wholes lives around getting little girls. They marry women so they can get to their children. Go into occupations where they can be around them. It's the fantasy. They can't resist it—they don't want to."

"It's sick," she said. She knew that technically the guy she was after wasn't sick. He was a sociopath—perfectly sane. But calling him "sick" relieved the pressure in her head, made her feel better.

"You'd be surprised at how many people—doctors, lawyers, beggarmen, chiefs—think that doing a twelve-year-old girl is acceptable. The evidence is there, staring you in the face. On the Net." He set his glass down on the table, spilling orange juice and champagne over his long, elegant fingers. He didn't seem to notice. "The Web has changed everything. People used to hide the way they felt, but now there are so many of them and they're all connected, they have strength in numbers. Now they're legitimate. They can rationalize it.

"So my question to you, Laura, is this: If more and more people believe something, might there not be some value to it?"

Before Laura could answer Jay called out, "You win, Freddy. I'm coming in." He backed his motorized wheelchair and deftly sped up the ramp and through the French doors into the house, leaving her to follow.

Freddy insisted that Laura wait in the living room while they "took care of some essentials."

She waited, feeling uncomfortable. Wondering if he was being cleaned up because he had overheated, wondering if he had, indeed, pissed his pants. Wondering, too, if he thought that just because a majority of people thought something was right, there was an excuse for cruelty. Did he really think that, or was he just playing devil's advocate?

Forty minutes later, Jay Ramsey reappeared, his hair combed nicely and his color better. "Let's get down to it, babe," he said.

Jay situated himself in front of the computer and connected to the Internet. Laura noticed that even with his limited hand motions, he was fast with his two index fingers; they seemed to fly over the keyboard like ten digits.

Laura watched as he pulled up a no-frills site, devoid of graphics.

Ramsey said, "Welcome to WiNX. This is the quintessential Internet relay chat program."

Laura tried to remember what Buddy Holland had told her. "Does it have something to do with instant messaging?"

"That's the currency. People talking to each other in real time. You've probably done something like it on MSN or Yahoo."

"Uh, no."

He twisted in his chair a little, smiled. "The principle is really simple. You put yourself out there and pretty soon someone wants to talk to you."

He hit a couple of keys and brought up a screen that reminded Laura of her first experience with a computer, back in the covered wagon days. "That looks like DOS."

"See? You know more than you think. WiNX is a DOS-based system. See these?" He keyed down through several lines of old-fashioned Courier print and pointed with a thumb. "These are channels—rooms where people with like tastes can meet. There're probably twenty thousand channels on WiNX right now." He flinched again, moved in his seat. Looked at her. "Am I confusing you?"

She remembered how Buddy had thrown technical terms at her without telling her what they meant. Enjoying her discomfort. She hesitated to make a fool of herself, but couldn't help asking, "Are they kind of like TV channels?"

He grinned lopsidedly. "That's as good a description as any. Imagine a station with unlimited channels on everything you can imagine." He clicked on another page. "WiNX has been around forever. The thing you've got to know is that this is the real underground. There are no controls. Nobody's watching you to see that you don't go over the line. There's nothing to stop you from doing anything you want to do. It's a no-man's-land."

Laura felt a kinetic snap in her spine. A no-man's-land. She got the feeling that she was on the brink of knowing something she'd rather not.

He scrolled down what seemed like miles of print. "Ah, here we are." He clicked on something called Warezoutpost, and a list of titles came up, all after the word "warez."

"Warez is 'wares,'" Jay explained. "As in 'let me show you my wares.' See? Software for games. Movies, music. This is where the kids are at because they can download stuff for free."

He showed her how to locate what he wanted, a movie called *Ghost Recon*. "This is what draws the kids. Free music, movies. I'm next in line if I want it."

With a few clicks to the keyboard he moved on.

"The kids are always the first to know. You can get anything you want off these boards. They cater to every taste. This one is general, but there are channels where kids talk to each other." He pulled up another window. "Let's see what we've got in the Girls' Room."

"The Girls' Room?"

"I call it that. It's used by lots of preteen girls."

He pointed out the list of names on the sidebar to the right. "Those are the people in the room now. What I'm going to do is . . ." He hit a key and then typed in a name, erased it, and typed in another. "Gotta have a nick." He added helpfully, "Nickname." He typed in "nick1amber/." This was accepted, and then he typed "hi."

It showed up like this:

Amber:   hi

Laura heard a chime and a message box popped up. Jay pointed to the status bar and Laura saw the name Gitmo.

Gitmo:   how old r u?
Amber:   13
Gitmo:   pic?

"He wants a picture."

Amber:   ok were you fro?????????
Amber:   from
Gitmo:   CA u?

Laura heard a chime. Another person wanting to talk to Amber. Jay hit a key and another instant message box popped up.

Podunk89:   a/s

"He's asking her age and sex."

Amber:   alost 13

Jay nodded to the status bar at the top of the screen. Podunk's name changed from red to black. He was gone. "Wrong age," Jay said, going back to Gitmo.

Gitmo:   where you been?
Amber:   My mom calledm e
Gitmo:   send me a pic

A flurry of chimes. Four new names lit up the board.

Amber:   well see   how old r you?
Gitmo:   you ever had sex?
Amber:   I had a bf last year

"Bf?" asked Laura.
"Boyfriend."

Gitmo:   Did bf getta bj?
Amber:   You sonud mean!!!!!!!!!!!!!!
Gitmo:   can't handle a joke LOL

More chimes, the board lighting up with suitors. Jay opened another instant message box.

Smooth Talk:   Amber u a little girl?
Amber:   im thrteen how old r u????????????????
Smooth Talk:   let me see a pic
Amber:   I have 1 at shchol school not here
Smooth Talk:   where d you live
Amber:   I live in az

Smooth Talk dropped out. Back to Gitmo:

Gitmo:   I want a pic
Amber:    not fair if u don send me pic toO
Gitmo:   you playing games little girl
Amber:    fairs fair my pic for yours
Gitmo:   if you don't want to fuck your wasting m time

Gitmo's name went from red to black.

Jay sat up straighter, twisted, adjusted himself against the back of the chair. "That's what you're dealing with. These creeps are on these boards all day, trolling for kids."

Laura was about to say that she didn't think any child would fall for that, and then shut her mouth.

Children would fall for it. Teenagers would fall for it. Because they had not yet developed the distrust that life ground into you over the years, like grime into clothing.

"We did a survey," Jay said. "Among parents. They think of computers as just another appliance, like a TV set. They don't realize it's like leaving the back door to your house open. Anybody can come in, and some of these guys are really smart. They know how to push the buttons."

"How do you find someone like this? Can you find his ISP?"

"Doubtful. Guy like that, he'd use one of the big servers, like EarthLink, MSN—it's easy to be anonymous. There are search engines that you can look on, but I'm pretty sure this guy wouldn't have a local ISP."

"Oh."

"But there's an easier way. That's what's so interesting about technology. Sometimes the best things are simple. You know the photo you have of him? We can probably trace him through that." He hit a couple of keys and a beach scene came up on the screen.

"This is why you need me." Sounding cocky. "Not many people can get their hands on this kind of software."

He explained that there was something called image recognition, software that could break up every photograph into its elements, then run each element against all kinds of databases, looking for a match. He zoomed in on a man on the beach. "See this guy's T-shirt? With the software I'm going to use, I can run a search for exact matches. It's like a search engine, instead of searching for like words, it searches for images. I'm going to need the original photo, though."

"From what Endicott said, it was a digital photo, and the only thing we have is an ink-jet picture." She nodded to the black-and-white photocopy. "It's not all that much better than that."

Jay looked troubled. "It might be harder, but we can still do it. Where is the original?"

"Endicott's FedExing it—I should get it today."

"What we'll do," Jay said, "is rescan the picture, using high resolution. Then I'll compare it to the databases. It might take a few days, though."

"You sure you can't find him with the ISP?"

"I'll try that, too. I'm warning you, though, this guy isn't your average Internet user. I think you know that."

"But this image recognition software, it'll take a few days? That's a long time."

"How many days has it been so far?"

Too many, she thought.

# 27

"This is what CloneImage came up with," Jay Ramsey said, rolling his chair to the computer monitor.

It turned out that Jay Ramsey's image recognition program had been quicker than expected; Laura had gotten the call this morning, not twenty-four hours after she last saw him. Jay had already found two matches to the man in the picture.

Ramsey pulled up a site called TalentFish.com. "For a small fee, actors and models can put their pictures online. Kind of like a rogues' gallery. Lucky for us that young Petey is up on the latest technology."

"Petey?"

"Peter Dorrance. Actor, model, pretty boy around town. This was a virtual cakewalk." He laughed at his own joke— virtual.

The TalentFish home page opened up. There were several headings at the top of the page: Actors, Portraits, Head Shots, Actor and Model Composites. Jay pulled up Peter Dorrance's page under Actor and Model Composites.

"CloneImage got this hit pretty quick, since one of these is the same picture he sent that little girl."

And there it was. The photo of the young man, the house behind him. This was a three-quarters shot, showing his excellent physique, but there were others, including two head shots.

Laura looked at the other photographs, the ones she'd never seen before. Dorrance had three photos taken in front of the house: two in black and white and one in color. In the color photo, he leaned against a blue sports car, arms folded over his chest. He wore a cable-knit sweater and looked like a print ad from Lands' End. The house behind him was yellow with white trim.

"Nice wheels," Laura said.

"Hard to get into," Jay said. "Unless you're his age. I also found the house, if you're interested."

"In a minute."

She looked at his résumé. Age twenty-two. Six foot three and a half. Forty regular. Several acting roles in plays Laura did not recognize (she wasn't a big patron of the theater). Print ads: Hair and Now; Leslie's Department Store; Eat at Joes. Television ad: Ralph's Car Sales and Gulf Chiropractic. Not a lot there, but he had gotten a crack at the big time, a cameo as a corpse on *CSI: Miami*.

"Eat at Joes is in Panama City," Freddy said.

"Take a bow, Freddy," Jay said. "The Florida Panhandle—just like you said it would be. Prince Charming here lives on the Forgotten Coast, the Redneck Riviera, or—if you're thinking red and blue states—Bush country."

Freddy pointed to the bottom of the page. "There's the address of the talent agency." The Strand Talent Agency, Panama City Beach, Florida.

"So there's good reason to believe he lives in Panama City," Laura said.

"Thereabouts. I got another match, though." Jay clicked through to another site, the Franklin County Home Buyers Guide.

Laura found herself staring at the house. "St. George Island?"

"Down the coast, east of Panama City," Freddy explained.

"An old listing," Jay said. "This site hasn't been updated since 2002." He zoomed in on a pale plaque near the top of the steps. It was blurry and hard to read, but Laura was able to make an educated guess.

"Gull Cottage?"

"Shouldn't be hard to find. St. George Island isn't all that big." He clicked on MapQuest. The barrier island looked like a narrow boomerang, bisected by one main road paralleled by a few ancillary streets. "Twenty-nine miles in length, and no more than a mile across at any one place."

He clicked onto some photographs of St. George Island.

"It doesn't look like a place Peter Dorrance could afford," Laura said. "Unless he's independently wealthy." Considering the sports car he leaned so casually against, that was a possibility.

"I did a few searches on him. The only times he comes up is in regards to acting jobs—and not very many of them. But at least you've got a place to start."

Laura stared at Dorrance's head shot. Was this her killer? If she went strictly by the FBI profile, he skewed young for this kind of crime. Usually, it took time to build up to precise ritual like dressing up the girl and posing her that way. It took time to develop that kind of self-confidence, time to become a full-fledged sexual predator.

"Something you might want to think about," Ramsey said, as if he'd read her mind. "You saw how easily I found this site. Could be your killer looked for the best-looking hunk he could find and sent it to the girl to impress her. Easy enough with gullible little girls."

Laura thought he had a point. But it had always been her experience that most people stayed within their comfort zones—including sexual predators. Even if the man in the photo wasn't her killer, she was willing to bet they had crossed paths sometime or other.

A call to the Panama City Police Department revealed that there was no one by the name of Peter Dorrance in either

Panama City or Bay County, Florida. While she had the detective on the phone, Laura described her own case and asked if he had anything similar.

"Nothing that comes to mind, and that one would. But I'll check around, see if anything like that's turned up in the other counties up here."

Next, she called Detective Endicott in Indio, the detective who had investigated Alison Burns's murder. She laid out what she had and asked him if he wanted to accompany her to Florida. He declined but asked her to keep him updated.

The rest of the afternoon she put her case together, wondering if she should go to Jerry Grimes or directly to Galaz. She didn't like the idea of going over Jerry Grimes's head, but she also knew that Mike Galaz would be more enthusiastic. After debating back and forth, she finally went to see Jerry. She couldn't leave him out of the loop.

He was gone for the day. She tried his cell, got a message and left one of her own. Looked at her watch. She needed to make reservations if she was going to fly out there tomorrow. She went looking for Mike Galaz.

He was practicing his putting. "How'd it go with Ramsey?" he asked her.

"That's what I'm here to talk to you about."

She ran it down for him.

Galaz didn't take his eye from the ball. "Jay has a point, don't you think? It could be the guy, or it could be someone else who got his picture off the Net."

"Either way, I think he's from around there. Other than Lehman, it's the only real lead we've got, and I think I should go and check it out. This guy isn't going to stop with Jessica Parris."

Galaz tapped the ball, which rolled up to the lip of the cup and hung there. He frowned.

Laura waited as he adjusted his stance and nudged the ball in.

Without looking at her, he started over. She knew better

than to say anything. Lucky for her, the ball made it in right away this time.

He looked up at her and smiled. "Ah, much better." Then he retrieved the ball and set it up again.

Laura contemplated grabbing the putter and whacking him on the shin with it.

She wondered if he was getting a perverse pleasure out of making her wait. He sure was milking it: the stance, the grip, the way he rocked back and forth, squatting down and stretching the putter out toward the cup before doing it all again. At last she couldn't take it anymore. "Sir? I've got to get moving if I'm going to go."

He held up one hand: Just a minute.

So she waited, the tasteful cherry-and-brass mantel clock on the shelf behind the desk ticking out her presence. After another successful putt, he palmed the ball and studied her. "Is this coming from logic or from your gut?"

"Both."

"But if you had to choose. You think this is woman's intuition?"

Woman's intuition? *Jesus.* She tried to figure out what he wanted but couldn't read him, so she picked one. "I have a real gut feeling about this, sir. I think Jay does, too."

He didn't answer right away, but seemed to be weighing her answer—an answer she had tossed on a fifty-fifty throw. At last he said, " Go ahead."

He was setting up the next putt when she left.

Next, she called Victor, who had been in Bisbee all day, working the case from there.

"Don't you think you're jumping the gun?" he asked.

"I think it's the guy. Or he can lead me to the guy."

"Are you that sure these killings are connected?"

"The similarities are pretty striking." Feeling defensive.

"There's a lot that doesn't add up." He enumerated the same dissimilarities that had bothered her. "Shit, a twelve-year-old and a fourteen-year-old. That's a big difference on the Tanner chart. You know how choosy these guys can be."

Thought about telling him her theory, but realized that arguing would get her nowhere. "There's something I'd like you to do personally. Check with Jessica's friends again. I never did get a straight answer from Buddy about whether or not she used the computer at school. If she didn't use it at school, find out if she used one at the public library."

"Anything else?" His voice was cool.

"That should do it."

After he hung up, she stared off into space. She realized she was skating on a very thin edge. Going over Jerry Grimes's head, working with Jay Ramsey, her less than enthusiastic investigation of Lehman. Working just as hard, putting in the hours, but more and more certain that with Lehman, they were heading down the wrong road.

# 28

Laura rented a car in Panama City and drove in the direction of the Strand Model and Talent Agency in Panama City Beach.

Panama City gave Laura the impression of a beach town being swallowed whole by Wal-Marts and shopping malls—a battle of old versus new. Fast-food chains vying with mom-and-pop burger stands, bait shops, and boat rentals in the shadow of superstores. Colored pennants and tacky signs marked mobile home sales and car dealerships adjacent to tracts of land marked for sale as "unimproved" property.

As if you could improve on inviting lanes disappearing into stands of southern pine.

The Strand Model and Talent Agency was located three blocks from the beach. Blue with gray trim, the modest salt-box was bordered by a row of immature banana trees and sat in one corner of a parking lot roped off by a giant, sand-encrusted hawser stretching from piling to piling. The plastic sign out front had stick-on letters, like many a drive-by church she'd seen on the way out here.

She was impressed by the pelican statue on one of the pilings—until it flew off.

The Strand Talent Agency must have been a doctor's office at one time. A partition divided the front office from the receptionist's window, and next to the window was the door to inner offices. Posters of sullen-faced models lined the gray fabric walls. A blond, equally sullen-faced receptionist sat behind the window, concentrating on her nails. She would be pretty if not for her spoiled expression. Laura asked to see the owner of the agency.

"You'll have to wait your turn," the girl said, and went back to filing her nails. Ludicrous. Laura was the only one here. She wondered how talent agencies made a living on the Florida Panhandle. She glanced at the stack of brochures sitting in the receptionist's window and saw the rates for runway modeling and deportment classes. Now she understood.

A young man carrying a portfolio emerged from the door to the inner offices and Laura took the opportunity to duck past him. If she expected a protest from the blonde, it wasn't forthcoming. She found herself in a hallway, poked her head into the first room. A heavyset woman with jet-black hair and white sideburns was making photocopies. She wore an outfit that could have looked great on the streets of New York.

"I'm looking for the owner of the agency."

"I'm the owner. Who are you?"

Laura introduced herself. "I need to get in touch with one of your actors." She handed Myrna Gorman the composite of Peter Dorrance. She could have found his address in Public Records in Apalachicola, but had another reason for talking to her.

Gorman led Laura into another room lined with file cabinets. For a big woman, her movements were swift and economical. "Peter. A great look, but we haven't been able to do much with him. He's one of those people who can't act." She opened a file cabinet and ran Turandot nails over the files, scooped one out. "Here it is. We sent him out on two modeling jobs this year. He lives far enough away that we don't send him too many places."

"But he did make it to *CSI: Miami*."

"They wanted the most beautiful male corpse they could find. Last I looked, corpses don't have to act."

"These head shots . . . Did he use your photographer?"

"We don't have a photographer on staff. There are two or three we use. I have their names and phone numbers if you want them."

Laura did.

"What do you know about Peter Dorrance? Other than he can't act?"

Ms. Gorman returned to her office chair and drummed her fingernails on the desk blotter. "He's one of those with stars in their eyes. I know he's planning to move to L.A."

"When was the last time you saw him?"

"Months." She looked inward. "April? I had an audition for him in Tallahassee—a national commercial. He didn't get it. What brings you here, all the way from Arizona? Did he do something illegal?"

"I can't discuss that."

"Well, I think you should tell me what he did. I have a reputation in this town and I don't want to be associated with something like that."

"You sound like you think he's capable of bad things."

Myrna Gorman's stare hardened. "I know he knocked up one of my models. But I guess that isn't a crime."

"How old was your model?"

"Alissa? Twenty-two."

"Are they an item?"

She shrugged. "Who knows? It isn't very often we get a production company coming through here to film. I landed that girl a good role. The day before filming was due to start, she had a miscarriage and ended up in the hospital. They had to recast, and City Confidential got the commission. You could say that Peter Dorrance has cost me more than he ever made me."

\*     \*     \*

Laura took Highway 98 going east past Tyndall Air Force Base, past miles of slash pines, then into a pretty town called Mexico Beach. Late in the afternoon, the sky, though clear, had a metallic quality—grayish green down at the horizon. The beach was on the right side of the road. An incoming wave caught the sun, the shape and color of a 7Up bottle lying on its side, and crashed down into foam. Laura wished she could pull over, buy a bathing suit somewhere, and go for a swim.

She drove through Apalachicola just after six p.m. According to her map, Apalachicola was once a major port city in the South. The place struck her as gracious: neatly gridded streets, live oaks draped with Spanish moss, a fisherman walking down a street spattered by shadow. Following her map, she drove over the Gorrie Street Bridge and across Apalachicola Bay to Eastpoint.

Peter Dorrance lived at the Palmetto Cove apartment complex in Eastpoint, the jump-off point for St. George Island. Two stories, Palmetto Cove Apartments reminded Laura of a TraveLodge. She followed the stairs up to a swaybacked concrete walkway and found his room overlooking the parking lot. When she knocked, the orange door rattled in the frame. Cheap. He was probably at work.

On to Bennies at the Beach, where Dorrance worked as a waiter. Laura backtracked to the St. George Island Causeway and drove across to the island. The bay shimmered in the lowering sun, brimming with oyster boats and sparklets of late light. The first thing she saw on the island was a water tower. It looked like a plastic golf tee.

Bennies at the Beach was just down East Gulf Beach going east. Easy to spot: three stories of weathered wood topped by a thatched roof, colorful surfboards lining the walls. She counted at least thirty cars parked along the road.

Laura was almost to the restaurant when she spotted a house on the right that looked familiar. She pulled over to the side of the road and looked across a vacant lot of sand

and sea oats to the pastel-colored houses facing out onto the Gulf.

They appeared to be relatively new. From what she'd seen in the renters and buyers guide she'd picked up at the airport, prices for homes on the Florida Panhandle were going up exponentially. Beachfront property was at a premium. Laura guessed these were vacation rentals. The house nearest to her looked like the Gull Cottage from the photograph.

She got out of the car and walked up the road for a closer look. Pale yellow siding, white trim, a red metal roof, widow's walk. She recognized the steps to one side, the palmetto, and the garage under the house.

What clinched it was the sports car: a blue BMW Z4.

The neighbor must be some nice guy to let an out-of-work actor pose with his car.

Or maybe Peter had waited for the owner to leave, and then had his photo session. Laura glanced at Bennies at the Beach, approximately fifty yards up the road. Every day Peter Dorrance came to work, he would have driven by this house.

She revised her notion that the house was a vacation rental; the publicity photos were at least five months old, yet the Z4 was still here. She debated talking to the owner, but decided that she would talk to Dorrance first.

The sky was turning sherbet colors—flamingo pink, orange, lemon—as she drove the rest of the way to Bennies.

Bennies was a Parrot Head paradise: fishnets hanging from plank walls, sawdust on the floor, middle-aged men in loud Hawaiian shirts. The noisy babble rose to the rafters. A sign above the bar: OYSTERS—HALF DOZEN FOR A DOLLAR. Exotic-sounding drink specials with names like "Banshee Breeze" written in colored chalk on a blackboard.

A waitress in a white dress shirt and black trousers whipped by, holding a huge tray overflowing with colorful food, making Laura hungry. She pressed her way through the crowd to the bar and yelled over the music until the bartender understood. He pointed to a tall young man with shoulder-length black hair.

Laura waited for Dorrance to finish taking his order and stood in his path. He smiled absently at her.

"Mr. Dorrance?" she asked.

"Yes. Hi. I'll be right with you." He expertly sidestepped her and headed for the kitchen. Laura couldn't follow him— the way he threaded through the crowd could have made him a star on the football field.

She waited at the kitchen entrance. "Mr. Dorrance. I need to talk to you." She held up her shield.

"Department of Public Safety? What's that?"

She found herself shouting. "An Arizona law enforcement agency." She watched him carefully, but saw only confusion. "Is there a place we can talk?"

He looked around doubtfully. Handsome, almost pretty. His hair was thick and slightly frizzy from the humidity. Startled blue eyes, heavy brows, cleft chin, full lips. "A twelve-top just sat down. Can you wait until I get a moment?"

She waited by the bar, watching him in action, tried to picture him picking up a young girl, keeping her with him, dressing her up.

Peter Dorrance was a waiter who lived in a crappy apartment because he couldn't afford to live on the island where he worked. Even used motor homes cost in the tens of thousands of dollars, especially the long one Mrs. Bonney had described. Peter Dorrance didn't seem like the kind of guy who could afford that.

Laura stepped up to the bar and caught the bartender's eye. He made it over eventually and slapped a cocktail napkin down on the bar. "What'll it be?"

"I'd like to speak to the manager." She showed him her shield.

A few minutes later a middle-aged man in a knit shirt and khakis appeared at her elbow. He was solid-looking, with dark hair and a face hewn by the wind and sun. "I'm Buddy Gill," he said. "You were asking for me?"

"Could we go to your office?"

He assessed her, then turned on his heel. "Come on," he said over his shoulder. He led her to a small room dominated by a maritime clock of polished brass and teak, a swordfish mounted on the wall, and photos of a woman and four blond boys. He sat down behind his desk in the only chair. He swiveled back and forth, staring at her.

"Eric said you're a cop?"

"I'm a detective with DPS, the Arizona state agency. I need to know if Peter Dorrance worked here last week."

He considered her for a moment, then reached into a side drawer of his desk and dropped a schedule on the table.

"According to this, he was scheduled for four days?"

"That's right. Tuesday through Friday."

"What about the week before?"

He produced that schedule, too. Laura saw immediately that Dorrance had worked both Friday and Saturday nights. Friday was the day Jessica was kidnapped and killed.

"This is penciled in. He actually worked these days?"

"I remember him being here."

She stifled her disappointment. Someone must have used Dorrance's picture. All this way, and anyone could have picked his picture up off the Internet.

"What's this about?"

"He's an investigative lead—a possible witness to a crime committed in Arizona."

"How could he witness a crime there if he was here?"

"He couldn't," she said. She pushed open the door and walked back out into the crowd.

Back in the bar, Laura saw Peter Dorrance was coming her way, a big friendly grin on his face. When he got close he dipped his head near her ear, so close she took a step back and jogged someone's drink.

"I'm on break," he said. "Let's go outside so we don't have to yell."

He nudged her through the crowd.

Outside, they stood on the deck overlooking the ocean. The sun had turned into a blood orange, sinking into a lavender sea. A hot wind tugged at Dorrance's pirate hair, and for a moment Laura felt she was in the middle of a Hallmark card. Especially the way he was looking at her, a cross between "Aren't I irresistible?" and "You're not bad yourself."

"I wanted to talk to you about your composite." Laura showed him the one she'd printed up from the TalentFish site. "Do you remember when you had these taken?"

He leaned close. She could smell his aftershave and a dash of garlic, probably from the plates he handled. Giving her his best smoldering look. "Last year some time. I had some old shots that didn't really represent what I look like now, so I needed to update them."

"You worked with a photographer affiliated with the agency? One of these?" She handed him the slip marked "From the Desk of Myrna Gorman."

He tapped the third name on the list. "Jimmy. Yeah. He gave me a good price. What's this about?"

He seemed truthful. Impinging on her space, though, trying to make a conquest. Too concerned with his own image to think about anybody else.

She told him how she came across his picture.

He stared at her, his seduction forgotten. "You mean someone used my photograph on the Internet? Pretended they were me?"

"That's what it looks like."

"Oh, man! If they found out at TalentFish I could be blacklisted!"

"That's one of the ramifications, yes," Laura said dryly. "Besides two dead girls."

He stared at his feet. "I can't believe this."

"This Jimmy. What do you know about him?"

He shrugged. "I don't know. He was just some guy Strand recommended."

"Do you remember what he looked like?"

"Average. Kind of . . . insignificant."

"He gave you that impression? That he was insignificant? Why was that?"

"I don't know. He was kind of short. Not good-looking."

Not good-looking. In Peter Dorrance's world, that probably had greater significance than the Mason-Dixon Line.

"What about his coloring?"

"God, I can't remember." He wanted to be helpful, though, so he added, "I think his card said he lived in Apalach."

"Where'd you take the photos?"

He pointed across the vacant lot. "That yellow house. Belongs to the owner." He nodded at Bennies. "Good guy, always looking out for his employees. He even drove the car out so I could pose with it." He shook his head. "Nice wheels. I didn't even want to lean against it, afraid I'd hurt the paint job."

"Was that his idea or yours?"

"Steve's? Oh, you mean the photog. It was his idea. He must have took ten, fifteen rolls."

"Is that unusual—that many?"

"I thought I was getting a really great deal. He said it was a special because he wanted to make his name as a fashion photog."

In Panama City? Laura thought.

"I only paid him two hundred dollars. Not that that's chump change, but for everything he did, it was a great deal. We must have been out there three or four hours. I went through a whole bunch of clothes."

"This exchange—" Laura showed him the phone number. "That's in Apalachicola?"

"I think so."

"Anything else you can remember about him? What did he drive?"

"I can't remember . . . wait a minute. It was an old beat-up truck. I remember because he parked it way down the road so it wouldn't get in the shots. So this is identity theft, right?"

"I'd say so." She circled her cell phone number and handed him her card. "If you can think of anything else about that day, or what he said or did, anything at all, please call me."

She started down the steps.

He called out after her, "You think I have enough for a lawsuit?"

"You're going to have to stand in line," she said.

# 29

The moon was up when Laura drove into Apalachicola. As she came off the curve of the Gorrie Street Bridge into town, she spotted the massive hotel she'd noticed on the way out. The Gibson Inn, blue clapboard with white trim, had wraparound galleries populated with Adirondack chairs. The inn looked like a riverboat all lit up and ready to steam away.

She parked out front and went in. Cigarette smoke lingered with the potted palms and plush Victorian furnishings of the lobby. A tabby cat lounged on the desk, partially covering the bell with her paunch. Laura stroked the cat and asked for a nonsmoking room. She paid with her own money. The woman at the desk led her upstairs to a nautical-themed room with wooden shutters and a king-sized bed.

For a moment she thought about Tom Lightfoot. Felt this overwhelming desire to have him here with her, a pair of lovers on vacation, having fun.

But this wasn't a vacation. If the photographer, Jimmy, didn't pan out, she'd go home empty-handed.

Unpacking didn't take long: putting away her other suit, two sets of casual clothes, and a small makeup case, toothbrush, pajamas. Her gun, her protective Kevlar vest, Jessica Parris's murder book she had compiled so far.

Then she called Jimmy de Seroux. The phone rang ten times, no answering machine.

She had to make another phone call which couldn't be put off. She reached the dispatcher at Apalachicola PD and left a short message, asking for an appointment with the chief.

"Just come by tomorrow anytime," said the dispatcher. She promised to pass on Laura's message.

Laura did this as a courtesy, although she had mixed feelings about contacting them. Jimmy de Seroux could be a dead end. Still, she didn't want word to get back that she had been asking questions around town.

Which it surely would. Laura had lots of experience with small towns.

After dinner in town, Laura took a glass of red wine from the bar out onto the porch. The air, which had been so heavy and hot during the day, was leavened by a breeze from Apalachicola Bay. She could smell the fecund richness of the bay, the sea life.

The waitress came out and asked her if she needed anything.

"Have you lived here long?"

"Grew up in Port St. Joe."

"Do you know a man named Jimmy de Seroux?"

"Dot would know." She nodded to the bar. "She's the bartender."

There were only a few people inside. The middle-aged woman wiping down the bar looked up and smiled.

"Jimmy? Of course I know him. What's he up to? Haven't seen him in a coon's age."

"I heard he's a photographer and he lives somewhere around here."

"I didn't know that. Photographer, huh? Must be one of those multitalented people." She sighed. "Some people get all the talent. The rest of us have to work for a living." She flicked a dishrag over the polished bar top.

Laura said, "He does something besides photography?"

Dot pointed at an autographed photo above the bar. "Jimmy used to play the piano here. Pretty good, too."

Laura peered at the photograph. Hard to see in the dim light. She asked Dot if she would take it down, and Dot obliged, handing it to her.

Laura stared at the picture. She felt the skin of her scalp tighten.

She'd seen many photographs like it, mostly in bars: a black-and-white photo in a black frame, typical publicity shot. But this wasn't just any photo.

Looking into that face, Laura had a bad feeling—a visceral reaction rather than anything based on logic.

If she'd glanced at the photo on the wall in a dark bar, she wouldn't have looked twice. The guy wasn't attractive. He wasn't even interesting. Just an average guy, mid-thirties, pale face and narrow mouth. The distance between nose and mouth was long and simian, like Homer Simpson. Wispy hair on the longish side, combed across a domed forehead. A white short-sleeved shirt that would have gone well with a pocket protector. He looked soft, almost effeminate— harmless.

He looked like a lot of people. The kind of person you've seen before but couldn't place.

But his eyes were dead.

Dot ducked back behind the bar and snapped down a business card on the bar. "I knew I had it somewhere," she said triumphantly. "People are always leaving their cards with us."

The card said, JIMMY DE SEROUX * PHOTOGRAPHER * MUSICIAN * PIANO LESSONS * PIANO TUNING. An address, a phone number, and an e-mail address.

"He gives piano lessons to kids?"

"Oh, yeah. My neighbor's daughter studied with him for a while. I went to her recital. They had it at the Elks Hall."

A pedophile who had access to children through his job.

A man who could play a wedding or photograph one. A mild, unassuming little guy.

She looked at the eyes again. Dull. As if she were looking at them instead of into them, not even a pinpoint of light to show the way to his soul.

She had seen him somewhere. Maybe in one of the photographs she'd taken on Brewery Gulch near the crime scene.

"Is this address close to here?"

"Just go west on C, that's the street right out front, and you'll run right into Fifteenth Street."

Laura glanced around. The other two patrons were gone and she and Dot were alone. "How long since he last played here?"

"A few months ago, at least."

"Can you remember when the recital was?"

"What *is* this?"

Laura produced her badge and ID.

"I don't have to talk to you."

"I know, but I wish you would."

"What did he *do*?"

"Nothing, that I know of. He's one of many people we're looking at who might know something about a crime in Arizona."

"What kind of crime?"

"Do you mind if I ask the questions at the moment? I promise I'll tell you what I know if you'll just humor me."

Dot's eyes darkened. Definitely hostile.

Laura asked, "At the recital. Did he spend a lot of time with the girls?"

"What do you mean?"

"Did he enjoy their company more than that of adults? Did you notice anything like that?"

Dot's mouth flatlined. "You've got it all wrong. That doesn't sound like Jimmy at all."

"You may be right. But why don't you think it sounds like Jimmy?"

"He's . . . it's hard to explain. You don't know what he looks like in person. He's kind of small. You ever read that story about Walter Mitty? He's like that. And respectful of women."

"How do you mean?"

"He was raised up right. You can tell. He's almost old-fashioned—giving up his seat at the bar when the place is full or opening the door, just a bunch of ways."

"Do you know his family?"

"No." She took a deep breath. "All I know is he minds his own business and I can't see him wanting to hurt little girls. It just doesn't fit the kind of person he is."

Laura thought Jimmy de Seroux was precisely the type of man who would go after little girls.

Inadequate.

# 30

The windows of the twin-gabled Victorian cottage on Fifteenth Street were dark. The yard was overgrown and leaves from the enormous live oak out front littered the roof. Wild vines snarled and matted the screened-in porch, as dark and secretive as the night surrounding it.

Hand near her weapon, Laura stepped into the porch and knocked on the door. She expected and got no answer. Although the place was neat and had been kept up, it had an abandoned feel to it, as if its owner had been gone for a while.

A breeze blew, heavily laden with the smell of the Gulf, and a few acorns pelted the walk. Grass grew between the cracks.

He wasn't here. The feeling Laura had about Jimmy de Seroux solidified. He hadn't been here in a long time. Months, maybe.

She glanced around. The house next door was boarded up. The rest of the street was quiet, a mixture of large houses and small. A few porch lights were on. But nobody looking out their windows, nobody on their front porches, no one driving by. It was too hot, even at this time of night.

Laura walked along the side of the house, peering at the windows. Most of them were draped, but she could see through the back door into the kitchen. She flashed her light, holding her hand over the top to keep the glare down.

Yellow linoleum. Honey maple cabinets. Very neat. A Felix the Cat clock on the wall.

She closed her eyes. Smelled the fecund earth, growing things. The slight mildew smell of the concrete. She tried to absorb the vibrations of the place, put herself into his place.

She knew he was gone. Traveling.

A breeze shifted the massive oak branches, their shadows playing over the crushed gypsum drive to the right of the lawn, bone white against lush darkness. There was a cleared space beside the drive, scars on the grass where someone had parked.

An old truck sat inside a carport fashioned from banged-together wood and corrugated plastic sheeting. Parked behind the truck was a smallish boat covered by a blue tarp. The truck fit Peter Dorrance's description—a 1967 Chevrolet pickup. Blue, dented, and splotched with rust around the wheel wells.

She walked around and peered through the side window, which had been cracked a couple of inches. Old, but clean. None of the usual detritus you'd find in a car someone used a lot. It had rained in; the seat covers were water-stained and wet leaves had drifted in through the crack in the window, sticking to the floorboards like tea leaves at the bottom of a cup.

Laura walked to the front and then the back of the truck. No license plate. She pulled on the latex gloves she always carried with her, reached through the passenger side window, and pulled up on the door handle. The door squeaked open. She paused, looked around, thinking how loud it sounded. Opened the glove compartment and shined her light in. A tire gauge, a few maps, registration two years old. The maps were for Georgia, Alabama, and Florida. Buried among the change and paper clips was one of those cards where if you get it stamped ten times you get a free meal. A Port St. Joe address. This card was for the Zebra Island

Trading Post and Raw Bar, in Port St. Joe. It had been stamped eight times.

He was a regular there.

Jimmy de Seroux was a pianist, which could mean he played piano at the Zebra Island Trading Post and Raw Bar. Someone to talk to.

She started back down the driveway and stopped at the place on the grass next to the driveway where someone had parked. Tire tracks that had sunk deep into the ground and dried that way.

They belonged to a heavy vehicle. They looked familiar.

Laura memorized the tread style and walked back to the pickup and looked at its tires.

The treads on the truck were different. Something else had been parked here on the berm. Something bigger, like the tracks on West Boulevard.

Back in her room, she couldn't sleep. She was worried that Jerry Grimes or Mike Galaz would call her back any time. She had nothing to show for this expensive trip except a gut feeling and a digital photo that could be downloaded by anyone.

Laura turned on the light. The only thing she'd brought to read was her mother's files on the Tucson murders and the six chapters of *Death in the Desert*. Laura removed the files from her suitcase and slid out Alice Cardinal's unfinished manuscript, held together by an industrial-sized paper clip. She realized that she never did follow up with the detective on the Julie Marr case. There had been too much going on.

Laura skimmed through the chapter on Julie Marr, still feeling it was strange—almost creepy—that her mother could write about a girl Laura used to see daily at school.

Alice Cardinal's book echoed much of what Laura had already read in the clippings. The car used in Julie's abduction had come from A & B Auto Wrecking. Laura's mother had interviewed the owner, Jack Landis.

Landis told detectives that the car in question, a 1955 Chevrolet sedan, had been one of the few vehicles at the junkyard that was drivable.

"Probably he took it because it was parked outside the fence," Landis said, pointing at the tall chain-link fence bordering the yard full of twisted, rusty car hulks. Landis explained that he also did muffler repair, and that he used the orange-and-white car as a "loaner car" to people who needed transportation while they waited.

"I guess he didn't want to face Luke and Laura," he said, nodding to the two Dobermans inside the yard.

Had the killer stolen a car just to use in commission of this vicious and brutal crime? It seems likely that he did. The Tucson Police detective on the case certainly thought so.

Laura found herself drifting off to sleep. Whatever lessons she could learn from the murder of Julie Marr would have to wait.

"I want you to run somebody on NCIC for me," Laura said when she reached Victor the next morning.

"Can't you do it yourself? We're a little busy here."

"What's up?"

"Lehman's about to give it up."

"What makes you think that?"

"His lawyer wants a meeting. This whole thing could unravel in the next couple of days. You really ought to be here."

"I'll try to hurry it up," she said. "Do you have the lab report on the tire treads taken up on West Boulevard?"

"Hold on, let me look." She heard him shuffle papers. "Got a whole shitload of stuff from the lab yesterday. A lot to plow through."

Hinting that without her there it was twice as much work.

She waited as the paper shuffled for an inordinate amount of time, thinking that if she was wrong about Jimmy de Seroux and had wasted the DPS's limited budget on a whim, Galaz wouldn't back her up. She'd be on her own.

"Here it is," Victor said at last. "They're Michelins. XRVs."

"What kind of tires are those?"

"Big ones. The kind you get on trucks, motor homes."

"Anything else? Was he able to get the wheelbase?"

"I'm looking," he said impatiently. She could tell he resented having to do it. "Here it is. Looks like it was a motor home. *That* narrows it down. There are only thousands of them all over Arizona."

"I'm sending you photos of some treads I found out here. I'm also faxing you the photo of a possible suspect, his name is—"

"Suspect? Didn't you hear a word I just said?"

She ignored that. "I'll FedEx a copy of the original as soon as I can get it done. The guy's name is Jimmy de Seroux." She spelled it for him, and gave him the registration number of his truck. "Be sure to run him on NCIC."

"Can't you do it?"

"I don't have access to NCIC right at this moment."

Silence. Then, "I've got to get going. Lehman's lawyer's gonna be here any minute."

# 31

The Apalachicola Police Department offices took up the second story of City Hall near the Apalachicola River. From its proximity to the water, the building could have been a cotton warehouse when the town was a bustling port.

A giant standing fan dominated Chief Redbone's office, blowing like a blizzard across the cluttered space.

A large man with thinning blond hair and a strawberry complexion, Clyde Redbone heaved himself out of his chair and held out a hand. In his late forties, more muscle than fat, he looked like a former linebacker.

"I'm Laura—"

"Cardinal. I know. Couldn't forget a pretty name like that. My secretary told me you'd be coming by." He directed her to a leather couch that had seen better days. "Sit down, take a load off."

He skimmed his bulk expertly from behind his desk and aimed the standing fan at her. "How's that?"

Gale force, but in this heat and humidity, necessary. "Thanks."

"Something to drink? Coffee? Co'Cola?"

She asked for water and he filled a mug with water from the cooler. He sat down and folded his hands on the green felt blotter. He wore a short-sleeved shirt that exposed massive arms mottled with freckles run together under a nest of blond hair. "What can I help you with?"

"I'm interested in a man named Jimmy de Seroux. Do you know him?"

He leaned back and regarded her through watery blue eyes. Something going on behind them, but she couldn't tell what it was. "I know Jimmy, but not well. Good piano player."

"I'm trying to locate him."

"Think he lives over on Fifteenth Street." He reached for the phone book.

"I know where he lives. I thought you could give me assistance."

He stood up and reached for his hat, hooked on an old-fashioned hat stand beside the desk. "Why not?" He checked his watch. "Tell you what. It's lunchtime. I was just going to go down to the park and have my sandwich. We could talk there. I try never to miss my half hour outdoors."

Girls' voices from the stairwell, giggling and strident.

"Hi, Daddy!"

"Hi, Daddy!"

A couple of teenage girls—twins—clattered into the office on tall sandals. One blond, one redhead. The blonde wore her hair long and straight, parted in the middle. She wore a short, flouncy skirt. The redhead wore short shorts, much more makeup, and enough chains to pass for Marley's Ghost. Identical twins, but each of them had developed her own look. Laura guessed it was a way to maintain their individuality.

Redbone looked stricken. "Holy moly, you walked down the street like that?"

From the looks the girls gave him, Laura had the feeling he'd said words to that effect before.

"Can we take the car?" asked the blond one. "Graham wants us to help him look at boats."

"You think that kid can afford a boat?"

Gum snapped. "Dad. We're just looking."

"Graham should be studying for the SATs, and so should you. By the way, this is Laura Cardinal, from Arizona. That one who thinks she's in the Navel Academy is Amanda, and this is Georgette."

Georgette lifted her hand in a tiny, lacquered wave. Amanda rolled her eyes.

"Please? Can we have the car or not?" asked Amanda, for all her makeup and chains sounding like a Southern belle in training.

"Yes, you can have the car. But you gotta be back by five. Your mother's cooking roast chicken. Got that?"

They were already out the door, their thank yous banging off the walls behind them.

Redbone shook his head. "Don't ever have girls," he said. "They'll give you an ulcer, then break your bankbook."

"There was a girl," Chief Redbone said, in response to Laura's question. He had to talk loud over the riding mower negotiating the lawn at the far end of Battery Park. They sat at a picnic table under a canopy of oaks, eating sandwiches bought from a deli on Market Street. Laura had asked the guy at the deli for a hoagie and he'd looked at her as if she'd come from another planet. Chief Redbone interceded and got them over the language barrier. Next time she'd ask for a sub.

Laura looked out at the little marina at the edge of Battery Park, enjoying the sight of the sailboats drowsing in the paint-peeling Gulf sun. Watching them rocking gently in the hot light had a soporific effect.

"Linnet Sobek," Clyde Redbone said. "Thought she was a runaway." He took a bite of his sandwich and chewed thoughtfully. "She ran off twice before. Got herself in all kinds of trouble. You know. Boys, drugs, getting drunk, fighting." He shook his head, his eyes sad. "Only thirteen years old."

Thinking about his daughters?

"Couldn't really blame her. She had a rotten home life. Mother was a meth head. Lots to run away from."

The aroma of cooking meat drifted across the park in a smoke haze. Laura glanced over at a large family group taking up two tables across the park. Kids, dogs, overweight adults in shorts and tentlike tees. She remembered Victor's pictures from Lieutenant Galaz's cookout. "When did she disappear?"

"Early summer 2002—June, I think. I've got the file back at the office. She was last seen hitchhiking on C30-A, near the turnoff to Indian Pass. Telephone repairman up on a pole saw her go by."

"You questioned him?"

"What do you think I do here? Trot myself out for the Fourth of July parade every year?"

"I'm sorry."

"No offense taken. Man's got to stand up for himself, especially when the big guns from Arizona come callin'." He grinned, his expression saying "No offense." "Humility is a Southern trait, since we have so much to be humble about. You're gonna choke, you scarf down that sandwich so fast."

"It's good." She wiped her mouth with a wispy napkin from the deli. "Those times she ran away. Did she come back voluntarily?"

"Nope. Her brother found her both times."

He nodded to the cold thermos at his elbow. "Sure you don't want to try a little of the local brew?"

Sweet tea. "No thanks. What did she look like?"

"That's the funny thing." He balled up the butcher paper his sandwich came in and threw it into the garbage can nearby. Three points. "Those photos you showed me of your victims? She looked a lot like both those girls. Pretty and blond."

After lunch they took a tree-lined rural road, C-30A, out to Zebra Island Trading Post and Raw Bar at Indian Pass.

Laura glanced at Redbone. He drove in a desultory fashion, the seat back all the way and one freckled hand steering from the bottom of the wheel.

"Zebra Island Trading Post?" she asked.

"This is the turnoff for St. Vincent Island. St. Vincent was owned by a rich man who thought it would look good with a bunch of zebras on it."

Before they left the park, the chief suggested that he take the lead, since he knew the owners and probably knew the clientele as well. Laura agreed; she was a fish out of water here.

Redbone swung the wheel and the patrol car slewed into a sandy parking lot, nose in to an old-fashioned country store. Under the pitched roof was a collection of weathered murals depicting an Indian chief's head—complete with warbonnet—a pastoral scene of zebras grazing, and a giant oyster. A GONE FISHIN' sign hung in the window.

"Well, that's strange. I didn't know Gary was going fishing," Redbone said. "Guess we should've called first."

They were still thinking what to do when a dull red Blazer of indeterminate age pulled into the lot. KC lights up top, jacked-up wheels. A sinewy man in a black T-shirt and camo pants emerged from the Blazer and went to the newspaper vending machines out front.

The chief buzzed down his window and cocked his elbow on the door. "Ronnie! How you doing?"

"Hey." Ronnie came over and bent his head inside the driver's door. "How're you?"

Chief Redbone nodded Laura's way. "This pretty lady here is Criminal Investigator Laura Cardinal from Arizona. You know Jimmy de Seroux, don't you?"

"Jimmy? He photographed my sister's wedding."

Redbone turned to Laura. "Ron's cousin owns this place. Where is Gary, anyway?"

"Went down to St. George for a couple of days of R and R. I'm keeping an eye on the place."

"Was Jimmy a regular?"

"Sure was. Came in at least once a week."

"He tell you he was going anywhere?"

Ron rubbed the bristles on his chin. "As a matter of fact, he did. Said he was taking a trip to see the country."

"When was this?"

"Long time ago. It was still cold—I remember talkin' to him outside, and as I recall there was a hard frost from the night before."

"He say anything else?"

Ron thought about it. "I don't think so."

"You know Jimmy very well?"

"Just, he likes his burgers. Every time he come in here he ordered a burger medium rare. Gary don't cook medium rare anymore. They'd go round and round on that."

"Jimmy have a girlfriend?"

"Never saw him with anybody. I don't remember him socializing with anybody, male or female. Real quiet guy, kind of kept to himself."

"How come he told you he was going on a trip?"

"I don't remember how that came up. Is it important?" He peered in through the window again. "Did he do something in Arizona?"

"That's what we're trying to figure out," Redbone said. "Somebody still breaking into those vending machines?"

"Nope. But it don't hurt to check."

Laura asked, "Do you know if he had an RV? Camper, motor home?"

Ron shook his head. "Heck, I was surprised when he told me he was going on a trip. Must have been feeling talkative that day."

Back at Apalachicola PD, Redbone showed Laura the file on Linnet Sobek. It was a thin file because she was considered a missing person. The photograph attached was eerily similar in appearance to that of Alison Burns. Same heart-shaped face, big blue eyes, child's small nose. Blond hair.

They could have been twins.

Scanning the file, Laura saw nothing that Redbone hadn't already told her, but she asked for a copy of the file anyway.

"I'll just run him on NCIC and see what comes up," Redbone said.

There were no wants or warrants on a Jimmy de Seroux. No previous convictions. If he was who Laura thought he was, he had been very successful as a criminal, sailing under the radar all his adult life.

Next, Redbone checked the Motor Vehicle Division records. Jimmy de Seroux owned only one vehicle, the blue 1967 Chevrolet pickup.

"So much for the motor home theory," the chief said. "You ask me, it's pretty thin."

"What's pretty thin?"

An Apalachicola PD officer appeared in the doorway and the room decreased in size by twenty-five percent.

"Just helpin' a fellow peace officer run down a suspect." Chief Redbone introduced Laura to the officer, Jerry Oliver.

Oliver took off his hat and Laura saw the sweat line in his hair above his moon face. She also noticed that his brass was unpolished, his nameplate so filmy she couldn't read his name.

"So who's the guy?" Oliver said. "Maybe I know him."

"It's none of—"

"Jimmy de Seroux," Laura said.

"Jimmy?" Oliver snorted. "No way. No way he'd do anything violent, considering what—"

"Jerry, did you go by Mrs. Darling's?" Chief Redbone said. "She's mighty agitated about that Buckner kid and his loud music."

"I've talked to her three times. The kid doesn't play that loud."

"Well, go talk to her anyway. See if you can work it out. Use your negotiating skills."

Oliver's face turned stubborn, and he rested his hand on his nightstick. "Let me at least get a drink of water. It's hot as Hades out there." He crossed over to the water cooler. "Arizona, huh? How'd you get a line on Jimmy?" he asked Laura, pouring water on his hands and rubbing his face.

"Jerry, I want you to get your butt out there now." Red-bone's voice boomed. Laura looked at him. She saw a hard light in his eyes.

"I'm goin', I'm goin'."

Chief Redbone watched him leave.

"That boy is the laziest sonofagun I ever saw." Back to his easygoing, affable self. Smiling, expansive. "Can't do a thing about it, though. His daddy's on the city council."

When Laura got back to the Gibson Inn, she checked at the front desk for messages. Victor still hadn't called back. She called him and got his voice mail. Left her own and paged him, too.

She wondered if Lehman had confessed. There might already be a deal in the works. And here she was in Florida, with nothing.

Tilting at windmills.

She looked at her list again:

Alison Burns—similars
Dress patterns—Inspirational Woman
Motor home seen at Brewery Gulch
Motor home seen near primary crime scene
Digital camera, jewelry sent to Alison/Internet connection (?)
CRZYGRL12
The man in the photo—beach house?
Serial killer, organized type
Differences between Jessica and Alison—period of time
    kept, age, manner of death
Postmortem vs. antemortem

She had added five items to the list:

Dorrance—J. de Seroux photog
Tire treads at J's
Linnet Sobek—last seen near oyster bar

J. S. regular at oyster bar
Linnet Sobek looks like Alison and Jessica

Chief Redbone was right. Pretty thin.

De Seroux had no criminal record. He didn't own a motor home. And as Victor had pointed out, anyone could have downloaded Dorrance's picture from the Internet.

Laura stared at the picture of de Seroux she had photocopied. The deadness in his eyes didn't translate to the dark photocopy, or it could be that she had attached too much significance to it. A lot of people looked dull. Her conviction that he was Jessica's killer was starting to evaporate.

To cheer herself up, she went out and treated herself on her own money to a good dinner. Oysters, crabcakes, and merlot at the Owl Café. The place was small and intimate. The rest of the diners were all couples.

Usually, she wasn't bothered about dining out alone. But tonight she felt self-conscious, as if people were looking at her. That wasn't true—one glance at the other diners told her that. They were too concerned with each other.

Maybe that was it. She pictured Tom opposite her, their heads bent together over wineglasses. Pictured them walking out on the marina dock over a plain of marsh and sawgrass, holding hands and watching the sun set on the water. Or on the porch at the Gibson Inn, listening to the night sounds, making out if no one else was around.

In the king-sized bed.

His presence, the way he looked at her, the quiet way he talked. Never ever in a hurry. His life just the way he wanted it. Something to be said for that.

Except his life wasn't exactly the way he wanted, or else he wouldn't want her.

As a cop, she always worked with a partner. Someone to watch her back, an ally. Not being alone . . .

It always came as a surprise to her that she didn't have any family. There were relatives back east, people she hardly knew. She doubted they would welcome her intrusion and she didn't want anything from them. She was used to being alone; only children were, as a rule, self-reliant.

Still, she'd always thought she would find someone. She had thought that Billy Linton would solve all her problems, that he could wipe out the idea of her parents dying by gunshot at close range. Of course that had not worked. She and Billy didn't have the stuff to sustain even a normal relationship, let alone one that had been banged up from the beginning. Ever since, all she had to show for a personal life was a string of failed relationships.

Now Tom was asking her to give it a try one more time. Living together wasn't marriage, but it was a commitment. She couldn't even think about getting married again, but she could think about sharing her house.

She paid her check and walked back to the inn, decided to prolong the night by having another drink out on the gallery. She walked into the bar, glancing up at Jimmy de Seroux's publicity photo.

She'd seen him before . . . well, of course she had. She'd studied that photograph more than a few times in the last two days. But there was something else.

Then it came to her.

Where she had seen him.

# 32

"What a day," Victor said when he finally got back to Laura that night. "We really thought he was going to take a plea, but he backed out at the last minute."

"Lehman? What did he say?"

"Nothing. He demanded to talk to his lawyer in private and that was it, man. Never came back. Is Cruller pissed!"

Roger Cruller was the county attorney.

"I knew—*knew*—he was going to confess. Why else did Glass call this whole fucking dog and pony show? And then, nada."

Laura wondered about Lehman's attorney, Barry Glass, who had a reputation for winning big cases. Why had he called the meeting if he didn't want to work out a deal? Maybe if Lehman himself got cold feet.

"And the bad thing? We don't have enough to arrest him at this point. The forensics on the computer could take *months*. You should hear the lame shit his attorney tried to feed me—like the screenplay? He said it was in the refrigerator because, get this, he wanted to protect it in case there was a fire."

She let him rant for a while before changing the subject. "Did you run my guy's name through NCIC?" she asked.

"I've been so busy, I must've forgot. You still want me to do it? I'll get to it first—"

"That's okay, we ran him at the PD here. He doesn't have a criminal record."

"Well, I guess that's it."

"Maybe not."

He ignored that. "I have some news you might be interested in. Timmy Judd's in intensive care. He tried to kill himself today. Drank some drain cleaner. They don't know how he got it. But you know he's gotta be suffering."

Laura thought about Shannon Judd, only seven years old, having the presence of mind to make her way into the crawl space underneath her house—the house she had lived in all her short life—to hide from her own father. The pain and fear she must have experienced as her life drained away along with the blood from two gunshot wounds.

"Hope it destroys his throat, his esophagus, his digestive tract—I hope he gets cancer."

"He's feeling it, that's for sure."

They were both silent for a moment.

Laura sensed that whatever rift had been between them was healing. She might as well make him even happier. "I'm thinking about coming back soon."

"Oh?"

"I want to get into his house, but I don't have enough to get a warrant."

"Come on, do you really think he's the one? I'm telling you, Lehman was this close to telling it all."

Laura mentally shrugged. "I would like you to do one thing for me. The photographs I took at the crime scene that first morning—of all the people hanging out there? Could you FedEx them to me?"

"I came straight home from Bisbee. I'd have to go back to the squad bay to pick them up, then FedEx—"

"I know he was there, in Bisbee. I saw him. You did, too."

"Where?"

"He was the pianist at the Copper Queen Hotel."

# 33

Musicman. Hot Wheels. Warlock. Smooth Talk. Traveler.

It was like having a wardrobe full of costumes. You could change your clothes whenever you felt like it. You just decided what person you wanted to be that day—whatever fit your mood—and donned the name like a favorite shirt or jacket.

His favorite right now was "Traveler," for a couple of reasons. One, he had always loved the open road, loved to drive. Just pick a route—back road or freeway, it didn't matter—and follow it. Go where he pleased, always looking for what was beyond the next bend in the road. But the most pertinent connotation of the word "traveler" came from the books the profilers used, those books about people like him. Men who killed—serial killers—had a tendency to go from place to place so they wouldn't get caught. They were called "travelers," and he thought it the height of irony to use that for one of his e-mail names. It was a hint, even though no one had ever picked up on it. A clever nod to fair play.

He had not done much traveling lately, although he had moved ninety miles to the north. Tucson was an easy town to disappear in. He had melted right into the Tucson melting pot. He was careful, though, staying close to the freeway in a Motel 6, only venturing out of the neighborhood to a UPS Store to pick up the money Dark Moondancer had sent him.

He was in the Motel 6 now, doing what he loved best—trolling the Net. But even that paled in comparison to what was on his mind: the e-mail from LVRGRL@livewire.com.

Intrigued, he'd opened it—and knew right away it was her.

She told him what happened—how her parents had discovered the camera and jewelry he'd sent her and demanded to know where she got them. She'd refused to tell, and her father, the son of a bitch, took away her computer privileges.

But his girl had spunk. It took her a while, but she managed to talk her mother into letting her use her computer for school, and immediately she set up a new e-mail account.

Kids these days.

I was scared but now I know how much I really luv U and I know its right. They cant keep us apart

Reading that, Musicman couldn't help experiencing a tiny kernel of hope.

He had to be sure, though.

He went through all his CRZYGRL12 messages—the messages which had lured him to Bisbee, messages he now knew were false:

I have to go visit my dad in the poduk town. Boriiiing. Theirs nothig to do there.

A lie.

I've been thinking. Your right. Its time we got together.

Lie, lie, lie.

I know a park were we coud meet
I want to do it now
I luv U

Musicman went back through each e-mail, scrupulously, trying to figure out when the imposter had taken over. Looking for changes in syntax and content. He couldn't see anything different. She used "lay" instead of "lie," a common grammatical mistake. Lots of smiley faces and sad faces, depending on her mood. The same misspellings: "their" for "there"; "coud" for "could."

He printed everything up; sometimes you could spot stuff on hard copy that you missed on the screen. Went through the e-mails again, starting with the most recent, going backward in time.

And then he saw it.

Theirs nothig to do *there*.

He rummaged through the twenty-seven pages of correspondence he had saved to disk, scanning rapidly, pulse thumping in his ears. Did she use "their" and "there" indiscriminately?

No. Thirteen times she'd written "their." Never "there."

Whoever intercepted their e-mails—and pretended to be CRZYGRL12—had slipped up. A common mistake; it's hard to misspell on purpose. Spelling was a habit like anything else. Like if you tried to change your handwriting. As careful as you might be, you had a tendency to revert to what you were.

How had he missed it?

Now he had to figure out if this latest e-mail came from the girl, or the imposter.

# 34

Back in Chief Redbone's mildew-smelling office, Laura removed the top two photographs from the envelope Victor had FedExed her and spread them out on his desk beside the photograph of Jimmy de Seroux.

"Kind of looks like him," Redbone said. "If you take away the mustache." He was in the process of eating a slice of apple pie from a Styrofoam box.

"I saw him myself. Playing piano at a bar in Bisbee."

He sat back and folded his hands over his stomach. "That may be, but you're not what Judge Lanier would call an impartial witness, and he's who we gotta get around if we want a warrant." He sighed and pushed the photo back across the table. "Sounds pretty circumstantial to me. Judge Lanier doesn't like circumstantial evidence. Honestly, I don't think he's gonna bite."

"The tire tracks outside his house are the same make and type as the ones found near the primary crime scene—Michelin XRVs." She pushed the lab report that Victor had faxed along with the photos across the desk.

Redbone picked it up, holding it out in order to read it. "Says here it's the same kind, but there must be millions of these things all over the country. There's no anomaly to show these are the exact same tires." He put his hands behind his head. "Lanier's not going to like that."

Laura had experience with recalcitrant judges. She always sought out the toughest judges because if they okayed a search warrant, the defense attorney would be left with one less piece of ammunition. "I'll take my chances."

The chief shook his head. "I can tell you right now he'll dearly love tearing this apart. Lookie here, the dress—the link to that Alison Burns killing. How many people use those patterns? They're on the Internet. And how many people could've downloaded this boy's picture? He's got it out there for everybody to see."

He scooped up some melted ice cream, licked the plastic spoon.

"Nope," he added morosely, "I don't see Judge Lanier liking this at all."

Judge Lanier had them in and out in ten minutes.

"He's got a golf game at ten," Chief Redbone explained as they were ushered out by the judge's white-haired bailiff. "He sure as heck shot us down. I'm sorry about that."

"Whatever happened to Southern hospitality?"

Redbone held the door open for her. "He's a transplant from Rhode Island."

Laura tried to think if she could have done anything different, but it had all happened so fast. Judge Lanier had said few words to them inside his stuffy, smoke-filled chamber, but the ones he did use were scathing. "A waste of the court's time." "A snipe hunt." And: "I don't know how you do it out in the Southwest, Miss Criminal Investigator of the DP of S, but here we have laws and we have precedents. You will not turn this court into a Star Chamber. The de Serouxs have been through enough, and I will not permit this witch hunt."

"What was that about the de Serouxs?" Laura asked Redbone as they walked down the steps of the courthouse.

Redbone said, "The judge doesn't like extra work, and

this qualifies. He doesn't want to come under any scrutiny. He just keeps a low profile so he's retained every few years. Well,"—he patted her arm—"I've got to be going. Gotta keep the streets safe for posterity."

He got into his unit and drove sedately down Market Street. She saw him turn in the direction of the police department.

Laura realized he never answered her question.

Hungry, she walked up Market to the Cloud Nine Coffee Shop. Taking a red vinyl booth by the window, she pulled the photos of Jessica Parris, Alison Burns, and Linnet Sobek out of her briefcase and spread them out on the Formica surface.

There had to be a way to get into that house. Her conviction was growing—this was the guy. She just had to look harder, find something she'd missed.

She stared at the photographs. All three girls looked alike. The same type. Similar hair length, if not style, same pert nose. A dusting of freckles. Innocent, wide blue eyes.

Jessica was the anomaly. Brown eyes. Light-boned, small for her age. Jessica was the mistake. The abduction of Jessica Parris was an act of impulse, after de Seroux failed to get the girl he wanted.

The waitress appeared and upended a brown ceramic mug. "Coffee?" she asked.

Laura nodded. The blond waitress looked to be in her sixties. Laura was mesmerized by the woman's upper eyelids, the color of purple grapes and almost as puffy, ending in eyelashes heavily lined in black. Her nameplate said MAR-LEE.

She glanced at the photograph of Linnet Sobek. "I sure hope she landed someplace good." She gave Laura a searching look. "You a reporter?"

"No."

Laura just wanted to be left alone, but the waitress was friendly. "You don't sound like you're from around here," the waitress added.

"I'm from Arizona."

"Well, isn't that a small world? I lived with my daughter and her husband in Phoenix up until a year or two ago. Where you say you were from?"

"Tucson." She wished the woman would leave her alone to think.

"I grew up here, never wanted to leave, but my daughter wanted me to come live with her and I wanted to be near my grandchildren . . . now the kids are grown and I just couldn't stop being homesick for this little town. So I finally made a break and came on back. One thing I've got is really good feet, that plus stamina, so I figure I can work until I'm seventy at least. Plus, I like the work, being around people."

Laura could appreciate that, but she just wanted to be left alone with her blue funk.

"What'll it be? The biscuits and gravy are good."

She remembered how when she was a kid she always ordered a BLT on white toast with a side of pickles. She hadn't eaten white bread for years, but suddenly craved it. Must be the influence of the South.

The waitress pushed back a strand of brittle hair and said, "Sure thing, honey." She whisked away with the menu and headed for the kitchen.

There was some kind of heating vent near the back wall and Laura could feel it on the back of her neck, steaming her clothes. The place looked none too clean, either—a greasy spoon. Her dad loved greasy spoons. She'd forgotten about that.

Laura replaced the photographs of the girls with the picture of Jimmy de Seroux. Maybe she was wrong—what if it *was* Lehman?

She reached into the wooden bowl of dried olives in front of the table jukebox, suddenly starving, took one and bit. It wasn't an olive—the thing was salty and kind of mushy. She had no idea what it was.

"Never had a boiled peanut before?" asked Marlee, coming by with a fresh pot.

"Who'd want to boil peanuts?"

"You just keep on eating them, and sooner or later you're gonna be addicted." She set the plate with the BLT down on the table with a plastic click and glanced at the photograph of de Seroux. "You know Dale?"

"Dale?" Laura was confused.

"Dale Lundy. That's got to be Bill Lundy's son. What's that say?" she added, craning her neck to see the writing on the bottom. " 'Best Wishes . . . Jimmy.' "

Laura said, "Jimmy de Seroux."

Marlee frowned, as if she were trying to access something on her hard drive. "No. That just can't be."

"This is Jimmy de Seroux. He plays piano at the Gibson Inn."

"No, that's got to be Dale Lundy. He looks just like his daddy."

Laura felt as if she'd just slipped down the rabbit hole. This woman obviously didn't know what she was talking about. Everyone she'd talked to had assured her that this guy was Jimmy de Seroux. He'd signed his name Jimmy. It was Jimmy de Seroux. Laura reiterated that.

"Nope, that's Dale Lundy. He looks so much like his daddy." The woman's conviction was unshakable. "Maybe you're getting them confused because they were neighbors."

There was something about the way she said it — as if she were holding back an unsavory detail. Laura remembered something Judge Lanier had said: *The de Serouxs have been through enough.*

"The de Serouxs and the Lundys were neighbors?"

"Next-door neighbors."

"You knew the de Seroux family?"

"I surely did. They used to come in every Saturday. Henry always ordered biscuits and gravy. Never ate anything different. That could have been a warning sign in itself."

"Henry?"

"Henry de Seroux. More coffee?"

Laura put her hand over the mug, natural curiosity getting the better of her. "What did you mean by 'warning sign'?"

Suddenly, Marlee looked uncomfortable. "It was a long time ago. You don't want to hear about that."

Something bad—Laura could feel it. The judge's statement, Chief Redbone's evasions. He hadn't told her anything about the de Serouxs. "What did he do?"

"I guess it's no secret. He killed his own family."

# 35

Laura stared at Marlee's mouth, the net of wrinkles moving. Now that Laura had finally pried it out of her, Marlee was happy to share the gory details. "Slaughtered his wife and two little girls one afternoon, then turned the gun on himself. Shotgun—heard he had to use his big toe."

"What about his son?"

"His son? Oh, the little boy. He died when he was younger—had leukemia. Can't remember his name."

"Then who's Jimmy de Seroux?"

"Well, he could be a cousin. But that's no de Seroux." She tapped one long lacquered nail on the photocopy. "That there is Dale Lundy. I know that because his daddy died must be eight, nine years ago and he's the spitting image of his father."

Laura was having trouble absorbing this. "Dale lives here?"

"He might've come back, I don't know. When his father died, an aunt took him in. She lived in Alabama."

"You knew the father well?"

"Just to say 'hi' to. Not that he was what you'd call friendly. Bill was an oysterman."

"And this Dale—did you know him?"

"Not hardly. I don't think anybody saw much of that kid."

Laura couldn't make sense of what she was hearing, but she asked anyway. "Why was that?"

"His mother homeschooled him. Nothing wrong with that, plenty do, but there was more there than met the eye." Marlee refilled Laura's cup. "That's a story in itself. She ran off and left the boy and his father to their own devices."

Laura was still trying to reconcile the one man and two names.

Marlee continued. "Alene Lundy belonged to some religious group. These days you'd call it a cult. Everybody knew she was a little strange and she seemed to get worse, keeping to herself, keeping that son of hers away from other kids, and you know that's not natural. If any family was going to end in tragedy, I'd'a bet it would have been them, not the de Serouxs." She nodded to the photo. "I don't know who's been pulling your leg, but that's Dale Lundy."

Laura caught Redbone as he was coming down the stairs of the police department. "Why didn't you tell me about the de Seroux family?"

He paused in the stairwell, a Co'Cola in his hand, the heat making his proximity stiflingly close. Laura saw little lumps of ice on the bottle. A Co'Cola would really hit the spot right now, but for once he didn't offer her one.

"Can't talk now. I'm on my way to a meeting," Redbone said, continuing down the stairs. Laura followed him out into the heat haze.

"I want to know why you didn't tell me about the de Seroux murders."

"Holy Jesus *Lord*, it's hot today." He pressed the Coke bottle to his sweating cheek. Perspiration like giant inkblots soaked his shirt. Looked at her. Good ol' boy with eyes of steel. "That de Seroux story was a long time ago. That's why."

"Maybe so, but it could have affected my case."

"And how would that be?"

"Whether it did or not, you should have let me know. At least then I'd have some idea what I was dealing with."

"He's a cousin from the outside," he said, stressing the word "outside." "He had nothing to do with any of that."

"You had to know I'd find out. A mass murder in a small town isn't—"

"That's all water under the bridge. Folks here don't like to talk about it. We don't like to even think about it."

"So the piano player is Jimmy de Seroux."

"He is to the best of my knowledge."

"What does that mean?"

He shrugged. "I know the family had cousins somewhere. He showed up and said he was a cousin. He owned the house. That was good enough for me. People here mind their own business."

"But didn't you wonder about his resemblance to Lundy?"

"I thought that wasn't any of my business, either."

"What? Oh." She got the inflection. "You think Bill Lundy might have—"

"I think we've aired enough dirty laundry for one day." He unlocked his car.

She persisted. "How would that happen?"

He took off his straw hat and placed the Coke against his forehead, smearing his dripping coils of hair. "The way it always happens, I guess."

"You're saying Bill Lundy and Mrs. de Seroux had an affair?"

"Look, missy, I don't know. Could be a lot of things happened. Henry had a sister, a real spinster type, if you'll excuse the saying. She lived there for a while. Don't ask when because I don't remember. Now if you'll excuse me, I'm late."

"I want you to run Dale Lundy for me."

"When I get back I'll do it first thing," he said, hefting his bulk into his unit.

\*     \*     \*

The doors to the *Apalachicola Times* were locked—closed even though it was the middle of the day. So Laura went looking for the library.

The library was located on a quiet Apalachicola street: a redbrick one-story building with white trim. Laura asked the librarian if she had newspapers or microfiche dating back to the time of the de Seroux murders.

The librarian looked at her, a vague uneasiness creeping into her deep violet eyes. She was a pretty woman, powdered and small, somewhere in her thirties. "The de Seroux murders?"

"That's what I heard. Someone named Henry de Seroux killed his wife and daughters here in Apalachicola."

The librarian looked shocked. "When was this?"

"A long time ago. It's not something that people would forget, though."

Definitely flustered. "Excuse me, let me take a look, see what I have on the database."

She went into the back room. Laura waited.

At last she returned. "I couldn't find any references on the computer, but that doesn't mean anything. We have back issues of the *Times* going back to the mid-seventies."

"So you never heard that story? Have you lived here long?"

"Twelve years."

"I guess it would be before that, then." A mass murder would appear on the front page, so all she'd have to do was look for the headlines. She'd start with 1990 and work her way back from there.

The librarian took her to the little alcove where the microfiche machine was. She showed Laura how to wind the tape on the spool, and Laura let her, although she'd done this many times before.

There was no reference to a mass murder in 1990. Or 1989, 1988, 1987.

By the time she got to 1983, her neck was beginning to ache.

And then she saw it: Page one, June 12, 1983.

### LOCAL MAN KILLS FAMILY, SELF

She read quickly, getting more excited as she read.

Henry de Seroux, a respected dentist and family man, had canceled the newspaper subscription, the water, the electricity, and the gas, gave his golf clubs to his surprised receptionist, and went home to kill his family and himself.

No mention of a young man who could be a cousin. No mention of any other family at all.

There was a picture of the family, though. A studio portrait with a gauzy blue background. The two girls were pretty and blond. One of them, sitting on her mother's lap, was five or six. Her name was Carrie. The other, standing, was older—eleven? Twelve?

Marisa.

She looked familiar, and Laura suddenly realized why. Marisa de Seroux looked a lot like Linnet Sobek.

And Alison Burns.

And Jessica Parris.

Laura hit the button to photocopy the page.

Back in her room, Laura started a fresh page of her legal pad. Looking for links.

1) The XRV tire treads in de Seroux's driveway are the same make and type as the ones found up on West Boulevard.
2) The resemblance among Alison Burns, Jessica Parris, Linnet Sobek, and Marisa de Seroux is uncanny.
3) Jimmy de Seroux might or might not be a man named Dale Lundy, the son of the next door neighbor.
4) Dale Lundy/Jimmy de Seroux—whoever he really is— had access to the original proofs of Pete Dorrance's publicity photos.

Laura, herself, had seen him at the Copper Queen Hotel.

She stared at the list. A couple of things occurred to her immediately.

Punching in 1411, Laura requested the number for the Copper Queen Hotel in Bisbee, Arizona, then called the hotel. The front desk answered.

"I wonder if you could help me," Laura said. "I was in the bar last weekend when you had the pianist there. I liked him so much I asked if he could play for my wedding. We exchanged cards, but I can't find his anywhere, and the wedding is in three weeks. Could you help me out? I think his name was . . ." She looked at her notes. Jimmy or Dale: Pick one. "Dale."

"Let me take a look," the woman replied. "Hold on." The phone clattered.

A minute passed before the woman picked up again. "Dale Lundy, right? He's playing this weekend, too. All I have is a cell phone number." She recited it.

"Thanks so much! This will make all the difference."

"Just make sure you have a good photographer. I stinted and it was the worst mistake we ever made. Good luck!"

Laura loved small towns. People still saw strangers as human beings.

Next, Laura opened her laptop and connected to the Internet. She'd already bookmarked TalentFish.com. She opened it up now and compared the TalentFish photos of Peter Dorrance to the one Detective Endicott sent her.

One of the TalentFish photos, the three-quarters shot in front of the house, was almost identical to the photo from Alison Burns's computer. Laura held the five-by-seven digital printout up near the computer, eyeballing one and then the other.

In the TalentFish photo, Laura could see half the saw palmetto fronds behind Dorrance, but in the Burns photograph, she could see only one-third. Dorrance's smile was different, too. Just a millimeter this way or that.

Laura had been to photo sessions before. A photographer

took many shots of one pose. The TalentFish photo and the Burns photo were in the same sequence, but slightly different.

She reached Myrna Gorman at the Strand Talent Agency on the first try. "How many different photos do you have of Peter Dorrance?" she asked.

"I'll have to look to be sure, but usually we get a head shot and a composite."

"How many in the composite?"

"Three or four."

"Did he send his photos to TalentFish.com or did you?"

"We did. We have an agreement with them. You want to hold? I'll get his file."

When she came back she said, "It's what I thought. We sent the composite. Four pictures."

"Can you describe them for me?"

They corresponded with what she saw on the screen. Laura found Chief Redbone's card and asked her to fax them to the Apalachicola Police Department.

She didn't need any more convincing, though.

The digital photo that had been sent to Alison Burns did not correspond to any of the photographs up on TalentFish.com. That meant that no one could have downloaded the photo and sent it on to Alison Burns. Either Peter Dorrance had placed publicity shots on another site, or the person who sent the photo had access to all the rolls of film they shot that day.

That meant either Peter Dorrance or Dale Lundy sent the photo to Alison Burns.

And Peter Dorrance wasn't playing at the Copper Queen Hotel next weekend.

"He's not gonna like seeing us again so quick," Chief Redbone said as he turned onto Avenue B. "If we get the warrant, let's do it tomorrow. That old house hasn't been lived in for a long time. It can wait till morning."

Thaddeus Lanier lived in a large Federalist redbrick

building with a gracious white portico and two tall live oaks dressed in widow's weeds.

Laura was feeling good—especially after they ran Lundy on NCIC. Unlike Jimmy de Seroux, Lundy had two arrests for sexual offenses: peeping and masturbating outside a grade school, both in Dothan, Alabama. One when he was twenty years old, another when he'd just turned twenty-one.

Nothing since then, but if he was the man she thought he was, Lundy had learned to fly under the radar, graduating from peeping and masturbating to taking young girls. His crimes fit into a predictable timeline, a clear trajectory. He had been given time to develop predilections and rituals—like dressing girls up in his doll dresses.

He'd learned his craft.

Laura had no doubt he kept a rape kit in his motor home, with all the tools he needed to capture, subdue, and kill his victim.

She had been right about the motor home. Dale Lundy owned a 1987 Fleetwood Pace Arrow. He also owned the house next door to the de Seroux house—the one she'd noticed because it was boarded up.

Vindication.

The Lundy house had been empty and boarded up since Bill Lundy died all those years ago, but had never been put up for sale. Dale Lundy had used the address when he bought the motor home, and it was the address listed on his credit cards.

They crossed the neat lawn and knocked on the front door.

Lanier appeared in khakis and a knit shirt—relaxing after a hard day of torpedoing search warrants. A dour, long-faced man with wire glasses perched on his nose, he looked down that nose now. Two grouchy-looking King Charles spaniels barked and yapped at his feet. "What do you want now?" he asked.

Redbone scratched his ear. "Well, Thad, more evidence just turned itself up. Looks pretty convincing to me."

"Very well." Lanier opened the door and stood back.

The front room was palatial. High ceilings, plaster rosettes in the corners. A gleaming hardwood floor. A grand piano with a mirror finish. Striped silk Queen Anne chairs.

Lanier led the way to his study, followed by the two muttering King Charles spaniels. He sat down at his massive mahogany desk and directed them to sit, too.

His sigh was long-suffering. "Let's see what you've got."

He perched the glasses farther down on his nose and started reading.

Twenty minutes later they had their search warrant.

# 36

"Here's what I want to do," Laura said to Chief Redbone outside the police station early the next morning. "I want one officer on the back door, and the rest of us will go in the front."

"I don't know we need to do that," Redbone said. "The place is boarded up and you said yourself this guy is in Arizona. We don't have to go running in there like we're looking for terrorists or something."

He had a point, but it was not one Laura would concede. She didn't care if the place was boarded up, she wanted a safe entry. She outlined it for him: She, Redbone, and one officer would take the front, and the third officer would take the back. She would position herself to the left of the front door and Redbone and his officer would take the right.

She said to Redbone, "I'll go low and you go high. Your officer will go low. That way I'll cover the right side of the house and you'll take care of the left."

He shrugged. "You're calling the shots."

Jerry Oliver drove up and got out of his car.

Redbone called out, "Jerry, you ever check that steak knife of Ginny Peacock's into evidence?"

"Don't worry, it's safe in the trunk."

"Why don't you do it now?"

"Can't it wait until after we do the entry?"

"No, it can't wait." Redbone looked at Laura. "Tell you what. You go with Officer Descartes, and Oliver and I'll be right behind you."

Warning her, perhaps, what caliber of officer Jerry Oliver was. She hoped Descartes was better.

Officer Descartes, it turned out, was much better.

"How's that strep throat, Andy?" Redbone asked as a young man in an Apalachicola PD uniform emerged from the City Hall building. Redbone turned to Laura. "Got him out of bed for this thing."

"I'm fine now, sir," Descartes said. "The antibiotics pretty much knocked it out."

Redbone introduced them. "I hope that pretty wife of yours is taking care of you." Redbone winked at Laura. "Newlyweds."

Laura noticed the unmistakable outline of a protective vest under Descartes's uniform. That made two of them. She'd asked Redbone earlier if he had Kevlar vests, and he'd said that the city council was still considering if it was a necessary expense. Evidently Officer Andrew Descartes had ordered the vest on his own. And, unlike Jerry Oliver, Descartes's uniform was pressed and his brass polished.

The trip to Lundy's house covered only a few blocks, allowing Laura to get a feel for the third member of the Apalachicola PD. She ran down her plan.

"Are we clear on that?"

"Yes, ma'am."

"You might think because the place is boarded up that this should be a cakewalk."

Before she could continue he said, "I don't think that, ma'am."

"Why not?"

"I was taught at the Academy you always need a plan. I mean, think about it, the bad guy might—have a plan. And if he does and you don't, you could get yourself and others killed." He came to a stop at an intersection, scanning the street with sharp eyes. "Besides, you know what you're going to do, you practice it, then if things go bad on you you'll probl'y come out all right because you fell back on your training."

"You sure you feel up to this?" she asked. "Strep throat is nothing to fool around with."

"I'm fine. Those antibiotics kick major— They really do the job."

On Fifteenth Street now, he made a pass by the Lundy house. He didn't slow down, didn't give any hint that this was the house he was interested in, although his eyes missed nothing. He reached the end of the block, turned, and parked out of sight of the house. He turned off the engine, tapped the wheel with his fingers. Geared up.

"Have you ever done this before?" she asked him.

"No, ma'am."

"I'm not worried," she said. "Just trust your instincts."

Right now, her instincts told her that at least one member of the three-man Apalachicola Police Department wasn't up for this. Even sick, Descartes looked like the better bet.

She stepped out into the warm morning. The grass and hedges were still soggy with dew and the street was quiet— no one around. Good. A tickle of excitement in her own gut. Nervousness. Not unusual, but something to acknowledge. Mentally she took inventory: the SIG Sauer forty caliber under her blazer, the S&W nine millimeter in her boot, handcuffs tucked into the back pocket of her slacks. Flashlight. Pepper spray. Gloves.

They walked up to the corner. An Apalachicola PD patrol car came up the street. To Laura's dismay, it stopped right in front of Lundy's house. Might as well be a flashing sign. Laura wasn't surprised to see Jerry Oliver emerge from the driver's side.

She regretted not pushing Chief Redbone to request a SWAT response from the sheriff's office. She knew the chief was smart, and there was no question he knew his town. But he might be out of his depth here. If it weren't for the fact that the house was boarded up, she would call this off now.

She let Redbone outline the problem, only interjecting to say that she wanted Descartes to take the back and Oliver to remain in front with them. She wanted Jerry Oliver where she could keep an eye on him.

As Redbone parroted her earlier instructions, Laura looked the house over. Like its neighbor, it was clapboard—modest compared to some of the houses on this street. The original color was Wedgwood blue trimmed with white, but the wood had weathered to gray. Plywood had been hammered across the windows, the front door barred by several planks. As they crossed the leaf-littered yard, an enormous magnolia tree swallowed them in dark shade. Some kind of hedge Laura didn't recognize grew around the house, something with thorns. It had gone wild, obscuring several of the windows. The porch was festooned with Virginia creeper that in some places had died but remained, snarled and gray like a spiderweb.

Gun ready, Laura crept up to the house at an angle, even though no one could see out the windows. She stood to the left of the door, which would open inward. But first, it would have to be stripped of the planks that had been hammered across it.

Redbone nodded to Oliver, who pried up the boards with the sharp end of a crowbar. When he was done, Oliver threw the crowbar on the grass with a hollow bang.

Laura crouched down, looking over to see that both Redbone and Oliver were in position. She caught Oliver's eye and nodded toward the gun on his hip. He sighed heavily and drew his weapon. Redbone checked the radio to make sure Descartes was stationed at the back door.

The radio crackled. He was in position.

Redbone tested the knob on the door. Locked. He nodded to Oliver, who reholstered his weapon, retrieved the crowbar, and bashed the lock with repeated blows. The door creaked open a couple of inches.

This time when Oliver threw the crowbar, it nearly took out Laura's foot. He caught her look and had the grace to look sheepish. He again drew his weapon, but held it loosely at his side, pointed down and dangling a little behind his leg.

She thought, *I hope his complacency doesn't catch up with him someday.*

She dropped into a crouch. Looked at Oliver again. He assumed a crouching position and raised his gun. Redbone remained standing, aiming his weapon toward the left. Laura shouted, "Police! Search warrant!" and shoved the door the rest of the way open, swinging back and forth into the dark, her weapon leveled on empty air.

# 37

The word that came to her was "surreal." As if she were in the middle of a snow globe, but the snow was the dust motes that floated in the golden light from the open doorway—glittering snowflakes falling across the jumping beam of her Maglite.

It floated out of the darkness at her, this strange, cluttered room. Too much to assimilate right now. She didn't have time.

"Clear!" she called as she ducked into the doorway to her left. Another light—Redbone's—jumped into the darkness, a weak ray. She was in the kitchen. Counter, sink, refrigerator—

"Kitchen is clear!"

Her flashlight swung in the other direction as Laura heard Oliver scrambling toward the doorway on the other side.

"Bedroom is clear!" Oliver shouted.

They went through the house, systematically clearing every room. Laura saw things that she did not expect to see, but it was so dark she would reserve judgment until they could get light on the situation. They returned to the first room, the living room.

Despite her wariness, respiration was beginning to return

to normal. They'd checked every closet, every alcove. No one home.

The place smelled stale.

Oliver holstered his weapon and stretched his neck as Andrew Descartes entered through the front door. Jerry Oliver would not be punished for his inattention today.

"Let's get some light in here," Laura said. "Get the rest of that plywood off."

# 38

Once the plywood was off, there was enough light to search some of the rooms, but not all. Redbone got on the horn and made arrangements for a gas-powered generator and a pair of 500-watt quartz lamps from the Franklin County sheriff's department.

There was enough light, though, for Laura to think she had stepped inside an old photograph of a Victorian house—something you'd see in a history book.

The front room—the *parlor*—seemed to press in on her. A stamped tin ceiling, an old-fashioned chandelier, dark furniture, burgundy velvet drapes swagged to reveal immaculate white lace. Everything fringed, shirred, swagged, or flocked. The wallpaper was dark, the floor dominated by a large Oriental carpet. Oval portraits on the walls in old, convex glass. Bric-a-brac everywhere: china cabinet, ottoman, settee, footstools—

So *much* of it.

Ottoman, settee . . . Words people didn't use anymore. A room out of the nineteenth century. The operative word here was "fussy."

"Good Lord Jesus," muttered Redbone. "It looks like a museum."

Laura's attention was caught by a sewing machine, modern vintage, on a table. Another sewing machine that looked exactly like the first one, except smaller—a child's machine?—sat on a shorter table.

Laura's throat felt dry as her latexed hand pulled open the many drawers and searched alcoves neatly stacked with patterns, thread spools, bobbins, measuring tapes.

Him and his mom, sewing together in the good old days?

But it still confused her.

This room confused her.

A Bible on a stand in the corner of the room, old and well-used. On the inside it said, "This Bible belongs to Alene Davis."

His mother's maiden name.

This room had a surreal quality, as if all she had to do was close her eyes and when she opened them again she'd see an abandoned house with plywood windows and cracking plaster.

She ran an index finger across an oval rosewood table. Dust. Several layers. But other than that, the place was clean. The dust was the only sign that Lundy had not been here for a long time. Everything was neatly *displayed*, a tableau.

A shrine?

She bent to look at the underside of the rosewood table: Ethan Allen—the store.

Not an antique, then. An *approximation* of an antique.

She flashed her light on the ceiling. It might have been stamped tin, or plastic made to look like stamped tin.

Watching where she walked, Laura went down the hall.

She looked in on a bedroom. It, too, looked frozen in time: a single bed with lace and eyelet Victorian linens, a down comforter, heaps of satin pillows. A wooden rocking horse. Enormous dry flower arrangements in tall vases. Dolls on a window seat.

A little girl's room, but Dale Lundy was an only child.

Onward, farther down the hall.

A boy's room. This one had Darth Vader sheets and

posters from the seventies. A hooked rug on polished floor-boards. Cowboy and Indian wallpaper, cornflower blue.

Dark in here. On an impulse, Laura walked to the window. Carefully, she moved aside the cowboy and Indian patterned drapes with her latexed hands. She was right. Blackout curtains.

He'd used plywood to cover up the windows, but he'd added blackout curtains as well. Why? It was as if this house had to remain a secret. As if it embarrassed him in some way. Maybe the kids at school had called him a mama's boy.

But he had been homeschooled—isolated from other kids.

Lonely?

At the end of the hall was what Laura assumed was the master bedroom.

She opened the door.

From every wall, Marisa de Seroux stared down at her.

Eight-by-tens, four-by-fives. Posters, blown up and fuzzy. Photo after photo after photo, a collage from floor to ceiling. Mostly black and white. All of the same girl. Most of them candid shots, where the girl wasn't posing or even looking at the camera. Many of them had been blown up to catch her face. But the majority of them were good: professional quality. Taken with a telephoto lens, pictures of the girl, unaware, going about her life in the small town of Apalachicola. As if she were being followed around by paparazzi.

The photos were cracked in places, as if they had curled up at one point and then been flattened again and again, glued into place.

She called Chief Redbone in.

"What does this look like to you?"

"I'll be damned. He sure had a thing for her, didn't he?"

"So this is definitely Marisa de Seroux?"

"Oh, I'd say so. That's Misty."

"Misty?"

"That's what everyone knew her by."

Laura walked to the first wall. "She didn't know he was taking them."

"This makes no sense."

"Maybe it does. It looks to me like he was obsessed with her." Enough to come back to town and pretend he was a member of her family? She had seen stranger things in her career.

She inhaled. It was musty in here; the place had been closed up for a long time.

"Hey, look at that." Chief Redbone motioned to a shelf crammed with books. "That one on the end. Looks like a scrapbook."

She walked over to the shelf and gently lifted out the scrapbook. More dust, like a blanket. The scrapbook was a cheap one he must have gotten from a drugstore. It had a bright yellow sunflower on the front.

She opened it up, careful not to smudge anything. The first thing she realized—it was less than a quarter full.

The first few pages were some of the best photos of Marisa de Seroux. Pale skin, blond, with serious eyes and a heart-shaped face. An angel.

Then she came to a yellowed newspaper clipping. Laura recognized it: The *Apalachicola Times* article about the de Seroux murder-suicide. She turned the page and saw the photo from page two, a white coffin under a mass of lilies being hefted up the steps into a church.

In the margin someone—Lundy, she assumed—had written in faded ink, "Liars!"

She made a note to save it for handwriting analysis.

Chief Redbone bent to see over her shoulder. "What does he mean by that?"

Laura knew. She felt it, that tangible truth that occasionally revealed itself at a certain point in a case. "He didn't believe she was dead."

"What? Why would he think that?"

"It was a closed-casket funeral, right? He could have gotten the idea she somehow escaped."

"Escaped?"

"Uh-huh." Laura remembered the news reports on TV after the Judd murder case in Safford. The hope everyone had that one of the children had escaped when all that time she lay underneath the house, dying.

"He must have been delusional," Redbone said.

"They say love is blind."

"What? Are you saying he was in love with a twelve-year-old girl?"

"Is it really that much of a stretch? How old do you think *he* was?"

Redbone frowned. "I don't know. A teenager, I guess."

"Probably not that much older than Marisa—Misty."

"She didn't escape, though. Everbody knew that. No way anyone could escape something like that—Henry shot up the house."

"The paper didn't publish any crime scene photos."

"No, of course not."

"There was no trial?"

"Nobody to prosecute. Everybody was dead."

"I'm guessing Lundy didn't want to believe it, so he didn't. What do they say? Perception is reality. Misty escaping—that was his reality."

"We can't know that for sure."

"No." Laura turned the page. It felt fragile in her hand, crackly. Another, shorter article describing the murder-suicide. Laura read through it quickly: nothing new.

But on the opposite page was something that made no sense at all.

It was a small news item in a Vancouver newspaper.

## WOMAN IN ALERT BAY SUCCUMBS TO INJURIES
### Live-in Boyfriend Charged with Capital Murder

"Misty Patin of Alert Bay, British Columbia, who has been in a coma for half a year, died today, paving the way for Robert Lewis to be charged with murder . . .

Laura read quickly. Misty Patin, age twenty-eight, had been beaten so badly she had been on life support for six months before succumbing to her injuries. She left behind a girl, thirteen, and a boy, five. This had been one of two traumatic events in Misty Patin's young life. Her daughter, Kim, had been kidnapped from a Wal-Mart in Vancouver during a family shopping trip two years before. Tragedy was averted, though, when she was found shortly afterward in the custody of a cabbie several miles away. According to the cabbie, he had picked up a nervous man and young girl in the Gastown district. The girl started crying and told the cabbie that the man was not her daddy. The man then jumped out of the cab and disappeared into the crowd.

The Pakistani cabbie described the man as "not a tough guy, you know? He was more like a gay."

Gay, Laura thought. Or just effeminate? The kind of guy who grew up sewing alongside his mother. She said aloud, "How would he get the idea this woman was his Misty?"

"Lundy?" The chief stared at her. "What, you think he followed her there? Because of her name?"

Laura was thinking on her feet now. "My guess, it was Lundy who kidnapped the girl."

"I thought he was in love with Misty."

"I know." It didn't make sense. Something was missing. Maybe it wasn't him. Maybe he didn't follow her there. But she wondered how a man in Apalachicola, Florida, would get his hands on a newspaper from Alert Bay, Canada. She wondered how many people in Apalachicola, Florida, knew of the *existence* of Alert Bay, Canada—or vice versa. She herself had never heard of Alert Bay until now.

Laura said, "There must be some link."

"You think he tracked down every Misty he could find?"

"Somehow he got on to this one."

"That's crazy. How would he get the idea that was Misty de Seroux?"

"I don't know." She was stuck on the kidnapping. If it

was him—and she felt sure it was—why did he kidnap the girl when it was Misty he was after?

He was attracted to young girls. That had to be the reason. Maybe he went looking for Misty. And then he saw her daughter.

He'd gone looking for Misty. It was the only thing that made any sense. "If you thought you'd been lied to, that the girl you were in love with got away, how would you track her down?" Laura asked the chief.

"It's too unbelievable."

"I know. But remember that story about Anastasia, one of the czar's daughters? A lot of people believed she escaped. They made a movie about it. If you thought Misty had somehow gotten away, what would you do?"

"I guess I'd get in touch with her people—if she had any left."

"Do you know where her family were from?"

"I have no idea. I know they moved here from somewhere else. But they weren't from too far away. Their accents."

"Why'd it take him so long?" Laura said.

"What?"

"Why did he go after her in 1998?"

She looked down at the scrapbook. That was the last page. It was as if he'd abandoned it. Or started a new one.

She stared at the sunflower. It sat in a turquoise water can. Behind it, through a window, a man stooped behind a plow. She thought that Jay Ramsey could have used his image recognition software to pinpoint the water can, the man, the mule, the plow.

"The Internet," she said.

"What?"

"He found Misty on the Internet."

"How would he do that?"

"He did a search on Google or another search engine. Probably found himself a bunch of Mistys, then whittled them down."

"How would he do that?"

She shrugged. "Age. Coloring, height—maybe he knew how to get information from driver's licenses. Maybe he hired a private investigator. For whatever reason, he zeroed in on this Misty. Maybe because of the name. Patin."

"Makes sense. Patin's French. De Seroux's French."

"Maybe he found a Misty Patin, found out she once lived here in this part of the country."

"That's crazy."

"He was there, in 1998. He took her daughter."

"You don't know that for sure."

"No, I don't."

Redbone scratched his head. "You think he was the one who killed her?"

"It says in the article her boyfriend killed her. I think that's probably true. Lundy wouldn't hang around. He wouldn't kill her two years later. He would have moved on by then."

To preteen girls.

"Found something here!" yelled Officer Oliver from somewhere else in the house. He sounded excited.

Laura didn't like being dragged away from her thoughts. Hard enough to keep track of them—they kept doubling back on themselves, trying to make sense of Dale Lundy's actions.

"In here!" Oliver called again.

She left the scrapbook and made her way to the kitchen.

The kitchen was utilitarian, with a round-shouldered refrigerator and sunny yellow chintz drapes and matching covers for the kitchen chairs. The large hooked rug in the center had been pushed aside to reveal a trapdoor in the old floorboards.

"Want me to open it?"

"No," Laura said.

He gave her a hostile look. "What do you want me to do?"

"Nothing for now. We'll get to it later."

He scratched his head. "I don't see why . . ."

"Because she told you, is why," Redbone said behind her. "Leave it be."

Oliver shot him a look of undisguised contempt. He was the son of a city council member, probably felt he was entitled.

"What do you want to do?" Redbone asked Laura quietly.

"I want to make sure we don't have any surprises." So far, Lundy had been full of surprises. "I want us to make sure we have cover and do this right. We might need assistance from Hazardous Devices."

"Good enough for me." Redbone looked at Oliver and nodded to the door. "You mark the evidence I pointed out in the living room yet?"

Oliver stared at him, fuming, before brushing past them without a word. Redbone followed him out, ostensibly to make sure he did what he was told.

Laura looked at Descartes, who had witnessed the exchange from the hallway. "Andrew, wait a minute."

"Yes, ma'am."

"Keep an eye on Oliver for me, would you? Under no circumstances is he to open that trapdoor. It's a safety issue."

"I'll make sure, you better believe it, ma'am."

Laura got Victor on the phone and gave him a rundown of what they had found. She read off Lundy's credit card numbers and gave him a detailed description of the motor home he was driving, the 1987 Fleetwood Pace Arrow.

Victor broke in. "Chuck Lehman confessed—"

"What?"

"But not to killing Parris. He was sleeping with her."

The moment Victor said it, all Lehman's actions, his evasions, made sense. Hanging out with Cary and Cary's girlfriend, the falling-out between them.

"It would explain a lot. The lipstick, for one. He's gonna plead to the probation violation and contributing to the delinquency of a minor. That'll put him away for a while."

"So you believe him?" Laura asked.

Victor sighed. "I believe it. Especially after I looked at the timeline and it didn't fit with the Burns killing. Do me a favor and don't say you told me so."

They talked about Lehman, but Laura's mind was still on Dale Lundy and his cross-country adventure. The idea that he was looking for someone like Misty de Seroux was, in a way, a hopeful sign. He was looking for an emotional connection. That might mean the difference between life and death for the next girl he took.

He'd kept Alison Burns for five days. Most sexual predators who murdered their victims killed them within the first few hours.

". . . with this?" Victor was asking.

"What?"

"You want us to go to the media?"

"No. I think we should keep it within law enforcement agencies for now. Put out an Attempt to Locate, make sure everybody gets pictures of him, the motor home, the credit card numbers. We don't want to scare him out of the area. This weekend he's supposed to play at the Copper Queen Hotel."

"We might get lucky if he used his credit cards, too. Find a paper trail."

"I'm hoping."

After he hung up she said into the phone, "I told you so."

She started photographing the bedroom, paying particular attention to the evidence she had marked: the scrapbook, the wall of photos, the contents of the closet. Chief Redbone had gone back to the evidence room at the PD to pick up more evidence bags—they'd need them.

She had just walked into the master bathroom when the roar of a shotgun blast reverberated through the cheap wallboard, stunning the air into silence.

# 39

In the first few moments after the blast, Laura heard nothing. She ran to the kitchen like she was running through a dream—like those movies where the woman runs from her pursuer, the soundtrack screeching and thrumming along with her thoughts, tracking her with a shaking handheld camera as she blunders through tilting corridors and jack-in-the-box shadows before stumbling onto a scene of unrelenting horror.

She knew it would be bad.

Two men down. One breathing, one not. Laura radioed Apalachicola PD, got no one. No one minding the store—the chief en route? Shit shit shit! She called 911. The phone still cradled between her shoulder and her ear, she dropped to her knees beside Andrew Descartes, compressing the carotid, her mind ticking between clinical observation and a panicked string of thoughts: just a kitchen towel and the gloves between her and his blood—unlikely he had AIDS but you never knew—his life leaking out, the phone slipping out from under her chin and dropping to the floor. The air was bright, every airborne fiber, every dust mote, every speck of blood delineated, every sound magnified. Knowing it was hopeless but unable to stop trying.

*Descartes.* Jesus.

Oliver moaning, then screaming, like a stuck pig.

Looking at Descartes, knowing he was finished. One shot to the carotid. Gone.

Let him go.

Move on to Oliver—more wounds. Find the worst one and compress that.

Later.

More sounds: radio static, a paramedic talking into his shoulder; ripping sensors and snatching bandages and sucking oxygen; the pneumatic wheeze of the gurney bearing Jerry Oliver down the steps to the waiting ambulance, a few blocks to Weems Memorial Hospital, and from there a medevac to Tallahassee Memorial—if he didn't die before he got to Weems.

Jerry Oliver had been shot in the cheek, eye, left shoulder, and upper right chest. Oliver, whom Laura was sure had been the one to open the trapdoor, was going to Weems and, if he was lucky, on to Tallahassee. Andrew Descartes, who had tried to stop him, was going nowhere—not for another couple of hours at least. First he would lie in his own blood while he was photographed from every angle. Then he would be transported to the morgue, evidence tweezed from his wound, his statistics read into a recorder, his organs weighed and measured, his skull sawed in half.

Andrew Descartes was now evidence in a crime.

The responding officer—a sheriff's deputy—looked sheepish after yorking his guts out on the linoleum floor. Uniforms coming, but where the hell were they?

Where were the techs from the Hazardous Devices unit?

They would be the ones to handle the twelve-gauge sawed-off shotgun still resting in its brackets on the underside of the trapdoor, everything but the muzzle concealed by a homemade plywood box. This she saw with brilliant clarity; her clinical mind divided right down the middle from her more emotional side, the emotional side lagging behind, still in shock. A simple principle. When the trapdoor opens, the shotgun fires: Chief Redbone's police force wiped out in an instant.

Laura stood in the torn, blood-spattered kitchen, hands tucked up under her arms from long practice.

She would not touch anything.

A paramedic entered the room, pulling another gurney bearing a body bag.

"You can't do that," Laura said.

"Who are you?"

*I'm the person who caused all this.* She held up her shield and gave him her name and rank. "He's not going anywhere."

"The chief—"

"This is a crime scene. He's staying here."

The sheriff's deputy stepped up. "She's right, man, we have charge of this scene now."

Only then did the paramedic leave.

The room narrowed down to just Laura and the body of Andrew Descartes. She made herself look at him. She was used to looking at the dead, but this was different. She knew him. She'd shared a joke with him not an hour ago. She saw his promise—a good cop who might have grown into an exceptional cop.

*I wonder who will tell his wife.*

She should be the one to do it because she felt responsible. If she hadn't come here, none of this would have happened. He'd still be at home, getting over strep throat, his new wife babying him with chicken soup . . .

The thought suddenly occurred to her: Where was Chief Redbone? She didn't remember him being around here. Had he already gone to tell Descartes's wife?

She wondered how it felt to have your whole police force devastated in the course of a split second. She thought of how his life had been laid out just the way he liked it, his teenage daughters, his sleepy town, dispensing his good ol' boy wisdom.

*In twenty-three years, I never had to draw my gun in anger.*

*That* record was shot to shit.

Laura kept her eye on Andrew Descartes, feeling dizzy.

Never before had her job felt moot. Never until now did she realize what a small dent seeking justice made into grief. Yes, she helped pick up the pieces, but they were still pieces. The aftermath of a tornado. In the face of that destruction, you were helpless. Now it had struck home, and she wondered if her job was worth anything at all.

She continued to stare at him, like serving some godawful penance. Filling her eye, her soul with him. Her mind straying away, and she, patiently bringing it back, around and around again to the fact: *You did this. You're responsible.*

But now she had to do the right thing. Look around, figure it out. *Do your job.*

Buckshot. Double aught buckshot, she guessed from the look of the wound. A single pellet, slicing through his carotid like a tiny razor.

Tears formed at the edges of her eyes, threatening to brim over, a still pool. That, she could not allow to happen. So she blinked. She blinked so hard and so fast she could feel it in the back of her skull, a corresponding ache to the one inside her gut.

Where was Chief Redbone? The deputy was the only other member of law enforcement here, but when she looked for him he was gone.

Out to meet the reinforcements, she hoped.

She heard the toilet flush somewhere in the house. The kid had used the bathroom at a crime scene.

She'd ream him out when he came back.

And then she realized it: *You have no standing here.* She would not be the investigator of this crime. That would fall to the state police, her counterpart in Florida.

But Laura couldn't leave. She couldn't leave Andy Descartes here alone.

*        *        *

Late in the afternoon, Laura and Chief Redbone drove up to
the Florida Department of Law Enforcement regional office
in Tallahassee to give their statements after handing the crime
scene over to two FDLE agents. Both of them were preoccupied with their own thoughts and did not speak. Laura found
refuge in the scenery as they drove in and out of the lengthening shadows. The grass along the roadside was a dazzling
kelly green from the rain earlier today. The sun's horizontal
rays ignited the trees and shimmered on the blacktop like
gold. Laura found herself looking back at the sunset behind
them, the leftover clouds turning from tangerine to cherry red
to dark plum.

Andy Descartes would never see another sunset.

At FDLE, Laura gave her statement, as clear and detailed
as she could remember. When she was through, Special
Agent Jack McClellan shut off the tape recorder and smiled.
Laura noticed he smiled a lot, but she wasn't sure why.

"That should do it. You're free to go."

Free to go where? Laura thought. She pictured herself
getting a ride to the Tallahassee airport, changing her ticket,
boarding the plane. Maybe sipping a cocktail as they passed
over the Mississippi and she put the South behind her. Just
a quick trip in and out of Florida, leaving an obliterated
Apalachicola PD and broken lives in her wake.

But that wasn't who she was. "There's the disposition of
the evidence. We need to work that out."

"I wouldn't worry," said Jeremy Poitras, McClellan's co-
agent. He was a massive black man with an exquisitely
shaped shaved head. He wore an expensive suit. "I'm sure
we can come to some accommodation."

A fancy-ass word for a fancy-ass man. Laura said, "We'll
need to do forensics on the computer, if you find one."

"We can work that out," Poitras said. "We have very
good people here—we can do the specific computer forensics."

"I want the computer to go to the DPS lab in Phoenix."

McClellan broke in smoothly. "First of all, we don't know he even has a computer. But if your agency can make their case to us, there's a good chance we'll release to you all the evidence that doesn't pertain to our investigation."

"I want to go into the de Seroux house. You understand I have a vested interest in this. Your guys are going to be looking for other things."

"That's fine by me," Poitras said. "You can certainly tag along, but . . ." He consulted his watch. "You'd better get down there soon. I have a feeling they've already gone in."

Laura felt her hostility rise to the surface. "I hope nobody opened any trapdoors," she said.

The de Seroux house itself seemed normal compared to Lundy's secret place. Cheap generic furniture. Plenty of fingerprints but little else. There was a desk for a computer, a cheap printer, split phone lines, a surge protector and APS, but the computer (or computers) were gone.

Again, Laura had the feeling that Lundy wasn't coming back. He had left the furniture but taken all his paper trail with him: checkbooks, statements, records. There was a square of less-worn linoleum in the room where the computer had been—she guessed it was where he kept his file cabinet.

The place felt like an abandoned ship.

The first to enter the de Seroux house was the FDLE Hazardous Devices unit, entering through the tunnel from Lundy's side, past the deployed weapon, looking for traps along the way. They found nothing on the other end except a corresponding trapdoor in the floor of de Seroux's tool-shed.

Laura wondered if Lundy expected his house to be searched and planned for that eventuality.

She had never been so tired. Perhaps it was because she felt like a guest at her own scene. She was allowed to gather evidence, but always under the watchful eyes of the FDLE special agents. She chafed; she never did well where she didn't have some control.

They finished processing the house early in the evening of the next day. Laura realized she was starving. She went by the deli on Market and got herself a submarine sandwich and a bottle of water, took them down to Battery Park. It was the first food she'd had all day.

After finishing her sandwich, she walked out onto the long dock. There was a slight squall out in the bay tonight, the scent of rain hanging in the air, and the sky alternated between bruised blue and copper when the sun came through. Fishing boats—she guessed a lot of them were charters— were coming in at sunset.

Why did he booby-trap the tunnel? That bothered her. If he was protecting the de Seroux house, did he really think the booby trap would stop the police? Or maybe it was just to kill whoever got that far—because he could.

Maybe he did it because he was embarrassed by the house itself, what it said about him: his obsession with Misty, his shrine to his mother's memory, the Victorian parlor. Mother and son sewing together. Maybe he wanted to hurt whoever became privy to his secret life.

Impossible to know what was in his mind.

Tomorrow morning they would search the tunnel again. Maybe she'd find her answer then. But she was beginning to believe it was just what her mother used to call pure bloody-mindedness.

She'd have to ask him when she met him face-to-face.

A pristine white sportsfisher was coming in, dropping down into idle just inside the no-wake zone. *Freedom's Daughter* was written in blue cursive on the bow. Laura felt her spirit lift just looking at it.

"I've always wanted a boat like that," Chief Redbone said behind her.

For a big man, he was light on his feet.

"Lot of work though," he added, leaning on the dock railing. "Time and money both."

The light had turned red now.

"That's a beautiful name for a boat," Laura said.

"I sure do second that."

Laura felt uncomfortable around him. The only time they had spent together since the tragedy was on the drive to FDLE in Tallahassee. She had not seen him since.

"How's it going over there?" he asked now.

She shrugged. "We haven't found much."

He sighed. "Glad I'm out of it."

He didn't sound devastated. He sounded like his old self. Laura wondered if that was a front.

"How's Mrs. Descartes doing?"

He leaned his back against the railing. His eyes looked like dark pebbles in his face, which seemed unusually slack. "About as well as you'd expect, which is not good at all."

"I should have gone with you. I feel responsible."

"It wasn't your fault." He said it, but she could tell he didn't believe it.

"Will she be all right? Financially?"

"She and Andy belong to the Church of Christ. Don't have to worry about making ends meet, not in this town. We take care of our own."

Laura opened her mouth to tell him she wished she could help, but said nothing. She could tell from the tone of his voice that she in fact wouldn't be asked to help. She was the stranger here.

And so she watched *Freedom's Daughter* glide under the bridge and into the Apalachicola River. Such a beautiful town. Easy and slow. She'd brought her big city troubles here, destroyed lives.

Chief Redbone stared straight ahead. "Thought you'd want to know Jerry Oliver's been upgraded to guarded. They think he'll be all right, although he lost the eye."

She nodded. "There are a few things we need to discuss. Will you be in the office tomorrow?" she asked him.

"Nope. I'm pretty much done here."

"What do you mean?"

He leveled his gaze on her. "I'm through with this. It wasn't what I signed up for."

"You mean you're quitting?"

"Been there, done that, as they say."

"What will happen now?"

"There's plenty of folks wanting this job. They're welcome to it."

"What are you going to do?"

"Me?" He thought about it. "First thing I'm gonna do is go fishing."

She thought he was done but he stared back out at the bay and continued. "Hasn't been one bad thing that a few days of fishing didn't cure, at least for me. Even my divorce. Thing is, though,"—he massaged his forehead over one eye—"I don't think I can ever get that picture of Andy out of my mind."

# 40

Chief Redbone left not long after that. Laura remained until it was dark, staring out at the bay and the ocean beyond. It was a short walk to the Gibson Inn, but as Laura started back she became aware of someone in the corner of her eye angling toward her at a rapid pace.

She was reaching for the SIG Sauer on her hip when she smelled the aftershave.

Old Spice. A familiar shape.

She left the gun where it was as Frank Entwistle materialized beside her. She heard the tiny wheezes through his nostrils he always made whenever he tried to keep up with her.

"What are you doing here?"

"Thought you could use some backup. Emotionally speaking."

"Emotionally speaking."

"Yeah, you know. Be your sounding board." He waved his cigarette and the cherry danced around them like a flying saucer.

Laura was weary of this.

"If you're so tuned in to me and my problems, why didn't you give me a heads-up on the booby trap?" *Why didn't you save Andy Descartes?*

In the dark, his face was the color of ash and about as

amorphous. "Could you slow down a little? You know I have a bum knee."

He stopped, so she stopped too. "To answer your question, I'm not a mind reader. I don't have a crystal ball, either."

"Then what the hell are you?"

He shrugged his shoulders in his ill-fitting coat and loosened his tie.

"I been tryin' to figure it out. You're not the only one who's affected by this situation." He swiped at his forehead with the back of his hand. "Damn, it's humid here. This is only a hunch, kiddo, but it could be I'm part of your subconscious."

Laura watched as a stream of cars came down the Gorrie Street Bridge, headlights flaring behind the dead homicide dick and turning him into a silhouette.

"Why are you here?"

He shrugged. "Beats me."

"Then why do you keep showing up?"

"Look, you're the one who's pulling all the strings. It's pretty clear you need me."

"Need you?"

Her phone chirped. She recognized the number that flashed on the screen—Victor's home phone.

Frank was saying, "If I were you I'd—"

"Just a second," she said to Entwistle, holding up a hand. She wanted to catch Victor before it went to voice mail. Maybe he'd had some luck tracing Lundy.

Entwistle said, "You sure you want to answer that?" just as Victor said something in her ear.

Laura stared from the phone in her hand to Entwistle. "Why wouldn't I want to an—"

"Why wouldn't you what?" asked Victor.

Laura looked at the spot where Entwistle had been. Gone. Gradually it came through, what Victor was saying.

Frank Entwistle was right; Laura wished she could somehow deflect the words coming out of Victor's mouth.

# 41

## Summer in Tucson

Summer didn't like lying to her mom, but she knew she'd never get to meet James if she didn't. There was no way she was going to miss out on the most important day of her life.

"You sure Chrissy's mom'll bring you home?" her mom said as they pulled up in front of McDonald's.

"Uh-huh."

"I don't want to impose."

"She doesn't mind. She likes driving."

"You have to be home by nine o'clock. No later."

"Sure, Mom."

She got out of the car, holding her new shoulder-strap purse that went with her sandals, leaning in and giving her mom a kiss on the cheek. And then she was free.

Her mom pulled out and nearly got wiped out by a bigger SUV. She never did pay attention to her driving. She was just totally unaware, driving away but looking back, waving. As if she'd never see her again.

She always did that.

Her mom treated her like a kid in so many ways, but she also treated her as if she was already an adult. She really liked to "talk things out." Communication was a big thing in their house. Her mom—who had just recently asked Summer to call her Beth—always said, "There's no problem too big to tackle if we just communicate."

Summer glanced at her watch. Seven o'clock. She was glad about the timing. Butthead Bryan was coming over tonight, and when that happened, her mom, who was usually pretty levelheaded, kind of lost it. She would do *anything* for him. She acted like a servant, waiting on him hand and foot. Bryan would be *thrilled* that she, Summer, was out of the way, over at a friend's house. That way they could do the nasty.

She knew that James wouldn't pat her butt the way Bryan patted her mom's, right in front of her. James had respect for women. When she and James made love, it would be beautiful. It would be right.

She found a table by the window inside so she could see the parking lot. It wasn't dark yet, but it was getting harder to see, especially because headlights were just coming on and they glared in the plate glass windows. Still, she'd know a Z4 anywhere.

She waited, and she waited.

It was getting darker by the minute. Every time a car pulled into the parking lot, she felt this incredible thrill. But none of them was a Z4. She glanced at her watch again. Had it really been ten minutes?

That was when the first doubt crept in. Maybe he was going to stand her up. She pictured having to walk to Chrissy's in the dark and face her friends, telling them he didn't show up.

No. He wouldn't do that. She and Jamie had some very open and honest conversations in the two and a half months since they'd met on WiNX, had talked for hours online and on the phone. She had fallen in love with him even before she knew what a hunk he was.

She knew he loved her. He sent her the MP3. He wouldn't have done that if he wasn't planning to meet her.

Of course her dad found out and took the MP3 player. He even read their e-mails!

Her face flamed as she thought of that.

"Summer?"

She looked in the direction of the voice. A middle-aged guy was making his way through the restaurant toward her.

"Are you Summer?" he asked.

"Uh-huh." She waited for him to come up to her. He was breathing through his mouth and sweating from the heat. He wasn't much taller than she was and looked a little like Mr. Murray, who taught fifth period math.

"I'm a friend of James. He got tied up and couldn't make it, so he asked me to pick you up." The man added, "I bet you're thinking you shouldn't go with me, but really, it's all right. James is staying with me while he's here."

"You're Dale?"

He looked surprised. "He mentioned me? Well, that's cool. All he's been talking about is Summer Summer Summer. I didn't think he'd even mention me." He smiled. His smile was so homely it made her feel good. "Let's go rustle up old Jamie."

She followed him through the parking lot to a white Geo Prism—not exactly what she'd been dreaming of.

He held the car door open for her, and for a moment she almost balked. Technically, he was a stranger. But if she didn't go with him, it would all be for nothing. She wouldn't get to go on her date.

Plus, James had mentioned Dale.

Dale was looking at her, frowning a little. As if he thought she didn't trust him, and this disappointed him.

She got in.

They pulled out of the parking lot and drove south on Swan. She was aware that he kept sneaking peeks at her. She knew she looked good in her denim skirt and her pink peasant top; getting looked at was nothing unusual. "Why couldn't James come?" she asked him.

"He's working on his folks' motor home. The air conditioner is on the fritz."

"His parents are here too?"

"Yeah. They're good friends of mine. That's how I got to know Jamie. He was the one who got me into dirt bikes."

James had told her that he raced dirt bikes. He also loved to hike and camp. They had that in common; when her parents were still together they had a camper and would go all over the place.

But now she had another worry: James's parents. What if they thought she was too young? What if they called her mom? Worse, her dad? She thought about this as they drove. Pretty soon she noticed they were driving through an ugly area, past a big electric plant. Dale glanced at her. "Almost there."

He turned onto the Old Benson Highway. This was a scrubby part of town: desert, old motels, and mobile home sales. She wondered why James would stay way out here.

They drove past motels with Western names, crummy old places with peeling walls and rusty signs. Past a vacant lot that seemed to go on forever. The headlights picked out the desert broom that grew alongside the road. Her mom had a constant battle with the stuff in the little yard of their new town house.

"Here we are," Dale said.

A weathered sign under a light on a tall pole said, EL RANCHO TRAILER COURT. Dale turned onto a narrow lane between two rows of trailers jam-packed together.

"He's staying *here*?"

"It's close to the airport."

Gravel popped off the Geo's tires as they drove slowly up the lane. The trailers looked dented and ancient—one of them had painted-over windows and was the color of dried blood.

That carnival ride thrill again, only this time it didn't feel so good.

She glanced at Dale. He was humming a tune under his breath, like he was the happiest man in the world.

The window shades of the trailers they passed were all pulled down, dim light seeping out from underneath, flickering blue. She pictured hillbillies in their underwear watching TV and drinking beer in front of an electric fan. They drove by a dead palm that looked like a witch's broomstick, and stopped behind a motor home parked at the end of the lane.

"Here we are," Dale said.

Suddenly she felt queasy. James was going to college in the fall. He owned an expensive sports car. His father was a surgeon. What were James's parents doing in a place like this, when they could have stayed at one of the inns by the airport?

"Come on," Dale said, getting out. He came around to her side and opened the door.

At least the motor home looked good. Clean-looking. New tires. That dispelled some of her worries. The other thing that made her feel better was, for some reason, THE ROPERS wheel cover under the back window. It had to be James's last name. She tried it on for size. James Roper. *Mrs.* James Roper.

And she liked the curtains in the window. Not blinds, but lace curtains. Something a mom might make. James's mom?

Still, she balked. "Where's James?" she asked.

"He's inside."

"I thought he was working on the air conditioner."

"He's probably finished by now. Come on, let me introduce you to his parents."

That made her hang back even more. She didn't doubt they would call her mom the minute they saw her.

Dale gave her a little nudge. "Come on, don't be shy." He unlocked the door to the motor home and stood there, waiting for her to step up inside.

The confined space was stuffy like it had been shut up. It didn't seem to her that the air-conditioning had been on recently. And wouldn't you have it on in order to make sure it worked?

"Jamie!" Dale called into the interior. "Come on out here! Milady awaits!"

That convinced her. She stepped up into the tiny living room.

"Oh," Dale said, as he closed the door behind them. "You know something? I just remembered, Jamie went to the store."

"What about his parents?"

Dale was looking at her, his face sad.

Alarm bells were ringing in her head now. Her stomach tightened, and her heart started pounding in her chest, her throat, her ears. She suddenly felt an overwhelming premonition that she had just stepped off the face of the earth.

# 42

Beth Holland had been watching TV, one eye on the window. Any moment she expected to see the sweep of headlights announcing Marie Lansing's car.

She had gotten Bryan out of the house by quarter of nine. It was for Summer's sake, because the two didn't get along, and things were tough enough on children of divorce. Even though Summer knew they were involved, she didn't want her to have to face the evidence firsthand. And so she had hustled to make her own bed and even wash the wineglasses and throw the wine bottle into the recycle bin.

Everything had been straightened up by nine o'clock. But nine became nine fifteen, then nine thirty. And now she was starting to worry.

She'd put off calling because she didn't want Summer to think she didn't trust her. But this was ridiculous. Steeling herself, she went to her address book and found the number.

Marie Lansing answered the phone.

"This is Summer's mother. May I speak to her?" She didn't want to embarrass Summer by telling Chrissy's mother what it was about. They would have their talk and that would be it.

Confusion in Mrs. Lansing's voice. "Summer? She's not here."

The girls couldn't still be at McDonald's, at this time of

night? "She told me she was going to meet Chrissy and Jenny at McDonald's, and then go to your house."

Marie Lansing said, "Chrissy's here. Let me put her on the phone."

As she waited, Beth started to feel more than worry. She told herself not to be silly. It was probably a misunderstanding.

"Hello?"

"Hi, Chrissy? Do you know where Summer is?"

"Huh-uh."

Fear sharpened to a point. *Take a deep breath.* "I thought she was meeting you and Jenny at McDonald's."

"No," Chrissy said carefully. "I think she said she was busy tonight."

"Busy?" She could hear her own voice, up an octave.

"I don't know what she—I mean, I don't think we had any plans," Chrissy said quickly. "You could call Jenny. Maybe she knows."

She gave Beth the number.

Dreading what she would hear, Beth called Jenny Conley's house and started praying as she waited for Mrs. Conley to go get her daughter. Went through the same questions, the same elusive replies.

Whatever Summer had going, it didn't include Jenny or Chrissy. Summer had lied to her.

Shaken, Beth put the phone down.

She stared at it for a moment. Then she picked it up again and called Buddy.

Buddy Holland was in the process of opening the door to his house in Bisbee when the phone rang. He locked the door behind him and carried the pizza from the Greek place and the beer from the Safeway over to the kitchen counter.

Then he stood over the phone, waiting for the message. He never answered the phone because of telemarketers. He hated them with a passion, but there was nothing he could do to them so he didn't waste his energy. Two things you had to just let slide in this world: spam and canned phone calls.

After the beep, Beth's voice—strained and anxious—came on. "I don't know where Summer is—"

He grabbed up the phone.

"Ohmygod, Buddy, she lied to me! I can't believe it . . ."

The moment he heard her voice he knew what had happened.

She was babbling. "I dropped her off at McDonald's and that was the last—"

"Beth, stop it. You need to calm down. Tell me exactly what happened. Don't leave anything out."

She told him. About the friends at McDonald's. About Summer's promise that Mrs. Lansing would drive her home at nine. He glanced at the clock. It was a little after ten now.

Summer had been gone three hours.

When she was through talking, he said, "Listen carefully. I want you to call TPD right now. Have them send someone out to the house. Ask for either White or Cheek. I'm on my way."

"She could just be meeting a boy. Don't you think we should look—"

"Call them. Do it now. I'll see you in an hour and a half."

"You don't think—"

"We don't have time to think. Call them."

When he hung up the phone, he sat down and closed his eyes.

This would be the end of his career. He had to face that. But his career was, at this moment, as unmourned as the uneaten pizza in the cardboard box. It meant nothing.

One thing for sure: He wouldn't want to live if he never saw his little girl again.

He swallowed his pride and made the two calls: one to the Tucson Police Department, the other to the Department of Public Safety. He managed to convince the people who mattered that they needed to recall Laura Cardinal from Florida—now.

By the time she arrived, he would have psyched himself up sufficiently to tell her the truth.

# 43

She was a wily one—a cop's daughter—but just like the others, she'd ended up doing what he wanted. That was the secret about girls. They aimed to please. Girls could be easily pressured, talked into things—they didn't trust their own instincts. They shut that part of themselves down because they didn't want to appear to be uncool, or rejecting, or out of the loop. So they were malleable.

Even now, he could tell she didn't believe it. She was still trying to apply the ways of the world she knew to this new circumstance. She'd been raised to be polite. She'd been raised to be a good girl. His heart ached for her. Politeness could be a dangerous thing in this day and age.

And yet it was what had attracted him to her. That aura of innocence. Oh, she pretended to be wise in the ways of the world, but she wasn't. She was like a kitten with its hair standing up, making itself seem bigger than it was.

That quality—that politeness, that *kindness*—that was what he had loved in Misty. Sadly, Misty had grown out of it. She'd had disappointments, she'd fallen into bad ways, she did drugs, but he preferred to remember her the way she was when they were in love.

He watched Summer's face. She was staring around, her bewilderment turning to panic.

"What's going on?" she asked.

He kept his voice steady and low, as if talking to a frightened animal—and really, that was what she had been reduced to. "I'm not going to hurt you."

"I think I'd better go home."

"In a minute. Just let me explain to you—"

"Where's James?"

This was always the part he didn't like. He hated that moment when he had to tell them the truth. Still, he had learned that it was better to get it over with rather than to scare the girl even more. "James is not coming."

"Where is he?" She had that look in her eye now, a dawning. He reached behind him, made sure the plastic handcuffs were there, stuck down the back of his jeans. He didn't want to use them, but he would if she didn't see reason.

"I want to explain this to you so you understand that I have only your best interests at heart. *I'm* James. I'm the person you wrote to, I'm the person you fell in love with."

Her mouth dropped open. She started for the door. "Let me out of here!"

He moved quickly and barred the doorway. She couldn't stop herself and stumbled into him, her face almost even with his, her tiny breasts in that peasant top brushing against his chest.

That did it. He wanted her now. Right now. Wanted her badly.

He closed his eyes, sidling away from the proximity of her breasts. He couldn't let her touch him again. If she did, that would be it. That would be it because he had such a tenuous grip on himself now—

He slid away farther. Aware that he was hard as a rock.

No, he told himself. He knew it wouldn't work that way. It just wouldn't. He'd learned from experience. Girls needed to be wooed. His mother had told him that.

He closed his eyes and started to pray. As he prayed he pictured what it would be like, the two of them, driving all over the country, going wherever they pleased . . .

"You don't know how great it will be," he said to her. "We can go all over—the Grand Canyon, Disneyland. Have you ever been to Six Flags Over Texas?"

"I don't want to go anywhere. I want to go home. You take me home right now."

"I can't do that."

"Why not?"

"I just can't." He held his hands up, open. "It's for your own good."

But he was looking at those small breasts. Like tiny buds, just barely stretching the peasant top. And her skin. Golden, like honey. There were white stripes, tan lines where she'd worn a swimsuit or sundress that had tied in a knot at the back of her neck. He could see it because of the blouse's scoop neck. And the skirt. So short, so tiny, the narrow little girl hips. The smooth long legs. Like satin.

Misty had dressed like that. His mother used to talk about how slutty she looked. How if Misty were *her* child she'd dress her in nice dresses. He agreed with that. They hid a girl's wares. Even pure girls had wares. It was just the way God made them.

"Take me home or I'll scream."

"Go ahead. I've heard two screaming fights since I've been here." He tweaked open the shade, the lace curtains. "See—nobody around now. They're all at work or inside their trailers."

"Why are you doing this to me?"

"You'll understand. I know it's going to take a while to get used to this, but we've got a lot of good times ahead. Just the two of us—"

If only she *could* understand. He felt the same way when he watched the vet shows on Animal Planet—when he saw the frightened animals struggling against the people who would help them. They just didn't understand that they were only making things worse by fighting.

He made himself turn away from Summer, the thin top, the smooth denim skirt.

He walked over to the closet and pulled out a dress. Girl's size 12. He had made it last year.

He held it out to her. "Would you do me a favor?" he asked. "Would you go into the bedroom and put that on?"

He saw she was about to argue. And then he saw the intelligence, the cunning, come back over her face.

Nothing like Misty.

Had he made another mistake?

She took the dress, turned on her heel, and walked into the bedroom at the end of the short hall, closed and locked the door.

In the bedroom, Summer stood back from the door, her heart pounding.

This wasn't happening. Where was James? What happened to James?

*"I'm James."*

She couldn't think. Her mind was racing but she couldn't think. She was stuck on the man who said he was James when he wasn't. She was stuck on what he said—God it was so creepy—*"Have you ever been to Six Flags Over Texas?"* Like he thought if he offered that to her everything would be all right, like she was some little kid, and the idea of going anywhere with that ugly balding little worm—

Creepy, the way he looked at her.

He was probably her *parents'* age.

This couldn't be happening. This couldn't be.

She became aware of the dress in her hands. It was like a little girl's dress. She was way too old for it—why'd he want her to wear that? But when he handed it to her, she just took it.

*Why didn't I fight? Why didn't I scream? Why didn't I try to escape?*

Instead, she just accepted the dress—maybe she even said "Thanks." What was wrong with her? How could she have gotten herself into this mess?

Because she knew this was something very bad. She

knew enough about sex—three of her friends weren't virgins anymore, and they had told her everything—she knew what this guy wanted.

He was old. He was ugly. The thought of doing it with him made her sick to her stomach. But here she was, in this smothering little room, all alone. Her mom didn't know where she was. Her dad . . .

He was a cop, but he lived in Bisbee. Of course they'd start looking for her, but how would they find her here? She had a pager in her purse, but what good would that do? He'd just turn it off. She wished her mom had gotten her a cell phone. She said to wait until her birthday. *Now I probably won't have a thirteenth birthday.*

She had seen enough on TV to know that she was in deep trouble. He would probably rape her. And kill her.

Adrenaline poured through her, a muscular current of fear. Her hands and legs shook.

*Get hold of yourself. You're not dead yet.*

Maybe, maybe if she cooperated, put on the dress, tried to talk with him. Get him to see her as a human being. Make friends with him. Maybe she could get to his phone, or his computer or something.

She needed to be smart. Observant, like her dad was. He didn't miss a thing. She remembered when they went to restaurants, he always sat with his back to the wall, scanning the room constantly, always *aware*. She needed to be like that. Careful, and smart.

She'd put the dress on. She'd try to get Dale to talk to her, to make friends with her.

Suddenly, she had something to do. She imagined herself as her dad. He was always in control. He'd be looking for her. He was a cop—he'd know how to find her. But in the meantime, she would picture herself as him. She would act like him, and think like him.

Musicman waited for her to come out. He'd seen this before, the girl going into his bedroom and locking the door, as if she could really escape that way, when in reality she was only putting off the inevitable. One of them—the girl in Colorado—had stayed in the room a day and a half. But she had been so hungry and thirsty, she finally opened the door.

The bedroom door lock that came with the Pace Arrow didn't really work, but he knew it gave them a sense of security. They felt they could get away from him, and that put them at ease. What she probably didn't notice was the hasp on the outside of the door. He could padlock it, but he didn't. Let her think she had the upper hand.

The bedroom was soundproofed. The lace curtains in the bedroom windows looked nice from the outside but they hid the fact that they weren't real windows—not anymore. He had boarded them up. She had locked herself in there, in that soundproofed room, and she could just think about it.

# 44

Laura massaged her back and stretched her legs. The cabin was dim—hardly anyone else on the plane. Nothing between her and her guilt over the killing in Apalachicola, an itch she could not scratch. *Your fault. You didn't trust your instincts. You knew there was a problem with Oliver but you ignored it.*

A police officer dead, lives that would never be the same.

She kept seeing Chief Redbone's face. The sense of failure she saw in his eyes.

Frank Entwistle used to call her—jokingly—the gunslinger. As in: The gunslinger come to town to help the townspeople chase out the bad elements. Like Wyatt Earp. But this time she'd brought only devastation and death before slinking off into the night like a coward. She was going home to her little house in Vail—but what would Linda Descartes do tonight?

"This is getting you nowhere," she muttered.

She needed to concentrate on what was happening now—Summer Holland's abduction.

Her conversation with Victor had been brief. Summer Holland disappeared from a McDonald's in Tucson. She'd lied about who she was meeting. And Buddy had been insistent: He needed to meet with Laura face-to-face.

He knew something.

Laura saw Dale Lundy in her mind. His pale, almost feminine face. The soft wet eyes that had no soul behind them. The Victorian-style room where he sewed with his mother. The photos of Misty de Seroux.

The twelve-gauge shotgun nestled in a homemade plywood box on the underside of the trapdoor.

She closed her eyes, trying to think. Could it be Lundy? How many kidnappers could there be, operating in that relatively small part of the world?

Suddenly, lights started dancing in the corner of her eye. She opened both eyes and stared at the seat back in front of her, expecting them to go away. But the lights kept on blinking.

Pulsing on and off at the corner of her right eye.

A thin edge of panic poked its way under her heart. She remembered the same thing happening at the Jonquil Motel the night she found the matchbook.

Her hand on the doorknob, the strangeness she felt.

Laura looked down at her hand. Again, it looked funny but she couldn't figure out why. The one side of her eye— it was like her vision was bleary from being underwater.

She got up and walked to the back of the plane, heading for the restroom, pushing down the beginnings of panic. Halfway down the aisle, the flashing lights went away.

She blinked. Nothing there—she could see fine.

Walking back to her seat, she thought, *It's got to be stress. After what happened in Apalachicola, she had a right to be stressed out.*

Musicman had just dozed off when he heard the door to the bedroom creak. He sat up on the couch and glanced at his watch: almost two in the morning. He'd taken care of his needs twice since she had disappeared into his bedroom but it hadn't taken the edge off. He felt like one long nerve.

In the light seeping in from under the shades from the

sodium arc light above the trailer court, he saw her edge into the hallway.

She wore the dress—he almost lost it right there.

He made sure to hide the sock he'd used as he fantasized about her, then turned on the light.

She looked like a burglar, caught red-handed.

*Talk to her gently.* "I'm glad to see you," he said.

She looked at him, and he rang like a tuning fork.

He was not expecting his reaction. Usually, seeing the girls in the dresses acted as an inhibitor, cooling his jets, so to speak.

But she was even more alluring, more exciting, in the dress. It was the juxtaposition of her innate beauty that had a definite sexual quality to it, and the way the dress tried to hide it. It did hide those tanned legs, the breasts, the curve of her ass, but it had just the opposite effect than he'd expected.

It titillated him.

She stood in the doorway, looking him right in the face. Calm, cool, alert. Just standing there, so serious. So dignified. And underneath—

No, he wouldn't think about it.

"Couldn't you sleep?" he asked.

"No." Her voice quiet.

"You sure look pretty in that dress."

"Do I?" Interested. Friendly, even. Like she was someone else, someone older. Like she was the one who was in control.

Those cool eyes on him.

There was a speck of brown in her blue-green iris.

That hit him square in the heart. Misty had that same imperfection. That was what they called it, but he always thought of it as a beauty mark.

"You have a brown spot in your eye," he said.

"I know. My mom calls it my beauty mark."

This had to be a sign from God—she was the one. He felt the rush of joy.

Not that he believed she was Misty come back to life. That would be ridiculous. He wasn't crazy, just nostalgic. Still, the resemblance was heartening.

His mind was babbling now. She was so like Misty. The spot in the eye, the words she used. *Beauty mark.* The way she tilted her chin—he hadn't noticed it before. The cool way she looked at him.

*This* time, it was going to work. He could feel it. Sure, he'd have to gain her confidence, her trust. He'd have to go slow. But this time would be different from the others.

"Would you like something to eat?" he asked. "I can cook anything you want. I'll make you something special."

# 45

Laura got in at two thirty in the morning. Victor Celaya and Buddy Holland were waiting for her, Holland bristling with negative energy. He had his keys in his hand as they walked down the steps toward the exit, his stride lengthening so he was way ahead of them, looking back periodically, impatient for them to catch up.

"He must be going out of his mind," Laura said.

"Jesus, can you imagine what he's thinking? What if it's Lundy?"

Laura said nothing, because she thought it *was* Lundy.

She remembered what Jay Ramsey had said before she left for Florida—there had been another girl. "How old is Summer?"

"Twelve."

"She lives with her mother? In Tucson?"

"Uh-huh."

The heat hit the moment they were through the automatic doors, a hot dry wind seizing the breath from her lips and nostrils. She'd gone from sauna to oven. It seemed to her it got hotter every year, the monsoon seasons of her memory dwindling down to a few thunderstorms, terminal humidity, and a plague of mosquitos. Maybe it was all due to global warming.

They drove the one long block to DPS headquarters. Laura had come back empty-handed. Nothing to check into evidence—that was still being decided in Tallahassee. Who got what, when. They headed upstairs to the squad bay, took chairs in the conference room. Buddy sat opposite Laura, and Victor sat between them at the head of the table.

Victor nodded to Buddy. "Okay. She's here. What was it you wanted to talk about?"

Buddy stretched his long legs out in front of him and stared at his feet. Laura thought he had aged ten years.

Victor said to Laura, "He won't tell me what's going on. He said he wanted to wait for you. So give it up, Buddy, what is it?"

Buddy's face was pale, his eyes like dark stones. He opened his mouth to speak, then abruptly launched himself out of his chair and started pacing.

"Come on, Buddy. What's so important we have to beg for it?"

He stopped and took a breath.

"I think I brought him here."

Laura wondered if she heard right.

"What do you mean, you brought him here?" demanded Victor.

Buddy started pacing again, head scrupulously turned away from them. He said, "I brought him here. It was me."

"How'd you do that?" Victor's voice loud in the small room.

"I found out my daughter was talking to this guy on the Internet. He sent her stuff—an MP3 player, earrings—"

Laura thought about Endicott's evidence list. She had been right. It was Lundy. She looked at Buddy, who was still talking. It took her a moment to catch up with his words.

". . . decided to intercept his messages. I knew he was a bad guy, a sexual predator. I'd been on the chief to let us start our own Internet sexual predator task force, but he wouldn't go for it. This guy was out there, and I couldn't just let him get away. So we set him up."

"Set him up how?" Victor asked.

"I took over for my daughter. Pretended I was her."

Victor whistled.

Laura said, "We? You said we set him up."

"Me and Duffy."

Duffy? Jesus.

Buddy slung himself into a chair. Now that he was talking, it all came out. How he and Heather Duffy had planned a sting, setting up a meeting with Lundy in City Park. "But he never showed. I think he saw something that tipped him off."

Laura thought, Duffy would look like a cop even in a negligee.

"He made you," Victor said. "He made you and he bolted, and on his way out of town he saw Jessica Parris. And you kept this secret all this time? What about Lehman?"

"I thought it could be him."

"That's a huge coincidence, man."

"Hey, his prints were on her *lipstick*." For a moment, the arrogant Buddy was back. "It could have been an unrelated crime."

"Come on! You expect us to believe that?"

"Where's Lehman now?" Laura asked.

"First place I called. He's at his house. He would have had time to get her to Bisbee. He had three hours."

"But he didn't," said Laura.

Buddy looked at her defiantly.

"You didn't go to his place, because you knew it wasn't him."

Buddy didn't say anything. He didn't have to. Laura asked, "Did he send her a picture?"

He nodded. Didn't look at her.

"What were you trying to do? Throw us off the track?" Victor again.

Buddy stood up and the plastic chair clattered, hit the wall. His fists clenched, he stepped toward Victor.

"Wait a minute!" Laura said, getting up to stand between them. "This isn't doing us any good. We've got to find this guy."

Buddy sat back down, passed a hand over his face. "Shit."

Laura cleared her throat. "We've got to compare notes. We know a lot more than we think." She looked at Buddy. "I know stuff about this guy now. The good news is, Jessica Parris was an anomaly. He keeps his victims for a while."

Buddy Holland shot her a look of gratitude.

She ran down what she'd learned, her belief that he was reliving some kind of relationship with Misty de Seroux. "That could work for us."

"Are you telling me he's looking for girls that look like this Misty?" Victor asked.

"I know—weird, but you've seen weirder." She looked at Buddy. "I don't think he's going to kill her—not yet. I think we have some time."

Buddy's gaze locked with hers. "Then what are we doing hanging out here? We've got to get moving."

"Where would we go? It's better if we figure out a few things first."

"He rapes and kills," Buddy said bitterly. "We already know that. He's probably already . . . oh, shit."

"If we recover her," Laura said to Buddy, "we can work with that. Get her counseling."

She reached into her briefcase and removed photographs of Alison Burns, Jessica Parris, and Linnet Sobek. And then she added a couple of candid photos Lundy had taken of Misty de Seroux.

She watched Buddy's face. He drew in a quick breath.

"Look at them, how much they look alike," Laura said quietly. "He wants a relationship. He wants someone like Misty."

# 46

"You just sit down and take a load off," Musicman said to Summer, bustling around the galley. "How do grilled cheese sandwiches and a Coke sound?"

Summer didn't like grilled cheese sandwiches, but she thought she'd better say she did.

He was trying to be nice to her. He brought the grilled cheese sandwiches to the table on paper plates, the kind you got from Paper Warehouse. These plates had purple, blue, and yellow fireworks and said HAPPY BIRTHDAY. Beside her plate was a present.

"Go ahead, open it."

She tore off the wrapping, feeling queasy. When did he get her a present?

"Could you be a little more careful?" Dale said. "We can use that paper again."

She did as she was told, gently parting the wrapping where the Scotch tape was until it revealed her gift: a Lucite photo cube.

"Well? Do you like it?"

"It's great," she said, trying to sound enthusiastic.

"That's for our trip. Here, let me put it away so we don't get food on it." He cleared the paper and put the cube away up in a top cupboard. He removed the bow from the wrapping paper and smoothed the paper out, folded it neatly, and put both the paper and the bow in a kitchen drawer. Then he sat down at the dinette table to watch her eat.

The idea of eating anything made her want to gag, but she smiled and bit into the sandwich. It tasted like cardboard. She chewed and chewed, trying to make the food small enough to swallow, and kept smiling. That seemed to please him. He acted like he had a crush on her—like he was shy or something. He reminded her of Justin Teeters in fifth period, who, whenever he saw her, got this look on his face that was really comic. She'd say "Hi" and he couldn't even answer back.

In that way, Dale was just like Justin. She knew he wanted to do *it* with her, but she also knew that he was holding back. Because he was shy?

Was he just like Justin, only older? She closed her eyes, imagined that her power was bigger than herself. That she was bigger and bigger and Dale was smaller and smaller.

When she opened her eyes he was looking at her. Staring. "How is it?" he asked.

"Mmmm. Really good."

"I bought ice cream for dessert. I know it's almost breakfast time, but hey, we can do anything we want."

Like a little kid. Jeez.

"Would you like some?"

She swallowed more of the cardboard. "Sure."

"I got Neapolitan," he said shyly. "That way you can choose what you want—chocolate, vanilla, or strawberry."

"Cool."

"You look so much better in that dress."

That reminded her. "What did you do with my clothes?"

"They're gone. Never you worry about that. You won't have to see them again."

She almost said she *liked* them, but bit her tongue. *Humor him. Humor him until you can find a way to get out of here.*

She set the sandwich down, sipped some Coke. Looked

at him, memorizing his face. That way, her dad would be able to track him down after she escaped.

*How* she was going to escape, she didn't know. But the more time she spent with him, the better she felt about her chances. He was kind of pathetic. She almost felt sorry for him. Sorry, and grateful that he wasn't the kind of kidnapper she'd seen on the Discovery Channel, the ones who murdered their victims. She couldn't see him murdering anybody.

"You like the sandwich?" he asked again.

"Oh, yeah. I just don't eat a lot. I'm on a diet."

He frowned. "You don't need to diet. Why do girls do that? You should be healthy, enjoy your life, not diet. I told Misty that."

"Who's Misty?" *Get him talking.*

"She was my first girlfriend."

"I bet she was pretty."

"Oh, she was."

"How come you aren't still with her?"

"We grew apart."

"I'm sorry . . . I don't know why she'd want to leave someone as nice as you. I mean, you're really pretty cool."

He stood up abruptly. "If you're not going to finish that, I'll throw it away."

She'd made him mad.

He shoved the picnic plates into the garbage. He wouldn't look at her, but she could tell he was angry by the way his shoulders hunched, the way he slammed around.

Finally he turned to face her. "Why do you have to be so *sly?*"

His face was dark red, his eyes like marbles. Suddenly he looked dangerous.

Her heart sped up. What was he mad about?

"Flattery will get you nowhere," he said.

"I just meant—"

"I know what you meant. You think you can wrap me around your little finger? Well, that's not going to happen."

He stepped forward, his hands clenching and unclenching. "That makes me so mad."

"I'm sorry, I didn't mean it. Honest."

"I think you'd better go to your room, young lady."

"Okay." She slipped out from behind the dinette table, had to pass right by him to get to the bedroom. She tried not to touch him at all, but her dress brushed against his thigh.

His hands came out and he whipped her around to face him. Bands of steel around her upper arms, nails digging in. His hands were trembling. His head was trembling.

His face was so close. It blotted out everything. His mouth was working, and his eyes—

His eyes were dark, like holes. Like there wasn't anything there behind them. Just black space. She opened her mouth to say she was sorry but nothing came out.

He shook her, once, hard, and slammed her against the stove. The edge of the stove whacked into her elbow, the shock running up her arm to her chin. She groaned.

He continued to stare at her. Eyes like holes. She was distracted by the pain in her elbow. Her funny bone.

Then she saw something else way down deep in his eyes. Pain? It was shiny, slick, desperate. He turned around and walked away from her. "Best get to your room," he said without looking at her.

She bolted for the room and locked the door.

A few minutes later she heard something bang against the doorjamb, then the sound of a padlock clicking shut.

# 47

Victor, Laura, Buddy, and Jerry Grimes set up a task force, calling their contacts at other law enforcement agencies — the FBI, U.S. Customs, her own DPS, Highway Patrol, U.S. Border Patrol, the sheriffs in all Arizona counties, the Tucson, South Tucson, Marana, Oro Valley, and Green Valley police departments. Laura contacted the detectives she knew with these agencies. Every agency was faxed a picture of a 1987 Fleetwood Pace Arrow, the head shot of Lundy, both names, and his license plate number. They also contacted law enforcement in New Mexico, California, and Mexico.

Anybody and everybody to help them out.

Buddy asked, "What about media?"

Laura was torn about that. "We have no idea if he's still in Tucson, but if he is, we don't want him to run."

"I think we should keep it to law enforcement," Victor said.

Laura agreed.

Buddy wanted the Amber Alert.

"It's too fucking late for that," Victor snapped.

Charlie Specter, a DPS intelligence analyst, started entering what data they had on Lundy in the Rapid Start system. Rapid Start was a computer program developed by the FBI for just this kind of situation. He would enter the data as in-

formation came in from various law enforcement entities—
one man in charge of everything.

"Too bad we don't have his computer," Charlie said to
Laura. "I guess he's had it with him all this time."

"Is there any way to track his movements on the Internet?" she asked. Just then her mobile rang. She excused herself, walking away so she could hear.

The caller was Barry Fruchtendler. She rummaged
through her overloaded circuits and pulled up the name—
the cop who worked the Julie Marr case—and told him
she'd have to get back to him later. He gave her his number
in Montana and she wrote it down. As she flipped the phone
closed she tried to recapture her line of thought. "What if we
had his e-mail address?" she asked Charlie.

"That depends. If he's gone wireless . . ." He shrugged.
"Worth a shot, though."

"How would that work?"

"If he's on the road, he'll need one of the big servers he
can access by an eight hundred number. All he needs is a
phone jack, and he can keep up on his correspondence, no
matter where he is."

Laura was puzzled. "The motor home wouldn't have a
phone jack, would it?"

"Nope, but there are plenty of places he can go. Cyber
cafés, anyplace he could get his hands on a phone line.
Which would give us a great way to find out where he is.
Once you have his e-mail account you could subpoena his
Internet server and have them intercept his e-mails. Trick is
to let the e-mails go through so he doesn't notice anything
unusual, but a copy comes here to us." He saw Laura's puzzled expression. "When an e-mail goes out, it has to go
someplace to wait before it's sent on—kind of like a clear-
inghouse. When you log on, you ask for your e-mail and
that's when the server sends it."

"And that could pinpoint where he was?"

"The general area where he's calling from. It goes by
area code. We'd know if he was in Tucson or Green Valley

or in New Mexico—wherever. We could even track him if he's moving, as long as he checks his e-mail."

Laura looked at Buddy. "It would be on your wife's computer, wouldn't it?"

"Better than that," Buddy said. "I've got his e-mails."

Musicman knocked on the bedroom door late in the morning. "Summer? You okay?"

No reply. He didn't blame her, the way he'd acted. What had possessed him?

"You're going to have to stay in the bedroom while I'm gone. Screaming won't help. A lot of people scream at each other around here, and everybody minds their own business. I just have a couple of errands, and then I'll be back. Is there anything you want me to pick up? Ice cream? Soda?"

Still no answer.

"Once we get to know each other, I won't have to take this kind of precaution."

The hot air hit him as he walked outside. The El Rancho Trailer Court was bad enough at night, but in the summer sun it looked as if it had been left out to rot. It was an ideal place to go to ground, though, for several reasons. The people here minded their own business. They remained inside, trying to stay cool. No doubt most of them were drugged to their eyeballs. An added bonus, the El Rancho Trailer Court was a short shot to the freeway and the airport if he had to get away in a hurry.

One of the best things about El Rancho was its proximity to the Motel 6.

He pulled into the Motel 6 parking lot and took his laptop into room 17. Inside, he set it on the round table near the door and closed the drapes against the summer heat. He turned the television to CNN and the air conditioner on high. Then he logged on.

When he wasn't on the road, he had to check his e-mail several times a day. He usually tried to find a cheap motel room—it didn't matter what color the drapes were, as long as it had a phone jack.

Every time he logged on, he felt an incredible rush of anticipation. His heart beat faster, his fingers practically itched. Maybe it was because his mother had so looked forward to getting the mail every day, as if she thought there might be a grand prize or a love letter from an old lover— something special. It got to be kind of a game. They would walk out to the mailbox together, and she'd say, "I wonder what I'll get today?"

Even if it was just a bill, she liked getting mail. It was always an adventure.

He was just like her. Even though he got a lot of spam, it was still mail.

He'd been hoping to hear from his friend Marshall, who lived in Chicago and had sounded interested in the pics of Jessica Parris. But all that came up were more messages from Dark Moondancer.

He had mostly ignored Moondancer. He'd sold him the pics, and as far as he was concerned, that was the end of it. But Dark Moondancer was nothing if not persistent. He must have sent thirty e-mails in the last week. All of them telling him to come and bring his latest sweetheart. Cryptic, subtle. Stuff like, "I'd love to meet your new girlfriend." And "I have such a cozy, out-of-the-way place, far from the rat race."

He opened the latest message.

I wish you'd think about coming for a visit. I could give you the run of the place. Please think about it. Yours, Dark Moondancer. PS, am enjoying my trips down memory lane.

Memory Lane was the title of one of the photos he'd sent to Dark Moondancer. A forest glade. But underneath it was a dark secret—Jessica Parris in the band shell.

The idea of that cretin coming near Summer sickened him. The man was untrustworthy and dangerous. It wouldn't be wise to put Summer into that kind of situation.

When he was through, he locked the door behind him and took his laptop back to the Geo. The room was so much cooler than the motor home, he'd debated bringing Summer here. Ultimately he'd decided against it. There was too much room for error. The motor home was a controlled area. He'd used it for all his girls, and had everything down to a science. You never wanted to do anything that could throw you off your game.

The Geo felt like an oven. The sour smell of cheap vinyl rose up around him. He started the car, yelped as his fingers touched the burning metal. He grabbed a gas receipt on the floor and used it to steer, narrowly missed running into a white panel van entering the parking lot. Feeling churlish, he flipped the driver the bird.

Hot air coming through the vents—the air-conditioning sucked on this thing. But it was his getaway car. If it got too hot, he could always leave the motor home and take off in the Geo.

Laura had Buddy print up three copies of all the e-mails and started going through them.

"So Summer was Crazygirl 12." She stared at Buddy. "Must have been a shock for you when that matchbook turned up."

He looked at her stonily.

She decided to move on. "Let's see what they've been saying to each other."

Laura had to admit that Buddy had a good ear. He had imitated his daughter perfectly, and Lundy had not suspected a thing. The only problem: He'd come early to their meeting and something had spooked him.

Laura read samples of Musicman's pitch:

I can't believe how sweet you are. You're not like other girls not in any way. You're different and I can't believe how lucky I am.

I want to be the one to make love to you for the first time.

The first time should be perfect. I picture giving you a bubble bath, get you nice and relaxed, candlelight, maybe a little something to drink. And when you're all warm inside and out . . .

She wanted to throw up—such a rasher of shit.

When can we meet in person? Your picture is not enough anymore. I think about you all the time.

He told her he was seventeen and would be a freshman in college this fall, premed. His parents had money but he "wanted to earn his way through college" so he worked two jobs. He described how beautiful Colorado was and how much fun it would be, just the two of them, camping out under the pines and falling in love.

"We need to get hold of Colorado law enforcement," Laura said. "It sounds like he knows these places. He might have had another girl there."

Victor leaned over her. "Durango, Mesa Verde, Ouray, Grand Junction, Glenwood Springs—I have a cousin who lives in Colorado. Most of those towns are on the same highway."

"He must have passed through." But when? She knew he had been in Indio five months ago.

"He really did take his show on the road," Victor said.

Buddy opened up the JPEG photo of "James," standing in front of the blue Z4, arms crossed.

"Only you and Duffy knew about this?"

"Yes."

"If you had this picture, why did you concentrate on Lehman?"

"You were the one who bird-dogged him, remember?"

"Yes. But I didn't have this." She motioned to the computer screen.

He shrugged. "I told you. I thought they were two different cases—"

"Bullshit." Victor.

Buddy shot Victor a venomous look. "I *did* look for him. So did Duffy. We must have stopped a dozen of those blue Z4s."

"We could have all been looking for him," Laura said.

Buddy Holland had gotten back his equilibrium, and blame bounced off him. "But that wouldn't have done us much good, would it?" He tapped the screen, the photograph of Peter Dorrance. "Because it *wasn't* him."

# 48

As Musicman drove the last block toward the El Rancho, his mind turned to the problem of Summer. He was angry with himself for treating her the way he did. Now he'd need to woo her all over again.

A street vendor had set up shop in an empty lot on the corner of the Benson Highway and Palo Verde. On an impulse, Musicman pulled into the lot. Under a parachute-type awning, an old man in a guayabera shirt sat behind a glass case of cheap-looking jewelry on velvet.

All his girls had loved trinkets. Of course, that was before they saw him. That was always a shock. They were always willing to accept gifts from a good-looking guy like Dorrance, but they turned their noses up at him.

He bought a pretty choker, the thin strand of silver almost liquid in the glaring sunlight. Little beads of turquoise were threaded on at intervals. He drove the rest of the way with a smile on his face.

As he switched on his blinker to make the turn into the El Rancho Trailer Court, he felt a sudden premonition. He'd learned to trust his instincts, so he flicked off the blinker and continued driving on to the next block. He turned there and turned left again, coming up behind the trailer court.

He'd been right.

From this angle he could see the revolving lights of a cop car.

Feast or famine, DPS intelligence analyst Charlie Specter thought as he got himself a cup of coffee and sat back down at the computer. Tips from law enforcement entities throughout the state had come in rapidly at first, then slowed to a trickle, followed by another onslaught. Like turning a faucet on and off. Right now was a downtime.

He checked his watch. Another thirty minutes or so had gone by since the last time he checked his e-mail.

Laura Cardinal had made sure that Charlie was specifically named in the subpoena to Lundy's Internet server. The messages that Lundy sent and received would be trapped at the server and then sent on to Lundy. After it had been sent to Lundy, an "admin copy" would be sent on directly to Charlie. Along with the text of the e-mail would be a header, showing the date and time of the e-mail, as well as the area code and phone number.

He took a sip of coffee and logged on.

Bingo! There was the e-mail address from Lundy's ISP log: musicman2@msn.com. The e-mail was from darkmoon-dancer@livewire.net.

Time sent: 1:57 A.M. Time received: 10:43 A.M.

Lundy's ISP had a Tucson area code. He was still in Tucson—a 628 exchange.

Specter called the 628 number. Familiar music came on— Tom Bodett inviting the caller to stay at Motel 6.

He looked up Motel 6 and found several. One of them had the 628 exchange.

He turned the corner and walked to Laura's desk. "How's this?" he said. "I know where your bad guy was, up to an hour ago."

*Get a grip,* Musicman told himself. There's no way she could have gotten out of that motor home. No way anyone could have heard her.

He parked the car by the side of the road, got out and trotted across the patch of desert toward the chain-link fence that bordered the park. The fence was woven with dried-out yellow plastic, so it was hard to see, but he could hear the yelling. It sounded like a drunk male, very angry.

He snuck up to the fence and peered through a hole in the plastic.

A shirtless long-haired man was bent over the hood of a Tucson police car as two cops struggled to handcuff him. His jeans were so low on his skinny waist they showed his butt crack and a bad tattoo.

"What'd I do? What'd I *do*?" the man kept screaming.

Even though the guy was obviously suffering from malnutrition, he gave the cops quite a fight.

The cop cars were parked four trailers down from Musicman's motor home. The motor home was quiet but Summer could be hitting her fists against the windows and screaming—no way to tell.

He watched the cops. They were so busy with the screaming man that they were oblivious to anything else. A few neighbors had come out, hanging back mostly, on their front stoops. A ragtag bunch.

Finally the cops wrestled the screaming man into the back of one of the patrol cars. Both cops had to pause for breath, and as they did, they looked at the crowd, which seemed to melt back into the rusting metal of their homes.

He didn't like it.

The first car, the one holding the prisoner, drove away. The second cop walked to his car. Was it his imagination, or did the cop give the Pace Arrow more than a passing glance? He even took a step to the side, so he could see more of it.

Then the cop's radio squawked. Whatever it was, he got in and drove off in a cloud of dust.

Musicman waited for several minutes, then got back into the car and drove around to the entrance.

Right before the entrance, the Geo stalled and he cursed.
Still, he was glad he'd bought the car.

He needed to get out of here.


Officer Ray Garcia wiped the sweat from his face. Even in the
squad car, Timmy Swanson was still kicking and screaming.
Let him kick. He wasn't about to break through that steel
mesh.

"D and D. Possession of crack. Resisting arrest. I guess
that'll about do it," said Sam Chilcott.

"Ought to. See you in a few." Ray knocked on the roof of
Sam's squad car and then walked back to his own.

He always told his kids he had eyes in the back of his head,
which wasn't far from the truth. He'd been trained to look at
everything as a potential threat, and had developed that eye for
detail. So as he walked to his car, he scanned the trailer park.
Maybe someone would resent the arrest of poor ol' Timmy,
maybe they would rush him, or take a potshot at him. Some
people would say he was paranoid, but it was a paranoia he
wasn't ashamed of.

A vehicle up ahead stood out from the rest. Every other
trailer looked as if it had been moored there and the vegeta-
tion—and junk—had grown up around it. But the motor
home at the end looked out of place. The trailers here had been
scoured by the sun and the dust, burnished to oxidation. But
the motor home looked as if it had been washed recently. It
also didn't look permanent.

He stepped out of the lane so he could see the back end.
Lace curtains in the back window, just like on the sides.

He'd heard something about a motor home recently, but
couldn't remember what kind or where.

His handheld crackled—a knife fight two blocks south of
here. He got into his unit and floored it on out of there.


Musicman unlocked the door to the motor home and called
out, "Oh, June, I'm home!"

It was a lame joke but it had become kind of a ritual. He

loved the old TV shows on TV Land. At his age, he'd missed the best ones, *The Andy Griffith Show*, *The Dick Van Dyke Show*, *Lucy.*

"There's been a change of plans. We're going on our trip sooner than I thought."

No reply.

"I'm sorry about what I did. I just kind of lost it. I won't act like that again."

Nothing. She was being stubborn.

He was surprised to realize that it excited him. He remembered one porno tape he played over and over where the man did a young girl and she fought and snarled and he kept saying, "You little wildcat!"

He couldn't think about that now. Sometimes he felt he lived inside a flame that wanted to consume him, burn him to nothing. This was one of those times. He swallowed. "We don't have any time to waste. We've got to go."

He unlocked the padlock. "Let's go!"

Still no reply.

Maybe he should just hitch the Geo up to the Pace Arrow and get out of here. That way he could leave her in her room. Deal with her later. She needed finesse, not force, and he didn't have time to play games.

"Okay, you want to play it that way, fine."

He walked outside and got into the Geo, drove it up to the hitch.

As he got out, he saw two cop cars zoom by on Benson Highway. Going fast and silent but with their lights on, headed in the direction of the Motel 6.

*Don't be paranoid.*

Maybe they were going to the Motel 6, maybe not. But what if they were?

What if it had something to do with him?

Shit! He didn't have time. He clambered back into the motor home and pulled the seat cushions off the dinette seat, flung it open and rummaged inside. He needed his duffel and his computer bag. He grabbed the duffel and started throwing things in. The main things were the laptop, the power cord, the disks, his Jaz drive.

His notebooks. His photo albums. His cameras, of course. His cash. And Summer.

It took him three trips to get everything into the Geo. There was a lot he was leaving behind, but he couldn't help that. Although no one had put his picture up on television, he could feel them breathing down his neck. He knew he was one step ahead of their snapping jaws—he could feel it. He always trusted his instincts.

They knew who he was. Maybe it was the way the cop had looked at the motor home. He should have jumped on that earlier. At least they didn't know about the Geo.

After he'd stuffed everything into the backseat, he stood by the car, hyperventilating, the sun beating down on him.

Where would they go?

Mexico?

He'd have to put her in the trunk. But what if the Mexican customs asked to see inside?

He'd cross that bridge when he came to it.

Or he could head east or west on the interstate. Or take the back roads, lie low.

Later. He'd figure it out later.

He went back inside, feeling strangely jazzed. She was going to give him a battle. He knew it. The wildcat.

And so he prepared everything ahead of time. The chloroform, the rag, his handcuffs, duct tape—all in the same place he'd stashed them after he'd used them on Jessica.

*The boyfriend, standing there in the doorway of the Pace Arrow. "What's going on?"*

The image so strong it seemed like real time. Stupid kid, surprising him like that. The girl, who'd just stopped struggling, a deadweight. He had no choice but to act—and act fast.

Still amazed no one saw him drag the kid down into the woods.

Now he had the rag, the bottle at the ready. Knocked on the door.

No answer.

He felt the beginning of impatience.

"Summer, we can do this easy or we can do this hard. I guarantee you won't like it hard." He tried not to laugh at the pun.

Nothing.

Bitch.

To think he'd bought a present for her. He reached into his shirt pocket and extracted the key to the padlock, unlocked the door, and pulled it open.

Something jumped out at him like a jack-in-the-box.

"What—?"

He saw the stick clenched in her hands and his mind had only a split second to wonder what it was when it hit him right in the midsection, punching into his side.

Pain, tingly and bright and blood-colored. He thought he screamed.

He grabbed at her as her impulsion carried her past him, his fingers snagging her dress—

She jerked away, and through a fine haze of pain he saw her bolt through the hallway and out the door, the door banging wham wham wham—

And he was aware that he was holding his side and it was kind of like hot pudding, slick as snot as his father used to say, and he staggered back, spun around, and that was when he saw the object on the floor. Wood tapering down to a band of brass glimmering at the bottom.

It was a leg off the swing-out table.

She'd sawed it off. Somehow.

Smart girl.

He grabbed a towel from the bathroom and pressed it to the wound. *Compress.* It hurt like a sonofabitch but it had missed everything vital. There were splinters, though, big ones.

Time slowed. His nerve endings screaming. The towel turning red. Still, he'd better go get her and think about cleaning this mess up later.

# 49

As Laura walked across the parking lot to the Motel 6 entrance, the overheated asphalt yielded under her shoe like brownie dough. Traffic hummed and sighed on the street behind her, a constant pedal point. She shielded her eyes against the glare and glanced back at the van parked unobtrusively near the edge of the property—a unit from the Pima County Sheriff's SWAT team inside.

The young woman at the desk looked like a college student. She wore a nice blazer with the nametag MARCI.

Laura asked Marci if she had either a Dale Lundy or a Jimmy de Seroux registered.

Marci looked through the book. "No one by that name."

"Anything close? Maybe a combination of the two? Dale de Seroux? Jimmy Lundy?"

Uncertain, the girl pored over the names again.

Laura looked at the names upside down. "That's it. James E. Lund. Could you pull the card, please?"

"I don't know—"

"We have a warrant."

"Oh. Okay." Marci found the registration card and pushed it diffidently across the desk.

The date of check-in was July fifteenth. James E. Lund,

Glenwood Springs, Colorado. Drove a 1994 white Geo Prism with a Colorado plate. He was in room 17.

A white Geo?

Laura wondered if he'd ditched the motor home, or if he'd just added the car. Sometimes the simplest things could slip under the radar. All the agencies were on the alert for a motor home. But they might not even see a motor home towing a car.

She asked Marci for the key to room 17. Marci handed it over without asking to see the warrant, which was good because Laura didn't have one. Victor Celaya was on his way with it.

"How did he pay for the room?" she asked. "Cash, check, or credit card?"

Marci looked up the receipt. "He paid cash in advance." She anticipated Laura's next question. "For a week." Laura counted up in her head. He had three days left.

She walked back out into the gunmetal haze.

At this time of day, between check-out and check-in, there were few cars in the parking lot, and no white Geo Prism with Colorado plates.

She walked back to the 4Runner, got in, and turned the air conditioner on full blast. Immediately her cell started bleeping. It was Charlie Specter. "A TPD officer spotted a motor home in a trailer court on Benson Highway that looked suspicious. He says it fits the description and the photo—the Pace Arrow. From the looks of the street numbers, it's less than two miles from where you are now.

"I got hold of the owner of the trailer court, asked him if he had anyone there by the name of Lundy or de Seroux. He said the guy with the motor home gave his name as John de Seroux."

Summer ran through the trailer park pounding on doors, screaming for help.

But the trailers just dozed in the summer sun. Nobody

was going to open their door to her. She didn't know why, but she knew it was true.

She started running up the lane toward the street.

Behind her the motor home door banged open and she heard running feet.

She knew it was him, but looked back anyway. Dale got into his car, backed it up and swerved around, heading toward her in a funnel of dust.

Summer knew she wouldn't make it to the road. She scanned the trailer court and saw a break in the fence near the last trailer she'd been to. She had to go back in the direction of the Geo, but the good news was, he'd have to turn around.

He saw what she was doing and hit the brakes, but by the time he had stopped the car she was past him and was already cutting across the concrete pad next to the trailer. Behind her, she heard the tiny engine roar as he put it in reverse. She darted toward the break in the fence, trying to figure out how to get through the clumps of prickly pear guarding it.

Behind her she heard the car slam into park and the door jerk open.

She had to get down on her stomach, which took time, and shimmy through, careful to avoid the cactus. Chain link snagged her dress and she had to yank at it, legs flailing. Then she was free, out into the desert and running.

"Summer, get back here!" Dale yelled.

Then: "*Dam*mit!" And the slam of the car door, the squeal of the engine again as he charged up the drive, spraying gravel.

What would he do? Could he drive into the desert? He'd have to get out onto Benson Highway and get past the other businesses before he could get to the empty lot. It would be fastest and easiest for him to make a right onto the highway and another right, so he would probably be up ahead. She switched directions, following a path through the scrub, her sandals scarfing up dirt like an open mouth and stickers pricking her feet and legs. She stepped on a doghead that went through the bottom of her sandal, and yelped. Pulled it out and kept on going.

She hoped she'd guessed right. As she ran she could see rooftops rising above the screen of creosote and mesquite—the next street, parallel to Benson Highway. A neighborhood. She ran for it.

# 50

Where did all this traffic come from? Musicman slammed the steering wheel with his fist. Summer was loose and here he was, just sitting here, waiting as a whole procession of cars drove by.

His mind raced. Where would she go? Would she stick to the desert or would she make her way back to the highway? Or would she head for another road?

Dammit! His side hurt. Raw, throbbing. Blood starting to show through the towel. If a cop stopped him now . . .

How could this *happen*?

Now he wished he'd chased her on foot. But even that would have been problematic; he doubted he could have gotten through the break in the fence.

One more car and he could turn right. But as he watched, the white van slowed down.

Come on, dammit!

The turn signal came on.

"Come on, come on," he muttered. "Shit or get off the pot."

But the van didn't turn in. It kept going, turn signal still on. He tried to catch a glimpse of what kind of asshole would play a game like that, but couldn't; the windows were too dark.

Suddenly he remembered the white van at the Motel 6, the one he'd flipped the bird at. He thought they were similar: a white Ford utility van with dark windows.

The van continued past and he pulled onto the street behind it. Suddenly, it U-turned four lanes and headed in the other direction. Cretin.

Down the road from the El Rancho was the next business, the Desert Rose Motel. The Desert Rose was a horseshoe of peeling white brick buildings around asphalt, a drained pool in the center. This was the kind of place that rented by the week. Place looked deserted, but he knew people lived here—if you could call this living. Could she have come here for help?

He swerved in off the road. He scanned the highway, the few buildings, tried to look between them at the desert. Finally he turned in and drove around the horseshoe. He didn't see anyone—it was too hot to be outside. Still, he looked, paying particular attention to the four cars parked nose-in to the cabins. Looking for movement, looking for feet underneath.

He came back around to the road. He didn't know what to do. She could be anywhere.

At the next street he turned right. He cruised along slowly, watching the desert, but he was thinking about the van. There was something about it that bothered him.

It was the stripped-down version. Blackwall tires. Nothing fancy. But clean. Government? He wished he'd gotten a gander at the plates.

Were they that close? He knew the FBI was involved—had seen it on CNN—but they'd been pretty closemouthed. Not even a press conference. If they knew what he looked like, they weren't letting the public in on it.

Why was that?

And then it occurred to him.

His ISP.

They'd used his ISP to track him to the Motel 6.

\*       \*       \*

Nobody home in the Fleetwood Pace Arrow parked at the El Rancho Trailer Court. The door was ajar, the screen door dented as if someone had bulled through it. No car, but Laura noticed a tow rack on the back.

The plates had been switched, but VIN numbers don't lie. The motor home belonged to Lundy.

After making sure the motor home was clear, Laura and Victor took a quick look inside as they waited for the tow truck.

Laura spotted some drops of blood on the floor near the bedroom, as well as a few smears where it had been hastily wiped up with a towel. "Don't come back here," she said to Victor. "We've got some blood evidence."

She retrieved a can of fluorescent paint from the car and spray-painted a circle around each drop of blood.

Victor said, "Not a whole lot of it."

"Unless he got a lot up with the towel."

"Look at this," Victor said, showing her the padlock and the way the door was configured. "Doesn't look anything like the floor plan we have back at the squad. The bedroom and bath have been modified. He remodeled the bedroom door into a swing-out door that locks from the outside."

He also noted the boarded windows. "His own personal dungeon."

Lace curtains squeezed between the window and the plywood. They looked like the ones at his mother's house.

Laura spotted a broken table leg on the floor. She squatted on her heels and studied it. "Blood on the end of this," she said, pointing it out to Victor.

"You think he stabbed her with it?"

"Or the other way around."

She took photographs of the table leg while Victor went back into the living room.

"What do we have here?" he said a few minutes later. She glanced back; he was holding two round, pleated stretches of vinyl. "Wheel covers. For the spare wheel on the back."

One of them depicted a quail under the legend THE AN-

DERSONS. The other, in cursive writing, said, "Happy Trails! Jeff and Pat Lieber."

He laughed. "Pretty cute. We're looking for a motor home with THE ANDERSONS on the back, and he morphs into Jeff Lieber and his lovely wife, Pat."

"Too cute," Laura said. "He's a little too elaborate for his own good."

Victor shrugged. "Seems to have worked so far."

Laura heard gravel popping outside, and ducked her head out the door. It was Buddy Holland in his plain-wrapped.

She understood why he was here, but couldn't let him in. He wouldn't do himself any good, and he sure wouldn't help Summer.

"Buddy," she said. "Two people in here is enough."

"What did you find?" Fear and hope warring on his face.

"She's not here."

His relief gave way to worry. He rubbed his hand over his eyes and then squinted into the sun. "*Was* she here? Did you find anything?"

"Nothing definitive," Laura lied. "We'll have to get prints—you know the drill."

"Where are we going to tow it?" Victor asked Laura from inside the RV.

Laura excused herself and went back inside.

Buddy peered in at her.

"We've got a problem. We need to use luminol—" Victor said. He saw her look and lowered his voice. "The DPS lab's too small."

In order to use luminol to look for more blood, the motor home would have to be in complete darkness. The DPS lab would not be able to enclose a supersized vehicle like this.

"The sheriff's has a big room," Victor said.

"Door's too small. We'll have to wait until tonight, I guess, unless we can find an airport hangar nobody's using."

She punched in the number for Charlie Specter. "We need to put an APB out for a 1994 white Geo Prism with either a white male or a white male and a twelve-year-old girl. Get a picture of the make and model and Lundy's picture and get them to the media."

She closed the phone. She would always wonder if she'd made the wrong call not going to the media sooner. One consolation, though, was that up until an hour ago, they didn't even know about the white Geo.

"I wonder if he bought that car here," she said.

"The Geo? It's got Colorado plates."

Laura just looked at him.

"Oh."

"Whether or not he changed the plates, we need to know the history of this car. He might have had it all along, or he might have bought it from around here."

"If he bought it from a private party, it would be hard to find."

"Buddy." Laura hopped down from the motor home. "Can you get me the Sunday *Star* from last week? And the *Citizen*." She described the car they were looking for. "Also the Sierra Vista and Bisbee papers, also last week. Oh. And a *Dandy Dime*."

He gave her a dirty look but got back into his car and took off.

It kept him away from the motor home, and the blood. For now, anyway.

# 51

Breathing hard now, Summer ran into the subdivision. The houses looked new, a cheaper version of her mom's town house in the foothills. The problem was, they didn't look lived in yet. She heard power saws and hammering, though. Up the street she saw construction workers up on a roof.

"Hey!" she called out, slowing to a walk. *Almost safe.*

One guy, up high stapling something to the wood frame of a house, looked in her direction and shouted something. She wasn't close enough to hear, but at least he knew she was there.

She'd escaped. Hard to believe that she'd done it, but she had. Her heart started to slow. Her legs felt like lead, now that she didn't need them for running.

Tires squealed. She looked back and saw Dale's car coming around the corner.

Desperately, she looked at the man on the roof, thinking she could climb the ladder up to him, but the house was too far away. She did the only thing that made sense—she darted between houses onto the next street.

The car kept going to the next corner. She knew he'd try to head her off.

This street was empty—she was all alone. The houses

were unfinished, sitting on a pavement of dried mud. Feeling scared again, she took a deep breath and almost choked on the smell of sawdust.

He'd be driving up this street any minute. She had to figure out what to do. Hide? There were plenty of houses around here to hide in, but she discarded the idea—she'd be trapped. No, the best thing was to let him start up this street, then run back through to the street she was just on.

Heart thudding in her chest, she squinted up the block, first one direction, then another.

Suddenly, she heard a car coming behind her. It sounded different from Dale's. It was a white van. It must be a construction van because the sides didn't have windows. She stepped out onto the new asphalt of the street and waved her arms.

The van slowed. He was going to stop for her!

Suddenly, Dale's car came around the corner at the other end of the street and accelerated. He lurched to a stop, got out, and ran toward her.

She had to turn her back on him to run to the van but she had a good head start. Dale knew it was over, didn't he? Still, as she ran she imagined she could feel his breath on her neck, smell the hot oil from the stupid car, hear his feet pounding on the pavement. Could picture him grabbing her at the last minute—

But it didn't happen.

A hand propped the passenger door open.

She started to say "Thanks" but the word froze in her throat. Something leaped out at her from the darkness.

Talons grabbed her, hard, pulled her around, a crushing grip around her throat as the thick arm levered her almost off the ground, elbow catching her chin and neck in a vise. She was dragged off her feet, her hip bumping hard against the side of the van. One of her sandals fell to the ground and with cold clarity she realized that she would never need it again. Then she was pulled in, backward, across the seat. Struggling as the driver put the van in gear.

"No!" Dale screamed.

Just before the door slammed shut she saw Dale Lundy's eyes, a mirror of her own bottomless terror.

# 52

Laura left the motor home to Victor and drove the few blocks to DPS. Hard to believe that Lundy had been under their noses all this time. Hidden in plain sight.

Although they had cops crawling all over the Benson Highway area, FBI agents at the airport, Highway Patrol and sheriffs in four counties looking for a white Geo with a Colorado license plate, Lundy had slipped through the net.

He could be anywhere.

She went to see Charlie Specter.

He looked up from his computer. "I was just going to call you. I think Lundy's got a soul mate."

He handed her a log of incoming e-mails to Lundy's account that his server had faxed over.

darkmoondancer@livewire.net
darkmoondancer@livewire.net
darkmoondancer@livewire.net
darkmoondancer@livewire.net
darkmoondancer@livewire.net
darkmoondancer@livewire.net
darkmoondancer@livewire.net
darkmoondancer@livewire.net
darkmoondancer@livewire.net

darkmoondancer@livewire.net
darkmoondancer@livewire.net
darkmoondancer@livewire.net
darkmoondancer@livewire.net
darkmoondancer@livewire.net
darkmoondancer@livewire.net
mortgagemike@mortgagemike.com
darkmoondancer@livewire.net
darkmoondancer@livewire.net
darkmoondancer@livewire.net
newsletter@studiomusician.com
darkmoondancer@livewire.net
darkmoondancer@livewire.net
darkmoondancer@livewire.net
darkmoondancer@livewire.net
darkmoondancer@livewire.net
darkmoondancer@livewire.net
darkmoondancer@livewire.net
darkmoondancer@livewire.net
darkmoondancer@livewire.net

Charlie leaned back in his chair, watching her face. "How about that? In my professional opinion, this guy is obsessive."

"Is there a way to find him?" Laura asked.

Charlie sighed. "Livewire's a big server with a one–eight hundred number. Which is fine—I was able to trace it to Coffee Anon, place on the west side—but these are old."

"How old?"

"They're from four days ago."

"Nothing since?"

"Unfortunately, no. Maybe they finally got together."

"Either they connected or Dark Moondancer gave up. I want somebody to go out and talk to the people at the coffee place. Call TPD and see if they can send Barry White."

She rapped her fingers on the desk. Where to go from

here? If Lundy was panicked, he might kill Summer anytime and ditch her somewhere.

She stared at the screen. Dark Moondancer. The name struck her as pretentious—extravagant. Like something from a movie. A fantasy.

She had seen or heard those words somewhere before. Recently. There had been something . . .

The word "fantasy" struck a chord. Lords. Lords and ladies. Role-playing.

*Role-playing.* She remembered now.

# 53

Because Laura had come directly to DPS from the airport, her mother's file and book chapters were still in her suitcase. She got them out and spread them on her desk. There it was—a notation on a scrap of notepaper: "Dk Moondancer?"

She called Barry Fruchtendler and got his machine. She pictured him out there in Montana, a beautiful sunny day, the retired cop out on a stream somewhere, casting flies.

"What's up?" asked Charlie at her elbow. "You heard of this guy before?"

"I know what Dark Moondancer is—*was*."

Charlie waited.

"A role-playing game, like Dungeons and Dragons. Knights, fairies, stuff like that. I don't know much about it. A few kids at our school played it, but it was really more of a high school and college kid's game."

Mostly males. She couldn't remember if the game was confined to Tucson or if it was popular throughout the country.

"A game?" Specter said. "You sure?"

Laura was thinking out loud. "Mark might know." Mark Hewitt, her landlord, had gone to school with her. She grabbed the phone book and looked him up. He was home, and he did remember the game.

"The object was to become Dark Moondancer," he said. "There were groups all over town. I think there was a point system, but it was pretty loose. Game had a bunch of different levels that you had to negotiate to get to the top, the top being the wizard, the powerful one. Only the people who made the top circle had a chance to become Moondancer. They were voted in by their peers."

"Sounds like *Survivor.*"

"Long before its time. I think . . . I think there was a certain time span—a month? Maybe it went by moon phases. Then they'd start over."

"How did someone get into the top circle?"

"I heard they did outrageous things."

"Like what?"

"Whatever was outrageous when you were a kid—there were tests. Stealing something, bashing mailboxes, waiting outside a store and getting an adult to buy beer. Running naked down Speedway. Getting a popular girl to give it up."

From buying beer to getting someone to have sex so you could get a few extra points in a game—a lot of leeway. "Did you know anyone who played?"

He rattled off a few names. Most of them were a year or two ahead of her and already in high school. She wrote them down.

"I'm leaving some of these guys out, I know it. I'll call you back if I remember." He paused. "While I've got you on the phone, we're having a wedding in the butterfly garden next weekend. A big one."

One of the conditions of living on the ranch rent-free was providing security for events whenever she could.

"I'll look at my schedule and let you know," she said.

Charlie looked at the list. "These the Dark Moondancer boys? You know any of them?"

"No."

"I guess it's something."

Not much, though. Who knew how long that game went on? Years, probably.

Laura spent an hour tracking down the names Mark had given her. Not much luck—she mostly got answering machines.

She wondered if she was wasting her time. Would Dark Moondancer even know where Lundy was? Probably not. All those messages he'd sent—it was clear to her that in their strange cyber relationship, Dark Moondancer was the beta dog to Musicman's alpha. But it was possible that Charlie was right and the messages had stopped because they had made physical contact.

Victor called in to tell her they had found an auto body shop which could be closed up and made dark so they could use luminol.

"How's Buddy doing?"

"Fine. There wasn't that much blood, so he knows he didn't kill her in there." He added, "You won't believe what that girl did."

"Summer?"

"She covered that bedroom with fingerprints—light fixtures, walls, chrome, you name it. We just filled up seven cards and all of them except one were the same. Plastered all over the place."

"How do you know they were hers?"

"Buddy picked up some prints from his wife's house—good enough to eyeball. Plus, the few places she didn't get to were wiped clean. Probably from the last one."

Laura wondered if "the last one" was Alison.

"Not only that, she pulled out her hair, *by the roots*. Left some hair in the sink, but some she hid. Like stringing one over the curtain rod, putting one under the lamp. Blond, so they were easy to see. And a barrette Buddy remembers because he bought it for her. You should see Buddy. He's glowing more than the luminol. Twelve years old and she does that. She's a cop's daughter, all right."

"See that the lab gets started on the blood right away. We

don't want Buddy wondering any longer than he has to—
with DNA it's going to be long enough as it is."

"You coming down?"

Laura saw Lieutenant Galaz in her peripheral vision,
holding a file folder, waiting for her to finish.

"Soon. Wait—you grew up in Tucson. Did you ever hear
of a role-playing game called Dark Moondancer?"

"Dark Moondancer? That's a silly name."

Laura told him about the game and the Dark Moondancer
who sent the e-mails to Lundy.

"Sounds pretty tenuous to me," Victor said.

"There's your big word for the day."

As soon as she finished talking to Victor, Galaz said,
"Why don't you take a look at this evidence list before I call
Tallahassee. I want to get this thing straightened out."

He dropped the file on her desk and walked across the
squad bay to talk to Richie Lockhart. She guessed that
meant he wanted her to do it now. She'd just started scanning the list when the phone rang: Barry Fruchtendler calling back.

"When I was looking at my mother's book, I saw a notation about Dark Moondancer with a question mark," she told
him. "Did that have anything to do with your case?"

Fruchtendler said, "It had a lot of bearing on the case. We
found some loose paper from Julie Marr's notebook in the
cemetery—must have blown over the fence. School stuff,
mostly. She wrote down that there was a party—I think it
was the weekend after she was killed. A Dark Moondancer
party. We didn't release that to the press, but your mother
knew about it."

"You followed that lead, Dark Moondancer?" she asked.
"Did you look at anyone in particular because of that?"

"Sure did. Talked to prob'ly seven or eight young men.
It's all in the murder book at TPD. I could make some calls,
get them to fax it to you."

More delay. "That would be great. I'll try to expedite it
on my end."

She was about to hang up when he said, "There's one name I won't forget. I always thought that kid had something to do with it, but no matter how hard I tried I just couldn't connect the dots. Not having a body, that was tough."

He paused to cough. His cough lasted a long time and did not sound good.

"He attended high school in the same district as Julie Marr," he said when he was finally able to talk. "His uncle owned A and B Auto Wrecking. That was where the car was taken from. Michael Harmon."

"*Mickey* Harmon?" Her voice loud in the squad room.

From his place near Richie Lockhart's desk, Galaz looked up disapprovingly.

"You know about him? That was his nickname, Mickey. Thought from the very beginning he was lying to me."

## Watch and Wait

Musicman glanced at his fuel gauge—almost empty. He had been parked among the big trucks outside the Crown Paper Company for an hour, keeping an eye on the warehouse at the corner of Seventeenth and Fremont, running the engine to keep cool. He'd have to do something soon, though. Waiting in one-hundred-degree heat, no shade in sight, wasn't an option. He supposed he could go get more gas. But what if they left while he was gone?

To Musicman's surprise, the white van hadn't gone far. The guy driving didn't care that Musicman was on his tail. He drove sedately down Old Benson Highway, took Park Avenue north, and turned into the manufacturing district near the railroad tracks. Musicman watched as the man unlocked the gate to a tall chain-link fence topped by razor wire. A derelict brick warehouse, the Chiricahua Paint Company, rotted in the sun beyond the fence. Once in the parking lot, the man drove around the back and out of view.

Since the road Musicman was on dead-ended, he had to turn before he reached the entrance. And so he drove around the block, trying to think what to do. By the time he came around again, he saw them at the side of the building, a big man holding Summer's arm, the man opening the door and ushering her inside.

Dark Moondancer.

The Geo was shaking from the air conditioner. He needed to do something, but what?

He did have options. He could make an anonymous call to the police and let them rescue her.

But he didn't want to give Summer up. She had the potential to be The One, and he could not let her go without a fight. The best thing to do was retreat and think about this. Wait until dark, when at least he'd have a chance to sneak up on them.

He only hoped she'd be alive by then.

# 54

Laura jotted down the words "Julie Marr, A and B Auto Wrecking, Dark Moondancer, Mickey Harmon."

Mickey Harmon worked for Dynever Security, Jay Ramsey's Internet security company. Jay had mentioned they'd grown up together. Jay might know something, either about Dark Moondancer or about Barry Fruchtendler's suspicions.

She called the Ramsey house and got Freddy, who gave her Jay's number at Dynever Security.

"I heard about that girl," Jay said when he answered. "If I can help in any way . . ."

"Maybe you can," she said. "You know Mickey Harmon pretty well?"

"We've been friends since we were in fifth grade."

"Did you ever play a game called Dark Moondancer?"

"Dark Moondancer?"

"It was a role-playing game."

"I know what Dark Moondancer is." It was not her imagination: His voice sounded strained. "What's this about Mickey?"

"Were you aware that the police considered him a suspect in the Julie Marr abduction?"

"Oh, that." He sounded relieved. "For a while there they really went after him. But Mickey wouldn't—"

She waited.

"Wouldn't what?"

"Do you mind if I call you back? I've got someone in my office."

"Sure," she said, but he'd already hung up.

Thinking he sounded spooked and wondering why.

Galaz caught her eye. She waved at him and held up the evidence list, pantomiming that she'd get to it now.

When she took the list over to Galaz, he and Richie Lockhart were laughing about something.

"What's so funny?"

Galaz said, "You missed all the excitement around here."

"Excitement?"

"While you were in Florida. Victor got a message from his mistress. Her plumbing went crazy and she was knee-deep in water, panicked that the water was almost up to her mattress."

"You remember the mattress he bought?" Richie said. "Top of the line, twenty-five hundred dollars?"

Galaz said, "He took out of here like a bat out of hell."

"When was this?"

"Couple days ago. Richie swears he took the message down right."

Richie looked at her, wide eyes innocent. "My *español* isn't that good, but I *thought* that was what she said."

Galaz said, "You should've seen Victor when he got back. He was running around the squad bay screaming for Richie's blood."

Richie beamed, looking like a pixie with his prematurely white hair, just long enough to touch the collar of his oxford shirt. "You get hold of Myra Maynes yet?" he asked innocently.

"Go look for your own remains," she said.

Richie and Let's Go People! thought that was hilarious.

Her cell phone vibrated. She sneaked a look at the number flashing on the screen: Jay Ramsey.

"Jay?" she said, turning her back so she could hear.

"We need to talk," Ramsey said. He sounded as if he were speaking from the bottom of a well. "I'll be done here in an hour and a half. Why don't I meet you at the farm in two hours. Say, six thirty? I'll leave the gate open."

"Six thirty, I'll be there."

He hung up.

That strange quality to his voice.

"What was that?" Galaz asked, his voice hopeful. "A break?"

"Nope," Laura said. "No break."

She stopped by the auto body shop to see how the lab techs were doing with the motor home. They were in the process of carrying out bags of evidence. There would be a lot to comb through.

Victor had gone to track down two private parties who sold white Geos in the last week, and Buddy was about to leave. He pulled out behind her but she lost sight of him when she headed in the direction of midtown. She decided to stop by Mickey Harmon's house and see if she could catch him off guard.

Harmon lived on a quiet street in the Sam Hughes neighborhood. His house was a Spanish eclectic mansion: arched colonnades, red-tiled roof, stately palms, and a lush desert garden which she could see through the gates set into the high stucco wall.

The security business must be booming. She rang the buzzer at the gate, but nothing happened.

She debated whether to go back to DPS or straight to Jay Ramsey's house. She had a little over an hour before they were due to meet—too short a window to get anything done at DPS and get back out to midtown. So she drove the few miles to Alamo Farm.

Unlike Harmon's place, Ramsey's gate was open. Maybe Jay had made it home early.

As she drove onto the property, the slanting sun poked holes through the windbreak of walnut and mesquite trees, throwing shadows on the lane like a bar code. She turned left on the lane leading to the house, driving into the sun. Dust from her car tires seemed to buzz in the air as sun and shade flickered across her eyeballs. The windshield gleamed gold and brown, like tortoiseshell.

A black SUV turned onto the lane from between the two eucalyptus trees marking the entrance to the Ramsey house. Funny. It looked like Mike Galaz's take-home vehicle.

He stopped and she stopped, window to window. "If you're looking for Jay," Galaz said, "he's not home."

"I'm meeting him here at six thirty."

"Have you talked to Mickey yet?"

"No."

"Two minds with a single thought," Galaz said. "Jay knows Mickey a lot better than I do—it occurred to me he could give us some insight."

"Same here." Laura stifled her resentment. She hated the idea of him micromanaging her case.

"You want me to come back with you and wait?"

"That's not—"

"Let me turn around, okay?"

She put the 4Runner in gear and drove on without waiting for him to catch up. Why was Galaz so interested? Was it because he was so close to Jay Ramsey and Mickey Harmon? She knew Ramsey was influential in raising money for Galaz's campaign for mayor. Maybe he was here for damage control.

She turned off at Ramsey's house, Galaz on her tail. Trees cast long shadows across the dirt clearing, the hard-packed ground reddish gold in the dying light. No cars. Laura knocked on the door anyway, and wasn't surprised when she got no answer. Cold air leaked through the screen door as she peered in. Nobody home?

Galaz wasn't good at waiting. He paced back and forth on the flagstone paving in front of the house, finally went around to the back. Returned and checked his watch over and over, whistling. Annoying the hell out of her.

A sprinkler stuttered noisily across the lawn, raining on a pair of shrieking grackles. Laura felt grateful for the cooling mist as the water spattered near her feet.

"I don't think he's coming," Galaz said after his second circuit around the house.

Laura was inclined to agree with him.

"That's it for me." Galaz got into his Suburban. "See you back at the ranch."

He started his engine to cool off the Suburban but didn't pull out right away. She could see him talking on the phone as she walked back to her own vehicle.

Something about this scene bothered her. Where was Freddy? She got out her phone and checked her messages. There was a message from Charlie Specter regarding the owner of the Geo Prism. The man was being interviewed by Victor Celaya now. But neither Freddy nor Jay had called to cancel the meeting.

The door to the house was open; only the screen door stood between her and the inside of the house. A guy who ran an Internet security company wouldn't leave his house wide open like that.

*I'll leave the gate open for you.*

Why? Why bother leaving the gate open when it was just as easy to do what he always did?

Abruptly, she had a bad feeling. It took her a moment to pinpoint it, although it had been in the back of her mind all afternoon.

She had interviewed and interrogated perhaps a hundred suspects and witnesses in her three years as an investigator, and in the cases where she got a confession, there was always that moment when the decision was made to capitulate. With some of them, it showed in their eyes—others, in their voices.

She had heard that kind of resignation in Jay's voice, realized that the sound of his voice was the main reason she had come out here. The link between Dark Moondancer and Musicman was tenuous and might come to nothing. Mickey

Harmon may or may not have killed Julie Marr all those
years ago. What compelled her to come here was Jay Ramsey's state of mind.

She walked back to the house, glancing at Galaz in his
vehicle, still engrossed in his phone call. She thought about
asking him to go with her, but discarded that notion. She
didn't know if he would be a help or a hindrance. Better to
do this on her own.

"Jay?" she called. "Freddy?"

She pulled at the screen door and was surprised that it
was unlocked.

Suddenly she remembered the last time she had walked
into this house uninvited, the night Jay Ramsey was shot.
For a moment the two incidents, decades apart, seemed to
meld together into this one surreal moment. She drew her
weapon. Heart slamming against her ribs, she cleared each
room she came to. Heading down the hallway to the master
bedroom, unable to shake the bad feeling growing just beneath her solar plexus. The air coming from the vents was
frigid, a vapor that seemed to seep like melting ice into her
bowels.

Something wrong.

The white carpet with the vacuum marks had long ago
been replaced by Saltillo tile. The tiles reflected the white of
the hallway walls and ceiling, gleaming yet cold, inviting
yet ominous. Ahead in the half-light, Laura spotted a sheet
of paper lying in the hallway. She picked it up. The freezing
air coming from the vents made the paper flutter in her fingers.

> *Dark Moondancer is a secret no longer worth keeping. I*
> *thought my penance was living the rest of my life as a*
> *quadriplegic, but it has become clear that I cannot live . . .*

The letter took up most of the page, twelve-point print.
Laura returned the note to the floor where she found it.

There would be plenty of time to look at it later; right now, she needed to find out if Jay was alive or dead.

She approached the open doorway to the master bedroom. The black iron dogs guarding the foot of the bed were gone, but she saw them as clearly as if they were here in real time, along with the indelible image of Jay Ramsey tangled in the sheets, bleeding onto the white carpet.

Superimposed by reality.

Now Jay Ramsey sat in his wheelchair. A bottle of whiskey and an empty pill vial lay in his lap. A plastic bag had been pulled over his head.

# 55

Laura holstered her weapon and was at Jay Ramsey's side in three strides. The bag had already been torn by his desperate fingers, leaving a hole, probably the last thing he did before he lost consciousness—suicides often had second thoughts.

A possibility then that he was still alive . . . she felt for a pulse. Weak, but there.

She removed the plastic bag and checked his airway—unobstructed. Breathing through his mouth. Good, she didn't have to give him CPR. She couldn't risk moving a quadriplegic from his wheelchair and laying him out on the floor.

Laura fumbled for her cell phone and pressed the TALK button.

"What's going on?" Mike Galaz called from the hallway.

"In here," she called. "Ramsey tried to kill himself, but he's still alive."

Galaz appeared in the doorway, his gun out and held at his side. "Is someone on the way?" Face pale, eyes dark in his head. Agitated. "Did you call Dispatch? 911?"

"I was just going to call it i—"

He put his gun away and crossed the space between them. "Let me do it."

Before she could object Galaz seized the phone from her

hand. He looked at the screen for a moment, raised his arm, and threw the phone savagely across the room. It hit the wall and exploded into plastic shards.

Laura stared at the wall and back to Galaz.

"Houston, we've got a problem!" Galaz shouted. "Do you hear me, Mickey?"

Laura heard a noise from the master bathroom and pivoted, but it was too late; her fingers had just brushed the grip of her SIG when two huge hands closed down on her wrists like a vise, wrenching her arms up against her spine. Her shoulders and neck protested as Harmon shoved his knee square in the small of her back. He pushed her hard against the bedside table with crushing force, knocking the breath right out of her. Cuffs ratcheted around her wrists.

She didn't feel the gun being taken from the holster, but knew he had it. Smelled his sour breath: pickles. Harmon yanked her upright, and as he did so Galaz darted in like a bantamweight prizefighter and jabbed her in the hip with a hypodermic needle.

He jumped back as Laura howled.

Galaz started pacing. "*Dam*mit!"

"Don't worry, boss. We can contain it."

"You don't understand! She's not some dime-a-dozen street hustler off Miracle Mile. She's DPS. This is *not* going to go away!" He crossed over to Jay and fiddled with the plastic bag. "There's a hole in this thing!" He tore the bag apart, crumpled it up, and shoved it into the pocket of his slacks. Breathed deeply. "The whiskey and the pills'll finish him off. All we needed was a little time."

He sat down on a chair by the window. "There's a way to do this, I just have to figure it out. I know what to do, I just need a little space. It'll come." He checked his watch, then looked at Ramsey. "He can't last much longer. While we're here, we might as well stay around and make sure."

Mickey kicked Laura's feet out from under her and she sat down hard on her tailbone, legs jarring as they hit the floor.

Shit-scared. What had he given her?

Galaz crossed one elegantly trousered knee over the other and stared down his long nose at her. "Under the weather, Laura? You should start to feel it anytime."

"What? What did you give me?"

"Do you feel hot?"

"Hot?"

"Not hot as in *Girls Gone Wild*—I mean hot as in burning up."

She did feel hot. She tried to bring her legs under her to stand up, and found she couldn't. Her legs weren't responding. They felt like wood. Rigid.

Her tailbone throbbed from the fall, and her hip hurt where the needle went in. The ache seemed to be spreading up into the small of her back. "What did you give me?"

*"Steatoda juliei."*

"What?" Her body was clenching. Sweat popped out on her forehead, her upper lip, her arms, trickled down her sides.

*"Steatoda juliei."* Galaz said. "It's a neurotoxin that comes from the false black widow."

It felt like she was cramping up—everywhere at once.

Galaz continued. "The term 'false' is misleading, since there are few differences between *Steatoda* and *Latrodectus*. The black widow is glossy black, as opposed to a matte finish—that's *Steatoda*—and the *Steatoda* doesn't have the hourglass on its belly, but otherwise, they're almost identical. Especially where their neurotoxins are concerned."

Locked in pain, Laura followed his words, but there was a lag. She could feel a buzzing in her brain and knew it was pure fear. This wasn't just pain, it was agony, her body slippery with sweat—soaking every inch of her skin, in her eyes, blotting her blouse. And clenching, God, her toes were clenching and the pain just wouldn't stop . . .

Galaz said, "There are variations in neurotoxins from species to species. Some are far more extreme than others. This particular neurotoxin is pretty severe, but fortunately for you, not long-lasting. One, two hours at the most, and then the effects wear off. Another choice of spider, and you could be in incredible pain for two or three days. But I chose *Steatoda juliei* because we don't need that long."

She looked at his crossed legs, the top leg moving back and forth. Using his knee as a fulcrum. He was smiling. "I gave this *Steatoda* its name. Since I spent months studying the effects of its venom on everything from bunny rabbits to horses, I can safely say this was, until now, an unnamed species. That's Phylum: Arthropoda; Subphylum: Celicerata; Class: Arachnida; Order: Araneae; Genus: Steatoda. Species: juliei."

Suddenly, her lower back bloomed like a bright red flower, pain so crushing and absolute that for a moment she couldn't breathe.

She closed her eyes and moaned. Her instinct told her to curl up in a fetal position on the floor, but her abdominal muscles were as stiff as a washboard. She gulped air, tried to roll with the cramping pain but couldn't: It was the bright screaming center of her brain.

Galaz was talking at her but she didn't understand much of what he said.

"When you find a new species you can name it after anything you want—other than yourself. That would be in bad taste. You just add an i to the end. So I named it *Steatoda juliei*. Do you know why I chose *juliei*?" He leaned his upper body as far forward as it would go so he was looking into her eyes.

Julie Marr. She didn't know if she spoke it out loud or if she just thought it.

"I meant this dose for Buddy Holland's daughter. I wanted to see how she reacted, but"—he shrugged—"The best-laid plans, you know the saying." He turned to Harmon. "How is our other patient?"

"He's dead."

"You sure this time?"

"Uh-huh."

Galaz stood. "We'd better go, then. You'll have to carry her. Give me her gun." Galaz removed his own gun from the paddle holster on his hip and traded it for Laura's SIG Sauer. Harmon tucked Galaz's gun into his ankle holster.

"That reminds me. Better check her boots, too. She should have another weapon."

Harmon's manhandling was excruciating. He found her second gun, her mace, her knife.

Galaz put his index finger to his lip. "What we'll do is, you make sure this place looks right. Doesn't matter about hair and fibers, lots of people come here. What about Freddy?"

"I saw him race out of here. He won't be back for a while."

Galaz said to Laura, "Freddy thinks someone stomped his boyfriend. He's probably just now figuring out his in-amorato isn't at St. Mary's Hospital. Pretty ingenious, don't you think? If only you hadn't come early and spoiled the party." He sighed. "I should have known—you never know when to stop."

Laura barely heard him. Her arms felt as if they were being pulled out of their sockets, handcuffed as they were behind her back. Every muscle—long and short, big and small—writhing, turning inside out, flopping like an oxygen-starved fish, wringing itself limp and squirting pain and adrenaline into her system.

"Aren't you even curious where we're going?"

Laura tried to say something but couldn't.

"You mean to tell me you haven't figured it out?"

He stood over her, the toe of his alligator-skin loafer inches from her face.

"We're going to see Summer," he said.

Buddy Holland trailed Laura Cardinal to a house in midtown, then to Fort Lowell Road. He knew from the way she was acting that Cardinal was onto something and he wanted to know what it was.

It was easy to get locked out in an investigation like this—he was just some cop from Bisbee with no power here. He also knew that Cardinal didn't trust him because Summer was his daughter. He understood how she could think that. But he didn't care how she felt; he wanted to find his daughter and no one was going to stop him.

He watched her drive through the gates to what looked like an estate. He got out and walked up the utility road along the east side of the property, lined with a new ten-foot-high chain-link fence topped with barbed wire, every panel marked NO TRESPASSING in big red letters. When he came to a place where the lane curved, he spotted a mirror by the side of the road to show the blind corner. The last time he'd seen something like that was in Germany, where he'd been stationed during his stint in the army. Fingers locked into the chain link, Buddy peered through the kaleidoscope of foliage at the narrow road, and saw Laura Cardinal's car stopped on the lane as she talked to someone in a black SUV.

The SUV turned around and followed her up the lane. They turned in at some tall trees—where he assumed the house was. Buddy wondered if the black Suburban belonged to the DPS lieutenant, Galaz. Whatever they were doing, he and Victor had been kept in the dark. Maybe it didn't have anything to do with Summer's kidnapping. Maybe their meeting was of a personal nature.

Still, he decided to stay around a while and see what happened.

He backed his Caprice under a tamarisk tree a little ways back from the road, where he could keep an eye on the entrance. The sun was low in the sky and the shade of the tamarisk, dense and inky, concealed the car well.

A little over an hour later he heard cars coming up the lane. Galaz's black Suburban drove slowly out the gate and turned right onto Fort Lowell, followed by Laura Cardinal's 4Runner.

The glass was dark on the SUV, but he thought he saw a

person in the passenger seat. A man drove Laura Cardinal's 4Runner. He was by himself.

Why wasn't Cardinal driving her own car? Was she riding with Galaz?

There was something secretive about this that seemed off.

Buddy realized he had a choice. He could go onto the property, or he could follow Galaz and the 4Runner.

He compromised by calling Victor Celaya. Victor said he would send someone to check out the property. That worked out, Buddy put his brown Caprice into gear and slipped into the traffic stream like an alligator into a river.

# 56

Ghostly letters spelled out the words CHIRICAHUA PAINT CO., in canary yellow on the dark red brick just under the roofline of the warehouse. Below that were two rows of multipaned factory windows, all of them either blacked out or broken. The property was wrapped in chain link. Behind the warehouse, an eastbound train rattled past. Laura wished she could scream to them. But even if she were able, they were too far away.

Mickey Harmon unpadlocked the gate and swung it open, waiting for Galaz to drive through. They jounced across the potholed parking lot around to the back and parked in the shadow of the building. Mickey got out of the 4Runner and into the backseat. Galaz left the engine running so he could run the air conditioner.

"Where's Musicman?" Galaz asked Harmon.

"Parked down the road between a couple of trucks. Must think he's invisible."

Galaz laughed. "I'll bet he's waiting for it to get dark. You should leave the gate open, make it easy for him."

"He might call the police," Harmon said.

"He won't. He wants her for himself. There's no way he'd give her up—not voluntarily." A smile flickered on his face, not reaching his eyes. "What do you think, Laura?

You've been hot on Dale Lundy's trail for some time. You think he's going to give up now?"

"No."

"See, Mickey? Cardinal knows her quarry."

She stared at him, feeling the ache in her eyeballs. Tried out her voice again. "You used me to find him."

He laughed. "It pays to have a crack investigator on the home team. At a certain point I didn't need you anymore, though—Jay tracked down his ISP before Charlie did." He turned to Harmon. "Just remember, Mickey, I want Lundy *alive*. I want the last thing he sees to be me doing Summer. I want him to know he's been dominated. He's got to learn that he can't defy me."

He tapped the steering wheel, the only sign that he was nervous. "I've got to figure out what to do with Laura here. Any ideas?"

Harmon grunted.

"I didn't think so. That's why you never got higher than the third level."

The third level? He must be referring to the game, Dark Moondancer. Pushing forty, and he was preoccupied with a kids' game. It was the first thing about this whole situation that made her want to laugh out loud. The feeling didn't last long.

Galaz's fingers drummed on the steering wheel: tap, tap, tap. "Jay was easy, but if one of our criminal investigators disappears, that's going to look bad. I really wanted to have some time with Summer, but it doesn't look like it's going to happen now."

"I dunno. You could maybe take her someplace else—"

"No. There's the time element. I'll be lucky if I have a half hour. Laura here is the head of a task force, people will be calling, they'll come looking for her. This whole thing could blow up in our faces. Better just go ahead and cut my losses."

Laura asked, "Why Dark Moondancer?"

"Why? Because it's more than a game, that's why. Dark

Moondancer transcends fantasy. To get to the highest level and become Dark Moondancer, you have to make it *real*. Things you would never dream of doing in your regular life, you'll do if you want to win. This game isn't for the faint of heart.

"The problem with Mickey here, and Jay—they always pulled their punches. They had no *commitment*. No vision."

Across the empty lot east of the warehouse, Laura saw cars crawling along a road that paralleled the railroad tracks, the last rays of the sun flaring off their back windows. Too far away to signal. She traced their movement with her eyes, though, watching them turn and go out of view, becoming swallowed by the rise of land and the creosote. One of them was a brown Caprice, the kind Buddy Holland drove. Now she wished she'd brought Buddy with her.

She said to Galaz, "After all these years, you're still playing this game?"

"It's not *just* a game. It's a way of life. There are smart people and dumb people, powerful people and losers. Dark Moondancer is a metaphor for power."

"Do you still play it, Mickey?" she asked.

Mickey grunted something unintelligible. Scared to say anything in front of Mike Galaz?

"Did Jay?"

Galaz said, "Jay was nothing but a rich crip who outlived his usefulness. Although he *did* buy me this warehouse for my extracurricular activities."

"Did he have anything to do with Julie's murder?"

"You saw the note."

"The one you wrote and planted?"

He smiled. "You think the three of us did it? That's what you think? Jay, Mickey, and me?"

Even through her pain, Laura was amazed at her own curiosity. She wanted to know how long Galaz had been killing. She wanted to know if Jay had helped him kill Julie Marr.

She *had* to know.

Galaz sensed that need and abruptly changed the subject. "You're not so different, you and the pedophile. There are a lot of things I can take, Laura, but being patronized is not one of them. I don't take that from anyone."

What was he talking about? "Patronize you?"

"Come on, Laura. Don't play that game."

"Honestly, I don't know what you think I did." In her mind she reviewed her actions of the last few months. She had always been polite, always did as she was told, was very careful, in fact, because she didn't know him well. She'd gone out of her way to stay under the radar, to do what he wanted, even going outside the department and working with Jay Ramsey because he asked her to. She had done everything—except show up at his party.

He couldn't be that petty, could he? Why would the fact that she didn't show up to his parties make a difference to him either way?

Galaz glanced at his watch. "Time's a-wasting. Mickey, you're going to have to do the honors."

Mickey Harmon got out and opened the passenger door.

"Better take the cuffs off. That would look bad if anyone driving by looked too hard. Laura, can you walk under your own steam?"

"I don't know."

"Get her on her feet and see."

At Twenty-second and Park, Buddy Holland got caught at the light. By the time he made the turn onto Park, both the Suburban and the 4Runner were gone.

He put on the afterburners, gunning it up to eighty to catch the cars ahead, but none of them were the vehicles he was looking for. Galaz must have turned off somewhere in between. He backtracked and found himself cruising through the warehouse district, his instincts telling him they were here somewhere. But where?

The sun was going down and it was getting harder to see. He scanned the roads, empty except for big trucks and semis parked for the night, the blank-windowed factories and warehouses. Then he saw something out of place—a small white car tucked in between two trucks.

A white Geo Prism, crammed to the ceiling with junk.

He drove down the road and pulled in behind an empty office building to think.

Buddy didn't know what kind of connection there could be between Dale Lundy and the meeting between Laura Cardinal and Lieutenant Galaz. Something was wrong, but he didn't know what. And now, here was this amazing coincidence. A '94 Geo Prism, parked between two trucks.

He got out of the car and slipped behind the empty building. He walked to the next block, cutting back between two warehouses, following an internal alley. He emerged fifty feet or so from the car.

Getting darker by the minute.

He drew his weapon, using the back end of a big tractor trailer for cover. He went from one truck to another until he was behind the truck parked to the left of the Geo. This gave him a good back view of the Geo, including the driver's side.

No signs of life. No movement inside that he could see, but with stuff piled that high, it was impossible to see past the backseat. Buddy squinted at the license plate. He didn't need to call in to get Dale Lundy's plate number; he knew it by heart.

He was right. It was Lundy's car.

He thought about going back to the Caprice and calling it in, but just then he heard footfalls down the road, the crunch of shoes on dirt. A hundred yards up the road he saw a figure almost obscured by darkness—just the white of his shirt. Walking north.

Headlights appeared at the other end of the street, lighting up the weeds along the side of the road. Buddy watched as the man ducked behind a paloverde tree until the car had passed. Then he was walking again, heading up to the street Buddy knew from his previous pass was a dead end.

He flashed his Maglite on the back of the Geo, approached it at a slant, gun trained on the driver's window. Adrenaline pumping, knowing he should identify himself but aware that the man walking up the road might hear. With every step he saw more of the interior of the car.

Empty.

Relief like a douse of ice-cold water. Summer wasn't there. But where was she?

Buddy looked up the road. The man was almost to the cross street. Buddy watched as he crossed the road and walked along the chain-link fence on the other side, then stopped. Too dark to tell, but Buddy assumed there was a gate. The man just stood there, peering in. Even from here Buddy could tell he was scared. It was in the way he hung back, the nervous movement of his head as he looked around.

*What do I bet it's you, asshole?*

Laura was able to hobble from the car to the warehouse door, every muscle screaming—her toes clenched, her teeth aching, her nerve endings shrieking like the high strings on a violin. Every shuffling step was an agony. She wanted to lie down. She wanted to curl into a ball. But Mickey had taken off the handcuffs so she needed to test her limits in case she had a chance to get her weapon back. Otherwise, she knew the end of her pain would also be the end of her life.

Once inside, her freedom ended.

"Carry her, Mick," Galaz said, his voice impatient. "Otherwise it'll take all day."

Mickey slung her over his shoulder.

The warehouse was empty except for broken glass. In the huge, cavernous space, their footsteps crunched on glass and concrete, echoing in the rafters high above. The last light of the day poked through the jagged holes in the many windowpanes. The intact windows had been painted over dark green, giving the place a murky, aqueous cast.

They didn't have far to go. Half of one side of the warehouse was a suite of offices; cheap wallboard painted mint green, doors removed. Their destination was the corner office, closest to the back door.

"Who's there?"

The voice belonged to a girl. It sounded creaky, as if she wasn't used to speaking. Just inside the door, Harmon set Laura down.

She was facing into the room, but her mind balked. She stared at her feet, at the floor, a kind of disconnect. She didn't want to see what had been done to Summer. Her job was finding the bad guy. Her job was to pick up the pieces. Her job was to comfort the families. There was nothing she had ever done that had prepared her for this.

She couldn't do anything for Summer. She was helpless.

Galaz said, "What's the matter, Laura? You've been looking for her all day—aren't you the least bit curious?" at the same moment Mickey Harmon poked her in the back.

She couldn't see this. It would do her in. She couldn't help Summer, she couldn't help herself. For the first time in her life, Laura wanted to give up. *Give it up, let it go.* Like slipping into a warm bath. A certain comfort when you knew it was hopeless and you were just waiting for death.

One more push from Harmon and she was in the room.

She smelled the stale air, fear riding on it. Fear and sweat and tears. And the coppery smell of old blood.

She squeezed her eyes shut, the way she did sometimes when the alarm went off and she insisted on sleeping a little longer, knowing that once she opened her eyes it was all over, she'd have to get up.

"Please . . ." the girl said, her voice drifting off. So pathetic that Laura felt a warm surge of emotion, tears climbing up into her throat.

When she heard Summer's voice, her resolve came back. She willed her eyes open.

\*       \*       \*

When Buddy was a kid, he was obsessed with American Indians. He read books about them, watched movies, pestered his parents to take him to Indian ceremonies—especially the Apaches, who were the toughest people on earth. During the Indian wars, an Apache could cover seventy miles a day on foot. The Apaches trained their infants not to make noise because they might alert the enemy. They lived on stealth because otherwise they would be eradicated. Now his days of stalking the low-rent neighborhood in south Phoenix where he grew up came back to him.

He was quiet. Like air, threading through the cracks of the world.

Silently he tracked Lundy through the dark parking lot of the Chiricahua Paint Company. Adhering to his training: Always find cover. Cover was something a bullet couldn't go through, like the engine block of a car. That was something that had been hammered into his head over and over. Find cover. If you can't find cover, find concealment. And if you can't find concealment, look for an escape route.

Lundy was a lightweight: a guy who picked on little girls. Watching him creep along the warehouse wall, flinching at every noise—it could have made Buddy complacent, but it didn't. The minute you let your guard down, that was when fate got you. He'd seen it many times in his twenty-three years in law enforcement. Just a little bit of inattention, and you were dead.

So he did not underestimate this man. Hated him, yes, but even the hate he had to push down deep inside. He had to clear the fear for his daughter out of his mind if he wanted to help her.

Not much cover around here, so he went for concealment.

The little man had his back to the warehouse wall, inching around like he was on a ledge twenty floors up. Clear he didn't know what he was doing.

Time to take him out.

Buddy was behind him in an instant, one arm around his

neck and his other hand over his mouth. He was tempted to administer a choke hold, tempted to take the choke hold too far.

He said quietly in Dale Lundy's ear, "Make a sound and I will kill you. Do you understand?"

A quick nod, his eyes bugging out.

He dragged Lundy backward, off his feet—the guy was as light as a feather. Dragged him under a tamarisk tree. The salt cedar's boughs trailed almost to the ground, affording him all the privacy he needed.

He had Lundy cuffed and on his stomach, one knee pressed into his back. Thinking about how much he'd like to pound his head into the pavement, crack it like an egg.

"Where is she?" he demanded.

"I don't know—"

"Don't fuck with me. Where is she?" Pressing his knee harder.

"She's in there."

"Why?"

"It wasn't my fault. I tried to save her but he got her anyway, I tried, I tried . . ." Blubbering. New blue Keds skating in the dirt.

Buddy fighting panic now—who got her? "Is she hurt?"

"I don't know—I don't think so. She looked okay when he took her in there."

"How long ago was that?"

"Two, three hours ago? I can't remember—it could be longer than that."

"Who is *he*?"

"Dark Moondancer."

He shook Lundy until he rattled. "Are you playing games with me? Because if you are—"

"No no no! Dark Moondancer. That's his *name*. It's the truth, I swear to God, it's his nick. He took her away from me, all I ever wanted was for her and me to—"

"Shut up!" He heard the savagery in his own voice. Out of control. Gritted his teeth, tamped down his revulsion. His voice quiet. "If you don't shut the fuck up about that I'll kill you." He took a deep breath. "Tell me about Dark Moon-dancer."

"I don't know him, really, except from the Internet. He . . . he and I have had transactions over the years. He knew I was in town and he wanted to . . . to meet Summer."

Buddy gave him a hard slap to the head. "Go on."

"He's evil. He likes torture. That's why I refused to let him meet Summer. I wanted to protect her."

"What are you saying? He's torturing my daughter in there?"

Lundy gasped. "Your daughter?"

"Answer the question."

"Oh God. Ohmygod, I'm dead. Oh God, please don't hurt me!"

His voice hopeless.

Buddy felt something crack in his heart.


Laura stared, taking in everything at once but unable to com-pletely assimilate it. Breaking it down object by object, things she could name. A gas can on the floor. A trouble light. Extension cords. A video camera. A worktable. Tools arrayed neatly on the table's pristine surface: pliers, a vise, an elec-tric drill, a staple gun. The tool cabinet was like the one her father owned—candy apple red. The kind you got at Sears.

Shackles bolted to the walls. Meat hooks dangling from the ceiling. A machine that looked custom-made, padded, something you'd see in a gym, but with shackles, chains, and pulleys at each end. A modern-day rack? Photos tacked to the wall, eight-by-tens of the hell he had commited on young women and girls—she counted three different women, photographed from all angles. Tied up, eyes bulging with fear. Before and After shots.

Digital photos of Jessica Parris after death.

A place for Let's Go People! to unwind.

Laura took it in, trying to stay clinical. She almost lost it as she stared at the mattress on the floor, though, soaked through with old bloodstains. So many reds, browns, and blacks, they formed a hard, shiny slick.

Mickey prodded her deeper into the room.

"You two girls know each other?" asked Galaz.

When Laura finally looked at Summer, she felt both relief and revulsion.

The girl was bolted to one wall, huddled down as far as she could get, but her arms were held high above her head. Wearing a little girl's dress.

Unhurt, physically. But how did you face something like this without losing a grip on your soul?

Twelve years old.

She looked at Galaz, the supercilious smile on his face. Seeing living, breathing women as something to torture for his pleasure, because he was so empty he couldn't get a high any other way.

*If there's a way for me to kill you,* she thought, *I will.*

Buddy secured Lundy to the tree with the cuffs after tearing strips off the man's shirt for a gag. Arms behind him, cuffs looped around a sturdy bough. Lundy on his knees.

That would hurt before too long. His back would be in agony. Good.

Buddy started for the back of the warehouse.

The cars were there, Laura Cardinal's and Galaz's. He made a circuit of the building, which was uniformly dark except for the one area near the corner, where a dim light leaked out through the holes in the painted-over windows.

That's where they were.

Buddy leaned his back against the brick, which still retained heat from the day. He needed to call it in. The cell phone would have to do. But before that, he took the knife he always carried and stabbed the tires on the two vehicles.

He called 911, explained who he was, that he was a cop. Gave the exact location. The South Tucson police were on their way. He got through to DPS, to Jerry Grimes.

He'd give them five minutes.

\*     \*     \*

Laura was aware of Galaz standing near her. He was smug, pleased with himself. But there was something else.

Something going on with him.

Working out a problem.

"Why don't you check her shackles?" Galaz said to Harmon.

"They're fine."

"Humor me, Mick."

Ponderously, Harmon walked over to Summer and bent down to check. He straightened, said, "I told you they were fi—"

The bullet took him in the chest, throwing him against the wall.

Galaz was holding Laura's weapon, looking down at Harmon.

"Sorry, Mickey, there's been a change of plans," he said.

Mickey started crawling along the floor.

Galaz crossed over to Mickey, his latex-gloved hand swooping in to take the gun from Harmon's shoulder holster. Harmon gasping, still crawling.

Galaz staring down at him. "You look like a snail, Mickey."

He followed as Mickey Harmon crawled, his fancy shoes inches from his face. Laura saw the narrow planes of Galaz's face—rapt attention.

She looked from him to the worktable. Less than two feet away, but her muscles had gotten cold again from not moving, and when she tried to move in that direction her body resisted like wood.

Had to do it.

Couldn't.

She looked at Summer. The look on her face. Jesus.

Throat constricted, aching, clenching—she inched her way, one eye on Galaz, the pleasure he got from watching Mickey crawl.

"Almost to the door, Mickey," Galaz said. "If you make

it before dying, I'll let you go." Pocketing her gun. Holding Mickey's.

Laura was almost to the table.

Mickey, two feet from the doorway.

Galaz, in a world of his own. The look on his face orgasmic.

The knife was closest. She didn't know if she could even wrap her crippled fingers around it. Even the idea was agony.

She heard a train horn.

Galaz still had his back to her, but he seemed to have lost interest in Mickey, who had fallen short of his mark and lay either dead or unconscious short of the doorway. Galaz oddly still. Thinking?

Laura's fingertips touched the knife. She closed her eyes, gritted her teeth, tried to grasp it. How she'd be able to do anything when she couldn't even wrap her fingers around the knife, she didn't know.

Suddenly, Galaz turned.

Laura started and the knife scuttled out of her fingers.

Galaz looked from the knife to Laura. "Can't do it, can you, Detective Cardinal? It must be frustrating, not being able to tell your body what to do when you've done it all your life."

Unconcerned, he crossed to the place Laura had been. Like a choreographer, he eyed the distance between that spot and where Mickey Harmon was shot. "This can work," he said, and nodded. "You shoot at Mickey and Mickey shoots at you. The problem is—maybe you can help me figure this out—what about all my hairs, fibers, fingerprints? Semen? What would you do?"

Laura needed to get the knife. But she'd pushed it even farther away, and her hands were cramping up even worse.

Galaz spun around and scanned the room. Frowning. "Have to burn the place down. That's the only solution, don't you think?" Talking more quickly now. "He shoots you but you shoot him, he's wounded. He's got to cover this up, though. So he pours the gas and lights a match and then tries to get out. Does that sound plausible?"

Not expecting her to answer.

"Or, he's about to pour the gas and lights it just as you shoot him—I don't think it really matters. The important thing is the point of origin. It's got to be right . . . here."

He strode over to where Mickey was when he was shot. Only a couple of feet from Summer. He had been checking her shackles just before Galaz shot him.

Outside in the night, she heard a train coming, horn blaring to warn people away from the tracks. Laura looked at Summer. Fear shiny in her eyes. Watching Galaz, understanding what he was saying, that the point of origin would be at her feet.

Galaz looked at Summer.

"Something I've always wanted to do—the Joan of Arc thing. Too bad I won't be here to see it all." He winked at Summer and walked to the gas can, hefted it up. Held it near her, watching her face. Completely absorbed in her fear.

He looked bemused. Oblivious to Laura.

Laura said, "What about Musicman?"

Startling him out of his reverie. "Musicman?"

The train was coming.

"Weren't you going to bring him here? To see Summer?"

"What? No." He shrugged. "You can't do everything."

"But he defied you."

Wheels ticking on the tracks, louder and louder.

"Can't do everything," Galaz repeated, uncertain.

The train upon them now, the rumbling shaking the room. A sweeping wall of sound, so big that for a moment it obliterated all thought. They were in the maw of sound.

*Concentrate!* She had to try one more time for the knife. She straightened out her fingers as far as they could go and pressed down on the handle, edging it to her by pushing the handle down against the wood.

The thundering in her ears. Fear pushing its way up into her throat. "Musicman wins, then," she said.

"He won't win. He won't get Summer now." Galaz un-screwed the cap and sloshed some of the liquid on the floor. The smell hit Laura, the rank high smell of pure gasoline.

The thing she feared most was dying in a fire.

Summer, whimpering with fear.

*Get your fingers around—*

Galaz produced a silver lighter from his pocket. Paused. Laura could see he was still working it out in his mind, see-ing the evidence the way the fire marshal would see it, the detectives, the ME.

*Get your fingers around the knife—*

The sound of the train abating now, the wheels the noisi-est part.

Laura curled her fingers. It hurt like hell, but fire would hurt worse. She closed her eyes and with an act of will, squeezed. The knife was in her hand. She'd have to rush him, but she could barely move.

She'd just have to aim herself at him, keeping the point of the knife to the front.

Five feet away.

She clenched her muscles even more, the pain excruciat-ing.

Galaz's back toward her. Splashing more gasoline on the walls, the windows.

Harnessing her adrenaline. Clamping down on muscles already stressed beyond the breaking point. Take a deep breath.

*Now.*

When Buddy heard the shot, he reacted immediately. Draw-ing his weapon, he tried the metal door but it was locked. He stared at the windows, looking for the weakest point. The panes were fashioned of glass and wood, and in some places the wood strips were broken.

There would be no element of surprise. They'd see him coming.

Then he heard the train. He realized the tracks went right

behind the warehouse. All he had to do was time it right. He doubted anyone would hear the breaking glass.

He took off his shirt and wrapped it around his gun. Picked the place where the wood had splintered, where there were stress fractures.

Waited.

The train coming, coming, the rumbling getting louder and louder until it enveloped him in an ungodly roar—

*Now.*

Laura pushed off from her feet and launched herself toward Galaz, flat end of the knife handle jammed into her side to keep it steady, using her body as a projectile. Trying not to think that it could poke her own guts out.

Landing far short, crashing on her hands, her knees, her chin, her hand cut, the knife skittering harmlessly across the concrete.

Galaz spinning around, his face a mask of surprise.

The stink of gasoline everywhere.

"You actually think—"

Shock in his eyes as a gunshot exploded through the small space, the momentum spinning him around and flipping him backward into the wall.

Head cracking—an awful sound. Holding his side, his mouth open and working.

In his hands, the lighter.

Manicured fingers flicking.

A rough male voice yelling, "Drop it! Do it now!"

Laura recognizing the voice but not sure—

An incandescent moment when metal struck flint, ignition. Spark—a runnel of flame swirling up Galaz's arm to his waxy face and up the walls.

The delight on his face turning to terror.

A blur beside her: Buddy Holland going to his daughter.

Laura thinking, *Shackles.*

Buddy from cop to father, his face twisted in terror as he

ran to his daughter, pulled at her shackles, saying, "Keys keys keys!"

Frank Entwistle, peering down at her. "You okay?"

*What do you think?* But she didn't say it.

"What about Mickey?" Entwistle asked.

"Mickey?" What about him?

Entwistle nodded toward the man lying in the doorway. "He had the key to your handcuffs, didn't he?"

Then she remembered: Mickey bending down to check Summer's shackles.

Suddenly, a loud whoosh! Galaz lit up like a burning straw man, sheets of flame spreading to the roof, the whole place getting darker, almost black. Boiling black smoke on a river of flame—

*Concentrate! He had the key to your handcuffs, didn't he?*

"Mickey!" Laura shouted.

Buddy looking up, perspiration running down his face, his face glowing in the flickering light, his eyes like a wild horse's—

Summer screaming.

Laura nodding at the man lying in the doorway.

Buddy, an acknowledging nod, then on the man like a jackal, coming up with a key ring, including three small ones—cuff keys. Buddy fumbling, Laura unable to move, Summer screaming screaming screaming—

*Get out now,* her brain told her, but she had no answer for that. The air buzzing at her mouth and nostrils like a swarm of bees, sparks lighting on her, in her hair, panic scrabbling like rats in the walls, the fear pure and hard and all-consuming.

*I don't want to die like this.*

Even with the incredible noise of the flames, she heard the click of the lock to Summer's shackles. Buddy cursing, praying, his breath hitching. Summer whimpering.

Laura, trying to remember where the doorway was because the air was now black except for the oily flames. Crawling, pushing her body to move.

Buddy running past her. She didn't see him but heard his boots on the glass, felt the wind of his passing, something soft passing across her face—the dress?

Fire feeding on oxygen. Blowing toward her—she could feel it on her feet, her back. Going toward the air? Or was that wrong? She couldn't think. Maybe she was going in the wrong direction. Where was the doorway? *I should have reached Mickey by now.* Her throat clogging up, her chest seizing with the need to breathe—

Banging, loud voices.

"Police!"

People in the room. Noise, men, legs, guns, SWAT.

Eyes stinging. Harder to breathe. Gasping for air. She could be dead any moment. Grateful that she lay on her face away from the smoke, that they were here. They were here, they would get her out now . . .

Legs milling, but no one coming to her.

*What about me?*

Entwistle looking down at her, his expression sorrowful.

Someone else—SWAT?—crouching down. Then she was borne up and carried like a bird in the grip of a hawk, up and out into the air, rushing headlong through the hurtling dark, the clean bright stars overhead.

# 57

Five days, twelve interviews, three interrogations, and reams of paperwork later, Laura decided she'd had enough. She had to go home, and not just for a few hours of sleep. They were at the point in the investigation where it was all mopping up and putting it in one place for the county attorney. Down the line she would have to make another trip back to Florida to testify in a related case, the death of Andrew Descartes, but not now.

That was good. Laura could barely wrap her mind around Andy Descartes's death. She had erred seriously in not asking for assistance from SWAT. She could rationalize all she wanted about giving the Apalachicola PD the benefit of the doubt, and that was true to a certain extent. But the real reason she had gone in that day with Chief Redbone and his two officers was hubris; she did not want to give up control of her case.

All the pieces of her case were falling into place. Mickey Harmon had survived the shooting, and he was talking—about his friendship with Galaz and Ramsey that had spanned twenty years, his lucrative position as Galaz's bodyguard, their blackmailing scheme. He cataloged a string of killings going back eighteen years, giving Victor the address of a warehouse in Phoenix where Galaz had plied his brand of sexual sadism while he worked his way up through DPS and planned a political career.

Dale Lundy—Musicman—confessed to killing four girls. He came off as beleaguered and confused. Laura thought his lawyer would argue for not guilty by mental defect, but after seeing what he'd done, she doubted any jury would go for it.

Victor was the lead on both the Harmon and Lundy interrogations. Laura sat in the room, watching Musicman, trying to figure the man out, but she couldn't. He gave them nothing—nothing except his "poor me" act. Unfailingly polite, small, insignificant, hands folded prissily on the table, he reminded her of a decent, churchgoing lady mortified at being placed in an impossible situation.

Laura asked him why he booby-trapped the tunnel.

He turned moist, frightened eyes on her. "Can I have a glass of water?"

After he had his water, she asked him again: "Why did you booby-trap the tunnel in your kitchen, but not the other house? What made you do that?"

He looked at her, uncomprehending.

She asked it another way. "You didn't booby-trap the front door, the back door, anything in the other house, so *what was your reasoning?* Why was that entrance so important to you when the others weren't?"

He gave a small shrug.

"I just felt like it."

*I just felt like it.* Laura had tried staring into his eyes, but there were no answers there. If she'd hoped for an explanation for Andrew Descartes's death, something real she could hold on to that gave this tragedy some kind of design, she wouldn't get it from Dale Lundy.

Buddy Holland was placed on administrative leave by the Bisbee Police Department. An Officer Involved Shooting investigation was the least of his troubles. Luring Dale Lundy to Bisbee would likely cost him his job. Fortunately, he had his pension from TPD. He was a young enough man he could find a good job somewhere in law enforcement.

"I hear Dynever Security is hiring," he'd joked.

He told Laura he was moving back to Tucson so he could be close to his daughter.

Laura had seen a lot of him lately. Summer had to give her statement, and Buddy was there with her. They went back and forth to DPS, to the courthouse: Buddy, Summer, and Beth.

Laura found herself envying Buddy Holland his family. Watching the bond between them. She remembered what it was like to have that kind of love, the love of her parents.

It wasn't over yet for them, though. Summer would need a lot of help to overcome what she had seen, what she had experienced, first at the hands of Musicman, and then Galaz. Unharmed physically, but emotionally devastated. Left alone in that room with the photos of the tortured women— knowing she would be next. Laura thought that with time Summer would heal. She would need counseling, and her family every step of the way, but she could heal.

Laura went to Jay Ramsey's funeral. It was sparsely attended. She recognized the younger brother, whom she had met only once close to twenty years ago. She noticed no one was with him—not a wife, not a child. He looked lost. Laura felt an odd kinship with him. He had no family left. She could tell from the shock on his face that he had never expected to be alone in this way.

He gave her a Post-it note that Jay had apparently intended for her. It had been pasted to his computer, Laura's name scribbled at the top. Below that it said, "Barbara Stanley" followed by a phone number. And the words, "Calliope's Music, 9 yr. old TB mare."

Laura thanked him and took the note, putting it in a special compartment in her wallet. She didn't know what to do with the information right now, so she would leave it there until she did.

After attending the funeral that morning, the fifth day after the Chiricahua Paint Company fire, Laura gathered up some of the paperwork that had yet to be done and told Victor she was going home.

"See you tomorrow?"

"I don't think so."

She headed home to the Bosque Escondido, after stopping at a little store squeezed into the middle of a strip mall on the south side.

# 58

"Where should I put the dishes?" asked Tom, carrying the box up onto the front porch.

Laura knew which dishes he meant. Cheap china, a brown-and-yellow design of bees and flowers. Tom had gotten them from a grocery store giveaway—buy so many groceries and pay a dollar for each dish. They went well with his two jelly glasses. "Couldn't we store those?"

"Sure. I'll put it with my sheets, my rug, my couch—"

"This is *my nidito*. You're just—"

"What? What am I?"

He stood there, looking at her, still holding the box. The man she had invited to live with her.

She thought of her nice Fiestaware. Thought of them nested one into the other, their fine solid colors, dark blue, green, tangerine, dark red. Okay, so there would be bees and flowers, too. She sighed. "Okay. Put them in the cupboard near the fridge."

Still holding the box, he bent awkwardly and kissed her on the forehead. "You're doing pretty well."

"You think so?"

"You've lived alone for a long time."

"So have you."

"But I'm not territorial like you are."

It was true. As he let the screen door close behind him, Laura realized this would not be easy. When she'd agreed to try it, in the middle of the night three days ago, it had seemed absolutely right. Love was love. It was supposed to conquer all.

But she'd seen him leave towels on the floor of his bathroom.

The morning after Tom Lightfoot moved in, Laura awakened to rain tapping on the roof just before dawn. It seemed to her that the temperature had dropped ten degrees. She crept out of bed, careful not to wake him. Looking down at him and thinking that this was how it would be from now on. She found herself thinking of Buddy and Beth. Were they healing the rift between them? Or would Buddy get a place nearby and hover around his daughter like a guardian angel?

She brewed some coffee and went outside, sitting down on the old steel glider, swinging back and forth. She'd found the art deco glider at a yard sale, complete with the original striped canvas cushion. Here on the porch of a house built in the twenties, the scent of the desert around her, she could pretend this was the early part of the twentieth century.

There were serial killers then—though not as many— and plenty of pedophiles, but people didn't know about it. How nice for them.

The rain was soft and steady—what the Navajos called a female rain. Water dripped off the eaves and splashed on the brick pavement in the few places the porch roof leaked. The smell of wet creosote wafting in, the trunks of the big old mesquites gleaming black as sealskin. The coolness good on her face, a balm to her singed eyebrows and the burn on her cheek.

Now was as good a time as any. She went inside, got her mother's old electric typewriter and set it on the wood drop leaf table on the other end of the porch. She needed an extension cord to plug it in.

It took her a moment or two to figure out how to install the ribbon she'd bought from Hart Brothers Business Machines. The guy had one ribbon left, taking up dust in a back aisle, saying it was fortunate for her this was a common typewriter in its day.

As she lifted the paper bale and rolled the first sheet of paper through, she smiled, thinking how Tom had liked the idea.

Zen and the Art of Unfinished Business. She liked it that her crazy idea had Tom's approval. But that was predictable; he admired simplicity in all its ways.

She stared at the clean sheet of paper, then typed "Chapter Seven." The action was strange, percussive. Both stiff and too fast for fingers used to a computer.

She was still staring at the words "Chapter Seven" forty minutes later when Tom came out and joined her. He'd brought her more coffee. He had put the right amount of half-and-half in it—a quick learner. She told him that.

"I read somewhere there's a big-shot designer in Hollywood who made up a swatch to show his maid what color his coffee should be. You're not that bad."

Glad she hadn't said she appreciated him using her Fiestaware instead of his supermarket china.

He bent to kiss her. Soon the coffee and Chapter Seven were forgotten.

After they made love, and were lying tangled together, listening to their heartbeats slowing back to normal, Laura felt a sudden strange bursting in her heart, as profound a moment as she had ever had. Tears unshed for eleven years suddenly came to the surface.

She lay in bed with Tom stroking her hair, her tears soaking the sheets and filling up her nose and throat. Enveloped in his comforting presence.

Feeling that, finally, she belonged.

## Chapter Seven

Mickey Harmon couldn't sleep. He kept dreaming that Julie Marr was alive. He had to see her again to make sure. He didn't know what he'd do if she really *was* alive—take her to a hospital? Maybe she'd be so grateful, she wouldn't rat him out.

He didn't know why he stopped by Mike Galaz's house. Maybe it was because he'd always gone to Mike for advice. In recent months, he and Jay had gotten tired of Mike Galaz always calling the shots, always being crowned Dark Moondancer. So they'd shut him out. But this was different.

He went looking for Mike Galaz by instinct.

Taking some chick's virginity would have been worth big points, but that didn't matter now. Mickey Harmon was scared. He couldn't face this alone, and he was afraid of how Jay—who had always been a mama's boy—might react. And so Mickey woke Mike up and they drove out to the place where he and Jay had dumped Julie Marr.

Mickey told Galaz the story on the way, how they had meant to seduce her—his euphemism for date rape—but she'd freaked, fought them, and in slamming around the car, she'd sliced her head open. So much blood . . . Mickey and Jay panicked, dragging her out of the car to a mesquite tree, covering her with dirt and trash.

But now he wasn't so sure she was dead.

It turned out that Mickey was right. Julie Marr was alive. They found her wandering dazedly in the desert, blood all over her face.

"What are we going to do?" asked Mickey, getting that panicky feeling.

Galaz didn't look at him; he just walked out to meet Julie Marr. When she saw him, her face lit up with relief. Mickey could swear he saw that. She thought Mike was here to rescue her.

He wasn't prepared for what Galaz did next.

Mickey watched in horror as Galaz raped and strangled Julie Marr. When she wouldn't die, he stabbed her repeatedly with a knife he produced from his Windbreaker.

He should have said something, but his voice was weightless, silent.

This time, they buried Julie Marr under the mesquite tree, digging a shallow grave in the caliche and rocky ground, piling up rocks to keep the animals away.

Mickey was scared.

Mike always knew what to do, though, and he already had a plan. Jay Ramsey, Mike told him, should never know that they'd found Julie Marr alive. Jay came from money and Mike Galaz saw an opportunity for blackmail, a way to control Jay Ramsey and his money.

"Don't even think about going to the police," Galaz told him. "You're as guilty as I am. We're bound together forever—the three of us. You, me, and Jay."

It was the first of many times Mickey would keep his mouth shut.

The pact Mike Galaz and Mickey Harmon made that night lasted until the summer of this year, ending with Mike Galaz's death in a warehouse fire.

In the aftermath of the fire, Mickey Harmon, cuffed and shackled, led the Tucson Police Department to Julie Marr's remains. Retired detective Barry Fruchtendler was there to watch as the girl's bones were unearthed from their shallow grave.

After eighteen years, Julie Marr was finally going home.

# Monkeewrench

## by P.J. TRACY

"FAST, FRESH, FUNNY, AND OUTRAGEOUSLY
SUSPENSFUL...THE DEBUT THRILLER OF THE YEAR."
—HARLAN COBEN

People are dying for the new computer game
by the software company Monkeewrench.
Literally. With *Serial Killer Detective* out in
limited release, the real-life murders of a jogger
and a young woman have already mimicked the
first two scenarios in the game.

Now Grace McBride and her eccentric
Monkeewrench partners are caught in a vise.
They can go to the police and risk shining light
on things in their pasts they'd rather keep
buried. Or they can say nothing—and let
eighteen more people die.

"A KILLER READ." —*PEOPLE*

0-451-21157-X

**Available wherever books are sold or at
www.penguin.com**